# STAR ROAD

A NOVEL

## MATTHEW COSTELLO
## AND RICK HAUTALA

THOMAS DUNNE BOOKS
St. Martin's Press
New York

This is a work of fiction. All of the characters, organizations, and events portrayed in this novel are either products of the author's imagination or are used fictitiously.

THOMAS DUNNE BOOKS.
An imprint of St. Martin's Press.

STAR ROAD. Copyright © 2014 by Matthew Costello and Rick Hautala. All rights reserved. Printed in the United States of America. For information, address St. Martin's Press, 175 Fifth Avenue, New York, N.Y. 10010.

www.thomasdunnebooks.com
www.stmartins.com

The Library of Congress Cataloging-in-Publication Data is available upon request.

ISBN 978-1-250-01322-4 (hardcover)
ISBN 978-1-250-01336-1 (e-book)

St. Martin's Press books may be purchased for educational, business, or promotional use. For information on bulk purchases, please contact Macmillan Corporate and Premium Sales Department at 1-800-221-7945, extension 5442, or write specialmarkets@macmillan.com.

First Edition: January 2014

10  9  8  7  6  5  4  3  2  1

## ALSO BY MATTHEW COSTELLO

*Vacation*

*Home*

*Rage*

*Island of the Skull*

*Beneath Still Waters*

*Unidentified*

*Darkborn*

## ALSO BY RICK HAUTALA

*The Demon's Wife*

*Little Brothers*

*Nightstone*

*The Wildman*

*Indian Summer*

*Reunion*

# STAR ROAD

# 1

## THE THALOS MINING COMPANY

*Captain Marie Rioux stood by* a railing overlooking the massive hold of the mining ship *Seropian*. The cargo ship had been designed to do one thing and one thing only: to carry the rare ores found on distant, desolate planets back to an ever-hungry Earth and its colonies.

Rioux watched as one of the mine's ore ferries landed and dumped its supply of ore. Another small ferry ship floated outside, waiting to enter the airlock system, and still more were waiting below, on-planet, loaded and ready to link up with the cargo ship in geosynchronous orbit.

All day long—though who the hell remembered how long a day was here—the mining ships traveled from planet to cargo ship and back to planet.

Rioux had to wonder if this was what she had trained for all those years.

The excitement of space travel?

Certainly not here, sitting in the middle of nowhere, waiting until the cargo ship's giant belly grew full, and then making the trip to the way station, to the Star Road, and finally home. Well, not "home." A smelting plant on the Lunar Base Fourteen.

But close enough to home to count.

Over and over, this routine made her romantic notions about being a space captain seem . . . absurd.

*I'm a damned truck driver*, she thought.

The tedium was matched by a constant urge to get the hell away from here, back to where there were green growing things and the normal days and nights of Earth.

The small ore ferry below had finished dumping its load and started its return trip to the surface of Thalos.

*Moving along . . . Good.*

All Rioux could think was, *Hurry. Fill me up so I can leave this God-forsaken place.*

Because if there was ever a place the God had forsaken, it was the dismal planet below.


Sam Hatch looked up as another ferry moved away from the ore processors, engines blasting as it passed over the great grinding conveyors that brought the ore to the ferries.

Each ferry carried tons of ore up to the cargo ship that circled like a hungry bird of prey above the small, red-stained planet called Thalos.

The *Seropian* was up there, he knew. But damned if he could see the ship or even the stars through the clouds of red dust churned up by the mining operations.

When that cargo ship was full, it would leave to be replaced with another.

And another.

He looked at the open wound of the mine itself. Huge trucks crawled back and forth over the rubble. The giant diggers, like ancient, lumbering dinosaurs, endlessly moving into caves and then down, below the surface, back to the deep shafts where teams of miners armed with explosives and tools hunted for new veins of minerals.

Nonstop.

The mining operation was an endless machine.

So far, this planet, whose home star wasn't even visible from Earth, appeared to be rich with the rare ores and heavy metals that could be used to make everything from the World Council's computers to the good citizens' sex toys.

Giant lights covered the area, so there was no visible difference between the broiling days and the frigid nights. And the red dust shot constantly into the air as if the planet itself were wounded . . . a bleeding cloud created by the miners' endless digging.

Hatch was satisfied.

All was running smoothly. Unlike the miners—whose contracts were tied to how long they worked—his depended on meeting his weekly quota.

The faster he got the ore, the sooner he would get to leave this hellhole. Then he'd get six months of R&R.

On a beach somewhere. Palm trees. Blue water. Drinking, ogling women in and out of bikinis, and forgetting about this ugly rock, the grinding noises, the dull-eyed miners, and the constant pressure to transport more and more ore.

Everyone appeared to be working as fast as they could. The machines' mindless efficiency seemed matched by that of the men. All of them—men and machines—covered with the red stain of the planet.

But could he really tell?

Are the loads full?

Do the workers stop to bullshit, eating up precious minutes?

The whole operation of filling the cargo ship just couldn't go damn fast enough for Hatch.

He turned away and walked over to the miners' camp to have a few shots. And maybe see if any of the miners decided to go buggy tonight. Because some did go buggy. For some, it wasn't a question of *if* . . . but *when.*

Hatch took the shot glass and downed the dark rum in a gulp.

The woman behind the bar hadn't been picked for her beauty. But he supposed that a patron with enough booze would hit on her, drunk and wearing thick enough beer goggles to make him see double.

*Right.*

*Look, she has a twin sister.*

Before that patron keeled over and had to be hauled back to the miners' quarters and tossed into a narrow cot, where the noise of the miners' snoring was like a rocket engine's roar.

"Another," Hatch said, slamming his empty shot glass onto the counter.

"Don't dent the wood," the bartender said as she refilled him.

And as he took the second drink, Hatch looked around the bar.

Nice and quiet. Off-duty miners sitting at tables, talking about the day, making jokes.

This drill bit broke . . . that grinder shattered . . . this guy fucked up planting the explosives and almost blew his team to hell.

Others indulged in the biggest sin of all—talking about home.

Earth.

Holidays. Kids. Wives. Food.

*Sex.*

*Now* that *kind of talk would definitely turn you buggy,* Hatch thought.

Though it was in his mind 24/7, too. Even here, on this planet with its fifty-six-hour rotation, everyone operated on Standard Earth Time and thought about their home planet constantly.

Good thing the operation here was outfitted with an infirmary stocked with enough class-A drugs to sedate a city. No one could run this job without that safety net, even though the booze was usually enough to keep things in check.

He liked having a belt or two, and then standing there with his handguns at his side, wearing his weapons like some goddamned sheriff. It had worked in Dodge and Tucson in the 1800s. Maybe it would work here.

The only other guns were in the hands of the security guards who were posted at key spots with pulse weapons. You certainly wouldn't want any of these miners running around with guns.

The barroom door opened, and Parker—his assistant who watched the tonnage, who really knew how much ore was being moved—came in.

He scanned the room for Hatch, caught his eye, and then hurried over. Before he could speak, Hatch did.

"Parker. I'm off-duty. Whatever the hell it is—"

"We got a jam up on the ship, Mr. Hatch." Parker's eyes looked frantic. "Last ferry got engine trouble."

"Shit," Hatch said.

That would lead to a line of ferries burning fuel, waiting to get into the *Seropian*'s hold.

*Eating time, screwing the day's quota. Making me fucking lose money.*

"Great. Terrific. What are they—"

"Captain Rioux has her team working on it. Shouldn't be too long. But you said—"

"I know what I said. I want to know about any delays."

Before Parker could reply, Hatch turned away and nodded at the bartender—a tilt of the head signaling he wanted another hit.

A quick pour from the bartender, and he tossed the rum down, letting it burn his tongue and throat.

"You did your duty. Now get back to it."

It took Parker a few seconds to realize that he was being told to go.

And Hatch went back to what he thought would be his last drink of the day before crawling back to his private quarters to shower and sleep and dream about any damn place other than here.

●  ●  ●

Rioux paced the bridge of the *Seropian*.

The dead ore ferry still blocked the entryway for the line of others waiting outside.

How long was this holdup going to be?

She had a good engineering team. They'd find the problem and get things moving again.

But it would take time.

She could imagine that down below, Hatch was not pleased at all.

*Well, too bad*, she thought.

She looked at the bridge crew, all young . . . raw, inexperienced. Most of them were only on their second or third tour. Still excited at being in deep space.

The reality of what this really was hadn't sunk in yet.

The utter boredom.

She checked the time and decided her workday was over. The ore ship would be repaired. Eventually. Nothing much to do. Watching and pacing the bridge wasn't going to make them work any faster.

But then, something held her there.

Maybe just the need for one last look before she left for the night.

The sounds of the bridge—the beeps and pings mixed with bursts of static from solar flares of the system's star—all turned into meaningless background chatter. One monitor displayed the immobile ferry blocking the cargo bay while others showed the red planet below, the stars outside in strange constellations, and the distant, shimmering strand of the Star Road.

Other screens filled with endless streams of ship's data. Heating, cooling, oxygen, and gravity levels.

*All good. All okay.*

*Might as well turn in*, she thought.

Fahir, her communications officer, suddenly spoke up, breaking the silence.

"Captain. I'm picking up something."

Rioux wheeled around to face him.

"*Something*, Lieutenant?"

"Signal's coming in. Can't see how many yet. They're masking their ID."

"Masking?"

"I'm trying to raise them, but they're not responding."

Rioux turned to the navigation station. Miller, a woman half Rioux's age, looked up, her inexperience reflected in her eyes.

"Miller, can you plot their course?"

The navigation officer nodded, already working on it.

"Got it, Captain," she said. "They're vectoring right toward us. Five vessels."

Then Fahir turned to her and said the one word that crystallized everyone's biggest fear these days.

"Runners?"

*Can't be*, Rioux thought.

*Not this far in-system.*

*And not when their goddamn leader is on trial on Earth.*

*The Runners are finished. That's what people say.*

"Runners aren't going to raid a mining operation," Rioux said.

She tried to project calm even though she didn't know what the hell was going on. With that ore ship crippled in the bay, they were an easy target.

"Nearest Road portal is . . . how far?"

"Four AUs away, Captain," Miller said.

Rioux shook her head. "Why the hell would anyone come this far in-system? They *can't* be Runners."

But that forced the question: *Then . . . who are they?*

One monitor tracked the five ships, coming in quickly, heading toward the *Seropian*. Until, close enough, the first images appeared on-screen.

Rioux moved closer to the monitor.

And saw: a gunship and four smaller raider escorts.

She thought: *Why all that goddamn firepower? Heading here?*

And then—

*They can only be Runners.*

Rioux turned to face the crew on the bridge. From this point on, everyone would hear her voice, loud and clear. She hit a button on the security display, and the quiet of the bridge was shattered by the blaring of a Klaxon. Emergency lights flashed on scores of consoles.

"Battle stations," she said. "All hands to battle stations. Prepare for—"

She shook her head.

*Battle stations?*

Stalled in space with the open cargo hold, the ship was unable to take defensive maneuvers. All that was left was for the *Seropian* to take the first hit, while everyone waited to feel the shattering vibrations of that first blast.

# 2

## THE RUNNERS

*Like everyone else in the* bar, Hatch saw the brilliant flash of the explosions outside.

His first thought: *Something's gone wrong in one of the mine shafts.*

A goddamned explosion, another screwup that would set the timetable back days, if not weeks.

Miners scrambled to the windows of the bar and looked out. Several ran outside. Hatch saw them pointing to the sky, but he still could see nothing through the haze of red dust.

His mind raced, trying to figure out what the hell had just happened.

He pushed his way past them and went outside.

A quick look at the mine operation. Miners had stopped and now stared up at the sky, waiting for more lights, more flashes.

Then, through the haze above, he could barely discern the massive cargo ship.

It appeared to be—shit!—*exploding.*

And all around it . . . Were those fragments of the cargo ships or smaller vessels burning up on reentry?

His earpiece started to vibrate. He fished it from his pocket and stuck it into his ear.

"What is it?"

"S-something's wrong with the cargo ship, sir." It was Parker. "They've gone to—"

But another, even bigger flash cut off Parker's words.

Unnecessary words, since Hatch could look up.

Even through the red haze, he could watch it all.

And think: *We are so fucked.*

Rioux started firing off orders, following protocol for the endlessly drilled response to a major attack.

Everything moved with a surreal franticness.

She was still trying to believe this was really happening.

"Ready emergency evac stations. Power up the pulse cannons. All stations fire at will. Execute evasive maneuvers . . ."

Commands flew from her, and her officers shouted into microphones, hit buttons, looked at computer screens and data readouts.

In the panic, their faces masks of inexperience and fear.

The screens told the whole story. Those monitoring conditions outside the ship showed the Runners' ships buzzing around like gnats, firing at the *Seropian* mercilessly. As they fired, a rapid series of explosions made the giant ship shudder and rock with a slow, lumbering roll.

*Are we even firing back?* Rioux wondered.

Were any of those goddamned explosions from any of the *Seropian*'s pulse cannons? They were good weapons—powerful and accurate.

But against this onslaught?

With this inexperienced crew?

Then she had the next, unforgivable thought.

*I have to surrender. Now. While most of our systems are still running. While we're still mostly alive.*

"Fahir. See if you can raise them."

But Rioux knew that the ships outside had ignored all attempts at communication.

Why would they talk now?

They were minutes away from having the cargo ship dead in orbit.

Its ore . . . theirs for the taking.

And down below? What would they do on the planet?

"Captain, they still won't respond."

"Keep trying."

Another blast. The ship now bobbing in its low orbit like a cork in a raging river.

"Keep try—"

She never finished the sentence. The next blast didn't echo from thousands of meters away from some distant part of the ship.

This blast targeted the bridge itself.

Walls of electronics and computers that girdled the main deck exploded inward. Rioux was in the center as shattered plastic and twisted pieces of metal flew around and into her, slicing deep into her skin.

For a few seconds, she was still able to remain standing in the chaos despite the battering.

But then a second blast hit the bridge, and although she didn't see it, Rioux felt something ram right into her—a piece of metal, a structural section from the room, blown free and turned into a spear.

She had a moment's awareness of being hit.

And then she dropped to her knees and pitched forward.


"Parker!" Hatch said into his radio mouthpiece. "Did you get the data pod sent out?"

"Yeah, but it—"

The radio went dead in Hatch's ear.

At least the World Council would get the news and a few minutes of video of whatever the hell was happening.

A Runner's raid.

Who would believe it without film?

*They were supposedly over. Finished.*

*But they didn't look too finished now.*

Hopefully, the Runners wouldn't intercept the message pod before it got to the Star Road. Once there, its mass was so small, it would travel much too fast on the road for anyone to intercept.

Hatch pulled out his revolver. Old school. Antiques. Real treasures.

The Runners above had peeled away from the cargo ship, which was now sending off a steady stream of fiery, soundless explosions. Flaming chunks of metal flared, a fireworks display as they entered the atmosphere.

Hatch didn't want to think about how this attack was going to negate his chances of leaving soon.

*Guess we're all gonna be down here for a while longer.*

Then it hit him.

What an absurd thought.

*We'll all be goddamned lucky to live much longer.*

He looked at the miners, panicking, helpless as they realized what was happening in the sky above. Some scrambled for cover. Others stood out in the open.

*As if it mattered . . .*

Everyone knew how brutal Runners were. But why attack here?

And what would they do once they got here?

The miners had to be thinking about the possibilities of defending themselves and their chances of surviving an attack.

Some miners might hide deep in the winding corridors of the mines—especially if they were suited up in their mining rigs. There were caches of emergency rations placed throughout the mine system.

Maybe the Runners wouldn't take the time to hunt them down.

The Runners might blow up the mine entrances, trapping them underground to die unless they could eventually dig their way out once the Runners left.

They wouldn't stick around long.

Anyone on the surface would probably be lucky if the pirates took them as prisoners.

Force them to join the Runners.

But the most realistic possibility was that they'd all be killed.

The miners' security force—a half-dozen men armed with pulse rifles—had their guns down, looking up and around.

Waiting.

They didn't have to wait long.


The roar of Runner vehicles screaming over the rubble, surrounding the mine area, filled the night air.

Hatch watched the ATV bounce over the rocky terrain and fly over the pits in the ground with ease, their oversized composite tires handling the torturous terrain.

Each ATV had a gunner firing a small pulse cannon mounted on the front. Hatch looked around. The vehicles converged on the mining site from every compass point. The Runners started shooting, mowing the miners down. The security guards started firing back while others began running, looking for an illusory safe place.

Hatch soon understood what was going on here.

*A massacre.*

*And maybe . . . a message.*

He drew his handguns and started firing. They had always been more for show than anything else, to let everyone know he wasn't only the project manager.

He *ran* this place.

Did the guns have enough range to hit the Runners' ATVs?

Was his aim any good?

He fired at an approaching ATV, taking aim at the driver. A hole bloomed in his head, and the Runner slumped down in his seat, the ATV careening to the side. It went up in an orange ball of flames.

Hatch wheeled around to see another approaching vehicle. He took aim and fired again.

The first shot went wide. Deep down inside, he knew this whole effort was wasted . . . useless.

There were too many of them.

Until two ATVs converged behind Hatch. He spun around and dropped to a crouch, firing both guns as he did.

The two gunners fired back at him at the same time.

*No way they'd miss him.*

And then . . . Hatch's last thought, again . . .

*Why?*

# 3

## RELEASE

*The doors to the World* Council Court flew open.

Outside, total chaos.

Ivan Delgato, flanked by guards, with double-lock handcuffs holding his wrists together and leg cuffs around his ankles, knees, and thighs that made it all but impossible for him to walk, took in the scene.

*Everyone here, all to see me,* he thought.

Reporters filled the granite steps of the World Council Court leading down to a waiting line of armored vans. Behind the wall of cameras, curious onlookers jockeyed for a good view.

The trial of the decade, *his* trial, was over.

Delgato knew he didn't stand a chance, not when he'd admitted to being the leader of the Runners.

Loud cheers and catcalls battled as the guards held his arms, standing between two massive stone pillars of the court building.

*Got my fans,* Delgato thought.

He looked behind him. More heavily armed security guards and police poured out from the building to either side of Delgato.

*A goddamned army.*

*What the hell do they think I'm going to do?*

The crowd kept up its yelling. He looked at some of the signs they carried, the scrawled messages . . .

FREE DELGATO!

OPEN THE ROADS!

Off to one side, a few steps down, a young, attractive reporter faced the holocam, reading from a prompter. She barely glanced at the main attraction as she read her live report.

"In Washington today, the World Council Court handed down a sentence of guilty on all counts in the treason case against Ivan Delgato, the leader of the terrorist faction known as the Road Runners."

A few meters away from her, another reporter . . . doing the same thing.

*Yeah. I'll be all over the vids tonight.*

The reporter looked at Delgato, even seemed to raise his voice so he could hear. . . .

". . . Ivan Delgato has been sentenced to life without the possibility of parole at the Cyrus Penal Colony in the Movasi Sector. This may be the last you will see of the leader of the Road Runners."

His guards let him stay on display for the cameras and the crowd, speaking into their headsets, nodding.

*Cyrus Penal Colony.*

*Now doesn't that sound like fun?*

The guards began guiding him slowly down the steps. Reporters tried to thrust microphones into his face.

*"Do you plan to appeal?"*

*"Who leads the Runners now that you're gone?"*

But the other security guards fanned out to either side, pushing the reporters back.

They didn't want any Road Runners making speeches.

The cheers and jeers rose in volume.

Delgato looked up. The clear blue sky, the sun already hot. Beads of sweat formed on his brow.

He might have been strolling on a beach in the Caribbean.

*Wouldn't that be nice?*

"Free the Road . . . Free the *Road*," a large group off to one side began to chant. Before long, others joined in, but then they were quickly countered by another chant: "Death to terrorists!"

*Can't please everyone.*

Then: a marble pillar less than six inches from Delgato's head exploded. Chips of stone and stone dust flew into the air.

The report of a gunshot echoed from the giant stone walls of the courthouse.

The police escorts raised their shields and tightened the line around Delgato. He watched several security officers below wrestling a man to the ground.

If the guy had been a better shot, this show would have had a completely different ending.

The police hurried the guy away, the shooter's feet kicking at the air as they moved him down to the street to one of the waiting armored vans.

They expected trouble, and they got it.

Questions continued to fly as Delgato's guards led him down, pushing through the sea of reporters, his steps small, constricted by the cuffs.

Once at the van, the side door slid open and his guards lifted him off the ground and threw him into the back. Before the van door slammed shut, one of the policemen remaining on the street turned and spit into Delgato's face.

*Pretty brave*, Delgato thought.

But without cuffs?

*Now, Officer . . . wouldn't that be interesting?*

He smiled and wiped his cheek on the shoulder of his prison jumpsuit.

*What they don't know*, he thought.

*The secret that no one—not here at least—knows about.*

The shooter wasn't the only surprise today. Not by a long shot.

Still, as the van pulled away from the curb, Delgato felt . . . isolated.

As alone as he had ever been.

Whatever his life had been up until now, today it had been altered fundamentally and forever.

There was no going back, even if he wanted to.

The van started, and Delgato felt it quickly pull away, the sirens of the escorts wailing as the caravan left the courthouse.

# ONE

∴∴
∴∴
∴ ∴
∴ ∴
●  ●

## FELLOW TRAVELERS

# 4

## STAR ROAD ACCESS TERMINAL—PLUTO

*Dr. Dario Rodriguez tried to* take it all in and understand what he was seeing as the small transport shuttle skimmed over the surface of the planet.

His first thought: *No matter how many times you see it, it's always impressive.*

Whatever the thing was down below, it was massive—a giant abstract art construction made by a lunatic, consisting of jumbled chunks of red and gray stone, and steel girders jutting out at random angles.

The sky was as black as ebony. The planet had no atmosphere to diffuse the light from the infinite array of stars. Earth's sun was just a white pinprick of light against the eternal void of space.

Outside, on what long ago had been know as the planet Pluto but was now an insignificant planetoid, there remained . . . the ruins.

Vast remnants of a past civilization whose beings used to live here or come here—*for what?*—had been left on this dead planet out on the frozen rim of Earth's solar system.

But that had been eons ago for all anyone knew.

Then something happened, and they vanished, leaving behind only these ruins and questions.

And the Star Road Station.

The transport banked hard to the left as if trying to impress the passengers, giving them a different perspective on what may have been an ancient city. Bright lights dotted the shadowed work areas of the site as teams—all carefully controlled by the World Council—carried out methodical excavations to determine the origin and purpose of this place.

People on Earth knew nearly nothing about it except that it existed . . . and that it may have been destroyed well before the dinosaurs went extinct.

Yet the Star Road had been *untouched.*

Is that because whoever or whatever had caused the destruction below depended on the Star Road as well?

Or perhaps the Star Road was invulnerable.

So far, it had defied Earth's best physicists. All anyone really knew was that the Road was still here.

And it linked humanity to the stars.

So many questions, and Rodriguez knew that a lot of people were busy here and on Earth searching for those answers.

There were almost as many answers as there were questioners.

Whatever the case, the Road worked, and humanity used it. With the Star Road, Earth and its solar system suddenly seemed much too small—a coral reef in an infinite ocean of stars.

Travel through the galaxy, theoretically an impossibility, suddenly became possible. Systems hundreds, even thousands of light-years apart could be easily accessed by traveling on the Star Road.

An amazingly complicated highway system had opened up, and no one knew how far it went, where it ended, *if* it ended, or—*the big question*—who the hell had created it.

People on Earth referred to them simply as "The Builders," but that answered nothing.

The transport banked again, straightening out as it lost altitude, following the sharp curve of the tiny planet. The horizon looked impossibly close.

Rodriguez took a moment and glanced around at the shadowy confines of the shuttle, at the dark figures of the dozen or so other passengers.

Are they all getting onto the Road?

Or are some cycling back for another stint on the terminal base on Pluto? Most sat quietly in their seats, some dozing, some lost in their own thoughts as they gazed at the amazing scene outside.

Everyone, except for the young woman sitting across the aisle from Rodriguez.

In the scant light, he caught her fiddling with the chip recorder implanted in the side of her head above her left ear. As the woman literally squirmed in her seat, her head moving all around the oval porthole, Rodriguez knew that the woman—almost a kid, really—was more than a "Chippie," more than a user.

She was in "record" mode, *creating* a new chip even now, capturing this moment for others on Earth to experience as if they were here.

All the experience, none of the risk, none of the stress . . . none of the expense or danger.

None of the excitement, either.

If this Chippie wanted to make an amazing chip, she probably couldn't do better than a Road trip . . . unless she went in for the kinky stuff.

Scanning her face, her body . . . Rodriguez imagined that she just might. She turned and caught Rodriguez staring at her. A bit of a smile. Then a taunt:

"Some view, hmm?"

Rodriguez nodded, still staring.

"See anything you like?"

"Sure," Rodriguez replied.

Then, he turned away. No doubt he wasn't the only one on the shuttle who had secrets. Everyone has their secrets. But he was getting on the Road for a reason that no one—especially not a Chippie—could know about.

On that point, his instructions were clear.

And Rodriguez was nothing if not good at following instructions.

He turned back to his porthole and stared blankly as the shuttle approached the terminal.

The shuttle glided silently over the icy rocks that looked like the aged teeth of a mouth frozen in the act of arcing up to snap at the shuttle.

Ahead, a bright glow.

The transport base.

*Mobius Central.*

Named, Rodriguez guessed, because the first scientists who found it couldn't figure out how the hell the Star Road—seemingly an actual structure—could somehow stretch its spidery strands throughout the galaxy . . . and maybe beyond.

Totally impossible.

It beat all quantum physics into a pulp.

*What was it made of?*

*What powered it?*

All unknown. Even after over a decade of using the Road, humans had unraveled only a small part of the mystery of this impossible structure.

Impossible. Just like a Mobius strip.

The process of building a road map was slow, a lot of trial and error. Especially error, at first. A lot of vessels . . . and good men and women . . . gone and never heard from again.

A detailed map of the system could change everything.

But so far, at least, no such map existed.

Would Rodriguez's mission yield some answers?

He didn't have a clue.

The dome ahead started to fill the porthole view.

A giant bubble of light revealing the people and areas inside. On one side, a row of airlocks; on the other, terminals to access the Road.

A small beep sounded from the speaker above Rodriguez, and the holovid winked on, displaying the smiling face of a shuttle hostess.

Then:

"Attention travelers. Our shuttle is about to dock at the Mobius Central airlock. Please check to make sure your seat harness is firmly buckled and that you have no loose articles near you. We will be touching down on the surface of Pluto in five minutes."

Rodriguez checked that the harness, a belt and a pair of cross-shoulder straps, were tight.

Then a voice. The girl, the Chippie.

"That's funny."

Rodriguez turned to her, seeing more clearly now. Short, dark hair. And blue-green eyes that glowed catlike in the pale light.

"What is?"

"Why'd they name the planet after a dog? Not even a real dog."

And despite what lay ahead—the responsibility, the unknown, the sheer adventure of it—Rodriguez laughed. He decided not to tell her that Pluto was also the Roman god of the underworld.

The shuttle began its easy glide as it made its way into the airlock chamber.

Annie Scott watched the load lifter raise a massive metal crate and lower it into the SRV's cargo hold.

At first, it looked like the crate couldn't possibly fit. And then, as if to force it, the operator bumped the crate into the undercarriage of the Star Road vehicle.

"Whoa! Bloody hell!" a man standing close to Annie yelled. "Take it the fuck easy! Jee-zuz. Who's in charge here?" His accent was a thick Scottish brogue.

Annie saw the operator look down at the man, maybe measuring him for a fight if it came to that. Then he looked to Annie, who raised her eyebrows a bit. The operator stopped the machinery.

"You got a bunch of monkeys working this thing? Goddamn!" Then louder, directly at the motionless operator, "Where's your captain, genius?"

Annie took a few steps closer to the man.

"That would be me."

The man turned to her, his face registering . . . what?

*Disbelief? Confusion?*

*Embarrassment.*

As if he thought the Road was for men only.

In other words . . . total bullshit.

"Captain Annie Scott." She extended her hand for him to shake.

The man rubbed his chin, momentarily stumped. Then shook hands with her. His calloused hand felt like a slab of overcooked beef.

"That your load, Mr.—"

"McGowan, and it sure the hell is. My mining suit. You have any idea how much one of them things costs?"

"Actually, I do."

Annie knew that the far-flung mining operations relied on these kinds of freelancers, guys with the expensive suits built to their personal specifications, a necessary entryway into a lucrative, if often deadly, business of off-world mining.

Sure, miners made a lot of money. But most of them never came back. And if they did, they were never satisfied, and they went out again. Things happened once you burrowed into an unknown planet.

Which certainly explained the guy's jumpiness.

"Those suits," Annie said, nodding at the frozen load operator, "they're built to resist a lot of stress, right? Cave-ins? Meteorites and such?"

"Yeah, so?"

"You think"—and here she leaned closer, as if the two of them were sharing a secret—"a little bump from my ground guy here trying to edge it into the cargo hold could hurt it even a *wee* bit?"

The man's face remained set. Then a bit of a smile.

He certainly looked seasoned, to Annie's expert eye, but who knew? Something was bugging him. Maybe he was prone to roadsickness.

She'd have to keep an eye on him.

"I guess not." Then, a genuine smile.

"So how about I get him to finish getting your suit on board, and you can go to the bar and grab a cold one before we head out?"

"Sounds like a plan." Then, after a pause, "Captain."

Another smile, and McGowan headed for the bar, the not-so-creatively named Star Lounge.

Annie looked up at the load operator.

"Okay, Jackie, let's get 'er in. The clock is ticking."

The operator began to ease the crate inside the hold, this time getting the angle right so the crate slid into the open underbelly of the SRV.

*Crisis averted*, Annie thought, and then—as if that would be the only problem she'd have to deal with before they took off—a trio of high-pitched chirps signaled that she had a message.

She touched her earpiece and turned away from the SRV.

"Captain Scott."

"Annie, I got something you'd better see."

Humphries—the terminal director. Nothing came into or left Mobius without his approval. His voice sounded tight. No banter.

"Come up to the office," he barked.

"I'm in the middle of—"

"*Now.*"

Annie looked back at the load operator, who was now picking up smaller containers and loading them. He had a good twenty, thirty minutes more work before they could start boarding passengers. Close to another hour, Standard Earth Time, before they could leave.

"Be right there."

And she started hurrying through the open expanse of the terminal to the elevators that led up to the Sky Box, the director's office.


"Get you something, pal?"

From the bartender's demeanor, Rodriguez could have been in his favorite dive bar on 9th and 46th.

*Pretty damn far away from that . . .*

"Sure. What do you have that's cold?"

The bartender gestured at a tap. "Got a fresh barrel of ER Dark on tap."

"Sounds good."

"Brewed right here."

Rodriguez looked up to see if the guy was putting him on. Not a hint of a smile. "No shit."

"So fresh it'll slap your face."

"You convinced me."

The bartender turned away to grab a pilsner glass, and suddenly the seat beside Rodriguez was taken.

"I'm traveling with a lot of chips in case—you know, if you get bored."

He turned to see that he now had a new best friend and travel companion. The Chippie.

"I'll remember that," he said casually, not wanting his need to show.

She stuck out a hand with long, slender fingers.

"Sinjira Renku," she said.

"Is that one name or two?"

Ignoring his question: "Looks like maybe we're on the same SRV."

He took her extended hand and gave it a quick shake. Her grip was warm. Firm.

"Looks that way," he said, wishing the bartender would hurry up with that beer.

"What are you doing? Business? Vacation?"

"What's that?" Rodriguez said, then he grinned.

"Work? Whatcha do?"

"I'm a scientist. I do . . . science things."

The girl made a silent "O" with her mouth, but Rodriguez wasn't sure if she caught his sarcasm or not. With Chippies, you never knew. When the bartender slid the beer in front of him—with an actual frothy head—she said quickly, "Oh, yum. Me, too."

The bartender turned to get her a beer.

Then Sinjira turned and scanned the room, this waiting area for the SRV passengers. Rodriguez knew by the blinking red light on the side of her head that she was recording.

"What do you think of . . . her?" Sinjira said, nodding a bit too broadly at the woman sitting at a far table in the corner. A dark cowl shadowed her face. Obviously trying not to see or be seen.

"Looks like she wants to be left alone."

"My guess is she's one of those religious nuts. A Seeker. Going on the Road to find—what?" And here Sinjira made her two lithe hands explode in a display of fingers shooting out. "The meaning of life?"

"Could be . . ."

Sinjira's eyes moved on.

"How about that one over there? The big guy all by himself. What's *his* deal?"

"Beats me. People go on the Road for lots of reasons. He may not even be on our SRV."

"I hope so. He looks lonely." She shot Rodriguez a sly smile. "So why doesn't he come over and buy me a drink?"

Then: "He looks . . ." She touched her forefinger to her lower lip, which glistened with a deep-red lipstick. "Interesting."

Then she stopped as Rodriguez took a slug of the beer.

*Tastes as good as it looks.*

"Whoa. Look at him. That guy over there. Looks damn eager, doesn't he? He might be worth a chip. Edgy, anxious. Some freaks like that stuff."

"Go for it."

After another deep slug, Rodriguez turned and glanced at the man Sinjira had spotted. He wore a long coat even though it was a constant 71 degrees in here. Not exactly pacing . . . but he shuffled back and forth.

Stopped. Looked around.

Every move screamed *nervous.*

Then Rodriguez said, "Let's hope he's *not* on our SRV."

"Amen, brother," Sinjira said. The bartender placed a beer in front of her, but she ignored it and went back to studying the workers and passengers who filled the lounge.

Annie knocked and then entered the director's office.

"What's up?"

Humphries stood next to his desk. Beside him was a shorter man. She had obviously interrupted their conversation, although Humphries had summoned her.

The two of them looked at each other as if trying to figure out who was going to speak first. Humphries began.

"Hello, Annie."

But that was all.

"Sounded pretty urgent," she replied.

"Well . . ." Humphries looked at his companion.

"What the hell is it?"

"There," Humphries said, "there's been a problem along your route."

"A problem?"

"Near the Omega Nine Terminal."

"And?"

"An attack on the mining colony. Could be . . . everyone was slaughtered . . . or captured. It's gone quiet."

"Quiet?"

"No transmissions. Nothing at all."

"You think Runners?"

"Who else? But nothing's been confirmed." Humphries took a slow breath. "Not even why someone would attack the operation. Nothing of any value there except for the ore, which they could've grabbed off a freighter once it was carrying it back."

"And they have a processing facility . . . where?" Annie paused. "They're not *that* organized. They couldn't run smelters without the World Council catching on."

"Space is a big place . . . and getting bigger by the day."

"So how'd you find out about this attack?"

Another look at the man with him, and then Humphries tapped the large flat-panel screen behind his desk. It came to life, and after another gesture, a holovid started playing.

A face appeared.

Eyes wide with fright. Face streaked with sweat. Chewing his lip before he spoke.

Was the guy injured . . . or just totally terrified?

"This is . . . Thalos Station. We've been attacked." A burst of static scrambled the hologram for a second, and then: ". . . wiping us . . ."

His eyes darted around. *Time was obviously of the essence if he's gonna get the pod out in time,* Annie thought.

The last word ended it, though.

". . . out."

The image on the screen froze for a count of three and then dissolved into a pixilated mess.

Humphries tapped the screen again, and it went dark.

"When did this come in?"

No answer from either of them.

"This morning? Just now?"

Humphries lowered his gaze and shook his head. "Three days ago."

Annie took a step toward the man who was, on paper at least, her boss. He reeled back as she approached. "You *knew* about this, and you didn't think to tell me until *now*?"

"Orders, Captain Scott," said the other man—who hadn't introduced himself—speaking for the first time. "No one is to know about it. Other than the council heads, few do."

Annie scratched her head.

*Who the hell is this guy?*

"So, what now? You expect me to scrub the trip?"

"That's your call. As always. I'm afraid in this matter you can't even consult with your company. You get to know what happened, but for now, that's it. It's classified."

"Great."

"Odds are they made their point with the attack, and they moved on."

"'Odds are'?" Annie echoed. She whistled as she exhaled.

"Probably retaliation for Delgato's trial and conviction," Humphries said. Annie considered that for a moment.

"You know I love to gamble, but this . . . ?"

"Like I said. It's your call."

She raised a hand to end the conversation.

"Not an option, Humphries. I'm going. I just hate surprises."

And now she saw Humphries glance at the man standing next to him. She knew another surprise was coming.

Annie stood there, not saying another word.

*Let Humphries bring it up.*

"Okay. You leave in less than an hour. One more thing, though. This is Bill Nahara."

Annie still said nothing. She had a feeling she wouldn't like where this was going.

"He arrived on the shuttle just now. He's going with you."

"Why?"

"World Council orders, I'm afraid."

"For what goddamned purpose?"

"You gotta stop at the mining station."

"Oh. It gets even better, doesn't it?"

"Nahara will carry out an investigation there. Nothing big. Just taking a look. Then you're on your way."

Annie turned away and walked to the office's wall-sized window that overlooked the terminal. She looked out, staring blankly at the ant-sized people moving around below.

"Guess I have no say in this after all, huh?"

"Not if you want to leave."

"Council orders," Nahara said. She didn't like the sound of his voice. Too nasally.

"You can still say no."

"But then your clearance will be revoked," Nahara said.

"Just following orders, Annie," Humphries added, as if that would help.

She stepped closer to the window. The loading was almost done on the SRV. The passengers lingered outside or were in the bar, ready and waiting to board, and then: she noticed something.

First, just one of the passengers milling about.

His movements jerky, odd.

Never good to have anyone fidgety on board. Even at their best, Road trips were never a smooth ride.

Then she looked over at two security guards at the checkpoint where passengers entered the security area once they'd been through the security scan. Both of them had pulse guns slung over their shoulders.

She didn't recognize either of the guards.

"Hang on. Who are those"—she put a finger up to the glass—"those newbies?"

"Probably just rotated in. Your point?"

She looked closer at the man below. Now he was circling the passenger area, and her instincts kicked in.

*Something's not right with that guy.*

*And the two newbies aren't paying attention. They might have something to do with it.*

She turned for the door.

"Nahara goes!" Humphries called out as she ran past.

She didn't stop, but said over her shoulder, "We leave in thirty minutes. Be the hell on board, or we go without you."


Ignoring the elevator—she couldn't wait that long—she took the staircase down, hitting the steps two at a time.

On the ground floor, she pushed the emergency door open and raced to the enclosed area where the passengers were waiting.

The two newbies gave Annie a look, scanning her ID tag.

*How the hell old are they?* she thought. *Eighteen . . . nineteen? Kids . . .*

Annie slowed her pace when she got close to the other passengers, a few at the bar, most sitting at tables or milling around, guarding their luggage.

*Going to get to know each other real well soon enough*, she thought.

But first she was going to get to know the man in the long coat with the twitchy eyes.

As she got close, she could almost smell the guy's anxiety.

*Maybe*, she thought, *a Road trip isn't in the cards for you.*

She moved to a position so that when the man turned to resume his shuffling steps, he'd be facing her.

And when he did . . .

"Sir," she said, extending a hand as if to block him. "Hold it right there."

The man looked directly at her.

She fired a quick glance at the two young guards who—so far—had taken no notice.

"Are you booked for my SRV, sir?"

The man's eyes went wide. Bug-eyed.

And the guards just let him sail in?

*I don't give a damn what kind of clearance this guy has, he deserves a few questions.*

*Like . . . what planet are you from?*

The man hesitated as if she'd asked a trick question.

His tongue slipped out between his teeth, looking like he'd swallowed a fat slug that wouldn't go down. Then three jerky nods.

Annie forced herself to smile.

"Great. We'll be loading soon. The SRV is right over there."

She indicated it without taking her eyes off him.

The man seemed to fight to look away from her. Then he gave the quickest of glances at the waiting Star Road vehicle.

Annie kept the smile plastered on her face, but she kept her eyes locked on him, barely blinking.

"May I see your boarding chip?"

The man's eyes were glazed now. They didn't move.

Annie took another step closer to him.

She broadened her smile, thinking, *This cork is about to pop.*

"Part of a captain's duties, sir. A last minute—"

And then it happened.

The immobilized man was suddenly fast. The long coat opened, and he pulled out a pulse gun. A pistol.

In a fraction of a second, the barrel swerved and aimed at what Annie knew had to be a spot right between her eyes.

A few people in the area saw what was happening. Someone screamed, and then others saw and shouted as they scrambled for cover. Panicked sounds moved like a wave through the terminal.

Annie hoped no one did anything stupid.

Pulling a gun was stupid enough. If those two newbies raised their weapons now, they could probably take this guy down . . . but likely only after he burned a hole through Annie's skull.

"Hey, hold on there," she said. "There's no need to—"

"The Road . . . is meant . . . to be . . . *free!*"

*One of "those" guys,* Annie thought. *A "Free the Road" zealot.*

How the hell did he get a boarding-chip clearance? He must have paid a

ton of credits to someone. And the pulse gun? Maybe someone planted it
here for him, past the security.

*And his plan?*

Commandeer the SRV?

Take out as many people as he could before burning his own brains out?

Make a fucking statement with blood?

"Right. I hear you, sir. But there's no need to—"

The man's eyes darted back and forth now that he was off-plan.

*What's he going to do?*

Is he considering getting everyone on the SRV, leaving here, *and then . . .
what?*

*Kill them . . . or hold them for ransom?*

Perhaps the idea that he was trapped, that it was already over, was beginning to dawn on him.

In which case . . .

*What the hell is he gonna do?*

He has an SRV captain at his mercy.

A lot of passengers around.

Not a bad statement.

Bunch of dead bodies.

*Free the Road* indeed.

Annie took another step, maintaining steady eye contact with him, not
even thinking to look at what might be going on around her, locked in this
deadly standoff.

*Deadly for me,* she thought.

"Why not lower the gun, and we can talk?"

Another small smile, but Annie guessed that her partner in this dance
wouldn't opt for that.

Annie lowered her gaze to the man's hand, the outstretched arm holding the weapon. Was his grip tightening, or did she only imagine it?

Her stomach tightened. She felt like she might throw up.

The man licked his lips and then opened his mouth.

"Free the—"

His voice wound up higher and then broke.

Finger *definitely* tightening.

And then, from the side, an arm flew from out of nowhere, hitting the
man's outstretched arm—and the gun—knocking both to one side.

But too late. The trigger pulled.

The gun shot a pencil-thin pulse at Annie's head.

But the intervention had moved the man's arm just enough. A high-pitched sizzling sound whizzed by, inches from Annie's head. The hairs above her ear actually moved in response to the charged particle burst.

Then her savior grabbed the man's gun hand and almost effortlessly twisted it. The gun clattered to the tile floor. Now—finally—the hapless guards were running toward them while the assailant found himself in a firm choke hold, arms pinned to his sides.

And finally, Annie realized who her savior was.

She walked up to him.

"Jordan. What the hell—?"

"Nice to see you, too, Annie."

*Been a long time*, Annie thought. *A lot of water under a lot of bridges.*

Jordan. A gunner. But what was he—?

"Someone upstairs decided you needed me on this trip," Jordan said simply.

"Luck of the draw? Or did you ask to be with me?"

Jordan smiled and said nothing. Then he indicated the assailant, who was now being collared. One of the guards stretched out a length of yellow-green neoprene and looped it around the man's neck. The collar glowed as the neural interrupters made the man go as limp as a baby.

"Orders are orders." He smiled—barely. "So, I'm your gunner. And—"

They both watched as the security guards dragged the man away.

"And it looks like, once again, I've saved your ass."

Another tight grin.

Annie shook her head. "Jordan. *Damn.*" Then looking at him, "Thanks."

"My pleasure."

Annie smiled at that and then turned to the crowd, all of them watching as if this was some bizarre sporting event.

"All right, folks. Show's over. Time to finish up your drinks and get on board."

And then, with Jordan a few steps behind, she strode over to the ramp leading up to the opened hatch of her SRV.

It was time to get on the Road.


When he realized what was going on down in the lobby, Humphries left his office in a hurry.

And Nahara finally saw his chance.

Without any hesitation, he walked over to Humphries's desk and sat down in the plush, leather chair. He leaned forward, his face close to the desk, and whispered, "Computer."

Something inside the machine clicked, and a thin red laser beam shot out from the screen and scanned his left retina. After a few seconds, the computer's friendly female simulated voice said, "Hello, Bill. *¿Qué pasa?*"

After a nervous look around, Nahara whispered, "Download Matrix zero-eight-eight-zero."

"That's classified information, Bill," the computer voice said.

Naraha got up from the desk and went over to the window. Looking out, he saw Humphries down below, talking to the security guards. How long would that take? He didn't have much time.

Back at the computer: "I'm authorized to override security clearance with Protocol nine-six-nine-alpha."

After a moment: "Confirmed."

Nahara waited, counting seconds. His eyes kept flicking to the door to Humphries's office. The entire front wall was made of wide panes of glass, fifteen meters high. Humphries would be able to see him as soon as he got to the top of the stairway, if he didn't take the elevator.

"Sometime today," Nahara muttered, tapping his fingers on the desktop.

"Transfer processing complete in five, four, three—"

"For God's sake, hurry up!"

"Two, one. Transfer process complete."

From the terminal console, a thin, transparent crystal with multifaceted sides emerged. It caught and reflected the light in a faint rainbow. Nahara grabbed it, almost ripping it from the slot, and pocketed it.

As he glanced up and started moving away from the desk, Humphries appeared in the doorway.

He looked grim. Unsmiling.

"Well," he said to Nahara. "Now that that's settled, you'd best get down there and board your vehicle. It leaves in ten minutes."

When they shook hands, Nahara was keenly aware of how slick with sweat the palm of his hand was. He wondered if Humphries noticed. He smiled broadly, nodded, and then turned and left.

As soon as he was out the door and walking to the elevators, he was filled with a sudden panicked thought.

*Did I log out of Humphries's computer?*

He took a deep breath.

Held it.

And kept walking, forcing himself to keep a slow, easy stride.

*Fuck it. It's too late to turn back now.*

# 5

## WELCOME TO THE SRV-66

*Annie sat down on the*—for her—oversized seat and looked at the massive, intimidating control board in front of her.

Considering the size of the board, it always amazed her that the SRV actually had something that resembled a steering wheel.

That this . . . *vehicle* could take people across the galaxy, and if you held the wheel, and sat back in the pilot's seat, you might think you were driving an Italian sports car.

Except sports cars didn't come with a panel full of lights, switches, a bank of holoscreens, computer readouts, and a "Heads-Up Display."

Then another part of that thought.

*And I actually know how to* drive *this.*

Even more amazing.

She liked this moment—sitting in the chair, ready to run through her pre-journey checklist, minutes away from following Mobius Control's check-out procedure.

For these few moments, the SRV was all hers.

And then Jordan entered the cockpit, hurrying up the steps from the passenger and baggage area below. He had to bow his head to avoid hitting it against the overhang.

"How we looking?" he asked.

She turned to him.

"Not too shabby."

She waited to see if Jordan got it. That hint of innuendo. Jordan was mighty quiet but also very easy on the eyes.

He seemed, though, oblivious or else willfully ignorant of such things.

Innuendo? Not in his vocab.

She turned back to the SRV control board and threw some switches, watching the displays change as the ship powered up. A faint hum filled the cockpit.

"All good. Think we have some time before Control begins checking us out."

Jordan sat down in his chair, resting his hands on the console.

SRVs didn't normally travel with copilots. Annie imagined that was because an SRV was really more like a bus or a truck, or interstellar cab. Why have a copilot?

But they *always* traveled with gunners.

She also knew that Jordan, from both experience and training, could—in a pinch—operate the vehicle.

And when they were between portals, there wasn't much to do except keep the SRV centered on the ribbony twists of road, activating small jets that sprouted from all around the vehicle, little bursts that kept the SRV squarely in the center of the "road" even as it twisted and turned through hyperspace.

Despite the hundreds of lights and switches, the thing wasn't really that hard to operate.

Jordan started toggling switches.

*Checking his guns . . .*

For a few minutes, Annie didn't say anything. Then Jordan turned to her.

"I'm going to check the main," he said.

*The main.*

The massive gun at the rear of the SRV had a 360 view of the area around the vehicle.

A holovid screen in front of the gunner's seat showed the pod that housed the main. Smaller screens had panoramic views from the SRV, now looking down on the launch platform.

Jordan could operate all the gun remotes from the cockpit, even the big main.

But if anything happened, she knew Jordan would go back there, strap into the narrow seat at the rear, to be a hands-on gunner, and operate it from there.

She knew that, having seen it happen.

Jordan wanted to hold those controls in his hands and swing around in the seat, tracking whatever he targeted.

And whatever he targeted almost always got hit. Annie couldn't remember any misses when they were on the same flight, but she figured there had to have been one or two.

Not that Jordan would ever admit it.

She asked him once, after she saw him blast some Runners who thought they could get the jump on her small SRV.

"You do that . . . go back there . . . because it's more fun, right?"

Jordan—being Jordan—didn't smile.

"It has a better feel. More accurate."

*He's a dinosaur*, Annie thought. *Something out of freaking medieval times. Cowboy movies.*

Jordan had been born too late.

Or maybe, considering things, at just the right time.

It almost always got interesting on the Road.

"As long as you're heading back there, mind checking the freight? Looked like the loaders secured everything pretty well, especially after the near-miss with McGowan's suit. But still—wouldn't hurt to check."

"Got it."

Jordan slid out of his seat and took the gangway down to the passenger area.


Ruth Corso looked around for a place to sit.

She wanted quiet.

Time to think. To meditate about this journey, about what it might mean, why it was so important to her that she left her family without saying good-bye.

The SRV only held eight passengers—four sets of single seats on either side. She counted—what? Only four passengers so far.

*Good.*

There were bigger SRVs, but they, too, had to keep the passenger areas small. Moving freight for the colonies, supplying them . . . that was the important thing. Passengers were an afterthought. Speed and mass being relative, the smaller the vehicle, the faster it would travel on the Road. And even at the impossible distances at equally impossible speeds, time was still paramount.

But the cabin on this vehicle felt smaller than she'd imagined. Cramped.

A stairwell in the front led up to the cockpit. The hatch was closed and, no doubt, locked from the inside. Lavatory on the left, in the back.

She wondered about the pilot. She looked awfully young.

After another look around, Ruth decided on the seat farthest back, on the left. The one across from that one was still empty.

She hoped it stayed that way.

*Better to gather my thoughts.*

Just then, the cockpit door opened, and a man came down the short stairway, hurrying.

When he looked up, Ruth caught her breath.

*No!*

*Not him! Not Jordan!*

*What are the odds?*

Then he stopped, looked right at her.

She opened her mouth. But then caught herself.

Of course he wouldn't speak to her.

But he looked straight at her, as if sighting her down the barrel of a gun.

Then he hurried to the rear of the SRV.

As he passed, Ruth somehow found the courage to reach out and touch him on the right arm.

"Does it matter where I sit?"

Jordan stopped. Licked his lips, his eyes skittering from side to side. "Not to me."

He looked at her a moment longer.

Ruth smiled. He had a patch with an image of the SRV on it.

*Copilot now?* she thought.

He shook his head. "Let me guess," Jordan said. "You're going to Omega Nine?"

*Is it that obvious?* Ruth wondered. *So clear that I'm a Seeker?*

And: *He doesn't like it.*

"That's my plan. I know there's—"

"Nothing but trouble. Lots of crazy, desperate people there." Jordan's voice stung like a whip.

Instant anger rose up inside Ruth. There was so much she—and he—could have said . . . *should* have said.

But not anymore.

Then she reminded herself . . . *Anger isn't the way. It never is.*

"Yes. Other Seekers have gone there. A place where—"

Jordan turned away. She thought maybe he'd noticed that other passengers were listening to their conversation.

He mustered a tight smile.

"Farthest point so far. Until we go, as they say, farther."

"You've been there?"

There was a note of awe in her voice. She realized she asked the question as if he had been to Mecca, a holy place—and if so, how could he not want to know everything about this Star Road, about the Builders? There were so many questions that needed answers—

"Yeah, I've been there. Nice pile of rocks. A few communities of your people waiting for—for what? Enlightenment?" His thin smile faded. "Get ready to be disappointed. Now, if you'll excuse me."

Jordan kept moving, slipping past the other passengers who were standing in the narrow aisle.

His words didn't bother Ruth.

There would always be doubters.

She repeated one of her favorite Seeker mantras: *Doubt feeds on fear, and fear feeds on ignorance.*

Ruth closed her eyes . . . and waited for the trip to begin.


The lowest screen at the base of the SRV's control panel switched from the Mobius Station logo to Humphries's smiling face.

"SRV-66—ready to begin pre-Road checkout."

She smiled. "All set here."

Humphries looked to the side of his screen as if trying to see if someone was sitting to Annie's right.

"Where's your gunner?"

"Checking the main and the freight area. We had an issue with loading."

"We know. McGowan already filed a liability-for-damages report. Sorry about that . . . and the little incident before boarding."

*"Little incident?"*

The words echoed ironically for Annie.

"A lot of people could have been hurt . . . if it hadn't been for Jordan."

"Yeah. But all's well, right? We're showing green lights across the board for your portal exit."

*He's avoiding the situation.*

"You know as well as I do that things can change quickly. No Runner activity reported thus far, and no areas showing any anomalies."

Another euphemism. *"Anomalies."*

Anything that happened on the Road that they couldn't explain was an "anomaly."

Anomalies could kill you out here.

"Good," Annie said, focusing on her job.

"Let's run through your board check."

"Let's."

And Mobius Control Center began checking every switch, button, screen, readout, and HUD remotely while Humphries confirmed that each responded properly.

*A tedious process.*

*But,* Annie thought, *keeping your ass safe is worth a tedious process.*

Jordan pulled at the metal clamps and tension bars holding the pallets of freight to be dropped along the way to Omega Nine.

Near the back, large metal bands wrapped tightly around the large metal sarcophagus that held McGowan's mining suit.

Everything as locked down as it could be.

He turned and bent down to enter the low passageway that led to the main gun turret.

The turret itself was small. Not unlike the old gun turrets mounted on B17s two centuries earlier.

The addition of a gunner's chair here, though, seemed almost like an afterthought.

If the gun could be operated remotely, with the 360-degree space easily seen from the cockpit, why the chair?

*Somebody had the imagination to realize there would be gunners . . . like me,* Jordan thought.

Where no screen—no matter how damned crystal clear the 3-D was—could replace sitting back here, swiveling, turning, circling, as a human, hands on the controls, aimed and fired the gun.

And though this SRV was perhaps the smallest vehicle that worked the Road, her main gun was . . . something else.

Lots of power, fast response, and with amazing accuracy.

Capable of pin-point blasts as well as wide-angle scattershots that could take out a half-dozen attackers at once.

He had to admit . . .

*I hope something happens this trip.*

*Be a shame to let all that firepower go to waste.*

He sat down on the seat, and for a few minutes practiced targeting as the seat pivoted and swerved. He smiled, knowing Mobius Control Center was wondering what the hell he was doing.

•   •   •

"All right, SRV-66, all systems check out. Got you synced to the Mobius Cloud . . . Oh. Thought you'd want to know. Your gunner is still in the back. Practicing, it looks like."

Annie was about to tell them Jordan didn't need any "practicing."

But they probably knew that. That's why they put him on this flight.

"I'll get him back up here."

"And you're cleared to give your passengers their final instructions . . . and then we're good to go."

"Roger that."

The man on the screen turned away, looking at his own bank of monitors.

Annie hit a button below a screen showing the main gun pod.

"Jordan. Showtime. Starting final prep."

"Gotcha."

Normally, an SRV pilot would deliver the instructions over the intercom.

As if this was a commuter run from Sydney to L.A. Though there weren't many "airplane" flights these days, and certainly not too many passengers using that outmoded flight system.

But Annie liked doing it more personally.

After all, *it's just us*, she thought. *A handful of people, crossing a fair swatch of the galaxy.*

Might as well put a human face on things.

She got up and turned to the stairway leading down to the passengers' cabin.

She also thought there was another reason to do this.

Get a good look at these people who'll be sharing this trip.

Who they are . . . what they're doing here.

And . . . always . . . any concerns. They'd already been screened for their potential to get roadsick—but that screening was far from 100 percent accurate. You never knew. Someone could ride the Road a couple of dozen times and be fine.

And then: Nausea and vomiting were the typical effects of roadsickness. But sometimes brain aneurisms. Occasionally, a passenger could have startling psychological reactions. Get violent, need to be restrained.

Which is why every Road vehicle stocked emergency kits with neoprene collars.

And then there were the few times a passenger had to be "neutralized." That was another euphemism . . . for what had to be done to get them to stop.

Which, depending on the circumstances, could be anything. One rule of the Road was that was *always* the captain's call.

Telling herself this would probably be another smooth and easy trip—
routine—Annie headed down to the passengers' area.

Annie stopped at the front and looked at the passengers settling into their
seats.

She knew their names from the manifest, which confirmed that they'd
been checked out by Mobius Security.

And rechecked.

Then checked again.

*Nothing to worry about here*, she thought.

Unless, of course, Mobius Central screwed up.

*Just like the Road itself . . . the unpredictable could always happen.*

In those seconds, she took in the group before they noticed her standing there, watching.

Sinjira Renku. Beautiful, exotic, legs curled up under her, ready to watch
a holovid.

A Chippie, with the nub of hardware extending from her skull just below her cerebellum on the left side of her head.

But more than just a Chippie. She was a Creator. Such a lofty, pretentious
name. Living and recording experiences for the masses who preferred their
thrills to be vicarious.

Though experiencing a chip was so real it felt like anything *but* vicarious.

Still, Sinjira had to go places and do things to record. And she looked like
the adventurous kind. Which explained why she was here. To capture this
Road trip for all those who would never have the money or get past their
fears to leave their safe home, much alone travel halfway across the galaxy.

Now the Chippie was talking to a man sitting across the aisle from her.

Rodriguez. A doctor. He appeared to be disinterested. Looking away.
Nodding. But maybe he wasn't about to admit that he liked what he saw.

Before she could scan the others—she'd already taken McGowan's measure in the cargo hold—people noticed her and looked up.

*I should start*, Annie thought.

But she paused when she finally noticed the figure wearing a hooded
cloak sitting in the backseat.

Annie glanced at the manifest: Ruth Corso. A Seeker. Not much on her.

*Seekers.*

Then: That, *I don't get. As if we need—what?—a new religion?*

Shaking her head, Annie focused on the job at hand.

"Good morning."

She waited. Now, everyone—even the Chippie—looked up.

"My name's Captain Annie Scott. I'm your pilot for our trip on the Road today. Normally"—she gestured up to the cockpit area—"pilots do the announcements from the cockpit. We're going to be together for a while, so I like to make things a little more personal."

Just then, Jordan emerged from the back gun turret and started up the aisle.

"I'd like to introduce our gunner—Jordan. Maybe the best gunner there is."

He looked up at Annie and—was that a smile?

"No maybe about it."

"He's modest, too."

The Chippie laughed, looking at Jordan like he was something she wanted to eat.

"We're cleared to leave Mobius Central, but before we do, there are a few things I want to go over. More for myself than for the Star Road Authority."

All eyes were on her.

*Good,* she thought. *I want their eyes and ears wide open.*

"We can never predict what might happen on the Road. Who was the anti-Road politician who said it's the Wild West out here? He called the Road 'too dangerous.' Said that anything can happen. And you know what? He had a point."

Rodriguez, the scientist, owlish in his glasses, dark eyes, sitting behind the Chippie. He looked like he didn't like the word "dangerous."

"What about what happened at the boarding gate today?" Nahara said.

"And," Rodriguez said, "the news. I heard there was an attack on some mining colony."

The scientist's face was tight with tension.

*Had he been carefully checked out?*

"Runners?" Annie said "Yeah. Sure. They're a problem. That's why it's damn good we have Jordan along for the ride. Runners are his specialty. But there are other things, Dr. Rodriguez—"

Sinjira looked up. All attention.

"You're a doctor?" She leaned close to Rodriguez. "Think you can drop a few scripts on me? I'll swap you for some . . . interesting chips. Real personal stuff."

"I'm not *that* kind of doctor."

*This trip is already turning interesting,* Annie thought.

She glanced at the miner up front. Not a newbie. Relaxed but still listening.

*Good reason to do that*, Annie knew.

For even an experienced Road traveler.

Check out your pilot. Your gunner. The people you're traveling with.

All that could be vital information.

"Once we start moving, this SRV is under my command. On this vehicle, my word is *law*. Any of you get roadsick, you signed the waiver, and I'm permitted to collar you to keep you calm. We all good with that?"

She paused a few seconds as everyone nodded. Even the cloaked figure at the back.

Bill Nahara, who worked for the authority, held her with his steady gaze.

*What's he doing, taking mental notes?* she wondered. *Will I get a report card?*

"Final things, then. The Road manual you all got tells you what to expect as we leave. Your CL devices will all work internally, but once we're on the Road, they're useless for any standard commlink purposes. The only way we'll stay in touch with Earth is through the pod stations at our stops along the way."

She took a breath.

"Any questions?"

Nothing.

"Good. Well, then, welcome to SRV-66. Once you strap yourselves in, we're set to go."

She turned and started up the stairs, back to the cockpit.

"Oh—one last thing. Only Jordan and I can open the cockpit doors. If you need to tell us something—if there's an emergency or something—use your CLs and fire us a message. We will—as they say—get back to you."

Despite having done more trips than she could remember, she couldn't help but feel excited as she entered the cockpit for final prep.

Because no matter how many times you've done it . . . getting on the Star Road *is* one hell of an amazing experience.

She felt good as she slid into the pilot's seat.

"All clear, Mobius Central."

"Clear at this end, SRV-66."

"You good, Jordan?"

A nod. Nothing more.

Annie shook her head. A small laugh.

Then: "You're something else, you know that, Jordan?"

And she started the vehicle's engine. The entrance ramp leading to the Road portal was straight ahead. Annie turned quickly enough to see the hint of a grin on the gunner's face.

*He likes it, too.*

# 6

## THE FIRST PORTAL

*Sinjira looked out her porthole,* a chip in place. Nothing out there yet to interest anyone, and the chip recording her feelings would show that.

*But you never know,* she thought. *Things happen.*

She looked at the guy across the aisle. The one she had flirted with in the bar.

*Why didn't he pick up on it?* she wondered. He was good-looking, although maybe a tad on the ordinary side.

*Intense, though. Like he's hiding something. But then again, who of us isn't hiding something?*

*He might be a fun ride,* she thought.

"First timer?" she asked.

He nodded.

For some reason, she didn't believe him.

Still not talkative.

She moved her legs, leaned a little closer . . . as far as the criss-cross straps would allow. The straps lifted and separated her breasts.

*Oh, yeah. Now he's looking.*

"Me, too. Going to be something, hmm?"

"Could be." He took a breath. Another look at her. "Guess so."

*All on the chip.*

*Why so damned cold?* she wanted to ask.

*Lighten up and enjoy life.*

Then the vehicle began moving. She looked outside. Then back to the man.

He was doing a great job of showing absolutely no interest in her.

But then again: *Things can change.*

"I like things that are intense," she said, still trying to draw him out. "People say my chips are—"

The vehicle bumped, its frame shuddering, the engine noise a low hum. And then she—and everyone else—got pushed back into her seat with an acceleration that grew steadily stronger.

Another quick look outside.

Still nothing exciting.

Then back to the man: "How about you—?"

But the guy had turned away and was staring out his porthole.

She thought . . . *Plenty of time to make something happen there.*

She smiled over her shoulder at the hooded woman—the Seeker— sitting in the back, so still . . . so calm. Spooky.

She turned to look out her porthole window again.

Something was going to happen soon.

Yeah. She could feel it.


"Approaching escape velocity," Annie said, toggling switches while her eyes darted back and forth across the controls.

It all looked good.

Jordan grunted, his eyes narrow. Focused.

The wheels of the SRV, a nearly indestructible combination of traditional and off-world alloys, now rolling at a steady speed.

The first time a ship approached a Road portal, it had exploded. Brilliantly. Over time—and at the cost of so many lives—pilots learned when and how fast to hit the portal.

Too slow, and you boomeranged down to the ground, a white-hot fireball. Too fast, and once you passed through the portal, regaining control was impossible. They couldn't even find the crew's atoms at that point.

But people, brave and foolish, kept trying . . . experimenting, and eventually they figured it out . . . within certain parameters. Still plenty of margin for error because no one knew exactly *how* any of it worked.

The simple fact was, it *did* work.

Why? Scientists were working on the physics.

As to who designed and built this system in the first place?

Not a damn clue.

Leave that to the Seekers and all the other crackpots, like the people who claimed the Star Road was God's nervous system.

*Now* there's *a thought.*

Annie touched the intercom button.

"Ladies and gentlemen, we're on the entrance ramp and coming up to our escape velocity. Might be a bit bumpy with those 'wheels' digging in. Like a roller coaster, if you remember what those are. If you look ahead, where you see . . . nothing. That's the portal. As I like to say, 'seeing is not believing.' For this trip, you just gotta believe—and hold on. If you have any concerns, don't hesitate to contact us."

She flicked the switch off. And smiled.

Jordan didn't turn to her, but he spoke: "That's supposed to reassure them?"

"Might as well make sure they get as much fun from their trip as they can—especially if it's their first."

The control panel dials glowed and flashed with colors that tinted the cabin with faint, pulsing waves. The SRV rocketed on the ramp, its metallic wheels not really touching the Road's surface but still making the vehicle feel like it was going to shake itself apart.

Annie hit more switches, slight adjustments, centering the SRV.

And where a holoscreen had showed only empty space dotted with stars, there now appeared a shimmering, multicolored ring—a hole, with a deep, starless blackness at its center. Swirls of bright rainbow colors ringed the outer edges, getting bigger and brighter by the second.

The imaging sensors intensified their readings on the Portal.

All the screens confirmed the SRV's speed and trajectory.

"Looking good," Annie said, not expecting a reply from Jordan.

To anyone watching from down below on the planetoid, it would appear that the vehicle was about to go *flying* off the ramp and careening over the horizon.

*Amazing sight to see.*

She held the controls in both hands now, trusting the computers to adjust for any fluctuations. Some SRV captains still called it "the helm" but that sounded way too military and old-school for Annie.

For her, it was simply "the wheel," and she held it tight.

The SRV rolled on nicely, at the crest of the ramp, leveling off, heading straight now.

Once she was through the portal, she'd really start to earn her pay.

Things could get weird in a nanosecond once they were through.

They had long since passed any "stop" or "turn back" position. No more exit ramps.

Still, she asked Jordan: "Everything okay on your readouts?"

"Perfect."

"Good."

Exiting . . . amazing . . . She had done this too many times to be scared or even unnerved, but still—the experience never lost its power.

Through the cockpit window, nothing ahead. But the vid screen showed the swirling circle of colors with its rapidly decreasing dark center.

*What kind of reality* is *this?* Annie asked herself as she shifted her gaze back and forth between the nothingness she saw ahead of her and the quantum fluctuations the nav-screens indicated were lying straight ahead.

She held the steering wheel tightly.

The SRV shaking wildly now, but the sensation odder than that.

She felt a disturbance on a molecular level. A primal, disturbing feeling.

If any of her passengers—or her, for that matter—was going to get roadsick, now would be the time.

In her mind, she counted down.

*Ten . . . nine . . . eight . . .*

It seemed like the right thing to do.

*Seven . . . six . . .*


Rodriguez grabbed the arms of his seat although the criss-cross straps made any movement difficult.

He told himself he wasn't really *scared* just . . . *uncomfortable.*

Doing this was all new to him, and he had no one to talk to express what he was really doing.

*Not good at secrets,* he acknowledged.

And there was this: *How much did he really know about what had happened on Omega Nine?*

*How much had they told him—and how much would he have to find out?*

*Most important—how much* didn't *they tell him?*

Pressed back into his seat, he took a shallow breath and looked at his porthole.

*It's all normal. Everything's fine,* he thought, feeling the SRV pick up even more speed.

*And for God's sake, don't get roadsick,* he told himself when a wave of salty nausea swept though his stomach.

The air in the SRV suddenly seemed too thin to breathe.

Rodriguez told himself he couldn't *actually* feel the atoms in his body rearranging themselves as the SRV shot up the ramp that seemingly ended in a wall of nothingness.

He tried not to think about the disastrous fall to the rocky desolate landscape of the planetoid below that was seconds away.

*Next time, stay home,* he vowed as he closed his eyes and tried to settle in his seat. *Next time, send someone else.*


Annie checked a screen to her right, which showed the terminal's air locks shutting behind the SRV.

There was no turning back now, and—at this speed—no stopping.

She pulled back on the wheel and felt the SRV pick up even more speed. The alloy wheels on the ramp surface made the vehicle shimmy like it might shake itself apart.

Some of the first-time passengers might not be enjoying this part, sitting helplessly in a vehicle that was screaming up a ramp that looked like it ended in nothing but a solid, black wall.

Stomachs must be lurching, to be sure. Vision distorted. The dimensions of the cabin shifting, twisting.

It only lasted for a short while, but with the space-time distortions, it felt like forever.

She hoped people remembered to use the bags in the pouches on the seat back in front of them if they needed to.

She turned to Jordan.

"Still okay on your end?"

"I'd tell you if it wasn't."

Less than a minute away.

Annie's hands tightened on the wheel.

She thought: *This . . . never gets old.*

*No way in hell . . .*


Sinjira moved her head from side to side, taking in the vastness of space on either side of the SRV. It was difficult to get a clear view of what was ahead, but that might be because the physics of Road travel were warping space, time, and gravity—at least, that's how she understood it.

Hers wasn't the first chip documenting a Road trip. Not by a long shot.

But with their destination the farthest outpost of Omega Nine—where along the way anything was possible—she wanted it to be the absolute best.

She wanted it to be—*real.*

When a chip was *so* good, that was the only word you could use. Not amazing, not fantastic. Real.

She leaned against the window so she caught a view of the ramp ahead. It ended abruptly, and she suddenly identified with that crazy-ass Seeker back there.

Accept it.

*It's out of your control.*

She kept her gaze fixed on the edge of the ramp, eager for what was going to happen next.

Even if she wasn't ready.

No one ever is their first time.

On the screen just below Annie's wheel, the clear image of the portal swirled like the storms on Jupiter or the mammoth flaring sunspots on the Earth's sun, changing colors, shape, pulsing as if a living, breathing thing.

*Who knows?*

*Maybe it is.*

The trickiest part of her job was about to happen.

On the screen, the SRV's nose entered the portal. For a timeless moment, the SRV seemed to stretch out to an infinite length. Straight ahead, through the cockpit window, the SRV headed—seemingly—into absolutely nothing.

Even the most seasoned captain couldn't help but be rocked by the feel and experience of this distortion of length, width, height, depth, and time.

A single moment that one poet described as a "fall into the dark backward."

*It'll pass*, Annie told herself as she watched her hands—looking strangely disconnected from her—run over the controls.

And then: speed.

It was as if the vehicle hit something that sent it rocketing even faster. There was no concussive sound. No display of light. And—thankfully—the rattling and the dimensional distortion stopped, as if the SRV was flying through space, which it was perfectly capable of doing.

Except it wasn't flying.

It had entered the Road.

And one look out the window gave an indication of how fast they were going. Long distended streaks of light flashed by. Amazing arrays of color suddenly appeared and winked out before the eye could fix, much less identify them.

Despite the sudden sensation of increased speed, it certainly didn't match what Annie or any of her passengers could see outside. Ahead, through the cockpit window, stars approached and flashed by, receding like strands of diamonds leaving spiraling contrails.

Whole systems—galaxies, even—shifted, spiraling in ways that would take thousands, if not millions, of years at anything approaching normal traveling speed.

Here, it all happened between breaths.

And below the vehicle was the Road itself.

A shimmering, multicolored ribbon, amazingly translucent and solid, distorting and warping everything as it stretched out ahead, curving, looping, circling as if laid out over hummocks, or perhaps dodging outcrops of rock of some landscape—only this landscape was the galaxy, if not the entire universe.

What was the Road actually navigating past?

What unseen cosmic forces did it cross or bend or ignore?

Maybe—crazy thought—it *was* alive, and it reacted to the ebb and flow of some ancient dance of space and time.

Was it, in fact, the "event horizon" that ringed black holes?

Annie smiled at her thoughts.

*Outside of my pay bracket to figure* that *one out.*

*If Earth's best scientists didn't have a clue, what were* her *ideas worth?*

Still—that was the thing about the Star Road—it made people *wonder.* Even Jordan.

No matter who experienced it, who traveled it, they experienced: wonder, amazement, curiosity, passion.

And for some—more than the Road Authority would ever admit—fear.

"Nice entry," Jordan said, his expression flat . . . unreadable as things returned to normal.

"Thanks. Thought it was pretty smooth myself . . ."

The crossover between the SRV hitting the Road after speeding up on the human-made ramp could be jarring. Especially with an inexperienced pilot. More than a few early tests sent vehicles flying off the Road, stranding them and their crew . . . who knew where?

Dead?

Alive?

In this universe . . . or some other dimension?

Ultimately, it didn't matter. They were never heard from again.

A screen centered above and between Annie and Jordan showed their relative position to the nearest star systems.

Still days away from having Omega Nine pop up—the end of the line for this trip.

But not the end of the Road.


Now, Annie could breathe.

Things were quiet now. She could just settle in, think about the trip ahead.

Their path well traveled, fully mapped.

That was important. The Road Authority estimated it had mapped a small section of what could very well be an infinite system connecting not only stars but galaxies.

Since the early days, they had explored a mere fraction of the Road using materials and machines unearthed on Pluto as models.

They used the ramp left by the Builders.

But who were they? The Builders?

And were they still out there?

More mysteries, and without more of the map, Omega Nine was the farthest point humans had gone.

*And plenty far enough for me*, Annie thought, considering it was more than halfway across the galaxy in a star-impoverished area of the Milky Way spiral arm scientists described as being "outside the Goldilocks Zone."

"Okay—going to check on the passengers."

"I've got the helm."

Annie smiled at his use of the word "helm" as she got up. She was still smiling as she unlocked the cockpit door and headed down the stairway to the passengers' cabin.

# TWO

# ON THE ROAD

# 7

## SOMETHING AHEAD

*Annie walked down the narrow* aisle. Most of the passengers were still staring outside at the dizzying display. At first, they didn't notice her.

Then Bill Nahara—the company man—looked up.

She had to wonder again: *What the hell is he doing here?*

Had to be some official Road Authority business.

Checking up on me . . . or Jordan . . . or one of the far system stations?

*It's like he's some kind of spy.*

In a small group and the tight confines of the SRV, that made her a tad suspicious—and uneasy.

McGowan was leaning back with his eyes shut. Could he really have done so many Road trips that he was already napping? Bored?

A wonder of the universe, and you doze off?

Then again, she knew that colony miners saw lots of strange things. Like ice planets with entire ecosystems simmering in the geothermal heat below a half-mile-thick frozen mantle. Or caves where new alloys and metals were discovered that seemed to share some qualities of organic material, responding to heat, light . . . or even touch.

Miners got used to "weird" pretty quickly.

Not a bad job even if some—maybe most—miners didn't make it back, no matter how strong an excavation suit they wore.

The pay—fantastic.

She cleared her throat.

"Just wanted to check to see how you're all doing down here?"

A few people turned to her quickly, nodding. The Seeker at the back—Corso—remained with her head bowed. McGowan opened his eyes to slits and grunted something unintelligible.

"No one feeling any roadsickness?"

Shakes of heads and mumbles all around.

*Everyone's fine here. Thanks for stretching out the molecules in my body until they snapped back like rubber bands.*

But Annie had to make sure. She studied each of them, looking for any indication of physical or psychological distress. The portal left even experienced passengers disoriented, and recovery time varied. Annie had one guy snap a year ago, who totally bugged out, wanting off the SRV in the middle of who-knew-where in space.

They'd had to collar him until he settled down.

But this group looked good.

"Okay, then. And we're up here in the cockpit if—"

She was still looking from passenger to passenger.

Good. No signs of anyone looking edgy except for Dr. Rodriguez. But he'd looked wide-eyed even before he boarded the SRV.

"—if you need help with anything, your CLs will work now. Any questions?"

There were none.

"I'm about to run the authority's official message—standard PR stuff. So if everyone's okay . . ."


"How are they?"

Jordan hadn't been with her when she'd had a passenger "malfunction." Everyone working for the authority had heard about it, though. Everyone knew psych screenings were good.

But they weren't perfect.

"Nice and quiet for the time being."

He nodded.

"Good."

They both knew that if someone went off-kilter, it was Jordan's job to restrain that person.

Collar, restrain, or—if necessary—kill.

Annie pressed a button and started the official Road vid.

•   •   •

The holoscreen materialized at the front out of thin air, and Ruth Corso looked up at the image of a man sitting at a desk. Big smile. The logo of the Star Road Authority was behind him.

His hands folded in front of him on the desk as if he was a bank's branch manager, he began speaking.

"Welcome to your Star Road vehicle and the amazing journey you have now begun!"

Ruth leaned forward, her elbows on her knees. She looked around and saw that not everyone was paying attention. But this was all new to her. New and definitely exciting.

"For the past two decades," the man went on, "we've been able to travel within our solar system using hybridrive. You all used Quarter Light Speed to get to your embarkation point on Pluto. As many of you know, QLS ships made the amazing discovery of the Star Road portal on Pluto. And thanks to the brave efforts and sacrifices of hundreds of adventurers, portions of the Star Road have been mapped and are now open for exploitation and exploration!"

*How many portions?* Ruth wondered.

Among fellow Seekers, it was understood: no one knows how big the Road is, how far it stretches, what secrets it holds.

"Using this amazing transportation system, we now have safe, dependable, and fast travel to many star and planetary systems that are hundreds, even thousands of light-years away from Earth."

Then Ruth thought: *I'm really doing this.*

*Leaving Earth.*

*Looking for those answers about the Road, humanity, and the universe itself.*

"Although the origin and full extent of the Star Road remains—for now—unknown . . . perhaps unknowable, we want you to relax and enjoy your trip in total comfort and safety. We are pleased to welcome you—"

The smiling man faded from the screen to be replaced by a twisting section of Star Road, unbelievably beautiful, shimmering. Music swelled.

"—to the Star Road!"

The screen dissolved into a thousand glittering pieces and vanished with an audible sizzle.

"Something, hmm?"

Ruth looked over at the Chippie seated in front of her, announcing her opinion to the small group.

Thinking: *I have nothing in common with someone like her.*

The man at the front of the cabin hadn't even watched the vid.

"So . . . who do you think made it?"

*Is this girl an idiot?*

As if *anyone* knows the answer to that question.

Still—everyone wondered.

Ruth spoke up.

After all, this was something she *believed*.

"I don't know. But they must have been . . . must *be* beings of amazing intelligence and understanding."

Sinjira turned in her seat to look back. "'Be'? You said 'be,' right? Like they're still around . . . ?"

The girl waved at the porthole, the vast flickering lights of space outside.

"You think they're still out there somewhere?"

Ruth looked away.

"I don't know," she said. "No one does. But I have faith that they are. That they're waiting."

"Waiting? Waiting for what?"

"For us—humans—to prove that we're worthy to meet them, to learn their secrets."

"Really?"

Sinjira grinned at the idea.

*I probably shouldn't say anything.*

Instead: "As soon as we leave behind all our evil, our violence, and when we prove that we, as a species, are ready."

"How's that working out for us . . . as a species?" Another big grin. "I think 'evil' is doing just fine."

*Pointless*, Ruth thought.

"We aren't 'done' as a species. No one knows . . . what's ahead," she said.

Sinjira nodded, still smiling.

"I like that," she said. *"No one knows.* That's so . . . so *real."*

Sinjira turned away.

And Ruth turned to her porthole and stared at the wonders shifting by outside.

Annie sat quietly, appreciating the smooth, gliding ride of the SRV.

In front of her, stars tilted and swirled as if part of a jacked-up planetarium show. She could almost imagine the hissing, crackling sounds the stars made as they slid by so fast.

The quiet in the cockpit, sitting here with Jordan, took on a deep solemnity.

*Like entering church*, she thought. Not that she had been to church in a few decades.

But something about a Road trip made her—and obviously Jordan—quiet. Maybe she'd engage the Seeker in a conversation later . . . if only to pass the time.

Her hands remained on the controls, making slight adjustments, but with the Road so straight here, stretching out to what seemed a vanishing point in infinity, the SRV nearly drove itself.

She focused on her breathing.

The feel of the cockpit space. The tremendous beauty outside. The steady humming sound of the SRV's engines.

*The wonder of it all*, she thought.

And then, without warning, a light on the screen to her left began to flash. The view ahead changed. Magnified. And a dark mass appeared far off in the distance.

A warning buzzer sounded in the cockpit.

"Shit!"

Annie's hands flew across the controls, calling up information.

"There's something on the Road ahead?" Jordan said simply.

Biting her lower lip, Annie nodded.

"Maybe just debris. Happens."

Jordan grunted and nodded.

"In which case, it's got maybe—what? Five minutes? Ten, tops, until the Road Bugs show up."

"We're closing fast," Annie said.

*Fast enough?*

She looked at the controls wondering if she should slow it down. The video display of whatever was up ahead was blurry . . . pixilated.

*What the hell was it?*

"Might be a Road Ship. A one-man Speeder. The mass is big enough."

Annie studied the screen a moment longer. Then hit the comm button.

"If I could have your attention, please."

She paused, imagining the various reactions in the passengers' cabin. Did they know they might have just hit trouble?

"We've detected . . . something on the Road ahead—" She didn't use the word "anomaly."

"Please make sure your harnesses are secure."

Now Jordan worked his console, trying to get a clearer image of whatever it was ahead of them. There were too many possibilities, but the first thought—as it was for any Road traveler—was: *Runners? Maybe an ambush?*

Mobius Control had said everything was quiet ahead.

But they'd been known to make mistakes.

"Just to be safe . . . might want to train your main gun on the Road ahead."

"What do you think I'm doing?"

Annie took a breath to calm down as she glanced at Jordan's fingers, so quickly adjusting the weapon's sights. He centered the object in his crosshairs.

"Road Bugs would have gotten to it and cleaned it up by now, don't you think?" Annie asked.

"Depends. Might have just happened."

He turned and looked at her.

"Could be anything, Annie."

Then he flipped a switch and said, "Got the front turret gun on it, too. Whatever it is."

Before Annie could say a word, he unstrapped his harness and got out. He unlocked the cockpit door and hurried down the aisle.

He wanted to be hands-on, no matter what it was.


"What's up?" the dark, twitchy guy, Rodriguez, asked as Jordan walked by.

Jordan ignored him. And ignored the Chippie, who looked up at him.

*Anxious?*

Definitely, but maybe just anxious to record what was about to happen?

But he didn't—he *couldn't* ignore Ruth when he passed by her seat. Their eyes met.

He could see her fear, her concern.

Still—best he kept his mouth shut.

After all . . . *it could be nothing.*

He moved out of the passenger compartment and opened the hatch door to climb into the main gun turret.

He settled into the seat and strapped in. Now he had direct control of the gun. The turret filled with the high-pitched whining sound of the charged pulse cannon, ready to fire.

He put on his headset.

Then—finally—Jordan smiled.

*I may get to shoot something after all.*

Through the patched-in comm system, he heard Annie saying something in the cockpit. Then a voice—a man's voice—broken by washes of static and shrill feedback. The Road always did weird things to communications.

"May-Day . . . -Day . . . This . . . damage . . ."

Over the headset, Jordan heard Annie's voice.

"This is Captain Annie Scott of the SRV-66. Identify yourself."

". . . chell . . . flying  solo . . . systems  overheated . . . possible . . . life support . . . port going . . ."

"Say again!" Annie said.

The commlink was weak, if not broken, but Jordan could piece enough together, and he knew Annie could, too.

". . . power  cores . . . induction  coil's  dumped . . . before  the . . . show up . . . me into rubbish . . ."

Whoever it was, he was minutes away from being "cleaned up" by the Road Bugs.

Having seen them in action, the only thing Jordan could compare it to was a frenzied shark attack.

*Whoever it is better hope the SRV gets to him first.*

Jordan took a breath, flexed his fingers, and waited.

"We're closing fast," he heard Annie say. "Are you capable of transfer?"

Jordan shook his head when he heard this.

No shooting today—unless the Road Bugs showed up first.

Just picking up someone stranded on the Road.

That was the code, whether he liked it or not.

*Stay frosty,* Jordan told himself.

# 8

## THE CODE OF THE ROAD

*This seemed strange.* Why a *breakdown?* Annie thought. Things like that ... just didn't happen.

"Why did your coil dump?"

The commlink turned clearer now. The man's voice steady—in control.

Pretty good, considering he might be facing a horde of Road Bugs any minute now.

"Please ID yourself," Annie said, her voice firm.

"Solo civilian vehicle. RA number IMT-9. My name is Gage ... Gage Mitchell."

"Individual Mass Transit," Annie muttered as she punched the information into the ship's computer. Moments later, the display flashed a message that the registration checked out as valid.

*So he's a civilian. Out on the Road. Alone. Doing ... what?*

"We're decelerating. Prepare for docking." Annie kept her voice steady. She could see Jordan in the turret.

"Atmospherics are low. I'm not sure I can pressurize the connector," Gage said.

"Have you got an EVA suit?" Annie asked.

"I'm wearing it as we speak."

*Good ... must be a resourceful and experienced traveler. Not some incompetent newbie.*

"You're damned lucky we chanced by," Annie said.

"Yeah ... all I have is luck."

. . .

Rodriguez looked out the porthole.

He looked back at the others—all also glued to their windows.

*We're definitely slowing down,* he thought.

*That's* not supposed to happen.

He looked around.

"Why are we slowing down?"

"We're not," said the old man—the miner—across the aisle from him. "Looks to me like we're stopping."

"Why would we stop out here?"

Rodriguez realized that he must have sounded scared.

Nothing he could do about that. Because he *was . . .*

"Probably—something on the Road ahead. Maybe some debris or a stranded vehicle."

"And . . . ?"

"Code of the Road. We have to stop and offer any and all assistance in the event of a breakdown."

*Sounds like he's quoting the damned manual,* Rodriguez thought.

"Shouldn't be a big deal. Not to worry, amigo."


Annie was the first to see them.

A glance to the image of Jordan in the turret, suddenly looking up at his camera, to her.

"Damn! Jordan—"

"Hell, yeah. Here they come."

Road Bugs.

If anything stopped on the Road, it was just a matter of time—usually minutes—before the Road Bugs showed up. Like much of the Road, no one had any idea what they were, but their function, *that* was simple, obvious.

Any debris on the Road that didn't keep moving—no matter the size or contents—would be engulfed by Road Bugs and seemingly consumed.

In minutes

*Destroyed. As if it had never existed.*

Annie leaned closer to the screen, seeing the bugs scrambling— apparently—from the underside of the Road.

They came in a variety of sizes and shapes, and they had gotten the name "Road Bugs" because of their weird superstructures and configurations that suggested—to the imaginative, anyway—Earthlike insects.

When these insects were through, even a vehicle as large as a World Council troop ship would disappear. Every atom. Where all the mass and energy went was anyone's guess.

And now, from both sides of the Road, the Road Bugs started swinging up and over the glowing edge of the Road, scuttling toward the stranded vehicle, IMT-9.

And the stranded pilot of the vehicle?

It didn't look like he had a chance.

# 9

## GAGE

Gage.

Ivan Delgato kept repeating the name in his mind even as the SRV and its captain came closer.

*Gage Mitchell.*

A mantra to remind him of who he was now.

*Got to make sure I respond to that name naturally. And convince her that I'm . . . what?*

Some digital supervisor doing his first on-site inspection? A manager for a mining operation, checking on output?

*Good luck pulling any of that off,* he told himself. *Just keep your mouth shut, and you might be fine.*

And what about his SRV's breakdown?

The trip just begun—and then the damned induction core failed.

*Sabotage?*

Could be. There were plenty of people who would love to see his mission fail and for him to disappear . . . forever.

*Better—and more permanent—than Cyrus Penal Colony.*

Now, he watched the Road Bugs . . . ten, eleven of them begin ripping at his ship, pulling it to pieces, cutting, slicing, and then the piece was gone.

*Not much damned time.*

He saw the approaching SVR on his screen, pulses already erupting from its main gun.

Bugs began flying off the road, exploding in a flash of light, then vanishing.

*Whoever's manning the turret gun is good . . .*

But the Road Bugs kept swarming toward him from both sides of the Road. Even with the gunner picking them off almost as fast as they appeared, it was only a matter of time until they made their way into the innards of the ship, to him.

Every blazing flash of his own pulse cannon ignited the Road Bugs, who then exploded in rippling lines of color, leaving behind twisted scraps of metal that other Road Bugs quickly stopped to ingest.

Now, though, he could hear them working in the back. Soon the SRV's big guns would be useless.

No good that close.

*Then they'll come straight for me.*

His breathing seemed loud inside the EVA helmet. The faceplate fogged around the edges, the compressed air inside not warmed up yet. The fringes of his vision took on the colors of a prism.

He kept his eyes on the gunner whose pin-point accurate pulses were keeping the Road Bugs in check.

*Still too many, though.*

Adrenaline surged through his system. All he could do was pick off any bug that came into his limited range. That, and wait, sitting there like bait in a trap, waiting to be eaten.

A vibrating shudder ran through his vehicle, shaking him side to side.

"You feel that?" The SRV's captain voice in his ear, crystal clear inside his helmet.

"Yeah—trouble docking?"

"That wasn't us."

*The Road Bugs. Must be a bunch in the rear now.*

"How long?" Ivan asked.

"Docking in . . . thirty seconds."

He took a breath, waiting.

"On my mark in three . . . two . . . one . . . mark!"

Another sickening rattle.

*That might not be soon enough.*

In the strange quantum void of the Star Road, he didn't hear the sound, but something—the Bugs?—was shaking his entire ship. He flipped on his external rearview.

And saw a Road Bug—bigger than any he'd ever seen—flanked by several others. He watched it take a huge bite out of the rear of his IMT.

*The thing. A monster.*

*Responding to the others getting blown away?*

Then: *Hurry.*

What little air was left inside the vehicle rushed out . . .

He watched the giant Road Bug's jaws close down from top, bottom, and both sides. The metal of his vehicle simply . . . vanishing.

*I'm next.*


Ivan turned and looked into the back of the cabin.

He raised his pulse rifle, but held his fire for a moment and stared into the gullet of the machine—

*Even if it is a machine*

—eating through his SRV.

The thing seemingly made of metal and who knew what other substances. But then, on the shimmering surface, the way it rippled . . . looking organic . . . biological . . .

*No time to study it now*, he thought, and fired.

The stream of light caught the Road Bug full on, blowing it back and away from the ship. Another blast, then another, and it turned into a glowing mass of fragments that flared for a moment and then disappeared when they landed on the Road.

"You here yet?" Ivan said into his commlink.

Longest damn thirty seconds he had ever experienced.

He tried to remain calm.

More bugs, maybe even bigger ones, would come.

"We're gonna have to do this on the fly," the SRV's captain said. "If I slow and stop, the bugs will be on me, too."

"Right. Got it."

The odds . . . turning worse.

Now a side section of his IMT disappeared, ripped away.

A smaller hole. But metal—*if that's metal*—jaws started digesting the skin of his vehicle, chewing from the side, right next to him.

"Go to your airlock and get ready to evacuate."

"Gotcha," Ivan said as he stood up from the helm.

A rattling from above.

Another Road Bug, this one landing on the top. The impact threw Ivan off balance, and he fell to his knees. His EVA helmet rang like a metal gong when it struck the cockpit wall.

*No way*, he thought.

He stood up fast, grabbing at anything for support. The suit—so damned heavy.

He wasn't sure if the spiraling pinpoints of light were outside on the Road or inside his head.

The support beams of the vehicle's ceiling started sagging inward from the crushing weight. And then a section of the roof three meters wide on each side simply flew away and disappeared inside the Road Bug's maw.

Shaking his head to clear it and keeping one hand on the wall to keep himself oriented, he crossed over to the airlock in three long steps.

"Ready whenever you are," he said.

Through the portal on the airlock, he could now see the metal flank of the SRV beside him, moving forward, then back, not daring to actually stop.

Amazing pilot, that's for sure.

Before the SRV captain said anything, he slapped the door control.

But the door didn't open.

*A Road Bug must have taken out the electronics.*

Ivan took a breath. Then he grabbed the manual override bar and pulled it. Nothing. Then another pull, and it finally moved. The outer airlock door slid open.

And then, there it was.

To his left, moving slowly past him—four meters away—the huge flank of the SRV. Leaning out over the Road and looking down the length of the vehicle, he made out the small, dark square of the open airlock hatch.

A black rectangle in the side of the much larger vehicle.

"Can you get closer?" he said.

Road Bugs might get him before he hit the airlock.

The SRV still sliding past him—slowing down but not stopping.

Then it started moving back.

*Now or never.*

Ivan placed both hands on the sides of the opened hatch and began shifting back and forth, getting ready, timing his jump as the opening moved steadily closer.

He would have only one chance at this. He saw bug activity on both sides.

He was totally exposed here.

Make it, and he would live.

Miss it, and he would find out all about the Road Bugs.

*If the fall doesn't kill me.*

The opening loomed larger as it came closer.

The SRV moved in tighter, closing the gap. But still several meters away.

Could he jump that far without a running start?

He was bouncing on the balls of his feet, flexing . . . tensing . . . getting ready, and then: with the airlock opening still not directly opposite from him, he jumped.

The instant before his feet left the deck, another Road Bug—maybe more than one—slammed into the sides of his motionless vehicle. The impact threw him off balance. He tried to adjust his jump, but the SRV—needing to keep moving—was already pulling past him.

His arms flailed wildly as he shot across the gap. Below him was the shimmering surface of the Road.

The SRV's airlock opening already looked too far away.

It had passed him.

But he twisted and thrashed in midair, legs and arms pinwheeling crazily, and—somehow—he caught the receding edge of the portal. A jolt of pain shot through him when his body slammed against the outer shell of the SRV. Without the EVA suit, he would have been squashed.

But his grip held.

Dangling above the Road, grunting loudly, he strained to pull himself up and into the bay. He chanced a quick look over his shoulder.

The Road Bugs had swarmed over and were busily devouring his vehicle. Another few seconds, and he would have been part of their "clean-up."

Ivan swung around and reached up to grab the door frame with his other hand. Then . . . slowly . . . arms aching from the angle and the weight of the suit, he pulled himself up. He kicked with his legs to get some kind of foothold.

Every muscle in his body felt strained to the breaking point.

One massive effort, and he managed to hoist himself up waist-high, to the bottom edge of the door.

He swung his right leg over the metal lip of the door and rolled to safety.

"Punch it," he said, breathing hard into his helmet mic.

The captain responded immediately, and the SRV started moving forward much faster. Ivan was still sitting against the airlock door, catching his breath, when the outer door slid shut, and the lights inside the airlock came on.

They were pressurizing the airlock and—thankfully—the door would open soon to let him inside.

And see just how he had rescued him.


"Thanks for picking me up," he said.

"Code of the Road," the SRV captain said. "SOP, as they say."

No emotion in her voice.

*Not exactly glad to have me aboard.*

And then: "Scanner indicates you're packing a sidearm. I expect you'll take it out and leave it on the airlock floor . . . once you can stand up."

*Drop my weapon?*

*Is she kidding?*

He never went anywhere unarmed.

"I don't think we should be arguing the point—"

"We're not arguing it. Lose the weapon, or you can stay where you are until we get to our first way station, and I'll let you and the council police work it out."

He shook his head, and slowly stood up, using the wall for support. He had no doubt the captain or the gunner—probably both—were watching him on the closed-circuit vid.

That's what *he'd* do.

So he made a show of drawing his pulse pistol, all nice and out in the open, dangling it from his forefinger, and then knelt down to place it gently onto the floor.

"I like your manners," the captain said. "You ready to come aboard now?"

"It would sure be more comfortable than staying in here."

Ivan stood by the interior airlock door. Head bowed. Hands braced on both sides of the doorway. He waited for the pressure in the airlock to equalize so he could enter the passengers' cabin.

When the light went green, he took off his helmet and prepared himself.


"You done good," Annie said, looking over at Jordan on the screen as he unbuckled his harness and then stood up from his station. "As usual."

Jordan nodded. He didn't need to be told.

But he liked hearing it.

"That big Road Bug. New to me."

Drawing his pistol, he walked over to the cabin door, unlocked it, and went down the short flight of steps to the passengers' cabin.

"That was *muy intensivo*," the Chippie said as he walked past her to get to the airlock. "I got most of it chipped . . . right up until when that guy jumped. Then he was too close to the ship. Would have been so freakin' *real*!"

"Good for you," Jordan said.

When he got to the door, he checked the readouts, made sure the pressure inside and outside the airlock had equalized. Then he punched the button.

As the door slid open, he stepped back to take a quick measure of the man standing there.

Slightly built but strong looking. Wiry . . . dark, intense blue-green eyes.

Eyes that said he'd seen and done things.

Calm . . . self-assured, especially considering the nightmare he'd just escaped.

He was sure the man was quickly assessing him as well.

"Welcome aboard," Jordan said as he stepped past him and into the airlock to retrieve the man's pistol—an Armstrong 49.

*Nice piece of weaponry. Lot of kick. And not cheap.*

"You the gunner?"

Jordan nodded.

"That was some fine work you did just now."

Jordan nodded again. Then: "Your name again?"

"Ahh, Gage . . . Gage Mitchell."

*Why the hesitation?* Jordan wondered.

"And you are . . . ?"

"Jordan."

When they shook hands, Jordan became aware that this new passenger, Gage Mitchell, was still taking his measure.

*Guy thinks he's tough . . . and maybe he is.*

And: *What's he doing out here, roading solo?*

"Thanks again for stopping," Gage said. "That was a little closer than I cared for."

"Good thing you jumped when you did. You hurt?"

Gage smiled. "A few aches. Bruises. Nothing to worry about."

"Good. Captain'll be down in a bit to talk to you. In the meantime"—he nodded toward the lavatory at the back of the vehicle—"you might want to get out of that suit and clean yourself up before you settle in. Close quarters here."

"Sounds good, thanks," he said.

Jordan watched Gage as he started down the aisle, ignoring the other passengers until . . .

The Chippie reached up and grabbed Gage's arm at the elbow.

"There's an empty seat across from me. I'd like to . . . get to know you better."

But the new arrival shook her off, ignoring her—and all the others staring at him—as he entered the lavatory and closed the door.

Back in the cockpit, Jordan sat down in his seat and strapped himself in.

"So . . . what've we got?" Annie asked.

Her fingers played across the controls, making adjustments as the SRV resumed its normal speed.

"Beats me," Jordan replied.

"Anyone get roadsick back there when we decelerated?"

"Not that I could smell."

Annie nodded. "Good. I'll go back and have a little chat with him in a bit."

"Excuse me."

Ruth leaned over and touched the arm of the man they just rescued, sitting across from her.

"This might sound, I don't know, strange. But don't you think it's wrong to kill those Road Bugs?"

The man glanced at her and shrugged. She could see that he saw her for what—not who—she was, a Seeker, and dismissed her.

"I mean, the Builders made them to protect the Road—"

Ruth was aware the Chippie was watching them both, always recording . . . even this simple question.

"Builders, hmm?" Gage said. "Never met one. And those things? No different from shooting a sonic cleaner or a blender."

Exactly the answer she expected.

*So ignorant*, she thought.

Still, the man, his voice, the way his eyes caught the light—he had charisma, no doubt about that.

Which is probably why the Chippie kept turning around and looking at him.

"That's funny," the Chippie said. "Blender . . ."

"Still," Ruth said, "if the Builders made them, we should treat them with the utmost respect. This is *their* Road."

"The only thing that gets respect—especially as far out as I'm going—is a gun and someone, like that Jordan guy, who knows how to use it."

Ruth lowered her head.

*Pointless.*

This guy was just another arrogant jerk who had bullied his way through life, taking what he wanted and damn everyone else.

Still, she had to try.

"Respect isn't something you *get*," she said, straightening her shoulders. "It's something you earn."

Then he turned to her.

"Is this a church or an SRV?" Gage sniffed with laughter at that and then, leaning closer and eyeing her steadily: "You keep on believing that, Sister. Live and let live. Me? I'll use the Road for anything and everything I can get from it."

Ruth thought, *Right . . . an arrogant jerk.*

She turned away from him just as the cockpit door opened, and the captain came down the flight of stairs.

Moving quickly, Annie walked down the aisle and stopped in front of Gage.

She placed both hands on the seats and leaned down toward him.

"Hi. Annie Scott," she said, extending a hand. The man shook it. A strong handshake.

*This guy's no office worker.*

"Your flight plan checks out with what I have in my computer. But I'll still want to send a pod back for confirmation once we reach the way station."

"No problem," Gage said.

"I'm curious what you're doing out along this route in a solo. Kinda unusual. And dangerous."

"Heading to Omega Nine . . . like you, I guess, if you're going to the end of the line."

"Yeah, but . . . a solo?"

"Uh-huh."

"And what's your business on Omega Nine?"

He smiled. The answer total bullshit.

"Family stuff."

"You have family on Omega Nine?"

Gage nodded and said, "Last time I checked—yeah. But, rescue or not, I don't see where it's any of your business. I do appreciate you stopping and saving my skin—for following the code."

"We don't get an option with that," she said.

She thought: *This guy needs to be watched. Something's . . . off.*

"And no worries—I'll make sure to transfer the transportation fee to your account when we get to the way station. What way station is it, anyway?"

"Way Station One—Epsilon Two Sector. So, why a solo?" the captain asked again.

"Only ship I could find at the time."

"So why not this SRV? I had a few empty seats."

The man shrugged.

"I left before you did."

"In a hurry?"

"You could say that. Still . . . I don't see where that's any of your business."

"Right. Okay. Good chatting. Just make sure you're no trouble to any of my paying passengers. Or me . . . or my SRV. Understand?"

"Perfectly."

Then she turned and walked back to the cockpit.


Ruth watched the captain leave and then looked back at Gage, slouched in his seat, hands folded across his stomach.

He looked at her and smiled.

He *likes* playing with people.

As if this *is all a game.*

Just like too many people she had met in her life. People like him were the reason she had joined the Seekers in the first place.

To get away from people who would say or do anything as long as they got what they wanted.

"If you don't mind . . ." he said, smile fading. His voice was low, edged with fatigue. "I'd just as soon not have any more sermons for the time being. That all right with you?"

Ruth stared at him for a moment, then adjusted her cowl as she turned to the window.

•   •   •

Ivan looked around at the other passengers.

Some of them—especially the Chippie—were watching him as well. The old-timer up front was dead to the world. The guy across from him looked like he was gone—lost in whatever chip he was using.

Behind him, a twitchy guy, eyes flickering around the passengers' quarter and then stopping on Ivan a few too many times.

But Ivan was glad there were so few of them.

It would make his masquerade a little easier to pull off.

Except for that gunner, Jordan.

Good gunner, no doubt. Rock solid. Someone who kept his guns and his suspicions close.

And what would he do if, for some reason, after all the planning, all the steps taken to make sure this worked . . . what if someone found out?

He needed to rest now, but even after a sonic shower in the lavatory, he felt wired. Maybe a few som-tabs would calm him down.

Too bad he had left his belongings in his vehicle—other than his pistol, which Jordan now had.

*Just the clothes on my back*, he thought.

Still—despite uncountable times on the Road performing maneuvers in places where there were no ramps—and Star Road portals could be anywhere, between mountaintops, hovering over vast chemical seas—Ivan kept a tight grip on the arms of his seat.

A primitive reflex.

As if that would help if shit got real.

Or was he feeling wound up because of his recent brush with death?

*All those Road Bugs. So close . . .*

No. He'd seen and fought plenty of those in his time with the Runners.

More than likely, he was worried Jordan had already seen through his "Gage Mitchell" routine. He'd had some micro-sculpting done on his face back on Earth, but when he looked in the mirror, he still saw his own face—Ivan Delgato.

Maybe Jordan did, too?

Like the other passengers, he was as firmly strapped into the seat as he could be.

He didn't like it. He should be piloting.

*I don't make a good passenger.*

It didn't help that he was unarmed and at the mercy of this Captain Annie Scott.

He looked out the porthole to his right. The light show and visuals of warped space were all hypnotizing. The display of interweaving colors and lights outside the SRV soon had him shutting his eyes. Sleep . . . would be good.

And then, just as he was dipping deeply into unconsciousness, the feeling so soothing, the cabin PA chimed, and Captain Annie Scott's voice yanked him violently awake.

"Attention passengers—"

# 10

## BOARDING PARTY

"*Just thought you'd want to* know we're coming up on Way Station One in the Epsilon Two Sector."

As she spoke, Annie fixed her focus on the forward screen, adjusting it for random fluctuations in the forces surrounding the SRV.

"Our layover will be three hours. Once we've docked and cleared security, it'll be a good chance for you to get out and stretch your legs. Get some fresh air. Indigenous life on Epsilon Two has some dangerous predators, so I highly recommend that you stay within the confines of the terminal."

*What am I? A tour guide? A babysitter? If anybody wants to venture outside and get eaten . . . so be it.*

Then she focused all of her attention on the screens and readouts flashing in front of her.

"All good?" she asked.

"Looking fine," Jordan answered.

"Portal entry in—"

She checked some more readouts. Toggled some switches.

"Five . . . four . . . three . . . two . . . one . . . contact."

Once again, the physical dimensions of the cabin—and the entire ship—altered.

Only this time, everything shortened as if the world—or the ship, anyway—was now at the wrong end of an old-fashioned telescope.

Annie enjoyed the rush of reentry. She hoped her passengers were ready for it. Even after doing this scores, if not hundreds, of times, she braced herself for the wave of strangeness that was a portal exit.

Fortunately, the physical and mental effects didn't last long.

She blinked, needing to focus quickly now.

The approach ramp appeared directly below her SRV.

*Easy . . . easy . . .*

*Touchdown.*

The SRV shuddered when it impacted physical reality, and then it started rolling along the long entry ramp. Its wheels squealed inside the cockpit as Annie braked the vehicle.

"Easy now . . . easy . . ."

This landing was trickier than most. Epsilon was a jungle planet—with some rugged terrain. Giant cliffs could pop up anywhere.

The approach ramps hadn't been laid straight. Like many planets with Star Road portals, the ramp curved and angled in a variety of directions to accommodate the topography.

*Made for some fun driving.*

She watched as dense vegetation flashed by in a green blur that eventually—as the SRV slowed down—resolved into individual trees draped with vines, creepers, and a riot of bizarre flowers of every conceivable color, size, and variation. Birds and large insects of species she had never seen or noticed before scattered into the forest and sky.

Some of the flowers, rumor had it, were carnivorous. One SRV had supposedly lost a curious passenger or two a few years back.

The atmosphere here was dense with moisture. On the horizon, massive gray thunderheads were slowly building up for a late afternoon shower and lightning show.

Fresh air and rain would be a relief—a luxury after the close, dry air of the SRV.

The daily storms, though, could be terrifying.

Jordan let out a gasp, and then muttered, "Son of a *bitch*!" Annie turned to him.

It didn't take long to see what had gotten his attention.

In the distance, parked beside the terminal, was a World Council Troop Transport.

Even through the gray haze at such a great distance, the vessel looked huge . . . undeniably impressive. Imposing. Its flanks bristled with gun turrets, observation ports, and loading bay doors.

Its giant wheels were taller even than SRV-66.

Smaller winged and ground craft moved around the troop ship like wasps swarming a hive.

Annie had only a second or two to stare at and admire the ship. Her commlink beeped and came to life. The voice from control center filled the cockpit.

"SRV-66. You are cleared to approach the terminal." The voice sounded metallic . . . hollow.

Annie's HUD flashed a map of the landing-ramp network. A glowing green line marked her approach path. The laser guidance system was locked on.

*This is the easy part,* she thought. *Sit back and enjoy the ride.*

Let the automatics navigate the winding roads and cloverleafs that lead to the terminal. Annie took another moment to look out at the huge warship.

"That's some ship, huh?" she asked.

Jordan grunted. Barely looked at it.

He didn't look happy.

*Not a big fan of the World Council,* she knew.

Not that Jordan talked about that kind of stuff.

"Makes me wonder what a World Council troop ship's doing out here."

Jordan sniffed and said, "If it's any of our business, I reckon we'll find out soon enough."

Even before he completed the sentence, control center came on again: "SRV-66. Please transmit you passenger's manifest to the tower immediately."

That got Jordan's attention.

He looked at Annie with surprise. *This isn't standard.*

*Something's . . . up.*

Annie almost replied that her passenger and cargo manifest, for that matter, were the company's private business.

But not with a World Council Troop Transport out there . . . within easy firing range.

*Best to comply.*

"Uh . . . roger that," she said. She didn't bother to ask if they wanted her cargo manifest, too. She'd only give that when—and if—they asked for it.

She called up the passenger list and stats on the computer. And stared at the list for a moment to see if anything . . . popped out at her.

She didn't see anything. Still . . .

*Might be that twitchy guy—Nahara. Or maybe this had something to do with the guy back at the boarding gate back on Pluto.*

*Or were they interested in her new passenger?*

Any questions, though, could have been dealt with in a message pod.

"Captain—we're still waiting for that passenger manifest," the voice of control center said. Sounded like a frigging robot. Probably was.

"Yeah, yeah, yeah."

Annie hit SEND. Then looked at Jordan, who shrugged.

*It's out of our hands.*

"Please make your way to gate four, and do not disembark your crew or passengers until you receive our say so."

"Gotcha," Annie said. Then she killed the commlink and whispered: "This is total bull—"

"Captain Scott."

Another voice—this one sounding chipper and bright—filled the cockpit. Whereas control center didn't use a holovid, this one did. The face of a young man—*a child,* Annie thought—appeared in 3-D on her main screen.

"And you are . . . ?" Annie was unable to disguise how pissed off she was.

"Commander Arno Lahti. World Council Security."

A security officer. Ice water ran in their veins.

Annie knew this Arno Lahti could see her and Jordan as clearly as she could see him. Still, she glanced at Jordan and made a sour face.

*I don't have to like this . . .*

"Prepare to be boarded," Lahti said.

The words were barely out of his mouth when Jordan's hand dropped below the console, checking his side holster.

"Jordan . . . chill."

*I hope he has the sense not to go up against a World Council commander.*


Ivan Delgato woke with a start.

Off the Star Road. Landed. Now, he felt momentarily disoriented. Confused.

He looked out the window and saw that the SRV had come to a stop on the tarmac by the terminal.

Ground crew swarmed the SRV, checking the wheels and preparing to refuel.

*What planet did the captain say this is?*

*Does it matter? It's not Omega Nine.*

*That's all that matters.*

He cupped his chin with his hand and stroked his face, feeling the bristles of beard stubble. His first and strongest sensation was: *hunger.*

*Maybe this god-forsaken backwater planet has a decent restaurant . . . and bar . . . and if the layover's long enough . . .*

*Women.*

*Been . . . awhile.*

The intercom beeped, and then: "This is your captain speaking. Please pay attention—"

The captain's voice tight, suddenly . . . formal.

"We're stopped at the terminal, but the World Council is sending a boarding party to the SRV before we're allowed out."

Gasps and muttered questions filled the passengers' cabin.

Ivan's first thought: *I'm unarmed.*

A lot of people back on Earth hadn't approved of his mission. Some people wanted him to fail. And spend the rest of his sure-to-be miserable and short life on Cyrus.

He glanced out the window.

Six World Council troopers—all of them dressed in crisp, blue uniforms and armed with pulse rifles and pistols, except for the man leading them—were marching toward the SRV.

*This might get ugly.*

"Do you know what this is all about, Mr. Mitchell?"

He heard the question, but it took him a second or two to realize the Seeker across the aisle was talking to him again.

He turned to her and said: "Please. Call me Gage."

"Fine. Gage. I'm Ruth."

He nodded but ignored her extended hand.

"So, Gage, do you know why we're being boarded? Is this routine?"

Ivan narrowed his gaze and shook his head.

"Not usually, but it . . . You have nothing to worry about."

"How do you know that?"

"Trust me."

He looked outside. The ground crew was hanging back. Watching. Interested. It wasn't every day an SRV or any other transport was greeted by the Council boarding party.

Ivan watched the captain as she exited the cockpit with the gunner a few steps behind her.

She didn't look intimidated at all.

She even smiled at the passengers.

"What's going on?" the old guy in front said.

The captain's smile tightened.

"I'm about to find out."

The gunner looked right at Ivan.

*Does this have something to do with me?*

*Mission orders rescinded?*

Ivan nodded.

Whatever was happening here wasn't routine, and Jordan apparently didn't like it either.

What could he do?

If they were here for him, it was over.

He watched Captain Scott punch the control, and the hatch opened. There was the clang of feet—many feet—on the metal steps. Then three troopers entered the passengers' cabin.

Everyone reacted. Sitting up straight as if in school.

The old-timer at the front asked again, "What the hell's going on?"

But the troopers ignored him. Each had his hand locked on their rifles, as if ready to take the passengers out.

Then their commander entered. He was smiling.

*Not always a good sign,* Ivan thought.

His stomach tightened. If the troopers were here for him, he was help-less.

*Unless . . .*

He looked at the troopers, their guns, weighing possibilities.

*If they come for me, do I fight?*

*Other people might get hurt.*

The SRV's gunner now looked at the troopers as if they were hostile invaders.

"Take it easy, old-timer. McGowan, right? The miner?" the commander said, still all smiles. "No need to worry, folks. We're here to help."

# 11

## COUNCIL'S ORDERS

Here to help?

*Yeah, right . . .*

Nahara placed his right hand on his upper leg and squeezed the data crystal in his pants pocket.

*Checking.*

*Paranoid now.*

Thinking: *Maybe they* know!

How could they have found out?

*I didn't log out of Humphries's computer. . . . Anyone with half an ounce of brains or suspicion could search the history and see what I did . . . the data I downloaded.*

*Dead easy.*

A sheen of sweat broke out on his forehead. His paranoia, so obvious, like the slick of oil on his skin when he wiped it with the flat of his hand. He tried to see if any of the troopers were focusing on him.

He glanced at the miner and saw his obvious reaction: he was pissed at the interruption. Maybe he was anxious to get out of the SRV and stretch his legs. Grab a beer.

Nahara thought: *I need to look . . . unconcerned.*

The tension inside him was so bad, he wanted to leap up out of his seat and run out the door, screaming: "You got me!"

How far would he get across the tarmac before they gunned him down?

And even if he avoided them, where the hell would he go?

He'd be trapped on this jungle planet.

*Carnivorous plants!*

He felt sick.

He took a breath.

Then: *No one's on to me. Humphries is too stupid to suspect a thing. All I have to do is—*

"We have orders to escort you to your final destination—Omega Nine," the World Council commander said.

Using his jacket sleeve, Nahara wiped the sweat from his forehead.

*It's all good . . . for now.*

Annie shook her head.

"Since when has a commercial passenger coach been important enough to warrant military protection?"

"We don't need your protection," Jordan added.

"Just following orders, Captain."

"Can we talk in the cockpit?" Annie asked, leaning close.

"No. Your passengers should know what's going on," Lahti said, turning around to face the cabin, his smile now faded.

"You all knew the risks when you signed on to come out here. That goes with the Road. But there have been reports of Runner activity that"—he turned to look at Annie again—"that *warrants* our protection. I'm sure you can all appreciate the added security of having a World Council troop ship along for the trip."

Already Annie felt like this wasn't her SRV anymore.

*A damned troop ship.*

*But what choice do I have?*

"We'll all be leaving—together—as soon as we refuel and re-ionize the ship's induction vents," Lahti said. "So don't wander too far." With that, he turned and exited the ship.

"Gage?" Ruth said.

Ivan turned. The Seeker raced to catch up with him, both with just an hour off the cramped SRV.

Ivan glanced at the troopers, marching back to their ship in stiff military order. All around him on the tarmac, ground crews and other way station personnel bustled about.

Half a dozen men tended to the SRV-66.

Ivan was headed straight for the way station bar. He considered pretending he hadn't heard Ruth, but then he stopped and turned to face her.

As he waited for her to catch up with him, he took a deep breath of the planet's moist, fresh air.

Dense . . . delicious.

The Seeker—*Ruth*, he reminded himself—had pulled back her hood . . . or it had fallen back—as she ran to catch up to him.

In the diffused sunlight of Epsilon Two, wreathed by a hazy glow because of the humid atmosphere, he found himself thinking that she wasn't so bad to look at outside of the dimness of the passengers' cabin.

Maybe she was even pretty.

*Too bad she's one of those religious fanatics.*

"Sorry to bother you, Mr. Gage."

"Drop the 'mister.' Just Gage," he said, nodding.

"Is it really so dangerous? I mean, where we're going that we need a Council troop ship?"

"World Council seems to think so."

He could see by her expression that his answer didn't help, and he decided to soften it.

"Look. Don't worry. We have a military escort now. So we're much safer. Besides, the Runners aren't the savages the media make them out to be."

"My . . . brother says they're nothing but a bunch of bloodthirsty pirates."

He caught the way she hesitated before saying the word "brother." That hinted at . . . something . . . some disconnect.

Thinking: *She has secrets, too.*

"He ever meet one? A Runner, I mean. Face-to-face?"

Ivan smiled at the irony because here she was, talking to the Runners' leader.

Former *leader, that is.*

"I . . . I assume he has," Ruth said. "He left home years ago and has been on the Road for a long time."

"Well, let me tell you one thing," Ivan said, stepping closer to her. "In my opinion, they're fighting for one thing and one thing only."

"And that is . . . ?"

"Freedom of the Roads. For everyone. I would think you, especially—"

He took a step back and regarded her with a long, sweeping glance from head to foot.

"—as a Seeker, would appreciate and support what they do."

"But they're cold-blooded killers, too," she said. "I can't support violence."

"And what the World Council does is okay with you?"

Ivan sensed his control slipping.

*Could make a mistake here.*

*Got to drop my support of the Runners. And fast.*

He shot a glance over his shoulder and saw the neon lights of the restaurant and bar. Its name was FAR OUT.

But clichéd name or not, if he was lucky, they either had some very fresh beer or some very old whiskey.

"Now, if you don't mind, *Ruth.*"

*Enough Seeker philosophy for now . . .*

"I want to grab myself a drink or two before we hit the Road again. And when I drink alone, I prefer to be by myself."

With that, he turned and walked away.

But all the while, he was aware of her gaze fixed on his back until he opened the door and entered the bar.

# 12

## ON THE ROAD AGAIN

*Ivan watched the female bartender* pour the brown near-bourbon—no one could make a profit bringing real bourbon all the way out here—with the enthusiasm of a lifer working a prison cafeteria's creamed corn station.

*Definitely not enjoying her work.*

He spent a few seconds looking at her face. How did they get her to come out here?

Hopeless life on Earth? Promises of bounties, bonuses?

Maybe she just didn't care. A lot of people didn't these days.

Her eyes looked at the glass as she put it down, but they might as well have been looking miles away.

"Thanks," he said.

The woman nodded automatically.

Then someone took the stool next to him.

The old guy . . . the miner.

"What he's having, please."

The bartender went to search for another glass.

Ivan sensed that the miner, elbows on the bar, was looking at him.

"Some kind of shit, huh?"

Ivan turned to the old guy.

The miner, probably a pro when it came to numerous Road trips, had slept most of the first stage of the journey.

Now, with a bar on offer, suddenly . . . he came to life.

"Meaning . . . ?"

"Troop ship? Escort? What the hell's up with *that* bullshit?"

His glass appeared in front of him, and he took a big gulp.

"Doesn't make any sense to me," he continued, wiping his mouth with the back of his hand.

*Me as well*, Ivan thought.

But he said: "Who knows. Maybe there are Runners ahead. Maybe it's no big deal."

The miner narrowed his eyes and shook his head. Then extended a hand. "McGowan."

They shook hands.

"Gage."

The miner held the shake longer than maybe he should have, and looked into Ivan's eyes.

A pro.

Someone who met lots of types on the road.

*Maybe he can detect someone who's lying?*

"I'm thinking there's something else going down. Don't know what, but—"

McGowan killed the glass and tapped it against the metal counter.

"Another, miss"

Hard worker, hard drinker.

Suspicious, too.

"My guess is they're escorting us for some other reason."

Another slug. "And you know, *Gage*—"

*Why the emphasis on my phony name?*

"That makes two strange things that have happened so far this trip."

"Two?"

"Picking up you—and now this."

The man smiled, and his thick mustache curled up on either side of his mouth, almost touching the corners of his eyes.

"Kinda makes one wonder."

Ivan was about to say that his being here had more to do with his engine shitting the bed than anything else.

*And how could that be connected with the troop ship escort?*

Except—even *he* had to wonder.

Once the World Council knew he had been picked up, that his mission for them might be in danger of being compromised, did they decide to provide a little extra insurance to guarantee he would actually make it to Omega Nine?

Because they definitely wanted that . . . some of them, anyway.

"I doubt that. See, when my Solo—"

"Attention. Passengers of SRV-66. Your Road ship is now boarding at gate four."

The voice over the speakers echoed in the wide, open area of the way station, girded with shops filled with the bare essentials and one odd kiosk selling souvenirs.

*Why would anyone want a souvenir of this place?*

Ivan looked around and saw Jordan in the doorway. He was expressionless as he came forward.

"We're heading out. Everybody on board—now!"

Ivan saw McGowan eyeing his near-empty glass number two. Maybe considering another?

Instead, the miner downed it and slid off the stool. He took some Council credits from his pocket and dropped them onto the bar beside his empty glass.

"Guess like a lot of things about the Road," the old man said, "we may never know."

As McGowan headed back to the SRV, Ivan sat at the bar for a few more seconds. He considered offering Jordan a drink, but Jordan didn't look like the kind of guy who would open up, even after a few.

But that old-timer McGowan had him thinking. . . .


Annie watched the passengers file in while Lahti checked a screen showing the freight manifest.

"Okay. Mighty full load there, Captain. Slowing you down at all?"

Annie shook her head.

The air here was so dense with moisture, like having a hot, wet woolen scarf wrapped around your face.

Might be good for the complexion, but it wasn't the easiest stuff to breathe.

"Got plenty of power. No problem."

Lahti nodded and lowered the screen.

"We'll take the lead. You follow. We see anything ahead, we talk."

Annie scratched her head, pushing a strand of hair to the side.

She wanted to ask the commander what this was all about.

Runners? Really?

The Runners could show up anywhere. In front or behind. What made this route suddenly so dangerous?

"You're in charge," she said grudgingly. "We'll watch our screens, too."

Lahti opened his mouth—probably about to say, no need for that.

Instead: "Let's get going."

Annie nodded and followed her passengers into the SRV.


Nahara had stopped at the top of the stairs that led to the passenger compartment.

Watching.

*The captain and Lahti.*

*What the hell are they talking about?*

*Sharing goddamned secrets?*

He rubbed his chin.

Then told himself: *Get a grip.*

He started down the aisle, back to his seat. His nose was filled with the sour smell of his own sweat.


Jordan sat in place at the console. Ready. As always.

"Learn anything?" he asked.

"Yeah. That there are"—Annie let her voice mock Lahti's—"reports of Runners ahead."

Jordan glanced at her. Then went back to his readouts.

"You don't buy it?"

"Do you?"

Jordan didn't answer.

She shook her head. "Not much we can do about it, though. Is there?"

"Exactly."

Lahti's voice filled the cockpit.

"Ready for portal approach, Captain. Give yourself some distance for any maneuvers we may need to do after transit."

"Right, Commander."

She couldn't bring herself to say "sir."

The troop ship jets on the side began to fire, the blue flames almost invisible in the humid air.

The ship's massive wheels had been tucked into the undercarriage of the gun-filled ship. Now the giant wheels lowered, the noise massive even inside the sealed compartment of the SRV.

A few troopers sat in turrets on either side, ready for anything once they went through.

The whole thing . . . something to see.

Then, almost as if the troop ship was some impossibly enormous truck, it began rolling along the entrance ramp.

The same ramp they had entered, but now they would be climbing up curves, swooping down, watching their speed the whole time, making sure they hit the swirling vortex that was the portal at exactly the right speed and deflection angle.

With the troop ship moving, it was time for SRV-66 to roll.

"Here we go," Annie said, pulling back on her wheel. She keyed the intercom. "All passengers. Please make sure your seat belts are properly fastened."

She did the same and, although there was no need, checked to see that Jordan had. The SRV was like a mosquito compared to the giant troop ship leading the way.

Annie kept well back as the troop ship fired more engines and, with surprising deftness, navigated the twists and turns of the ramp. Within seconds, it was gaining speed.

Down to a screen—and she could see Way Station One disappearing behind them in a blue haze.

Now the SRV was traveling over trees the size of city buildings, and then down into gullies, past walls of stone and vegetation, to finally hit a flat straightaway before making the fuel-hungry charge straight up the final section of the portal ramp.

Annie checked half a dozen screens all at once.

All looking good.

"Whoa," Jordan said, tapping the cockpit window. "Take a look."

Flying things—Annie didn't know what they were called—glided along beside the ramp. Their multicolored wings shimmered in the rays of sunlight that broke through the clouds.

"Got some friends," she said

A few of the winged creatures ahead flew beside the troop ship, kicking hard with what had to be ten-foot wingspans to keep up with it.

Then they fell back, flying beside the SRV.

Close enough so that Annie could see the eyeballs of the one on her right. Filmy, huge . . . with a big black marble at its center. The leathery skin around the beak and eyes was reddish but also streaked with faint shades of green and gold.

The beak, like a cormorant's but striped black and white, was closed tightly.

This fun for them?

Or are they just curious?

But in seconds, as Annie left the last section and followed the troop ship up the last incline, the alien birds couldn't keep up and fell behind, gliding over the treetops.

Ahead, she saw nothing.

But the screen directly below the wheel showed the swirling portal.

Like a multicolored washing-machine basin, sending off ribbony slices of whatever unknown energy powered it.

She'd love to watch it as they entered.

But concentrating here was vital.

"Ready for entry?" Lahti said, his voice clear and strong over the commlink. That would change once they were on the Road, where communications had a habit of breaking off.

"Roger that." She wondered if he caught the sarcasm.

Hands tightened on the wheel.

In an instant, the troop ship disappeared between blinks.

One moment there, the next . . . not.

Safely through the portal.

Or one had to assume.

Then: SRV-66's nose tipped into the portal, the front disappearing, the shaking rumbling toward her even before the cockpit was engulfed.

And then, like the troop ship, SRV-66 disappeared.

# 13

## STORMY WEATHER

*Sinjira watched the Road station* guy, Nahara, get up, leave his seat, and head to the back of the SRV.

*To the toilet,* she guessed.

And: *He's so edgy.*

Maybe rattled by the portal crossing? Roadsick?

Whatever—he looked more than just green. He was sweating. Haludon Fever, maybe?

Eyes looking around. Snapping back and forth. *Guy has something going on,* she thought. Some secret.

Quiet . . . edgy.

And for her . . . *interesting.*

As soon as he passed by, Sinjira got up and followed him to the back of the SRV.

She touched his shoulder, and Nahara jumped and wheeled around fast. *Really wired.*

"What?"

She leaned close. This little convo was for just the two of them.

"Gotta tell you, station master—I mean, that *is* what you are, right? A Road station guy?"

"I work for the company. Yes. But what does—"

Even closer. She could feel his breath—cold—on her cheek.

"Just wanted to tell you that you are giving off some serious . . . what do they call 'em? Vibes? Yeah, vibes."

His eyes widened and were fixed past her, over her right shoulder.

"I guess I'm a little sick. The portal—"

But Sinjira shook her head. "No, man. Not that kind of vibe. As someone who makes chips, I can, like, see emotions and feelings. They're like colors to me. That's what makes my chips so good. And what I see coming off you . . ."

A whisper.

"Fear. Anxiety. Maybe just a little bit of . . . paranoia?"

"I don't know what the hell you're talking about."

"I told you. It's a gift. But not to worry. Your secret's safe with me."

She turned an imaginary key in front of her lips and tossed it over her shoulder. "Totally safe. But one thing . . ."

Nahara looked directly at her now; she had his full attention.

Eyes on her eyes. Or maybe her lips as well.

This guy is still a guy, even if he *is* running scared.

"If you ever want to pop a chip in and share those feelings with me . . . I can use them. All kinds of freaks in the chip world, looking for all kinds of thrills."

He held her gaze steadily.

And now she picked up something else coming off him.

Below the fear. Under the paranoia.

Something new.

Danger.

*Maybe best not to push him too far.*

"You're one sick lady. You know that?"

"Me? A lady? I think you got the wrong chippie. Just think about it. For tapping into that"—her finger touched his forehead—"even for a just a bit . . . I'll bet I could find ways to make it worth your time and effort."

Nahara shook his head.

And yes, he had secrets.

But now she also felt a ripple of what he might do to protect whatever that secret was.

Nahara turned his back to her and walked into the lavatory, locking the door behind him.

As for Sinjira, she was glad she'd had a chip in during that little chat. Got the whole roller-coaster ride of her own feelings—real time—all recorded.

*They say there's a market for everything.*

Pleased with herself, she walked back to her seat.

•   •   •

Ivan looked over and saw Rodriguez staring at the young Chippie walking down the aisle, sitting down.

"Like what you see, Doc?" Ivan asked.

The man turned to him.

"And you don't?"

"Chippies—a little extreme for my tastes. Probably for you, too, I'm guessing."

Rodriguez pursed his lips and then turned away.

"I'm just looking."

Ivan smiled. Then he got to his real point of talking to Rodriguez.

"So, Doc, you're going to Omega Nine, too?"

Rodriguez nodded.

Another smile.

*Good to know what everyone is up to on this small SRV.*

*Would be best—but highly unlikely—if I'm the only one with a secret.*

It felt like everyone in the cramped quarters was hiding something.

Made for a lot of unknowns.

And Ivan didn't like unknowns.

"What are you going for?"

"My company investigates and researches any new life forms found on the Road systems."

"So—they found something new on Omega Nine?"

"I didn't say that."

"No. I did. Interesting, though. New life forms . . . usually the Road Authority makes a big deal about any discoveries. Even something microscopic. Proof that the Road is about more than commerce."

"I didn't say—"

Ivan reached across the aisle and put a hand on the man's forearm.

"Easy there, Doc. Your secret's safe with me. I don't really care about old life forms. So, new ones . . . not exactly my thing, either."

Rodriguez turned away.

And Ivan thought: *That's not his mission. I can smell bullshit.*

The truth would come out, he knew. One way or the other.

Everyone's secret on this ship. Bit by bit.

Before Omega Nine.

Before Ivan did what the World Council wanted him to do.

Something . . . that Ivan wasn't even sure he would actually do.

He'd have to learn everyone's secrets eventually.

But for now, he shut his eyes and let the steady rumble of the SRV lull him to sleep.

• • •

"Whoa," Annie said.

She tapped the screen to her right, the one that tracked near-space for any anomalies ahead on the Road.

Jordan turned to her.

"Whaddya got?"

"Not sure. Still pretty far away, but see those specks? What are they?"

Then the voice of the troop ship commander in her ear. Sharp . . . crisp. *Alarmed?*

"Captain Scott?"

"What is it, Commander?"

"We've picked up an ion storm ahead."

Annie had traveled past these storms before, but just a few. They weren't pretty. The noise, the light, the way it could rattle the SRV—all pretty disturbing. And it could bang up a SRV pretty bad.

Enough time in a storm could rip a ship apart.

But usually they lasted only minutes, like passing through a vapor cloud and momentarily losing all viz.

Then—in seconds—all over. Done.

*But this one? . . . Looks big.*

"It's directly ahead of us, Captain, and it appears to stretch all along the Road for quite a distance. Can't tell how far yet."

Annie could see it on her forward screen now.

The size of it . . .

*Shit.*

No goddamn vapor cloud they could pass through in seconds.

The hair on Annie's forearm prickled. Her stomach muscles tightened.

"There's a spur ahead. Small station. We need to get to there and off the Road." The commander's voice was beginning to break up as they got closer to the ion storm.

*Good call*, Annie thought.

Except that meant that they'd be in the storm for some time before reaching the spur. And if the storm was also affecting the spur . . . ?

"Yes, Commander," Annie said, not letting the concern show in her voice.

"We're going to go as fast as we can. Follow in our wake. We might be able to clear the way for you."

"Okay."

Then . . . nothing.

She took a breath.

"I'm gonna tell the passengers what's going on. No way around it. It's gonna get nasty."

Jordan nodded.

The gunner simply said, "Yup."

She pressed a button, and cleared her throat.

# 14

## VANISHING ACT

*"Attention. We are moving into* an ion storm ahead. Everyone *must* take their seats and fasten their safety harnesses immediately."

Ivan looked out his porthole, seeing nothing unusual off to the side.

*Must be right in front of us.*

Then: "What's that?" Ruth asked, looking out her porthole and then turning to Ivan.

Ivan had been through a lot of ion storms. Usually, he'd pass through quickly, and everything would be fine.

But he'd heard of other, bigger storms. Killer storms.

"What's what?" he asked casually. No sense scaring her.

"An ion storm?" Ruth said.

Ivan looked at her. Sinjira turned around so she could listen as well. She was probably recording the whole thing. Great. Just what he needed . . . his face in a chip.

*Can't avoid it now.*

"Ionized sub-particles," he said. "I don't know the actual physics of the thing, but the ions cluster together and collect. I always thought it was like a buildup of whatever energies power the Road. Anyway, running into them is a little like going through a sandstorm . . . only the sand has teeth."

"Teeth?" Her face, at least what he could see of it under the hood, had gone pale.

*So much for not scaring her . . .*

"It's bad?" Rodriguez asked.

Ivan didn't like that all of the passengers were now focused on him. Like he was the expert or something.

Nahara had turned back. If anything, his eyes looked even more haunted.

"Depends how big it is," Ivan said, wishing the miner—the old-timer—would jump in. "Some storms can be real bad.

"We'll probably get through it pretty fast," Ivan said. "It'll get bumpy, I'd guess, but that's all."

"And if we don't?" the Seeker, Ruth, asked.

No one touched that question.

*Everyone's scared now*, he thought. *Let's hope "bumpy" is the worst of it.*


Within minutes, Annie could see the cloud, like a huge weather formation back on Earth. A hurricane that sprouted too many tornadoes to count. It swirled . . . billowing over the section of the Road ahead with the troop ship heading straight toward it.

*No way we're gonna get to that Road spur before it hits.*

"Damn, that's big," Annie said.

"Biggest I've ever seen," Jordan murmured. Even he sounded a bit awed. And Annie knew he'd seen a lot.

They couldn't stop, she knew. If they did, the Road Bugs would swarm and make quicker work of them than the storm. At least with the storm, they had a chance.

As for going backward? Any storm moving that fast was moving faster than they could possibly go.

Not an option, either.

There was no other choice than to head straight into it as fast as they could and hope for the best.

She looked forward as the troop ship entered the swirling cloud. Shifting forks of static electricity shot through the swirling black mass.

And immediately, the huge ship began to react to the barrage of energized microparticles.

Huge electric-pinpricks, looking like fireballs, flaked off the troop ship's surface as the particles battered the ship. Spears of blazing light shot out in all directions.

"Shit," Annie muttered.

The troop ship looked like it was under attack.

"SRV . . . the storm . . . we are . . . maximum . . ."

*Lahti.*

Talking to her, warning her, but the message was garbled as the ionized particles wreaked havoc on communications.

SRV-66 was seconds away from hitting the storm.

Annie did a mental countdown, taking one hand off the wheel and adjusting her seat harness. As tight as could be.

For a moment, she lost sight of the troop ship. It was gone in an instant, and she feared the worst, but then it reappeared, wavering in and out of view.

She had the thought: *Never saw one this big before*, but saying that to Jordan wouldn't help.

*How can he remain so calm?*

"Here we go," she said.

Jordan said nothing.

The SRV entered the cloud.


A noise filled the passengers' cabin like a deluge in a rain forest pelting down on a metal roof.

Ivan shifted in his seat.

Swirls of particles roiled around outside. A tornado-like spiral encircled the Road like a snake.

The Road itself didn't react at all.

*As if immune . . .*

Whatever the particles did . . . they couldn't affect the Road itself. Maybe this was even good for the Road. Resurfaced it.

But whatever traveled on the Road?

Different story.

"It's so loud!" Ruth said, blocking her ears with the palms of both hands.

Nearly sobbing.

*People are gonna lose it if this keeps up for long*, he thought.

It sounded like boulders, now, raining down on the SRV.

Ivan himself felt immobilized. Nothing he could do but sit there and, like the others, listen to the terrible noise of the storm enveloping the ship.


"The troop ship . . . it just—" Jordan left the rest of his sentence unfinished, because now Annie could look ahead and see.

The ship's enormous size seemed to have attracted massive diaphanous billows of particles as it entered a swirling tunnel made of the cloud.

The intermittent sparks that had flown off before now turned constant. Bright streamers of light sizzled and crackled, the sounds faint but growing louder inside the SRV.

Then: She couldn't believe her eyes.

A giant piece of the ship flew away.

Just . . . *peeled* away from the ship, lifting off like a tin roof blown away by a hurricane and disappearing into the empty space off the Road.

Annie hit a commlink button.

"Lahti? Commander Lahti? Can you—?"

Nothing but a wash of static.

Subatomic particles washed across the shield, forming a vibrating, fiery screen. The SRV's cockpit windshield was designed to resist this kind of impact, but could it really stand up to such a pounding?

At this rate?

Not for long.

Annie saw that the troop ship was pulling away, Lahti making a run for it at top speed through the storm.

No way she could keep up.

But Annie pushed the SRV as hard as she could while still making sure she had enough control to navigate on the Road, which had started swerving and swaying as well.

*Just what I need*, she thought.

And then, when she thought that she absolutely didn't need anything more to handle other than the screaming noise of the storm outside, the road curving wildly, her hands on the wheel—two things happened.

Ahead, the troop ship—now careening on the Road, its bulk making the high-speed navigation even more difficult for its pilot—took a curve in the road.

Giant chunks of material began peeling off its sides. Explosions of blue and white sparks sprayed the area around it.

One chunk went flying back, inches away from smashing into SRV-66.

Then: the troop ship . . . *vanished.*

The ion cloud grew so thick and dark, so relentless in its battering of the ship, that the troop ship disappeared under the assault and then exploded into thousands of pieces that immediately turned into dust, swept up into the cloud.

*Gone . . . just like that.*

"Jordan. I think we're going to—"

He reached out. Touched her right arm locked on the wheel.

"Steady, Captain. Just keep it going as fast as you can."

But as soon as he said those words, the SRV lurched as if it had hit something in the Road.

The vehicle shuddered, and then: *no!*

Slowing.

Jordan looked at her. A question? Or a hint of panic in his eyes?

"What was *that?*"

Annie scanned the dials, the monitors, the screens as the SRV shook so hard its frame vibrated as it slowed even more.

Slow . . . slower . . . and finally coming to an almost complete stop.

"The deflection panels," Annie said, pointing to a small readout. "Something's wrong. They're not working. Engine needs to shut down, or it'll explode."

The SRV, with the cloud outside seeming to grow in intensity, slowed even more.

They couldn't stop now. Road Bugs would come and finish off what the ion storm had started.

Annie knew what she had to do, and she didn't like it. She was sure they didn't have enough time.

# 15

## McGOWAN

*Sinjira turned around.*

"The troop ship's gone!"

Normally she'd be so excited.

Imagine a whole troop ship *vanishing*! And she had seen it . . . recorded it.

But the noise outside the vehicle had grown so terrible, the particles—whatever the hell they were—constantly battering the ship. She imagined people, hundreds of people, outside the SRV, pounding on it to get inside.

The old miner in the front looked out his porthole and asked, "Where in hell'd the troop ship go?"

None of the others could answer that. But Sinjira had seen so clearly how it had simply shattered into pieces, and how those pieces themselves had disappeared. Reduced to atoms in a flash.

If you blinked, you would have missed it.

"What the hell—?"

McGowan suddenly making a lot of noise.

"You're right. It's . . . *gone!*"

"Why won't the captain tell us what's going on?" Ruth Corso asked. "We have a right to know what's happening!"

Sinjira guessed that Captain Scott had her hands full right about now.

And what would she say?

*We lost our escort.*

*And we're next.*

Sinjira fingered the button of her chip recorder. Thinking: *This is too much. I should shut it off.*

Nobody would want to see this, to experience this.

But she left it running.

As she felt what everyone else in the compartment had to be feeling.

The SRV bumping, then slowing.

Now—almost stopping.

Even she knew they couldn't stop on the Road . . . not for long.

*So . . . whatever just happened, it could get worse.*


Annie undid her safety harness and took one look at the console.

"Okay, you stay on the Road. Watch for the bugs."

Jordan looked at her. "We've got some already."

He indicated the right portal where, through the storm, Annie could see several indistinct shapes, pacing along beside the SRV.

"Shit," she whispered. She shook her head and added, "We're gonna have to clear those deflectors before we stop entirely."

"Or go anywhere. How you plan to do it?"

"I'm no expert, but I can run the SRV's engine with their safeties off."

Jordan shook his head.

"Maybe . . . and maybe not. You don't know how bad the damage is."

She saw him undo his harness straps and start to stand up.

"Stay here," she said. "Keep her as steady as you can. And shoot any bugs that get too close."

"If it's more target practice, I'll take the main gun."

"No. I need you up here to watch the screens. And . . ."

"What?"

"I'm going to ask Gage to take the other gun."

"What makes you think he can?"

"That's an order, Jordan."

He sat down and rebuckled his harness.

And Annie raced down the stairs to the passenger compartment.


Straight to Gage.

McGowan touched her as she passed.

"What's going on? Why the *hell* are we slowing down?"

The sleepy miner's voice was commanding now, booming in the compartment.

But Annie didn't stop.

Until she stood beside the man they had rescued.

"Can you operate a turret gun?"

Gage looked at her, but only for a moment. Then he nodded.

"It's aft. Jordan's on the forward guns. Stay in contact with him."

Gage got up and started down the aisle to the back of the SRV.

And only then did Annie turn to the passengers.

All eyes on her.

"The storm particles have damaged our heat deflectors. Not sure how much. The monitors are out. But the engines can't run without 'em."

"What are you going to do?" Nahara asked. He sounded more defeated than scared.

Annie hesitated.

*False confidence? Or the truth?*

"I don't know. I—"

She heard the snap of a seat harness being undone.

McGowan grumbled as he stood up.

"Mr. McGowan. You need to sit *down*. I can't predict what we may have to do—"

But McGowan, burly, filling the center aisle, walked toward her.

And faced Annie.

"You ain't sure what to do, is that it?" he asked

"I know what I have to do—I'm just not sure—"

"If you had your vehicle back at a way station, in a service bay, you could do the repairs no sweat, right?"

A curt nod from Annie. She couldn't stop wondering how long before the bugs decided they were moving slow enough and removed her vehicle from the Road, piece by piece.

"Only one thing we can do," McGowan said, his eyes steely, boring into her.

She knew what he was going to say.

"Someone's gotta clean them damn ion deflectors before the bugs get to us."

"And how, exactly, can we—"

"Someone's gotta EVA." A pause. "If you'll excuse me, I'll get on my mining rig and go out. We don't have much time just to stand around gabbin'."

Annie thought. But only for a second. Then another quick nod.

A bit of hope.

The old miner in his suit . . . out there? Removing ion particles from the deflectors? That's close to a suicide mission.

But it just might work. Like he said: Back on good ole *terra firma*? No problem.

Out here?

Not so much.

The big question was: Can the suit stand up to the steady blast of ionized particles?

And with the bugs already here . . . what else could McGowan do?

All pointless questions when McGowan's offer was the only option they had.

"I ain't a flight jockey," McGowan said, "so you'll have to talk me through it."

"I'll be in your ear."

McGowan nodded and grinned at that.

Then Annie stood aside. But before McGowan started to the rear of the cabin, Sinjira nabbed him by the crook of the elbow.

"Wanna be famous?" Her eyes were bright when she asked.

"What are you asking?"

"Chip up. Record it. It'd make a helluva chip."

Annie watched as she held out a small recording device with two adhesive nodes.

"For posterity? Think about it. The brave rescue attempt."

"Emphasis on the word 'attempt.'"

*We don't have time for this*, Annie thought, watching as McGowan took a breath.

"What the hell . . ."

He took the chip recorder and pasted the two electrodes to his left temple just below the hairline. Then he slid the recording device into his jumpsuit pocket.

"Let's go," Annie said, and she followed McGowan to the back of the SRV where she opened the utility hatch, and stepped aside so he could climb down into the hold.

"I'll help you suit up."

She wondered if her voice betrayed her doubts. He looked like he didn't care one way or another.

Just doing what he had to do.

Ivan settled into the gun turret, letting his fingers slide over the dull metal and worn plastic of the controls.

*Like coming home.*

The hissing sound of particles hitting the exposed ship was much louder here. It dulled when he slipped on the headset.

"You there, Jordan?"

Ivan adjusted the volume.

"You know what you're looking at back there?"

Not the same type of gun Ivan was used to, but he could figure it out soon enough. He studied the targeting grip, an old-school item that had to be fun to operate.

*Like something right out of the movies . . .*

He noticed a screen at the bottom showing the cockpit. Jordan was watching him. Like a hawk.

"I'm all good here," Ivan said.

"Targeting tends to drift to the right. Some of the old bearings in the turret mechanism need replacing. Just—when they come—make every shot count. Each miss will cost us."

"Got it."

Ivan paused. Took a breath.

It would be up to the two of them to keep the bugs away while the captain did what she had to do.

As to how she'd do it, he didn't have a clue.

And if Annie Scott didn't do it fast, sitting here with this killer of a gun would be useless.


McGowan moved fast, efficiently, unstrapping the metal casing for the suit quickly and undoing the neoprene clasps that held it tightly in place.

For such a big man, he eased into the suit as if sliding his feet into a pair of well-worn slippers.

"Battery's on reserve, but it's powered to max."

He pulled on the two special "gloves," more like metal pincer claws with other attached tools that he could activate if needed.

The gloves twisted around before they locked into place with loud clicking sounds. When McGowan opened and closed them a few times, they looked like lobster claws, snapping together. Only much stronger.

"Not really built for fine work," he said.

He bent over and picked up the helmet with the pincers. He grunted as he raised it over his head and then lowered it to the metal ring of the collar.

A few quick snaps, and it, too, locked into place.

In seconds, he was encased, waiting for the suit to fully pressurize.

He nodded at Annie

"Jordan, you hear me?" she asked.

Her gunner had to be watching this.

A delay . . . then: "Yes."

"We're all set for the EVA. Everything quiet up there?"

"No problems yet. The bugs are still tracking us."

"They any closer?"

"Still holding back . . . like they don't know what to make of us."

"Good."

*Maybe*, she thought, *the bugs were being held in check by the storm. Or maybe . . . they were only seconds away from scrambling out onto the Road.*

McGowan waddled to the airlock in the back, servos humming with each movement.

"Good luck," Annie said to his back.

The miner raised a hand, a wave as he entered the airlock, and the door closed behind him.

A red light above the door came on.

Then: green.

Through the floor of the ship, Annie could feel a subtle shaking as the air inside the lock vented. The outer lock opened, the hull resounding, and then the man who was hopefully going to save them all exited the SRV.

Annie turned and made her way back to the cockpit so she could watch—and guide—him on the monitors.

# 16

EVA

*The first thing McGowan noticed:* the total emptiness that surrounded him.

The vast void of space stretching away from the ribbony Road in a dizzying spiral.

As if he was in the center of his own empty universe.

A pinpoint in infinity.

The sense of being absolutely motionless while traveling at unimaginable speeds was totally disorienting.

*Don't think about it.*

And then he heard and saw the storm particles—

*Not as bad as I thought.*

—flicking across his suit, making tiny orange and white sparks when they hit.

Like subatomic insects.

*Nothing the suit can't handle,* he thought.

It's stood up to worse, he knew.

Explosions of stone and ore when a blast went bad, or when the rock face of a miles-deep tunnel suddenly collapsed.

Ignore the light show.

He turned to face the SRV.

"McGowan, there's one deflector on each side of the vehicle . . . about two thirds of the way to the stern. A short ladder leads up to it."

Annie's voice was surprisingly crisp over the commlink.

McGowan had a basic understanding of how the deflectors worked: they conveyed the excess engine heat generated by contact with the Road so the SRV's engines didn't overheat . . . or explode.

Road jockeys called it "dumping the core." Over time, though, the particles built up a residue that ground crews cleaned between each run.

Not hard to do . . . just bothersome.

But now SRV-66's deflectors had become useless, clogged. He'd have to see how bad.

He clambered up to the vent on the right, taking care to plant each step securely. Beside and behind him, indistinct forms—Road Bugs—suddenly appeared from under the edge of the Road.

"Great . . ." he whispered.

"Say again?" Annie's voice.

"We got company."

"We know. Jordan has them targeted. Don't worry. They won't do anything unless we completely stop."

McGowan nodded to the emptiness.

*Right. But still . . . the bugs were shifting closer. . . .*


Leaning across Nahara, who wouldn't yield his seat, Sinjira peered out the side window and watched the miner in his suit as he moved along the right side of the SRV.

Everything transmitted directly to her chip, so she saw and felt exactly what McGowan did.

She *felt* it when he knelt down in front of the vent and opened it by removing a large cowling.

She saw the total darkness as he leaned his head into the gap.

She couldn't stop thinking: *This is amazing!*

But also thinking: *I could die . . . we could all die here.*

*Not so amazing then . . .*

*Terrifying.*

There were rumors of some black-market chips, but to her knowledge, no one had ever been recording a chip as they were dying.

*But now's not the time. . . . Let's get through this. . . .*


Annie was seated in her command chair. Eyes fixed on two monitors that displayed the defectors port and starboard on the vehicle. She could rotate the cameras to keep McGowan in frame.

She felt herself hold her breath as he knelt beside the starboard vent. His arm moved clumsily as the metal pincers of his suit literally dug and scraped at the mesh.

*Don't make it any worse,* she thought.

Pieces of ionized mesh and metal flaked off from the ship—or his suit— and flew away in wild spirals of light.

"Looks like he's getting it," she said.

She watched, fascinated. The only sound—McGowan's breath. Slow . . . steady. She tried to ignore the glimpses of bugs she caught wavering in and out of view.

Jordan nodded but focused on the Road ahead . . . watching . . . waiting.

Annie knew he was ready to shoot the bugs if they came any closer.

*Do we have enough time?* she wondered as a cold tingle reached deep into her gut.

But time wasn't the only thing she had to worry about.

She glanced at the engine levels on the console. The heat and pressure building up fast in the core.

*And if the core dumps . . .*

"I've gotta slow down some more . . . blow some of the heat off."

Jordan didn't look at her, just grunted his agreement.

And up ahead, the dark cloud of the ion storm, dancing with energy, was rolling steadily toward them.

*A lull in the storm . . . it's going to get bad again.*

She hit the commlink button.

"McGowan. There's more bad weather coming. Big time."

Her eyes flicked back to the screen showing McGowan at work. His mining suit now looked like it had caught fire. Thousands of sparks streamed off it and spun away in the darkness behind them.

And the Road Bugs loomed closer.


McGowan heard the words.

But he kept his focus on what he was doing. No distractions. He could feel the presence of the Road Bugs closing in all around him.

Waiting to pounce as soon as the SRV stopped.

The ionized particles slashed like metallic rain against the hull. The heavy barrage from earlier had coated the deflector with an inch-thick crust that filled the shaft connecting directly to the engine.

Like liquid metal that had dried into a flaky, hard casing.

He hadn't studied the mechanics of an SRV in any detail, but he knew enough to know this was bad.

He activated a drilling implement in his right glove and started to dig directly into that hard surface. It chipped away a little at a time.

The hardened flakes flew off to either side of him. Like a shower of flame.

*Not too bad though,* he thought.

He looked at the arms of his suit.

*Holding up just fine.*

*Get this one done, then the other, and get the hell back on—*

He looked up.

The raging cloud closed in on the front of the vehicle. A nimbus of light surrounded the nose cone.

Then it slid over the SRV . . . like some kind of monster engulfing it in a fiery storm.

McGowan focused on cutting into the buildup with his drill.

So hard to see through the glaring light. But at least this deflector was nearly cleared.

And then the storm surrounded him.

All he could do was watch what it was doing to his mining suit and pray the suit was tough enough.


Sinjira let out a shriek when the Road Bug suddenly appeared out of the darkness and scuttled close to the side of the ship.

It was covered with pinpoints of bright, blinking lights. A huge gap opened up in its center and seemed about to engulf the miner, but then it veered away and disappeared behind the SRV.

Had someone—Jordan—shot it?

Even if that one "thing" was gone, the miner was still in trouble. The storm was wreaking havoc with his chip transmission.

But she'd seen enough.

She didn't have to be a scientist to know that if he didn't get back inside the SRV soon, he would die, his suit ripped to pieces.

It might already be too late.

His suit shredded away—especially the right arm and shoulder, which took the brunt of the storm's force.

Sinjira—connected to McGowan—started breathing in short, sharp gulps that burned in her lungs.

Then a tug on her shoulder and a voice sounded in her ear.

"Are you all right?"

Looking up, she saw the Seeker leaning over her, staring at her with wide eyes.

"Can you see what's going on?"

The other passengers—Nahara and Rodriguez—stared out their window, too.

"He's doing what he has to," was all Sinjira could think to say.

The Seeker stared at her for several seconds.

Then lowered her gaze. Shoulders slumped, she walked back to her seat at the rear of the vehicle and sat down. She belted herself in and folded her hands in her lap.

*Yes. She's preparing herself. She knows we're all going to die.*


The red lines on the console kept creeping up.

Annie glanced at Jordan.

Stone-faced. Waiting.

Not panicking . . . but feeling desperate, confused.

*Why isn't the heat going down?*

McGowan had the starboard vent clear.

Maybe not entirely, but enough so the engines automatically recalibrated.

*Unless the ionization dumped particles even deeper . . . already in the core.*

In which case . . .

"How's it going out there, McGowan?" She tried to keep her voice calm.

*Don't let a shred of panic show.*

"Best I can . . . not as . . . as I'm used to . . ."

The commlink was breaking up. The static was painful in Annie's ears, making her wince.

"That one's good enough. Best get to the port side fast and see what you can do."

"More bugs are showing up by the minute," Jordan said, his voice calm. "Should I waste a couple? Keep them busy with something to clean up?"

Annie shook her head tightly. She focused on the gauges . . . wishing they would start moving down—or at least stop rising. At least the starboard one was holding steady.

She watched, barely breathing, as McGowan tread slowly up the side of the vehicle, grabbing the service handholds and walking along narrow platforms along the way.

His movements were so excruciatingly slow. Sparks and streamers of energy flew off of him, surrounding him in a cone of fire.

*How long can even a mining suit take that kind of beating?*

"If you could move a little fas—"

"Damn it! I'm going as fast as I can! This is . . . disorienting. I'm used to solid ground."

McGowan's voice turned sharp and loud in the headset.

Annie leaned back in her seat. She wanted to ask him how his suit was holding up, but—

*What if it isn't?*

It sure as hell didn't look it.

"We can't wait much longer. I'm going have to punch it to shake these Road Bugs."

"Gimme two minutes!" McGowan said.

On the port monitor, she watched as the miner knelt down in front of the vent and started to work. His left shoulder now led into the blast of the storm and it glowed as brightly as an arc torch.

White-hot.

And then something much larger than a chunk of ionized metal flew away, skimming off the hull of the SRV.



Ivan sat in the gun turret, his hands on the controls as he watched McGowan through the transparent Plexisteel.

He had to give the man credit.

He had *cojones.*

Of course, McGowan might not be able to see what Ivan—and, no doubt, Jordan—could see.

Scores of Road Bugs . . . everywhere.

Now coming from every direction.

Swarming.

All shapes and sizes.

These mechanized monsters—designed to resemble horrific creatures— converged on the slow-moving SRV, pacing along beside it. Through the swirling glow of trailing embers that engulfed the ship, their faces with glowing eyes and gaping jaws closed in with slow, mechanical purpose- fulness.

Ivan's trigger finger began to twitch.

Just a little.

The sense of impending action sharpened his senses . . . He felt: *alive.*

He watched McGowan work on the port-side vent. He experienced no tension. No emotion. Just an intense . . . *interest* in what was going on.

The thought that they might all be dead soon was not sticking.

There were other things to think about.

Things he'd have to face if—not *if*—*when* they came.


McGowan drilled into the port vent and then a warning beep sounded inside his helmet, piercing.

He focused on the HUD inside his helmet and saw the problem the same instant the speaker inside his helmet said: "Joint rupture imminent. Zero atmospheres. Prepare for extreme life support."

His stomach tightened.

The words flat. Their meaning . . . dire.

He looked down and saw that the mining suit sleeve between his wrist and elbow started . . . disappearing.

A steady stream of glowing particles tore at it, leaving the suit—his impenetrable mining suit—in tatters.

"Christ," he whispered. Then: "I'm so close."

"Say again?" Annie's voice was sharp over the commlink.

"We have a problem."

"What kind of problem?"

"Let me rephrase that. *I* have a problem."

He winced as he said this. All he could do now was wait for the inevitable.

"Is the vent damaged? What is it?" Annie asked. Her voice calm . . . steady, but it rang hollow in his ears.

McGowan narrowed his eyes.

*Get ready for it.*

"Executing extreme life support measures." The mechanical female voice inside his helmet didn't betray an ounce of pity.

And then it came.

In a sudden hiss that changed the pressure in his suit so suddenly it made his ears pop, a jolt of ice-cold pain encircled his arm a few inches above the elbow.

The suit automatically injected a high dose of painkiller into his system, but it didn't take effect fast enough.

*How do you get ready for something like this?*

The pain came in a sudden white flash that made his skull ache as if it was hit with a hammer.

Tears filled his eyes, but there was no way he could wipe them away. The suit's ventilation system would dry them soon enough.

But his vision remained just clear enough to see the jet of blood that shot out from the now-shortened sleeve of his left arm. It froze instantly in the vacuum of space and the crystals blew away in a bright-red icy shower.

McGowan watched with vague detachment as his left arm—*what had been his left arm*—clattered against the deck of the SRV and rolled away, dropping into the Road below the ship.

Either shock or the meds finally kicked in, and then he didn't feel the slightest bit of pain.

"McGowan. What's happening out there?" Annie shouted in his ear, as if she were right there inside the helmet with him.

"Cauterizing wound," the mechanical female voice inside his helmet said.

The captain must be able to hear that as well. Did she know what it meant?

Doubtful . . . she probably hadn't had much experience with mining suits.

"Suit's not holding up," he said. "I thought it would, but—"

"How's the work coming?"

"It's a bit more difficult now—"

*Without my goddamned left arm.*

"I have to pick up some speed if we're going to shake those bugs," Annie said.

He listened as she paused.

"I need that other deflector online now."

"I've got to head back inside," McGowan said. He felt disoriented. Without immediate medical attention, the pain would eventually cut through the meds.

"How are the vents?"

"I've done what I could do."

*Not very reassuring. There was still some buildup he hadn't removed.*

*But had he removed enough so they could get going again?*

He heard the weakness, the shallowness in his voice. He didn't want to show panic . . . or pain . . . and he hated not finishing the job.

But then he looked down and saw that his left leg—the one taking the brunt of the storm—now glowed white-hot.

"Oh, no . . ."


"Jordan. I have to get more speed," Annie said.

Her focus was on the forward view, and she didn't like what she saw.

The storm bearing down on them, and so many more bugs.

*Can't count them . . .*

And how many more were hidden behind the cone of light and sparks that surrounded the SRV?

"If he doesn't get in here soon," Jordan said, "he's dead meat."

Annie toggled the mic switch.

"McGowan. Get into the airlock pronto."

No reply.

"McGowan! What's going on out there?"

Still no reply.

*Is he already dead?*

On the monitor, his body looked oddly misshapen as it trailed sparks into the void, like a statue of sand being blown away by swirling winds.

And then she saw him slump, lurching to one side.

"Go, Annie. Just go. Don't wait . . . for me!"


*I'm not being brave . . . just realistic*, he told himself.

He stared down at his left leg, watching the fabric of his miner's suit shred and flake away in large chunks.

And then the blinding pain. The constriction around his upper thigh. Dull . . . and cold . . . numbing.

"Leg rupture imminent. Zero atmospheres. Prepare for extreme life support."

He groaned and slumped to the side, shifting all of his weight onto his right leg.

"Executing extreme life support measures."

He collapsed completely as his left leg suddenly ripped away from him. His head smacked against the hull. Hard enough to jolt his vision. A metal clang rang like a gong inside his helmet.

His leg rolled away and disappeared over the side of the vehicle.

"Oh, sweet Jesus!"

The captain's voice in his ear . . . filled with panic.

"The vents . . . they're as clear as I could get 'em," McGowan said. It struck him as odd that he could think and speak so clearly. He knew about "extreme life support" situations, and he'd always thought—or hoped, anyway—he would remain calm if it ever happened to him.

*You're doing good.*

"So boost it, Captain. Get the hell—"

"Get back into the—"

"There's no time for that!"

"But you'll be . . ."

Before she could finish the thought, McGowan got up into an awkward kneeling position . . . so hard to do with just one arm and one leg.

He supported himself as best he could, struggling to maintain his balance as he stood up . . . and then pushed off the SRV.

And onto the Road.


McGowan didn't feel the impact when he hit the Road.

He felt like he was floating. Spinning out of control.

His only clear thought was: *If that Chippie back there in the SRV is getting this, she'll probably lose her mind.*

He lay there on the Road for what seemed forever. Weird energies surrounded him. And then a strange insectlike head with wide, gnashing metal jaws loomed above him.

And descended.

It was about to destroy him.

And yet, McGowan felt something else . . . something more than his imminent death.

In an instant, he learned things about the Star Road that no human was ever supposed to or probably would ever want to learn.

# THREE

· ·
· ·
· ·
· · ·
·   ·

# THE DEATH STATIONS

# 17

## EXIT POINT

*A sudden shriek bubbled up* from somewhere deep inside Sinjira.

Everyone in the SRV turned to look at her, but all she could see and think and feel was the last burst of "experience" she had gotten from Mc-Gowan before he hit the Road and the transmission shut off.

*What was it?*

*What did it mean?*

*Like seeing a vid run at light speed.*

*Then gone.*

She had felt his panic and horrible pain when he lost his arm, then his leg. And his sorrow, bringing her to tears, making her tremble when he realized he would have to die.

So brave. So defiant right up to the end.

*Not at all like me*, she thought.

And then: she couldn't explain it.

Not even close.

She had "experienced" things that she doubted she would ever begin to understand.

She looked around at the faces staring at her.

Their eyes. So wide. Staring at her with . . . with what?

Fear?

Concern?

Pity?

*They have no fucking clue.*

*I was there . . .* with *him.*

The images . . . the emotions and thoughts that flashed through her mind had been almost too much to handle.

Even now, she remained shaken, immobile.

Drawing her legs up so they pressed tightly against her chest, she covered her mouth with both hands. Eyes wide as she tried to absorb what she—and McGowan—had been through.

Together.

Then, despite all eyes on her, she started sobbing.


*No time for regrets,* Annie thought.

*McGowan knew the odds . . . that the worse could happen. And in the end, he had jumped. He made a choice.*

The SRV started gaining speed. She could see by the readouts that it was halting—sporadic—but moving. And the heat levels started to drop.

McGowan had done what he'd set out to do.

*He saved us.*

She thought of what happened when his body hit the Road . . . and the Road Bugs swept over him.

She hoped he was dead before they got there.

"He did what he had to do," Jordan said, echoing her thoughts.

Annie nodded, keeping her eyes fixed on the fast-approaching portal. She worried about what might be going on with her passengers. The fear. The panic.

But right now, she had more important things to attend to.

She turned on the link to the cabin.

"We're approaching the Nakai System Portal. Please . . . everyone into your seats . . . fasten harnesses."

She looked straight ahead.

*We have the speed we need, but will it hold steady for the Nakai Portal?*

The palms of her hands were sweaty.

That didn't usually happen. But now? Who knew?

*McGowan died to get us out of here . . . so don't muck it up now.*

They came closer and closer to the portal. Its display of light and seething energy on the screen were as fascinating as ever.

But Annie could only wonder if in spite of McGowan's sacrifice, they might not make it after all.

There wasn't much room for error. *If they hit the portal at the wrong speed—or the wrong vector—then . . .*

She blocked such thoughts from her mind.

"Steady as she goes," Jordan said, his voice calm and steady, cutting like a knife through her unsettled thoughts.

*Good old Jordan.*

*So much more than just a gunner.*

*Focus . . . this is where you earn your pay.*

The nose of the SRV hit the portal with a slamming jolt that tested the vehicle's framework.

The relative shortening of physical reality hit harder this time. A wave of roadsickness swept over Annie. Something that *never* happened to her.

As her hands flicked over the controls—boosting, adjusting—that old, familiar detachment settled over her.

"It's gonna be all right," she said, not caring if she spoke her thoughts out loud. She didn't glance at Jordan; he wouldn't have reacted anyway.

And then they were through the portal.


Traveling at blinding speed, SRV-66 burst through the portal and angled down toward a long, narrow stretch of landing ramp. Bright sunlight with an odd blue glow filled the cabin with a weird, shadowless light.

Annie let out a breath she didn't realize she had been holding.

The landing gear dropped into place, and the SRV touched down on the ramp with a heavy thud that shook every bolt in the vehicle.

*We made it.*

She finally took a moment to look over at Jordan.

Surprised to see the faint trace of a smile.

"Closer than I'd like," she said as she pressed the button on the commlink. "Not much of a ramp." Then—all business, "Nakai Control Tower, this is SRV-66, requesting an emergency landing plan at the terminal."

"Nakai," Jordan said. He squinted and leaned forward, looking out the front window at the alien world.

Annie nodded.

"New to me. Never been here before," Jordan added.

The scene outside wasn't inviting.

The way station was all but lost in a distant blue haze that wrapped the world like dense smog. Only this smog wasn't from any industry. The immediate landscape was a stark desert with little evidence of vegetation, other than some small, scraggly growths that looked more like carved rock than trees.

No other signs of life at all.

"Not much reason to come here." Annie glanced at him. "We're off the usual grid."

"But alive."

"Yeah."

Ruth fought to maintain her composure in front of the other passengers. She had been afraid that she was— that all of them were going to die.

Die on the Road.

Wouldn't a true Seeker want that?

*Maybe . . . but not with so many secrets still to learn.*

Gage walked back from the gun turret to get ready for the landing.

He fell into his seat without saying a word. The Chippie, still curled up, had at least stopped crying.

*If she had still been connected to McGowan . . . what did she see?* Ruth wondered.

She was mortified that a part of her wished she had been chipped when he fell.

What might she have seen and learned, experiencing someone else's death?

Then she turned to Gage. "Where are we?" A tremor in her voice.

But it was Nahara who turned and said, "Secondary Way Station is my guess."

She looked back and forth between him and Gage.

"What system?"

"Have to ask the captain that."

She preferred to talk with Gage. Somehow he exuded strength she found . . . comforting.

Nahara made her feel all the more scared.

"Don't you think we should turn back?" she asked Gage.

A faint smile played across his lips.

"Not very likely."

"The way I see it," Rodriguez piped in, "McGowan sacrificed himself so we could go on."

"You're kidding, right?" Ruth masked her anger as best she could. "Just like that? You write off the life of a man?"

"One life to save the rest of us?" Rodriguez's expression was flat. Emotionless. "Seems fair to me."

"He knew the risks," Gage said. "It was . . . a sacrifice. Best to remember him that way."

"What's the matter, Seeker?" Nahara's voice was low . . . and ice cold. "Losing some of your zeal to find the Builders?"

"It's not that, but I—without the troop ship—we may be in more danger than we can handle."

She saw Gage smile at that.

*Yes, she definitely felt better around him. Still . . .*

"Does anyone *else* think we should turn back? Get some help from the World Council before we go any farther?"

She turned to the Chippie. An unlikely ally.

Sinjira stared at her for a heartbeat or two. Eyes unblinking. Then she looked away.

Faintly, Sinjira said: "After what I've seen . . . I don't care either way."

"You're all right with going on? Just so you can make more chips?"

Sinjira shook her head slowly from side to side as if she had heard this all before.

"You recorded a man dying, and you—you're going to *sell* that?"

Her eyes refocused on Ruth. "It may be pain they like, but it also may be their pleasure. Don't forget that."

Frustrated—and outnumbered—Ruth looked away to stare out the side window, watching as the landscape flew by in a blue blur.

*There's no going back now . . .*

*No help coming.*

She had wanted to be on the Road.

And now, here she was.


The station remained silent.

"The ion storm might've knocked out the commlink."

Biting her lower lip, Annie nodded.

"Not sure. Looks . . . okay . . . no?"

All systems checked out. But there still could be all kinds of shorts and glitches, giving a false reading. She toggled the switch a few times. The monitor showed she was broadcasting.

"Control tower. Do you read me?"

Nothing.

She looked at Jordan. His face pale in the wash of the blue light. Ghostly. Then she checked the radar for the immediate area.

Nothing.

"This ain't right," she said. "There's no traffic anywhere."

Jordan shook his head.

"Not good."

"We'll have to raw dog it," Annie said.

Jordan smiled. "Do you even know what that means?"

"Sure I do," she said. Now smiling as well. Then, she shook her head. "No," and Jordan laughed.

She laughed, too. After such tension, it felt good to laugh.

She was still smiling as she steered the SRV along the winding roads and ramps leading up to the way station terminal.

"I don't like it," she said as they approached the small service area. "No one out. Not even a ground crew."

"Pretty damn quiet."

She looked out at the deserted station.

Dust devils swirled along the tarmac, like a ghost town from one of the many ancient Western movies she used to watch as a kid.

Powering down the engines, she rolled SRV-66 into the terminal.

"So, we'll have to de-ionize and recalibrate on our own."

"Done it before," Jordan said. "No biggie."

"No big deal when you're in a service bay, anyway."

Annie shuddered at the memory of McGowan, but she was sure Jordan could handle it.

But not before they checked out the station.


*This is bad . . . really bad.*

The thought kept circling in Nahara's mind.

When the cockpit door opened, and first Captain Scott and then the gunner, Jordan, came down, the only thought in his paranoid mind was: *Maybe they're on to me.*

Captain Scott looked at the passengers—*but especially me*, Nahara thought—taking them all in at a glance.

Evaluating them.

"Where are we?" Rodriguez asked.

"Well, Doc, after what we just went through, we're lucky to be on solid ground."

*Drop the snark*, she told herself.

"We're making an unscheduled stop. We're in the Nakai System."

"Can we get off the vehicle?" Rodriguez asked. "Stretch our legs?"

*Edgy. Tense. Something's bugging him, too*, Nahara thought. That actually eased his paranoia.

"You folks sit tight. We're going to have a look around. See what's go-ing on."

"Why?" Nahara asked, his voice shaking. "Is something wrong?"

"Looks like nothing out there but ghosts," the Chippie said.

Nahara turned and looked at Sinjira as she stared out the window. Her face was pressed against the Plexi.

"I have to get out," Rodriguez said, unbuckling and standing up.

*Tense*, Nahara thought, *but trying to hide it*. He'd make sure to keep an eye on this one. *He's up to something.*

*Maybe he knows something. Shit, maybe he's the one who's been on to me the whole time.*

"Sorry. No one's going anywhere until we check out the terminal."

"I have an important message waiting for me on the Pod System. If I don't get it—"

"I'm not risking civilian lives," Captain Scott said sharply. "Not saying there's any risk. Still—"

"I'm not a civilian. I'm traveling under World Council orders." Rodri-guez eased into the aisle, stretching to his full height. "I have to get that message."

*Yeah*, Nahara thought. *What's up with him? World Council orders to do . . . what?*

"This is an unscheduled stop," Scott said. "How do you know your mes-sage pod will even be here?"

"Because they took all contingencies into account and arranged to send pods that could be accessed at every way station along the route."

Nahara had to admire the man's tenacity.

Captain Scott struck him as someone who didn't take any shit from anyone.

*Definitely keep an eye on him.*

"I have to go, too," Nahara blurted out, surprising himself.

Now Scott turned to him, rolling her eyes.

Nahara stood up. "I know the standard layout of the way stations. I can get us in and out of here fast, if that's what's needed. Get any equipment you need for repairs."

Scott and the gunner exchanged glances. Obviously, they didn't like how this was going.

*But what choice do they have?*

Finally: "All right. You two can come. But stay close."

# 18

## THE STATION

*"Where's the main station office?"* Jordan asked, taking point several steps ahead of the group.

He had armed Naraha and Rodriguez, though he wasn't convinced either of them could handle a weapon.

He held his own pistol out, scanning the area, but his handheld thermal scanner showed no evidence of life in the immediate area.

"The station control office?" Nahara said. His voice was tight—high-pitched. "Standard layout. It's at the rear of the main building. We can access the main computers there, too."

"So where's the pod bay?" Rodriguez's voice was a bit shaky.

"Close to station control."

Jordan had taken an immediate dislike to this planet.

The gravity was Point 2 above Earth Standard, so he felt sluggish. Heavy. Slow reflexes.

The blue star that was its sun cast thin shadows; the entire world looked washed out.

*Like it's fading.*

Without having to be told, Annie moved to the right of the entrance doors of the main building while he swung to the left, signaling the others—Nahara and Rodriguez—to hang back.

Simultaneously, he and Annie nodded and stepped forward to trigger the automatic doors.

Jordan wasn't surprised when they didn't open.

Annie cast a quick glance at him.

"Power's out."

To Nahara: "Doesn't the terminal have auxiliary power?"

"Only for the essentials—computers and communications."

"I would think getting in and out of the building might be considered essential," Jordan said. He didn't like belaboring the obvious. But this didn't bode well.

Thinking: *What the hell happened here?*

Stepping over to the manual door, he pushed the metal bar to open it, but it, too, didn't budge.

*Locked from the inside?*

No choice, then.

He waved Annie away from the door. Then he gave the Plexi in the door a quick blast with his pulse pistol.

It shattered, spreading a wide, white spiderweb across the surface. Jordan stepped up to it and kicked it in. Shards of Plexi rained like spilled diamonds onto the floor.


As soon as they were inside, something to his left caught Jordan's attention.

Something on the floor.

*A body.*

*Human.*

He pointed it out to Annie, who nodded.

Performing a 360-degree sweep, they approached the body. Jordan wondered if Annie might be shocked by what she saw. But he'd seen enough death as a grunt fighting the Northwest Uprising.

You grew . . . kind of used to it.

*Kind of.*

Definitely a man—or what had *been* a man.

His face was a tangled mess of ripped flesh. His throat had been torn away in one large chunk, exposing the glistening white knobs of his spine. His eyes so *wide.*

And empty.

Staring sightlessly up at the ceiling. Is that where what killed him had come from?

"Jeezus—not good," Annie said, shaking her head.

"We know one thing."

"And that is?"

"We're not dealing with a human killer."

He looked down at the scanner.

The only life signs were from the small SRV party.

*Good*, he thought.

Annie nodded.

"Okay. Station control's this way. Up a level," Nahara said, signaling them over to the nonmoving escalator.

Still scanning their perimeter, Jordan led the way up the steps with Nahara and Rodriguez close behind. Annie brought up the rear. Heads pivoting like searchlights.

Then, just as they reached the top, Jordan heard a noise.

A low growl.

He looked at the scanner.

*We've got company.*

He dropped to one knee, pistol extended, gripped firmly in both hands.

Then, down the corridor—so dark—something moved.

And then—incredibly fast—it charged, and then launched itself at him.

He pulled the trigger.


Annie yelled when she heard the first shot. She started up the stairs, pushing past Nahara and Rodriguez to get to Jordan.

"Jordan!"

Only one shot.

Jordan usually didn't have to fire twice.

*But what if he missed, and . . . ?*

She heard an enraged howl—unearthly, a sound that made her stomach tighten.

It filled the air, echoing in the empty corridor.

Then the stench of singed flesh and hair filled her nostrils before she reached the top of the stairs. Nahara and Rodriguez froze on the dead escalator—and she saw what had happened.

Jordan was getting to his feet, slowly. Then he walked over to his kill.

He turned from side to side, looking in both directions at the upper floor.

*Checking for more visitors.*

"Why didn't your scanner pick up that life form?"

"It did. But not soon enough. Something's wrong here. Some kind of interference."

She looked at the dead thing on the ground.

"So what have we got here?"

"This?" Jordan gave a quick glance down at the dead creature but didn't lower his guard for an instant. "Not good."

The creature had to be at least four meters long, stretched out. A long snout . . . the wide anteater-like mouth lined with pointed fangs, fangs that could easily tear out a person's throat. Or remove a head. Or an arm.

*One nasty beast*, she thought.

And it reeked. The fur, smoking from the pulse blast, gave off a horrible stench of musk, fecal matter, and singed skin and fur.

Jordan's pulse pistol had ripped away the creature's right flank, exposing thick rib bones. The thick, matted pelt was marked with wide brown and black stripes. It was heavily muscled, especially the torso. Whatever it had for internal organs was spilled onto the polished floor, glistening, purple in the dim light that came through the high station windows.

"I'm not familiar with this," Annie said.

"I am." Jordan was still scanning the area with a cautious eye. "It's a warrow."

"Never heard of 'em."

"You don't want to. They don't—uhh—do well in zoos. Thing is"—he turned to Annie and lowered his voice—"far as I know, they're indigenous to only one planet . . . in the Janus System."

"We're a long way from Janus."

Jordan nodded. "No kidding."

"So what the hell's it doing here?" Nahara asked, suddenly coming back to life.

Neither of them answered.

Annie kept looking around the upper-level area, peering into the deepest shadows in the places farthest from the windows. The silence was unnerving.

"Thing is," Jordan finally said, "warrows always hunt in packs, like wolves, years ago on Earth. And they—" He caught himself.

Annie turned to him. Eyebrows raised.

"And?"

"Just stay frosty," Jordan said. "These things are clever stalkers, and like I said, they generally hunt in packs."

"How many in a pack?"

The waver in Nahara's voice made Annie tense even more.

"How many do you think they need?" Jordan said.

*We need get out of here*, Annie thought.

"Okay. Warrows. Maybe . . . maybe more of them. All right. So let's get to the damn pod bay," Rodriguez said, "so I can get my message, and we can get the hell out of here."

Annie nodded. Not a bad plan. Check the ion deflectors fast.

Then split.

They moved as a group down the long corridor, their footsteps echoing loudly, Annie still in the rear. Gun at the ready.

She said, so Jordan could hear, "I'd like to find out what happened here. The Authority will want—"

But then she and the others drew up short when, ahead, they saw something that confirmed her worst fears.

A dozen or more human corpses littered the floor and were draped over chairs and desks in awkward, unnatural poses.

Throats and stomachs torn open. Organs spilled across the floor. Blood splattered in wide swatches on the floor and walls.

*Not fully dry . . . Jesus, this slaughter didn't happen all that long ago.*

"Well," she said, "now we know why no one was here to greet us."

# 19

## THE BODIES

*Nahara took a breath, his* paranoia now replaced with something more primal.

The whole scene was surreal as he looked around station control. The auxiliary power had kicked on, so all the computer stations and monitors were up and running. No power anywhere else, though.

But there were no people left alive.

The room—a charnel house.

Jordan walked around, ultimately counting more than thirty corpses, including the ones on the second floor. It was hard to get an exact count because they'd been ripped apart, and so many body parts were scattered all around.

Some bodies were still draped across their desks and chairs where they had died. Others—and parts of others—were sprawled across the floor, sticky with drying, clotted blood. The filtered air still rich with the stench of excrement and death.

"Looks like this just happened. Maybe within the last hour or two," Rodriguez said.

Nahara remembered. Rodriguez. Scientist. Exo-biologist.

*Knows things about alien creatures. That could be good.*

"You have the computer passwords?" Scott asked Nahara.

He nodded.

*In a goddamned daze.*

He started rattling off the sequence of passwords that would bring the station's screens to life, the visuals floating in the air, ready to reveal secrets.

"Okay," Annie said.

With a few flicks of her hand, she moved one screen to the side and brought up others. The images from a series of monitors floated before her.

"Right," Jordan said, coming closer. "Let's check the monitors and security cams. See what the hell happened here."

"Isn't it *obvious?*" Rodriguez's voice was pitched so high.

*Is he freaking out?*

"They didn't just break in here and start killing," Jordan said.

Annie looked back to her gunner. "What do you mean?"

"I mean"—Jordan paused and, gun raised, looked all around—"someone set these animals loose in the station."

Annie looked at each of them in turn. Then she focused to Rodriguez.

"We have to report this . . . get a pod out," Annie said. "Doc, when you—"

"I just want to get my message and get the hell out of here," he said.

"You can. And you'll send word back to the WC Authority. Got it?"

Rodriguez nodded.

With the captain's attention on Rodriguez, Nahara moved over to one of the computer bays and sat down. A screen popped up in front of him.

Only then did he see what was resting on the terminal bay.

A severed hand.

Nahara gagged and, using a file folder from the desk, pushed it away. It left a thin smear of blood on the display. With a quick touch of a few keys, a display screen was projected in front of him.

From where the others stood, they couldn't see his screen as he waited for the computer to run through its initial boot.

He entered his authority password and called up the security files. After they finished scrolling onto the screen, he entered a single command:

Purge.

If there was going to be an investigation into what happened here—and he had no doubt there would be—he'd make sure no compromising files remained.

The computer screen ran down through the files before it flashed a message:

REQUESTED FILES PURGED.

But then . . . someone was walking toward him.

Scott.

His fingers flew across the screen, hurrying now as he called up the backup files and then entered another PURGE command.

The last of the files disappeared from the screen as the captain came up to the desk, leaning over his shoulder to look at the screen.

"Anything?"

Nahara grunted and shook his head.

"Picked clean. Security vids are gone here, too. Transport and incoming logs deleted. Inter-office memos—kaput. Everything."

Scott gave him a hard look.

An unasked question on her face?

"My guess? Whoever released those creatures into the station had enough savvy to come up here, get computer access, and wipe the security files clean."

Scott nodded. Then: "Maybe. But where'd they get the passwords?"

Nahara squirmed in his seat. He didn't like this dance. He wanted to keep his lies to a minimum so he could keep track of them.

"True. Could be they had someone . . . ?"

He left his thought hanging so she could complete it herself. She stared blankly at the computer screen and then said, "On the inside? But why?"

"Why what?"

"Why kill so many people in cold blood? On some backwater station. Revenge?"

"Or for fun?"

"Warped idea of fun."

"Could have been Runners?" Nahara said.

"I don't get it." Scott took a breath.

"We're not going to find out until the WC investigates," Nahara said. "And by then, hopefully we'll be long gone." He hoped that would end it.

And it did.

For now.

Scott left him at his terminal and walked over to the others. Nahara took the time to finish deleting the rest of the deep backup files. Closing every door. He never should have suggested this was the work of Runners.

Because he knew it was.

Once the drive was wiped clean, he felt marginally better . . . as long as any auto reports hadn't gone out between the attack and now.

*Maybe none of them suspect anything after all.*

He smiled, his first in a long time.


Rodriguez was tense . . . jumpy as they made their way down the corridor toward the pod bay.

He squeezed the grip of his pulse pistol even though he knew he'd be worse than useless in a fight.

*Probably end up blowing my own damned foot off.*

They passed several more bodies, all of them horribly mutilated.

The stench in the corridor—overwhelming.

When they arrived at the data pod bay, Jordan entered first with Scott close behind.

Guns raised. Ready.

Rodriguez exhaled.

But he saw movement.

To the right.

Something huge and dark, racing toward Jordan.

A strange sound filled the room as the creature launched itself into the air, its hind legs curled up, its front paws straight out—and the mouth, lined with razor-sharp teeth, wide open.

So fast. No time to think, much less react before the heavy thump of a pulse pistol blast filled the small room. Loud enough to hurt his ears.

But this time, the gunner didn't get off a clean shot.

The creature's snarl rose into a howl of rage and pain as it slammed into Jordan, knocking him backward, onto the floor.

Rodriguez raised his gun and waved it around, but he didn't fire.

But Scott did . . . aiming at the beast, up close.

In the thrashing scramble on the floor, it was impossible to distinguish man from beast.

Annie went right up to the creature pinning the gunner, pistol to its head, as it turned.

A shot.

And the head disappeared.

Bluish, nearly black blood sprayed the nearby wall and Jordan.


"Damn!" Jordan shouted as he threw the heavy carcass off himself and got to his feet.

Annie looked at him. His face, clothes . . . all stained with splashes of blue-black blood. He looked more pissed than shaken.

Jordan turned to Rodriguez and said, "Get your goddamned message so we can get the fuck out of here!"

Scott came over to him.

"Thanks," he said

"No problem."

Jordan looked around. "Gonna be more of them. We gotta move fast."

Rodriguez stood at the pod bay.

"Shit!"

Annie saw that the display showed . . . nothing.

"The message pods have been wiped, too. Nothing in or out."

Nahara walked over.

"Hang on, Doc." He looked at the screen showing incoming and outgoing pod messages. Then, with a few flicks of his hand, he paged past some screens and then: "You might be in luck, Doc. There's one pod that hasn't been logged in yet."

Rodriguez stepped back and waited while Nahara touched the screen. After a moment, a small, opaque metal capsule the size of his thumb emerged from the console.

"Give it to me," he said, holding his hand out impatiently.

Nahara took the miniature pod and held it up, rolling it between his thumb and forefinger. He narrowed his eyes as he looked at Rodriguez.

"We can run it right here," Nahara said. "See what it says."

"It's encrypted." Rodriguez was getting angrier by the second.

Nahara looked at Annie. All she could think was: *What are they, school kids?*

"I don't think we need to be keeping any secrets now, Doc."

Rodriguez flinched at the sound of her voice. He turned to her and took a deep breath.

"Look, Captain. I'm under strict orders to maintain top-level security with this."

His tone was sharp . . . something new from the nervous scientist.

She looked at him, wondering: *What the hell is this about?*

And: *We have to get out of here ASAP.*

She shook her head.

"Read your damn message."

•   •   •

After making sure the washroom next to the pod bay was clear, Annie stood guard at the door while Jordan went inside and cleaned himself up. He came out a few minutes later, his clothes still stained with warrow blood.

"Blood smells like shit," he said, sniffing the stain on his forearm.

"You look like you're back to your old self again," Annie said.

Jordan looked at her as if to say: *I'm* always *my old self.*

Before they started back, while they were alone: "So, what do you think about those two?" Annie asked.

Jordan was silent. Shook his head.

"Useless in a fight, that's for sure."

Annie smiled. "Nothing else?"

"Like what?"

"Always a pleasure, drawing you out," she said. "I mean—what do you think their deal is? Nahara's twitchy as a frog on a skillet. And who the hell knows what Rodriguez is up to." She paused. "I don't like it."

"None of our business," Jordan said. "Just have to get 'em to their destination."

"Not if it kills us."

She nodded.

"Haven't heard any screaming or shooting," she said. "They're probably okay."

"Or dead before they knew it."

Watching both ends of the corridors and every doorway, they made their way back to the pod bay.

And there they were . . . Rodriguez in a secure pod terminal and Nahara lingering nearby as if he were trying to eavesdrop.

Annie glanced at Jordan and whispered, not too softly, "I can't wait to get to Omega Nine and be done with these guys."

From Jordan, a small laugh.

"What?" Annie asked.

Jordan's mouth was a thin, straight line as he shook his head and said, "If I was you? I'd be more concerned about that Gage character."


In the security of the message cone, Rodriguez wondered if he would be safe from attack if another one—or more—of those creatures showed up.

*Wait in here while they kill everyone else? And then what?*

His hands were sweating and shaky as he slipped the metal pod into the console and keyed it in. He put on a pair of VR goggles, adjusted them, and then settled back.

*Relax . . . Just relax . . . It's all good . . .*

After a few seconds, the view before his eyes pixilated.

Then the three-dimensional face of Dr. Lucius Carroll appeared.

"Good day, Dr. Rodriguez. If you're watching this, I assume you're alive and well, and on your way to Omega Nine. What I'm about to tell you is classified top secret. You cannot reveal the contents of this message to anyone—even your SRV captain. I hope you understand."

Rodriguez nodded, then realized that the motion was unnecessary.

*All right,* he thought as mild tension gathered within his gut. *Here we go . . .*

Dr. Carroll's face dissolved to a view of a planet—Rodriguez assumed it was Omega Nine.

"Nice place to take the wife and kids," Rodriguez said softly as he stared around at the stony, bleak landscape. A small, feeble orange ball of light illuminated the landscape with a sickly glow. In the distance, a vast mountain range rose against a beige sky.

And in the foreground several small figures were moving about—and there were at least fifty—maybe more black metal capsules, about human-sized.

*Caskets . . . coffins . . .*

Carroll's voice continued: "Three weeks ago, we thought we had an outbreak of a previously unknown disease on Omega Nine. Of course, the likelihood that pathogens that would affect humans evolving independently on a distant planet is highly unlikely. What we found out . . ."

A short pause. Dr. Carroll stared into the camera.

*Do we really need the drama?*

"The situation on Omega Nine is worse, much worse."


Back in SRV-66, Ivan sat sprawled in his seat.

Eyes closed. Head propped against the bulkhead. Pretending to sleep even though that damned Chippie would occasionally let out a low groan or a stifled whimper.

*Give it a rest.*

*You're the one who decided to chip in.*

*Deal with it.*

Mostly, though, he couldn't sleep because he knew the Seeker, *Ruth*, was watching him . . . wanting to talk.

"Waiting's the hardest part, isn't it?"

Her voice was soft, soothing. In his half-sleep state, like a voice in a dream.

"Don't you think?"

Dream voice or not: *Leave me the hell alone*, he thought.

"Gage?"

A light tap on his shoulder.

"Not in my experience," he said sleepily, not opening his eyes.

*Will she get the hint?*

"I'll bet you've been to lots of interesting places. On the Road, I mean."

The Chippie.

*Ah, there she is . . . back to her old self . . .*

Ivan decided to let that comment pass. Next thing you know, she'd be wanting to make a chip with him . . . doing . . . God knows what?

Not that she wasn't attractive.

In fact, that was the problem. She was very much not unattractive.

"What do you think's happening? Out there?"

Seeker Ruth again.

*So much for a nap.*

Sounding earnest. Nervous. And maybe—yeah, scared.

Ivan slid his eyes open and looked up at her. In the hazy glow of blue sunlight, she actually looked . . .

*Interesting . . . maybe.*

"Isn't there *something* you can do?"

Ivan heaved a sigh and sat up straight. The Seeker might be right.

Waiting *is* the worst part.

*No, what's worse is not having a damn gun . . .*

"None of my concern," he said, and he meant it.

"But it's so . . . empty out there. Where are they? Why aren't they back yet?"

"Your guess is as good as mine."

"What if—"

She let the thought drop, but Ivan finished it for her.

"What if whatever happened to the station personnel happened to them?"

"Yeah . . . then what?"

*Then things would get interesting*, he thought, but he reminded himself that getting tangled up in other people's problems usually led to problems of his own.

And he needed to avoid problems . . . especially during this trip.

*Still . . . if I had a gun . . . I might go find out what's happening.*

Looking past the Chippie, he eyed the storage locker where Jordan had stowed his weapon when he'd first boarded.

A combination lock—with numbers and letters.

*Great.*

Besides, the locker probably had a failsafe that would lock it permanently if he entered the wrong code more than a couple of times.

It was strong, too. Judging by the looks, there was no way he was going to be able to pry it open unless he came at it with a laser torch.

*So let Captain Annie and the others figure out what's going on out there,* he thought even as his eye lingered on the locker.

*Yeah. That's what I should do.*

*Nothing.*

Instead . . .

"Pardon me," he said, standing up and easing past Ruth, who shied away from him as though fearing he might hit her.

*Why is she so jacked up?*

He made his way up the aisle, trying to appear casual as he approached the storage locker. Leaning his elbow against the ship's wall, he brought his face up close to the keypad and inspected it. Then—just for the hell of it—he tapped in a couple of numbers and letters.

At random.

*As if . . .*

He grabbed the handle and pulled on it, not at all surprised when it didn't open.

He sensed Ruth's presence behind him, turned, and looked at her.

But she was at the side hatch. It was open, and she was standing in the doorway, looking out. A thin, piping whistle sounded from outside.

Ivan focused on the combination again. Frustrated.

He entered another series of random numbers and letters, each key beeping as he pressed them.

The small, unblinking red light stayed red, and when he yanked on the handle—a bit more angrily this time—he muttered a curse under his breath.

The Chippie shifted in her seat behind him. He could feel her gaze fixed on him.

*What was she thinking? Time for some fun?*

He glanced at her and smiled. She was digging through a small leather case filled with chips.

*Good solution,* he thought. *Retreat into another safe little fantasy world.*

He turned back to the lock. Stared at it. Frustrated.

Then a voice said: "K-2-6-Y-Y-7-A-1-9."

Ivan turned.

"What's that?"

"K-2-6-Y-Y-7-A-1-9," the Chippie said. "The combination."

He looked at her in disbelief. Smiled. Shook his head.

*She putting me on?*

"What are you," he said, "psychic or something?"

A slow, sensuous smile spread across her face, and her almond-shaped eyes narrowed as she raised her right hand and tapped the chip implant on the side of her head.

"I was in recording mode when you first came onboard the ship. I watched the gunner open the locker before he opened the airlock to let you in."

"Son of a *bitch*." Ivan laughed.

He punched in the code.

After a second or two, the lock chimed, and the light started blinking green. When he triggered the handle, the alloy-plated door swung open easily. He glanced at the Chippie over his shoulder and nodded his thanks.

She licked her upper lip with the tip of her tongue.

*Yeah . . . she's feeling better.*

Then he reached inside . . . and grabbed his gun.

As he pulled his hand back and stared at the pistol, he smiled and thought: *Now* that *feels better.*

*Time to see what's going on out there.*

# 20

## PREDATOR AND PREY

*Rodriguez walked out of the* data pod bay, and Annie could tell from his expression that whatever he had just learned, it hadn't been good.

"You okay, Doc?"

His face pale, the scientist walked stiffly to the balcony railing that overlooked the station complex.

Annie glanced at Jordan.

Then she approached Rodriguez.

"You don't look so good."

Rodriguez didn't bother to turn to her. Instead, he kept staring out over the empty station below, littered with bodies and body parts.

Then—uncharacteristically—he banged a fist on the railing and turned to Annie.

"I can't tell you," he said, barely repressing his anger.

Now Annie was alarmed.

*What did he just learn in there?*

"What do you mean?"

"What I was told in there . . . is classified, Captain. By order of the World Council. I can only tell you once we reach Omega Nine. And even then—"

He looked away.

The man was sick with the knowledge . . . with whatever this secret was . . . and he had to hold it alone.

"—and even then, after reviewing things . . . *only* if the WC approves."

Annie was tempted to threaten the man.

If he knew something that jeopardized her ship, this mission, the lives of the passengers, then she damned well better know, World Council or no World Council.

But Omega Nine still lay some distance away.

There'd be time to work on Rodriguez. Get him to talk.

But not now. Not here.

Jordan was looking over at them.

*Picking up on what's happening here, maybe?*

Jordan came over and stood by her side without a word.

Then: "Annie, we gotta get moving. Been here too long. I don't—"

A high-pitched tone came from the pod bay.

A message scrawled across a holo screen floating above the bay.

The words: DATA POD SUCCESSFULLY LAUNCHED.

"What the—" She looked around. "Where's Nahara?"

Over in a distant corner, Nahara was sitting off to one side, his eyes wide.

*More damned secrets.*

"Nahara, did you just launch a pod?"

Biting his lower lip, he shook his head.

Too quickly.

"Then who the hell did?" Jordan said as he walked over to the man, bringing his face close to the authority agent. "The corpses?"

"I-I don't know. Maybe it's a station auto-update. Some of them—especially outpost stations—are programmed to do that."

"With all the files wiped?" Annie said.

Nahara looked from Jordan to her, his eyes wide. Staring.

"You know what I'd like to do, Annie?" Jordan said. "I'd like to—"

But his words were cut off. A low, sick sound came from behind them.

"Holy shit," she whispered when she turned to see what Rodriguez was looking at.


Ivan stared at the main terminal building and didn't like the emptiness that surrounded it. The broken door window. Already signs of trouble.

On the grounds and tarmac . . . nobody at all. No ground crew. No mechanics. No baggage handlers.

*Too damn quiet.*

If everyone was inside the terminal . . . why?

Might have been smarter to leave someone outside to watch the door. That's what he would have done. Jordan should have known.

So where were they? Inside, talking to the station manager? Finding out what was wrong here? Because something was most definitely wrong here.

He held the pulse gun out in front of him, sweeping the area.

A substantial weapon. Fully charged. And with a scope that would allow him—even a mile away—to hit a target with pinpoint accuracy.

His gut told him he was going to need it.

And now, with a gun in his hand, he vowed not to give it up so easily when Jordan and Annie Scott came back.

He quickened his pace, heading to the main building.

Annie looked down.

Warrows.

Dozens of them suddenly filled the corridor down below . . . like rats spilling out of their hiding places.

Sniffing the air, they looked around. Some sank their teeth into the corpses lying below.

Biting . . . chewing . . . feasting and squabbling over the bloody remains.

Annie stood stock still.

Then: a quick look at Jordan, who also wasn't moving. He was intently watching the creatures on the ground floor.

"These ones look bigger than the others," Annie said.

And they were. The ones they had already fought and killed were—what? Maybe three to four meters, stretched out. These looked like they were more in the four- to six-meter range.

"Those"—Jordan nodded at the massing creatures—"are the adults."

"What?"

"They let the young ones lead the hunt. To get the experience. Then the adults take the spoils."

"Jesus. Why didn't you tell me?"

Jordan sniffed and said, "I didn't want you to worry."

He was silent for a moment. Thinking, probably, the same thing she was: *We're screwed.*

"They don't know we're up here," Annie whispered.

"Not yet."

"Options?"

"Start shooting . . . and let them know we're here?"

And have that horde, scores of warrows, direct their attention on them up here?

As far as she knew, there was only one way up and one way down.

The math was clear. They couldn't do it. Not without losses.

For every warrow they took out, there would be three or four more coming up behind, ready to tear them apart before they could take them all out.

A moment of indecision.

Rodriguez was still holding on to the railing, but his arms were shaking, wobbling like skinny tree limbs in a hurricane.

Nahara was standing a short distance behind them. He was sniffing the air as if it had turned thin . . . rancid.

Annie didn't like hesitating like this. They had to do something—and soon.

But then the decision was taken out of her hands.


From below, sudden snuffing and whimpering sounds.

Jordan reacted first, probably guessing what was happening.

Moving his gun up, arms extended. Annie followed suit.

Rodriguez didn't go for his gun. He looked helpless. Useless.

She didn't say anything. Keeping quiet in case they misread the situation.

But then there came the sickening confirmation as a warrow leaped onto the balcony, claws grasping at the railing, legs scrambling to gain purchase on the wall.

Within seconds, the first beast flipped itself over the railing and landed directly in front of Rodriguez.

Then another warrow leaped up, scrambled, and landed to their left. Two more on their right.

The warrows had them in a pincer.

Jordan didn't wait. He began firing before other ones landed.

Annie yelled as she started blasting at them.

"Guns! Nahara. Rodriguez. *Shoot!*"

She barely took aim before firing at a warrow that came flying at her, teeth bared.

The dead weight sent her smacking down to the floor. Black blood that smelled like shit covered her midsection, but the open mouth didn't move.

But the weight—so damned heavy.

More blasts. Jordan shooting.

Then, as she pushed the weight aside, the thing rolled off her.

Jordan. Pulling it.

Annie leaped to her feet.

*Four . . . five of them up here now.*

After the initial outburst, they were wary, now circling.

Rodriguez had backed away, and two warrows had him cornered. The scientist held his gun limply in his hand, dangling uselessly at his side.

Annie fired at the back of one, and a massive hole opened up at the top of its spine, spraying blood and bones against the wall.

Rodriguez finally raised his gun and fired, actually wounding the other warrow, who skittered on the floor, howling with pain and rage.

But the shot wasn't nearly well-aimed enough.

Jordan spun around, crouched, and fired at it, then turned back to the railing. More were scrambling up and over the rails.

"Over there," Jordan shouted, pointing his muzzle behind her.

Annie turned and shot in the direction of the dead escalator where a dozen or more warrows scrambled, scurried up. Big ones, hungry . . . racing to the feast that awaited them.

Four of them charged together, side by side, their claws skittering on the tile as others came together to form a V-shaped phalanx.

She and Jordan were back to back, looking around, turning, firing as fast as they could as the circle of warrows tightened.

"How's your charge?" she asked.

"Below fifty percent."

*The numbers were overwhelming.*

Had to be only minutes—seconds—before the sheer weight of the surging beasts would break through the wall of pulse blasts and rip into them.

"Steady. Aim," Jordan said as he fired repeatedly, every shot wounding if not killing.

He didn't mean Annie, she knew. He was talking to the others. Encouraging them.

"Make every shot count."

Annie fired as fast as she could, knowing that all the good aiming in the world wasn't going to turn this tide.

Ivan hurried into the building.

He had heard screeches, blasts, weird ululating howls.

*Someone's alive. Jordan, Annie . . . but maybe not for long.*

He raised the gun to shoulder-level as he raced into the main corridor of the building.

Right into a line of huge animals ahead—

Warrows. He recognized them from his time in the Janus System.

They were running—surging—up the stairs.

Scrambling over each other.

Ready to swarm anyone who was up on that balcony, up near the offices where, Ivan guessed, the people from the SRV were trapped.

# 21

## ESCAPE

*Ivan stopped.*

Before he took another step, he fired four quick blasts at the column of warrows, madly scrambling to get to the top of the dead escalator.

Two shots sent the warrows at the head of the column tumbling backward, crushing the ones behind them. More blasts, and soon the room was filled with howls and screams.

*Wounded . . . and they don't like it.*

But the shots achieved his real purpose.

It drew the attention of the creatures, who halted their mad charge and turned to see where the shots were coming from. Their bloodlust was still high. They had been going in for the kill, but now there was new danger from below.

The ones at the bottom of the dead escalator turned. Their snarls echoed in the empty hallway.

Ivan stood out in the open, exposed.

*Easy prey.*

Eight or ten of the creatures climbed over the wounded and dead, moving swiftly toward Ivan.

*Sometimes*, he thought, *you get exactly what you wish for.*

He dropped to one knee and, with the warrows closing in, sucked in a deep breath, took careful aim at a spot between the eyes of the lead beast, and squeezed the trigger.

As a black fountain of blood and brains exploded into the air, he had already taken two more shots.

Annie backed up and bumped into Jordan, their backs touching, *almost*, she thought, *as if we're one person.*

So far, Annie and Jordan, backed by Nahara and Rodriguez, had been able to keep the creatures at bay.

*But for how long?*

But next to Jordan stood Rodriguez, who Annie could actually hear whimpering, moaning between the steady *thump* of the pulse blasts and the howling yelps of wounded warrows.

She didn't take a moment to look down at her gun to see how charged it was.

It wasn't a damn assault weapon. Not designed for a goddamned standoff.

At least Nahara—next to her—seemed to be taking some kind of aim and shooting with a reasonable degree of accuracy.

But then one warrow leaped in close and swiped at Nahara's gun hand. His pulse gun flew from his grip as Jordan blew the creature's face into a bloody mess.

"Shit," Nahara said.

*Right*, thought Annie. *Shit, indeed.*

Nahara responded by pressing himself tighter against the defenders, now with only two reliable shooters and Nahara, unarmed and exposed.

*Fruit ripe for the plucking.*

The steady punching sound of a pulse gun filled the air.

There were more blasts coming from somewhere down below . . . louder sounds, too.

Not some puny pea shooter, not the handguns they had, but something much more powerful.

More warrow screams echoed from down below. Wild snarls and thrashing sounds.

*Is this the cavalry arriving?*

Someone helping them. Someone who survived the initial onslaught? A security guard who had maybe been in hiding and who had come out now and was going to save them from this massacre?

A nearby warrow swung its head toward her. Mouth wide. Teeth gleaming as it went for her arm.

But Annie was able to tilt the gun in time so those jagged teeth met her gun barrel—and in that contact, with her finger pulling back on the trigger, the beast's head disappeared.

Buying seconds.

Any real hope, she knew, was riding on their savior, down below.

The last of the charging warrows fell inches away from Ivan, like a long-distance runner who simply couldn't go the distance.

No time to examine the things, since he could still see huge, dark shapes bobbing up and down on the balcony.

He lowered the gun, and bolted.

He made his way through the piles of bodies, most of them dead, but a few were writhing on the ground, some trying to turn their heads and catch him in their jaws as he raced by and up the escalator.

To the top of the stairs.

To see the four people from the SRV.

And even as his gun came up, he wondered if he was in time to save them, because the creatures had them surrounded and were closing in, their jaws wide . . . hungry for flesh and blood.

Annie saw him through a break in the circle of creatures.

*Gage.*

Gun up.

Shooting.

A surge of hope, but at the same time wondering: *How the hell did he get here . . . with a gun?*

Only seconds ago, she had accepted the hopelessness—the simple, dark, grim fact of their impending death.

Now . . . suddenly things looked different.

But in that hopeful moment, one of the creatures leaped forward and pulled Nahara out of the protective huddle.

Its claws closed on the man's midsection.

Nahara's trapped body swiveled, his eyes wide, turning. His mouth was open; he was screaming, but no sound came out.

He was being dragged away to where the warrows could feast in private.

Annie spotted other beasts crouched down low, avoiding the gunfire and creeping up on them, using whatever cover they could find.

But—a decision—she used her next shot to drill a smoking hole through the throat of the warrow that was about to eat Nahara.

Its traplike jaws didn't let him go.

Maybe a reflex action, an instantaneous rigor mortis that kept the man held in its grip.

Only then did Annie turn to shoot at the closest warrow who was crawling toward her.

She turned, almost too late.

This time, her gun wasn't coming up fast enough. She thought for sure she was dead.

Which is when she heard another one of those cannonading blasts, and the creature fell, sprawling on the floor, inches from Annie.

Gage's blast had taken it down, and behind her she heard Jordan shooting. Rodriguez kept making noises.

But ahead, Gage said—*yelled*—over the mayhem: "You gotta move . . . *now!*"

Between him and Jordan, the rest of the pack was either dead or dying. Savage snarls and howls filled the air.

Seeing a break, Annie hurried over to Nahara, freeing him from the clamped jaws and hearing Jordan right there behind her.

"Let me help."

Gage stood there, gun up, scouring the area, firing at anything that moved. Then, quickly, he waved them over to the dead escalator and down through the piles of warrow bodies to the floor below.

## 22

## GETTING OUT

*Ivan stayed back until the* others started down the gore-drenched staircase. The carnage was terrible.

But Jordan ran up beside him.

"We'll give them cover," Jordan said.

"You got it," Ivan said with a nod.

And then they, too, went down the slippery staircase, turning and pausing as they did. The corridor was empty but not silent. Whimpering and guttural growls filled the air, and Ivan was tensed—ready for one or more of the wounded creatures to suddenly leap at him.

Like Jordan, Ivan looked all around the empty room below for any signs of more creatures.

*Is that it? The entire pack is wiped out?*

The only survivors were the handful they had left behind on the balcony, intelligent enough to be cautious after all this carnage.

*And how soon before they regroup and come after us?*

Some may have started nibbling at their fallen companions . . . perhaps deciding that the tasty humans were simply too much trouble.

But as he neared the bottom of the stairs, Ivan saw that wasn't true of all the warrows. A few big ones began leaping—covering two or three steps at a time—as they came down the stairs, racing toward them.

"Fuck," Jordan said.

Then the gunner turned to the others.

"Run! Fast as you can! Get the hell back to the SRV!"

Jordan glanced at Ivan.

The look, the message was clear.

*It's you and me, pal. Let's see how much more you got.*

Bringing up the fucking rear.

They started firing, Jordan lethal with his small handgun. Ivan used his bigger gun with devastating effectiveness on the warrows that chased after them.

And all the time they ran backward, taking care not to trip over any of the bodies—human or warrow—that littered the floor.

A slip, a fall, and those seconds on the ground could mean the difference between life and death.

And all the time, he saw Jordan watching . . . waiting to open fire again.

"Charge low?" Ivan called to him.

A nod. Nothing more.

The others—Annie, the doctor, and the station manager—had reached the main doors and were hurrying outside.

*Are there more creatures out there, waiting to clean up?*

Then, when he and Jordan were almost at the door, the safety of the SRV only a minute or two away, Jordan nodded to the left and said: "Over there."

A gesture, Jordan's free hand came up and pointed.

More warrows were coming down the corridor to the left, joining forces with the survivors from the battle on the balcony who were spilling down the escalator.

Jordan glanced at Ivan, then to the door leading outside.

*The others . . . how far had they gotten?*

*All the way back to the SRV?*

Ivan hoped so. Maybe they had bought them enough time.

"We gotta go for it," Jordan said.

Now, instead of a slow, backward move mixed with gunfire—having given the others a gift of protective fire—Ivan followed Jordan, turned, and started running full out for the open door ahead.

He was about to see if he and Jordan—and the others—had what it took to outrun the animals chasing them.

Ivan was thinking: *About as primal a moment as the universe can deliver.*


Sinjira stood by the closed hatch, peering out through the small portal.

Annie and the others—most of them, anyway—were running across the tarmac, heading back to the SRV. The thin blue sunlight threw their nearly invisible shadows on the ground.

They were moving fast.

But where was Jordan . . . and Gage?

Sinjira unlatched the door and started to push it open.

"What—what are you doing?" Ruth asked.

Sinjira turned on her.

"Opening . . . the god . . . damn . . . door."

Ruth looked out her porthole, then to Sinjira. Her face was twisted.

*Fear will do that,* Sinjira thought. *Take those soft, smooth curves, and turn them into a grim mask.*

"They're n-not here yet! Wait."

*Yeah, right,* Sinjira thought, choosing not to listen to her.

Whatever they were running from had to be close behind.

No time for them to wait outside while the door opened.

She hit the controls on the door; a message on the display asked for confirmation as it ran a quick atmosphere and pressure check.

Another touch, and the door popped open, swinging outward just as the captain, Nahara, and Rodriguez raced up the staircase. Tears and sweat streaked Rodriguez's face, and Nahara was bleeding. His jacket was stained with blood.

Into the SRV.

Rodriguez out of his mind, the only one to speak.

*"Close it! They're coming!"*

Annie led Nahara over to a seat—the one McGowan had been sitting in. He was obviously hurt. Then she looked out the open door.

Thinking: *The crazy scientist might be right.*


When Annie settled Nahara into a chair, he let out a loud groan as his head slumped down onto his chest.

Annie hurried to the hatch, her gun ready—and saw the situation. Jordan and Gage were running hell for leather to the vehicle. She wasn't sure if she should risk a shot or two at the pursuing beasts.

Five . . . no, six warrows were racing toward them, quickly closing the distance with their long, leaping bounds. Jordan and Gage didn't slow down to aim and shoot. They sent off a few wild shots over their shoulders, but all went wild, scoring the tarmac and taking out a few windows in the terminal.

Judging the angle of fire, Annie could see that the warrows were too close for her to try to pick off one or two.

*Come on,* she thought.

*"Run, you bastards!"*

Not knowing if they could outrun those things or not.

Still, she could try to divert the creatures.

Aiming carefully, she fired to one side and then the other of the runners. Each blast scorched the ground and took out huge chunks of tarmac, but the warrows kept coming.

In the open doorway, Annie watched, her chest aching from not breathing.

The beasts were closing the gap . . .

Thirty yards . . . twenty . . . fifteen.

Until the two men were close enough, and she had enough elevation to shoot over their heads.

And then they were at the bottom of the stairs . . . and up . . . and in.

She slammed the door shut behind them and threw the bolts.

She turned to them. "What do you say we—"

She stopped talking when something—the lead warrow—slammed into the side of the vehicle. It sounded loud enough to rock it, and Ruth let out a squeal of fright.

Annie knew they were safe. There was no way the creatures could tear through the shell of the SRV. They were safe, and she was smiling with relief as she turned to Jordan.

He had gone straight over to where Rodriguez sat, panting heavily and bathed with sweat, and grabbed him by the shirt. He screwed up a handful of fabric and all but lifted him out of his seat.

Nose to nose.

"What was in—?"

He gave the scientist a shake, a human rag doll.

"—that god . . . damn . . . pod?"

*"Jordan!"* Annie shouted.

Eyes blazing, he turned to face her. His cheeks were flushed. She had never seen him like this.

Never.

"He knows something. About this trip. About Omega Nine." Jordan hiked his thumb in the direction of the terminal. "Maybe even about what just happened in there. And I want to know what it is."

Annie frowned.

"It could endanger all of us," Jordan said.

He gave the man another wild shake. Rodriguez's eyes rolled back. He looked like he was about to pass out.

"I can't—I'm not authorized," he said, his voice faint . . . defeated.

Annie stood immobile for a few seconds.

*What the hell?*

Bad enough replaying the Alamo with the warrows back there . . . but now this? Jordan—who barely spit out more than three words at a time, who never lost his cool . . . now his cool, was clearly gone.

"Jordan, can this wait—?"

Jordan stared at her. His eyes wild.

"I can't have you beating up my passengers."

She was trying to infuse calm into her voice, but after what they had just been through, everyone's adrenaline was soaring.

But Jordan turned back to Rodriguez.

"You'll tell me, Doc. One way or another, you *will* tell!"

Then another thought.

*Nahara.*

He was hurt. Slumped in his seat. Looked to be in shock. He needed medical attention now.

*Things are out of control*, she thought.

Her world would spiral out of control if Jordan lost it.

"He can't tell you," Nahara said.

"What?"

Jordan. Still holding on to the scientist.

"He— he's under World Council orders. He can't tell you *anything*. Not unless they say so. He'd get fired."

Nahara made a loud watery sound when he coughed.

Annie went to him.

"Or worse."

Only then did Jordan relent, slowly lowering Rodriguez.

Annie knelt down in front of Nahara.

"Let me have a look where it grabbed you."

All SRV captains had basic medical training, so Annie was able to deal with most minor medical emergencies.

She wasn't so sure when she slowly pulled up Nahara's shirt. He winced and let out a low moan when the material pulled away from a bloody spot.

The warrow's teeth had raked three parallel lines across his ribs. Already, there was evidence of swelling.

"I'll have to clean and disinfect those bites."

Nahara nodded.

Everyone in the cabin had their eyes on her.

She studied the three lines where the warrow had bitten him.

His left side was okay, only a bruise. Nasty-looking. Big. But the skin was unbroken.

His right side, though . . .

The gash could be deep. Blood was dripping steadily onto Nahara's lap.

Jordan—pulling it together—came over to her with the med kit, already open.

She grabbed a spray can that would sterilize and cauterize the wound. As she did that, Jordan took out a bandage and antiseptic. She couldn't put any Nu Skin on until the wound stopped oozing.

She looked closely at it, being careful as she placed the bandage.

"Not too bad, Mr. Nahara. All things considered."

Still, he needed to have a real doctor take a look at it.

*Next way station*, Annie thought.

She stood up.

"Okay. We're going to get the hell out of here."

Her eyes fell on Gage sitting quietly in the back.

Their savior . . . still holding his gun.

She looked at the storage locker, thinking: *How the hell did he get a gun?*

Maybe she'd ask one of the others. The Chippie, perhaps.

She turned to Jordan. Maybe both of them were thinking the same thing.

*We need to get that gun away from him . . . at least for the duration of the trip.*

Another thing to deal with later.

For now?

"Gage."

He looked up with sleepy eyes. The only one who didn't seem worried or stressed about what had just happened.

"Thanks for the help."

He nodded.

"We'd all be warrow food if you hadn't shown up."

In the back, Gage nodded again and raised a hand. A slight wave.

She thought: *Who is this guy?*

"We're leaving here now. Back on the Road. We'll have to get Mr. Nahara some help at the next station. For now, though, everyone sit tight."

She turned to Jordan.

There was a lot she needed to talk to him about.

That, though, also had to wait until they were in the cockpit, away from the ears of their ever-more-interesting group of passengers.

Annie climbed the stairs to the cockpit, Jordan following with none of the passengers saying a word . . . maybe from fear . . . maybe too numb to feel.

*What does it matter?* she thought. *We gotta get moving.*

# 23

## SUSPICIONS

*Annie didn't relax until the* SRV slid through the portal.

First, a check of the Road ahead. No signs of the storm, only the ribbony expanse of lights looking now serene—after what they'd been through—stretching out into space.

*And what about the ion deflectors?*

No more EVAs, that was for sure. So she'd have to wait—and hope they made it to the next station.

Only then did she turn to Jordan.

"So what was *that* all about?"

Jordan hadn't spoken since they got back to the cockpit other than single words during the preflight check.

Although he always kept his thoughts to himself, that total silence—after what had happened—seemed unusual, even for him.

She kept her eyes on the screen and gauges, making minor adjustments but mostly to simply keep busy.

*Engine's running good . . . core's well within parameters.*

*Thank you, McGowan,* she thought. *We're alive because of you.*

Jordan's response: "What's *what* all about?"

"With Rodriguez. I thought you were about to strangle the guy."

"I was."

She was aware that Jordan had turned and was looking at her. She gave him a quick glance but went back to her screens.

And since she wasn't exactly asking the question out of curiosity, she liked keeping her attention focused . . . elsewhere.

"Care to explain?"

"Okay. That son of a bitch has information from Earth. About what's ahead. About his mission, on Omega Nine, right?"

"So?"

"Any information he has could be vital for us. For our survival. It could give us a heads-up. Especially after that freak show back there at the station."

"It's classified, Jordan. *Classified.* By the World-freaking-Council. Don't you get that?"

His eyes were still on her.

Then, after a long, uncomfortable pause: "Yeah. So. It's still dangerous."

"The Road's always dangerous," Annie said, still not looking at him.

*He's not telling me something*, she thought.

Another quick look at him.

"You have to let it go, Jordan."

She knew him too well. She knew he wouldn't—or couldn't—let it go.

"I'm not asking," she said. "I'm *telling*. This is *my* ship, so you let it go. At least, until we get to—"

Jordan leaned close, about to say something. His breath was warm on the side of her face.

"It's that guy. Gage."

"You mean the guy who saved our asses?"

Jordan nodded. "Damn good shot, don't you think?"

"Lucky for us he is."

"Annie. Truth is, what I saw? He's an *amazing* shot."

Another silence.

"He knows tactics. Aiming . . . a firing retreat."

"Impressive."

Jordan shook his head. "You're not getting it."

He took a breath and held it as if he himself didn't like what he was about to say.

What it might mean for this trip.

"There are only two ways you learn that stuff. Two that I know of, any-way—"

She chanced to look away from the screens, the SRV rolling along smoothly, everything fine. A solid stretch of straight Road ahead of them.

No need to keep up the charade that the vehicle needed constant moni-toring.

"You might learn all that in the World Council Forces. Like me," Jordan said. "You learn it after years of fighting in those *pissant* shoot-out wars that seem to be the new normal on Earth. Weapons use. Strategy. Tactics. Marksmanship. Special Ops. The WC teaches its troopers well."

Now Jordan looked away.

"Kind of like . . . after all that . . . you're not much good for anything else?"

Jordan nodded, his mouth a straight line.

Annie nodded, thinking: *Jesus, I've learned more about my gunner in the last few minutes than from years of him riding shotgun with me.*

"And the other way?" she said, breaking the lengthening silence.

Jordan's face tightened. As if he didn't like the word . . . or the implications . . . or the fact that it was most likely the correct option.

"Runners."

"What? You think he's a Runner?"

"Not just any Runner. Someone key. The way he took command of the retreat—"

"A Runner, traveling with us."

The idea sank in slowly.

"And if he's who I think he is . . . and if Runners unleashed those warrows like unloading a crate of rats on a ship . . . if Runners are active along this route, following us, following him—"

"Or leading us on," Annie said as the realization hit her like a cold slap in the face.

"Then I'd say we're heading into a load of shit, Annie."

It was her turn to take a deep breath. Thinking . . . trying to absorb what Jordan had just said. His logic was damned good unless—

*Unless you're getting paranoid . . .*

But the more she thought about it, the more sense it made.

So where did that leave her?

Gage. Either a WC vet . . . or someone who had trained with the Runners, a paramilitary group using the same techniques, the same weapons, skills, tactics.

Finally: "So what do we do?"

"We have to do something."

Annie nodded.

*And try not to rattle Rodriguez, not if he has any information that could be relevant.*

"I've been running facial scans from the WC data banks, but so far, no matches," Jordan said.

"He might have had some reconstructive surgery," she said.

Jordan nodded.

"Let me mull it over. But you keep running through the files. See if you get a match."

Jordan nodded, and then, for a few moments, they both sat quietly.


Ruth leaned over to Gage, Touched his arm. It was thrilling to her . . . how solid it felt.

He turned to her slowly, eyes narrow slits.

"Can I tell you something?" she asked.

He nodded.

"I was scared back there. Terrified about what was going on. I could barely breathe. Or move. I've never . . . *never* been so scared."

"It happens."

"I know. Or at least I've heard about how dangerous the Road is, but when she"—Ruth indicated Sinjira, sitting a few seats ahead, curled up, maybe sleeping—"wanted to open the door with everyone running, and those . . . those *things* chasing you, I screamed—"

The fear still twisted inside her, but instead of screaming now, Ruth lowered her voice. Barely a whisper: "—for her to shut the door."

She looked down, but Gage hadn't looked away. "I was so scared. But now I'm just embarrassed. That was wrong. I mean—"

Gage took a slow breath.

"Look, people do stupid things when they get scared."

*Is that what you think I am? Stupid . . . and weak?*

"Fear's probably the biggest motivator for people. Makes 'em do things they don't think they'd normally do—until there's a crisis. I'm sure if we hadn't gotten to the door in time—"

"But you did."

"Yeah. We got lucky, maybe, but I'm sure you would have gotten the door open and done whatever else was necessary."

Ruth nodded, not entirely convinced.

"It ain't healthy to deal in hypotheticals."

She wanted to believe she would have risen to the occasion and done what had to be done despite her fears. Even if there had only been seconds, she would have opened the door despite the risk.

"Yeah," she said. "I hope I would have."

Gage smiled.

Ruth looked at him, feeling genuine tenderness. This man who had gone out there and saved everyone now suddenly so gentle in the quiet of the passengers' cabin.

"See?" he said. "Even when you're afraid, frozen—we all have our limits. That time when we *will* act. No matter what."

Another smile.

"So no more blame. Okay?"

She smiled back at him, glad that he could make her feel so much better about herself.

"And another thing," she said.

He nodded.

"What about you? What about *your* fears? What did it take for you to go out there and face those . . . those *monsters?*"

She watched his eyes narrow. A different kind of question, and now his face registered . . . what?

Caution? Reticence? Maybe he didn't like to talk about his own fears.

*Or . . . was it a secret?*

"Why weren't you afraid?"

A nod. Then another quick smile.

"Oh, I was afraid. Be crazy not to be. I guess I . . . I used that fear so I could do what I had to do."

Ruth nodded. "It's as simple as that?"

Gage nodded. "Sometimes the simple answer is the right one."

And then he turned away, maybe because the conversation had turned, she thought, uncomfortable for him.

And now it was over . . . along with that brief moment of tenderness.

Nahara felt his side.

The bandages tight, and the wound no longer oozing blood.

The pain, though, even with a strong local anesthetic, was a constant reminder that the creature had come so close to tearing him apart.

They could put on a layer of Nu Skin right now, he knew. But if the next station wasn't too far away—only a couple of hours—then he agreed with the captain that it was best to wait.

No imminent danger of infection.

And he could deal with the discomfort.

He looked over at Rodriguez, who had been shaken like a rag doll by the gunner. His eyes were shut; but Nahara guessed that he wasn't sleeping.

Probably just pretending so no one would talk to him.

Or was he in shock from the nightmare they had just experienced?

Nahara thought again about what he was carrying.

The Data Crystal and what it contained. Its value, its amazing worth.

His paranoia had ebbed during the melee at the station. But now, sitting so quietly, it returned—the fear of discovery, the panicked thoughts of what he would do if caught.

Wondering now if it was at all worthwhile.

He looked again at the scientist, who was faking it . . . or not.

And he decided that maybe closing his own eyes and sitting quietly, pushing aside his worries would be the best thing to do.

That is, if he could.


Annie turned in her seat.

"Okay. I say we ask him directly if he served in the WC."

Jordan nodded.

"And if not?" Annie frowned. "We ask him where he learned to be such a good shot. Could be other explanations."

"Possibly."

"There are how many Earth-based terrorist groups? Highly trained and funded. He could be with one of them."

"Doubt it, though," Jordan said.

"Anyway—that's no better than him being a Runner."

Again, all Jordan did was nod.

"Either way, we need to find out. Maybe we can talk to him privately, bring him up here."

"He still has that gun."

"I know," Annie said. "We should have gotten it back under lock and—"

"That's another thing," Jordan said. "How'd he get the gun locker open?"

"We'll have to ask him that when we talk to him."

Annie shook her head. This SRV didn't feel like hers anymore, not with this now intimidating stranger sitting below, a pulse rifle by his side.

"When do we do that?"

"I'm not sure. We don't want to spook him. Let him know we're on to him."

"You think he doesn't know that already?"

"Maybe when we stop at the next station. Make it casual. Ask a few questions."

Annie chewed her lower lip.

A physical reminder that for once in her life, she wasn't sure how to handle something. This wasn't like her.

Then she noticed that Jordan had unbuttoned his shirt cuff and was rolling up his right shirtsleeve. All the way up to his shoulder, exposing his biceps.

Jordan twisted his arm around to the right, exposing a spot under his biceps, then he held his arm up so Annie could see.

A series of black lines and squiggles.

A QR symbol burned into Jordan's skin.

"Every trooper, from grunt to central command, gets one of these. For security, for safety . . . for *life*."

And then it became clear what he meant.

She repeated his words: "For life."

A nod.

And with that vital, even dangerous bit of information they could plan what they were going to do.

"When we get to the way station," Annie said. She looked around, checking the flight readouts. "We'll deal with it then . . . where there's security to back up our play."

Jordan nodded.

Good, she thought. *But having a plan and pulling it off are two different things.*

They both fell silent as they prepared to enter the portal to the next way station.

# 24

HYDRA SALIM

"*I wonder if going through* the portal looks the same to everyone," Ruth said, her face turned to the window.

The light show streaked by in a dazzling array. "Or if it's like—what's the word? Subjective? What if it's subjective, and you see what you want to see?"

His nap obviously over, Ivan opened his eyes, looked at her, and shook his head.

*Why all the mystery? This wondering about the Road, the portals? The god-damned Builders.*

The Road was the Road.

*Take it for what it is—what it has to offer—and don't ask so damned many questions.*

He said none of this because, as much as he didn't want to admit it, he was finding her *attractive*.

Better looking than the Chippie, if he had to choose.

*Been so long. No time for any of that in his previous life.*

He let his hand drop to his side and touch the smooth barrel of his pulse rifle.

Now *that's* reassuring.

He was waiting for the confrontation—when the gunner or the captain, more likely, asked him—*demanded!*—that he yield his weapon.

*Not gonna happen . . . and they'd better not try to take it.*

"Attention please!"

Captain Scott's voice.

"Please secure your seat belts. We're coming up on the portal to Hydra Salim in a few minutes."

"Ohhh . . ." the Chippie said. Ivan watched her check to make sure the chip in the side of her head was secure.

He heaved a sigh of relief.

*Hydra Salim. A short hop from the last station. Still not even halfway there.*

So ready for this trip to be over.

He had something important to do, and he wasn't going to relax until it was done and over. Even if that meant he was dead.

"We're not sure what the conditions are at the portal or at the way station."

Before Captain Scott could finish, a low, rumbling shudder ran through the ship, vibrating it like a huge tuning fork. The lights streaking by outside appeared to grow brighter, more frenzied.

"And after what we just went through . . ."

Another, deeper shudder that made the vehicle's frame rumble like distant thunder.

The lights in the cabin dimmed. Went off. Then came back on.

*What the hell?*

"There's no cause for alarm."

*Really?*

The captain's voice soothing; but Ivan wasn't convinced.

Ivan glanced at Ruth, no longer thinking of her as simply *the Seeker*, and smiled—he hoped—reassuringly.

He liked the glint of light he caught in her eyes before she bowed her head and focused on her hands, clasped in her lap.

Ivan smiled to himself. That's what he always liked about the Star Road.

*Endless possibilities.*


As it came screaming out of the portal, SRV-66 bumped and shook from side to side as though being buffeted by a sudden blast of hurricane-force winds.

The jerky movement had Annie banging her head against the back of her seat. Hard enough that she saw stars.

Her hands quickly ran over the console, making adjustments as the landing gear dropped into place.

"You all right over there?"

Not a shade of concern in Jordan's voice.

"Yeah. I didn't recalibrate for barometric and the gravity dispersal. Damn. Sorry."

Thinking: *How could I forget? What happened back there really shook me up.*

"Keep us on the track," Jordan said.

"Lovely planet," Annie said, looking out at the landscape.

*No. Not landscape.*

A seascape, as far as the eye could see; this planet . . . a wide expanse of gray, churning water. Swells rose up like mountains, their tops blowing away with foaming spindrift. Heavy clouds—a weird purple that looked like a healing bruise—streamed by, closing down on the SRV.

This Road station was never one of Annie's favorites. She came here as seldom as she could.

*The damn entryway. Insane . . .*

Like a series of interconnected roller coasters, set on pylons that rose above the waves.

Usually.

The problem was—with Hydra Salim—sometimes the storms got fierce enough to wash over even some of the higher routes.

Like now.

A huge wave—it had to be thirty meters high or more—swept over the ramp in front of them. When it drew back, it left behind a tangled black mass of vegetation—a layer of the indigenous life smashing into the ship.

No intelligent life, though . . . unless it remained at the bottom of the vast ocean that encircled this planet.

Annie clenched her teeth as she steered the SRV along the amazingly complicated network of winding roads.

"Why do you think the Builders made it so damned complicated at this station?" Annie asked.

"Beats me," Jordan said.

Annie fought to keep control of the SRV. Rough winds buffeted the vehicle from every side, knocking it around like a kite. Pellets of rain lashed the windshield.

"Have to ask the Seeker we got onboard," she said. "Maybe she'll have a mystical . . . theory."

In the corner of her eye, she caught Jordan's grin.

It took her total effort to keep the vehicle on the road as wind-whipped plumes of spray shot up and washed over them, momentarily obscuring their view.

"Any closer to the water, and we're going to need a submarine," Jordan said without even the trace of a smile.

Annie focused straight ahead, watching the mad spiraling complex of ramps, interchanges, entrances, and exits unwind past her. All of the spurs and runways tied into one huge knot supported by towering gray pylons.

Dense mist and lowering clouds, veined by white lines of lightning, hid the terminal in the distance, but then—

She caught glimpses of what was up ahead, and she didn't like it.

Shifting blacks clouds. Darker than any fog or clouds she knew.

*Smoke?*

"Jesus, no!"

"Say again?" Jordan asked, looking at her.

Annie pointed ahead. Jordan said nothing for a moment or two as he stared at the heavy black billows partially masked by the shifting mist and smoke.

"I think we got more trouble," she said. "No way we can stop, get out of here."

Annie saw Jordan activate his main gun HUD.

*Not good.*

She punched the button for the intercom.

Her voice was pitched low, steady. "Please remain in your seats with your seat belts securely fastened until further notice—even after we come to a stop."

She didn't know what she might have to do once they reached the station, the smoke and whatever the hell it meant.

She flicked off the intercom, grateful she wouldn't have to listen to the passengers' reactions and questions.

Enough trouble to deal with up ahead.

Without a word or a glance, Jordan unbuckled his safety belt.

And headed to the back of the vehicle . . . to the gun turret.


Jordan ignored the upturned faces of the passengers . . . all except Gage, who wasn't looking at him.

*As if he isn't wondering and worried about what's going on, too . . .*

It wasn't easy, keeping his stride straight and steady, Annie still taking the sharp turns, left and right, twisting on the entryway, the SRV on a roller-coaster ride.

His knee bumped into the armrest on Ruth's chair, and she looked up at him.

Eyes glistening and bright with fear.

He could tell her not to worry, that they would be all right.

But he had no guarantee of that.

A cooling wave of relief swept over him as he opened the hatch and settled himself into the gun turret's seat.

A quick run-through to power up the weapon systems and visuals.

He nodded to himself as the weapons charged.

A look outside, to the world below and the station ahead. The black smoke rising out of this watery hell.

Heavy storm clouds pressed down on the portal runways. Huge waves topped by blowing spindrift surged in a roiling mass. The SRV, now down so close to the water, and Jordan feared the waves would engulf them.

*Kind of funny,* he thought. *The ship can withstand the quantum variations on the Star Road, but can it make it through water? The power of a raging sea?*

The smoking ruins just ahead now, as the vehicle swung around on one of the looping curves.

The closer they got, the clearer it became. . . .

Something was really wrong here.

Far in the distance, the way station—or what was left of it—was destroyed. As if a massive bomb—or several smaller ones—had gone off. Exposed girders, scorched and blackened alloy as thick as the SRV, lay in huge, twisted heaps beneath the lowering clouds.

Lightning spiked the smoke that billowed from the wreckage. Nearer to the terminal, the landing area all covered by debris . . . still smoldering rubble.

Orange blades of flame flickered inside the ruins.

"Jordan? Seeing this? This is *not* good."

Annie's voice sounded tinny through the commlink.

"Not good at all," Jordan replied as he hurriedly checked the scanners for signs of anything moving out there. "You still going to dock?"

The pause was long enough so Jordan thought their commlink might have gone down. Then: "Got to. After that bath, we at least need to check the deionizers."

The wheels of the SRV screamed as they left the ramp and hit the tarmac, the impact rumbling through the vehicle . . . jerking it from side to side.

Jordan could see that Annie had to pull the steering hard to avoid the larger chunks of rubble that were strewn all across the runway.

The wind slammed against the SRV like invisible fists, rocking it from side to side.

*Don't go skidding off the ramp . . .*

As they got closer to the terminal, the massive devastation here was perfectly clear. Wind-driven rain swept across the tarmac in shimmering silver sheets as SRV-66 rolled and then stopped more than a hundred yards away from the nearest terminal entrance.

"As close as we're going to get," Annie said over the direct commlink to Jordan.

"We going out?" Jordan asked.

He knew the answer; a clear Road rule. Investigate any signs of an attack. Offer help.

He began unbuckling the turret chair restraints.

Before he took off his commlink headset, he said: "We'll have to be fast."

"Don't worry about that," Annie said. "In and out."


"You want some help out there?" Ivan asked.

He nodded his head at the port window as Jordan made his way up the center aisle toward the main hatch.

Jordan paused, turned, and froze, as if studying him.

*He thinks he can intimidate me*, Ivan thought, smiling as if they were in on a private joke.

"No. Not till we know . . . what happened."

"I'm just saying"—Ivan shrugged—"I can— we can *all* see that something really bad happened out there."

Jordan stood silently for several seconds.

Ivan kept smiling. Then he continued: "I don't have to prove that I'm good with a—"

"You know how to shoot. Congrats. You're still staying here."

Ivan could tell that Jordan was close to asking for him to hand over the gun.

But he didn't make a move to take the weapon.

Ivan tightened his grip on the rifle just in case.

*If he wants it, let him try.*

"We're all in this together," Ivan said, still trying his best to sound friendly . . . helpful.

"You're a civilian, *Gage*—"

Ivan didn't like the emphasis he put on his fake name.

"So if I ask . . . *tell* you to stay put, you damned well better do it."

A nod. The smile still in place.

*Let's not make the gunner even more edgy.*

"Just trying to help," Ivan said with a casual shrug. And then, his hand still tight on the pulse rifle, he turned and looked out the window.

*It doesn't look good*, he thought.

And as to staying put?

If anything out there might threaten *him*, staying "put" would be the last thing he'd do.

"You ready?" Annie asked.

After what had happened at the Nakai Station, she wanted to be sure that they didn't take any unnecessary chances.

She and Jordan had pulse rifles and were suited up in full battle armor.

She looked at Jordan, finding strength in his confidence.

Annie checked her weapon, adjusted her gloves, and then put on her combat helmet.

The HUD on her faceplate came to life.

*All the readings looked good.*

A few seconds to boot up, adjust—and to make sure the sensors were reading.

She nodded.

"Okay. Good to go."

Jordan opened the hatch and, taking the lead, went down the steps to the rubble-strewn tarmac, Annie only a few steps behind.

The wind-blown rain lashed at them, almost knocking Annie over.

She braced her legs and hunched her left shoulder into the blast. Rain sliced across her faceplate, so forceful it made a metallic noise.

"Christ!" she said loudly.

She thought she had to shout to be heard above the howling wind. But when Jordan spoke, his voice sounded surprisingly close.

"Remember, quick. In . . . and out."

But even Jordan didn't look any steadier on his feet. His helmet swiveled from side to side as he scanned the area.

His rifle ready.

*The right person to be watching my back,* Annie thought as they headed across the tarmac toward the terminal.

Up close, the damage looked much worse. The terminal had been stripped to its girders, with gaping holes in the walls and all of its windows blown out. Below them, the ocean churned as towering waves crashed with a thunderous roar against the support pylons.

Annie knew: these weren't lightning strikes. This damage wasn't caused by any storm.

That much—at least—was obvious.

*But what—or who—had?*

Everywhere she looked, she could see scorch marks from pulse weapons and craters from what had to have been concussion grenades. The flames that had appeared so small from the distance were, in fact, huge, stories-tall conflagrations, sweeping through the buildings in spite of the driving rain.

And there were bodies . . . body *parts* more like it . . . strewn everywhere.

The tale here clear, obvious. The station had been attacked, the place destroyed, the personnel wiped out.

"Suggestions?" Annie asked, stunned by the devastation.

"None yet." Jordan shook his head even as he added: "I don't think we're going get to deionize here."

"I think you're right."

"And you know—this wasn't done by warrows."

"Gee, you think?"

"But maybe whoever hit Nakai did this."

Walking close to Jordan, Annie picked her way as carefully as she could through the carnage. The wind kept slamming into them, knocking them around. Annie kept her stance spread wide for stability, but that only gave the wind a wider area to hit.

"Well, lookie here," Jordan said.

He had stopped a few paces ahead of Annie and pointed down at one of the bodies on the ground.

Annie drew to a stop beside him. At first, all she could see was the mess of tangled, charred flesh. Even the internal organs were fried.

A man, she assumed by the large build, burnt to a crisp. The mouth, a ragged black hole.

The skin on the face was seared, peeled back, exposing both upper and lower teeth. A silent, sinister scream.

And the eye sockets.

Empty holes.

"Someone from the station?" she wondered.

Annie glanced at Jordan, then back at the corpse.

She saw that the dead man's left arm and his uniform were still intact, the torn edges burned and melted into his skin.

And sewn on the sleeve . . . an arm patch.

"Oh, shit," Annie muttered, seeing it.

A depiction of a spiral galaxy with a large *R* over it, stitched in red . . . and a blood-tipped spike driven through the letter.

Annie swallowed hard.

"Runners," she whispered.

Jordan nodded.

Then he knelt down and, taking a sharp blade from the tool kit on his belt, cut the emblem off with a few quick slices. Burned skin crinkled and blew away on the wind.

Before Annie could ask Jordan what he was doing, he looked up at her and said, "Evidence."

"For who?"

But Jordan didn't answer. He stuffed the emblem into his kit and stood up.

"I'm pretty sure the pod bays are gone," she said. "We can't even get word out, get help."

"That would be my bet."

"So how are we going to contact the WC?"

Silence from Jordan.

"Okay then." Annie squared her shoulders in spite of the buffeting wind, and looked around. "So we don't get a message out to report this attack, either." She shook her head. "I have to give 'em credit. They may be brutal, but they're damned systematic."

"Very thorough."

Annie kept staring out over the desolation, not even trying to estimate how many bodies she could see from where she stood. She didn't like the note of urgency she heard in her voice when she asked, "It's just . . . why are they doing this? What's their goddamn message?"

She heard Jordan in her ear, voice low, taking a deep breath.

"I think there's someone on board who can tell us."

# 25

## THE TRUTH

### [PART ONE]

*Ivan looked up slowly when* the swatch of cloth with an arm patch dropped into his lap.

Facedown. A tiny burst of adrenaline entered his system, his right hand steady as he slowly turned it over and saw: the Runners emblem.

He took a slow, steady breath and looked up straight into Jordan's eyes as the man said: "Recognize it?"

*How do you play this hand?* he asked himself.

*Act dumb?*

*Confess everything?*

*Go for the gun?*

It was all so wide open, as far as he was concerned, until: "What's wrong?"

Ruth's voice came from the back of the vehicle. He didn't want her to get into the middle of this, to confuse the options he had.

But she got out of her seat and walked up the aisle to them.

She stopped close enough to Jordan to put her hand on the crook of his elbow.

*How well do they know each other?* Ivan wondered.

*Something there.*

"It's none of your business."

Sharp.

Not the way you talk to just any passenger.

Then, softer, more understanding, and—*what? Concern?*

"Please. Ruth. Go back to your seat."

Ivan looked up to the front of the cabin at Annie, standing a few paces away, her pulse rifle lowered but ready.

The others—Nahara and Rodriguez—gawked at Annie and her gunner, and the drama being played out.

*She could easily get a shot off before I even touched my rifle*, Ivan thought.

And he knew how fast the gunner was.

*Game over . . . no reset.*

"That's a good idea," Ivan said, casting a quick glance at Ruth. He saw the worry for him in her eyes.

*Been a long time since anyone gave a damn about me.*

"Ruth. Take your seat." The tone in Jordan's voice . . . again suggesting that they knew each other.

Still, the Seeker didn't back down. Ivan kept track of her in his peripheral vision as he stared long and hard at Jordan.

"Anything to say?" Jordan asked, his voice low.

"Not really."

Ivan took a deep breath, still calculating—and not seeing—any way out of this without endangering the other passengers in the cabin, and probably losing the race to his gun.

"Well?"

Finally: "Yeah." Ivan shook his head, looked away. "I might be able to stop them."

Back to see the gunner's face. Set, ready for anything.

And maybe even enjoying this.

"That's what I figured."

Ivan exhaled to steady himself. His pulse pounding in his ears . . . throbbing in his neck.

"Or lead us right into a trap." Ivan braced. Jordan pointed his gun right at Ivan's midsection.

"What's been going on . . . out there, back at the other station. I see the patch. I get that. But that's not how the Runners operate."

Jordan laughed out loud. Then: "You mean *you*! How *you* operate."

Ruth let out a gasp behind him. Ivan shook his head.

*This isn't how it's supposed to go down . . .*

He considered pleading with Jordan, telling him everything. But he knew the gunner wouldn't believe a bit of it.

And if the situation was reversed, he wouldn't, either.

*And so here we are . . .*

● ● ●

Annie had never seen anything like it.

*Ever.*

Jordan appeared to be losing control. His face flushed, breathing fast through his nose. Sweat stood out on his brow, but his gun arm remained as steady as ever.

She never wanted him to look at *her* like that.

He looked like he was ready to reach into Gage's mouth and rip his lungs out.

She had to do something.

"Stand down, Jordan," she said.

She knew he heard her command because of the quick flick of his eyes—a millisecond—in her direction.

If anything, his body tensed even more.

*Can't have a damn firefight in here.*

"I said, stand *down*!"

"Sorry, Captain," Jordan said. "I can't do that."

"That's not a request, Jordan. It's an order. You can and *will* stand down—now!"

"Could I ask exactly what the hell is going on here?" Nahara asked, turning to Annie.

He started to stand up but then sat back down when Jordan fired a quick glance at him.

Ruth looked like she was working up her courage to intervene.

"I know who you really are, *Gage*," Jordan said.

He practically spit out the name.

"Oh, yeah?"

Ivan looked up at him as coolly as if Jordan were a waiter who had just asked him how his meal was.

"Yeah. Ivan Delgato."

*What?* Annie thought.

*Impossible. The Runner leader was in prison, on Earth . . .*

*No . . . No way . . .*

Ivan picked up the arm patch from his lap and studied it, letting it dangle between his fingers.

Then—amazingly—Gage . . . *Ivan* . . . didn't deny it.

"This isn't us. This isn't how we operate," he said in a low and controlled voice.

"Whoa—hang on!" the Chippie said, sitting up in her seat to get a better look at Ivan. "I *knew* it! I knew you were . . . somebody."

Now Nahara stood up.

*This is getting crazy here,* Annie thought.

"Nahara, sit the hell down," she said.

"You traitorous son of a bitch!" Nahara shouted, fists clenched, his face flushed.

"W-why doesn't he look like he did in the news vids?" Rodriguez asked.

*Great . . . now everyone's involved,* Annie thought.

"Micro-surgery, more than likely," Jordan said. "A bit of sculpting? Right?"

Ivan said nothing.

His pulse rifle still only inches away.

Jordan's attention didn't waver from Ivan.

From Annie's viewpoint, it looked as if the two men had locked eyes like big jungle cats about to engage in battle.

*Fucking primal.*

Annie and Jordan both knew how fast Ivan was—they'd seen him in action.

Hell, he'd saved their lives back there.

That had to count for something.

Would Ivan do something now that might get innocent passengers injured . . . or killed?

Then again, if he *really* was Ivan Delgato—the convicted leader of the Runners—he had proven that he had no regard whatsoever for innocent lives or people's property.

*And what the hell's he doing out of prison?*

Last she'd heard, Ivan Delgato was off to the Cyrus Penal Colony in the Movasi Sector.

*Enough,* she thought.

*Have to take control of the situation.*

Annie stepped forward, being careful not to place herself between Jordan and Ivan.

"Did you send that message pod from Station Two?" she asked. "Maybe our coordinates and routed them to your damn Runners?"

Holding her gaze, Ivan shook his head slowly. "I never even got close to the pods."

Jordan: "So you haven't contacted anyone, told them about this SRV? I have a hard time believing for one second that—"

Then, from behind Annie, a sudden shrieking noise, a shrill beep sounding a warning.

Filling the cabin.

"We have company," she said, turning to Jordan.

His expression—a stone carving.

Jordan nodded.

"Get me a neuro-collar," he said.

*Jordan? Giving orders now?*

"It doesn't have to be this way." Ivan cast a glance back and forth between her and Jordan. "I can explain."

"I knew we never should've picked him up," Nahara said.

Annie went to the emergency supplies compartment and entered a code. The container door popped open.

"So much for your vaunted code of the Road, huh?" Rodriguez piped in.

The alarm—still blaring.

Annie moved fast, getting the neuro-collar for Jordan.

Her gunner meanwhile gave Ivan a sharp nudge with the barrel of the gun.

"Who's coming, Delgato?"

"How the hell would *I* know?"

Now another, harder hit with the gun. To the face. A trickle of blood ran from the corner of his mouth.

Ivan looked ready to leap up at Jordan. Tear his throat out.

"Easy, Jordan." Annie handed him the collar.

"You've been leading us into this trap all along starting with your Speeder breaking down."

"If I wanted you dead," Ivan said softly, "believe me, we wouldn't be having this conversation now."

"Collar him," Annie said. "There's incoming. We don't have time for this."

The warning sound increased in volume and frequency.

The passengers looked wide-eyed, panicked.

The situation . . . *out of control.*

*Whoever's coming here . . . they're getting closer.*

"Everyone, I'm going to keep Delgato collared until we get to Omega Nine. Then the authorities there can straighten it all out."

"What authorities?" Jordan asked.

"You want the truth?" Ivan's voice was firm. He wiped his mouth on the back of his hand. Studied the smear of blood for a moment.

Jordan wrapped the collar around Ivan's neck and snapped the connectors in place.

"Yeah, you can tell us all about it later."

The neuro-collar signal lights came on, blinking green.

Ivan became immobilized, his body going limp.

"Jordan, let's move it."

But Jordan stayed where he was, watching, as if he didn't trust the collar.

Then he reached down, took Ivan's pulse rifle.

Annie turned to the passengers, their eyes on her.

"Get in your seats. Buckle up. We're getting out of here. Now."

And she darted back into the cockpit, her gunner finally turning and following her.

# 26

## RUNNERS

*Jordan followed Annie up the* stairs and into the cockpit.

But when he sat down in his seat and strapped in, glancing at the console, he didn't like what he saw.

Annie already had the vehicle's engines powering up. The SRV started rolling.

"We have someone—*a few someones*—coming in at two o'clock on the port side," Annie said. "They're on an upper level, but they're heading our way."

Jordan nodded.

"I'm picking up at least six vehicles," Jordan said, adjusting his scanners. "They're bunched close together, scrambling the signal."

"Shields?"

"Up to maximum, too."

"Can't be sure they're hostile," Annie added—a hopeful note as if to reassure herself. "We can't simply assume."

Jordan tapped the screen tracking the converging ships. "Tell me this doesn't look like a coordinated attack."

He unbuckled his harness. "I'd best get to the aft turret. Better safe . . ."

He got up and moved quickly through the passengers' cabin to the gun turret. He noticed that Ruth was looking at the immobilized Ivan.

Thinking, as he rushed past her: *Pity? For him? Seriously?*

He kept moving fast, and within seconds, he was strapped into the turret seat, gun powering up, headset on, and commlink working.

*Ready to go.*

• • •

"I still don't think they had to do this," Ruth said, leaning close and staring into Ivan's eyes. "Can you even hear me?"

She turned and looked at the other passengers—Nahara, Sinjira, Rodriguez. "Is he still conscious? He's like a zombie."

Nahara nodded as he cleared his throat. "He's fine."

Rodriguez looked away for a moment, then back at her.

"Yes," Rodriguez said. "With the collar, he can hear and understand everything perfectly. Just can't move or speak."

"He deserves to die, if you ask me." Nahara's face was flushed.

"What if he was telling the truth . . . that he's not with the Runners?" Sinjira asked. "From what I've heard, no one's ever escaped from Cyrus."

"Always a first time," Nahara said, more calmly. "Maybe these attacks have been, like, a diversion while his band of killers broke him out."

"Yeah. He had to have had help," Rodriguez said, staring at Nahara. "From inside the prison or from the World Council or . . . maybe even someone on this vehicle."

"What? What the hell are you suggesting?" Nahara's face was pale. His upper lip oily with sweat.

*A lot of fear and mistrust on this ship*, Ruth thought.

"*Someone* sent that damn message pod from *inside* the terminal."

"It wasn't me." Nahara looked furious.

Ruth watched the passengers as they looked around suspiciously at one another.

All of them, jumping to conclusions, making judgments. Calculations.

Paranoia.

*Now, turning on one another.*

"How about you, Doc?" Nahara leaned one arm on the seatback and stared directly at Rodriguez. Challenging him. "We still aren't clear why you're headed out to Omega Nine. What's the big secret, hmm?"

Rodriguez tightened his mouth and shook his head.

"If it was any of your business, you would know."

Then Sinjira got up and walked over to Ivan. A smile lit her face as she knelt down in front of him, Ruth inches away, taking it all in.

Leaning close, pressing her breasts against his arm, she whispered loud enough for Ruth and everyone else in the cabin to hear: "We should talk, Ivan. Perhaps when we get to Omega Nine"—she paused—"when they take off this stupid collar. We could license your life story for . . . millions. The stuff you've done, the things you've seen."

Ruth looked back to Ivan, a line of drool and blood running down his chin from the corner of his mouth. Like he was crazy, demented, looking so vulnerable . . . so harmless.

*How the hell can this be Ivan Delgato, the notorious rebel?* she thought.

*He's not a cold-blooded killer . . .*

"You should go back to your seat and strap in," Ruth said. Sinjira rolled her eyes and then stood up. She delicately traced the edge of Ivan's jawline with the tip of her forefinger.

"Are you his nursemaid?" she said, glowering at Ruth. "Or maybe . . . you're interested in the Runner for other reasons." The Chippie was grinning wickedly now. "Can't say I blame you."

Then, a sudden lurch of the vehicle threw her off balance and almost onto the floor.

The captain's voice came over the speaker.

"Please—everyone remain seated and strapped in."

Ruth checked Ivan's straps, and then sat down and buckled in as the Chippie made her way back to her seat.

And then SRV-66 started moving on the ramp leading to the Portal. Fast.

*Something*, Ruth thought, *is going on. . . .*

As soon as she powered up and started rolling, Annie saw the incoming vehicles on the screen.

She watched as they split up and took different ramps.

*Different vectors.*

*Circling like vultures . . .*

*Surrounding us . . .*

"Looks bad, Jordan," she said into the commlink.

"Go as fast as you can, Annie," Jordan said over the headset. "I'll keep them busy."

"Okay."

The SRV picked up speed as she moved it away from the demolished terminal building.

Fast, Annie trying to gauge how much speed she could muster as she hit the curved, fun-house ramp to the portal . . . just how much she could push it.

Zigzagging to avoid the still-smoldering rubble and scattered body parts.

Her breath froze in her throat when she brought up the rearview screen with a swipe of her hand.

A vehicle suddenly appeared behind them, and it was *huge.*

Almost as large as a WC troop ship.

And then she realized that's exactly what it was—a decommissioned troop ship that had been modified, almost unrecognizable. Its hull was scored with numerous pulse blasts and dents. Gun turrets bristling everywhere.

Even as she watched, the forward portals opened, and several small, bullet-shaped speeders shot out, heading toward her.

"Jordan, they're coming in fast. Speeders all over the place," she said.

"They have to stick to the Road like we do."

As if in response, a white spike of fire shot from the rear of the SRV. The shields on one of the speeders exploded in a shower of orange sparks and bubbling hot metal.

What was left of the speeder stopped dead on the road—a twisted wreck.

Annie's options of which ramp to take were numerous . . . and confusing.

The map configuration on her HUD displayed dozens of interlacing ramps and roadways, all curving around wildly and converging in gigantic Gordian knot–like intersections.

The entire interchange was supported by hundreds of massive pylons that faded away into the distance. Below the ramps, the oceans churned, hurling huge waves up to the sky.

The oncoming vehicles skillfully navigated the winding intersections.

*How the fuck do we get out of here?*

Even as she thought that, a group of speeders started to close the distance, speeding up behind them.

So far, they were holding their fire.

*Why?*

Annie had to make a decision. Moving to full power, she saw four good options immediately up ahead.

*They must want to take us alive.*

The speeders—still far enough away . . .

Maybe she could shake them off, get to the portal, get back onto the Star Road.

Get the hell out of here.

*Maybe.*

She decided not to take the obvious route—the most direct route to the portal.

That's exactly what the Runners would be expecting; so before she got to the junction, she cut the SRV hard to the left and onto a ramp that dropped down . . . toward the ocean.

*Has to be rocking the passengers . . . and if they see the speeders?*

They'd be getting the Road trip of a lifetime. She wondered briefly if the Chippie was recording all of this. No doubt.

Checking a screen, she saw that the maneuver had worked.

For now.

One of the speeders tried to take the unanticipated turn but, moving so fast, it flew off the edge of the ramp. It dropped in a lazy, dizzying spiral and then flared in a silent explosion when it hit the edge of another ramp thirty meters below. Still spinning like a whirligig, it plunged another hundred meters until it splashed into the raging ocean.

And disappeared.

Nothing left but a large, iridescent oil slick on the surging waves and bubbles rising to the surface, marking where it had gone under.

"Two down," she said into the commlink.

"Make that three," Jordan said.

Annie watched as a pulse cannon took out one of the two speeders that had successfully negotiated the hairpin turn, coming up fast behind them.

The other had forward shields up; but each turn exposed its flank . . . at least for a moment.

She watched as her gunner took full advantage and fired short, sharp blasts.

The speeder exploded in a glorious shower of sparks and twisted metal.

*That leaves two more left that we know of,* Annie thought.

And then she wondered: *Why aren't they shooting at us?*

She had no idea how many more speeders might come after them. There could be dozens more still inside the troop ship . . . or circling around out of scanner range or hidden behind the massive pylons to head them off.

Eventually, with planning, every section of ramp could be a trap for the SRV, and these guys looked like they knew what they were doing.

Frantic, she scanned the various screens, looking for more signs of enemy pursuit.

When her gaze flicked back to the rearview, she groaned.

"Shit . . ."

A speeder close on their tail . . . and all she could think of to say to Jordan, shouting into her headset, was: "Why aren't you taking that son of a bitch out?"

"Easy there, Annie. I can't get a bearing. He's too close, and this ramp is anything but straight."

Even in this situation, Jordan sounded calm . . . collected.

No pressure.

*Wish I could say the same.*

Annie took a quick turn and dropped down to another, lower level, as if she might be doubling back to the station, in exactly the wrong direction if she wanted to access the portal.

The SRV skimmed along the undamaged ramp surface, shifting from side to side as she adjusted for its winding curves.

She kept an eye on the speeder on her tail, but she had to focus on the path ahead. Its twists and turns made her stomach roil.

*Who the hell designed this?* she wondered.

Her passengers below had to be losing it.

"Okay. This . . . is going to be crazy," she said, as much to herself as to Jordan.

With a sudden jerk of the controls, she took a sharp turn onto an even lower level, one that nearly skimmed the surface of the sea. Foaming waves towered against the sky.

The SRV sped along the ramp at nearly sea level.

Massive tongues of water splashed across the ramp's surface and pulled away, leaving behind thick tangles of a strange kelplike substance that gave off an eerie red luminescence.

*Stuff looks slippery. Hit some of that on a sharp turn and . . . good-bye.*

In spite of a few reckless turns, the single speeder behind them kept up and now was gradually shortening the distance. Annie had no doubt that the driver was in communication with the troop ship, giving his exact location so they could send out more speeders and intercept her.

*Only a matter of time . . .*

"Still can't get a clear shot," Jordan said over the headset. "If you got to a straight section. Even for a few seconds . . ."

Annie checked her screen showing the ramp sections ahead.

"Okay . . . we're coming up on a straightaway."

"Copy that. I'll be ready."

Annie also saw that there weren't any other ships directly ahead of her.

*Not yet, anyway.*

*Coming down so near the surface threw them off.*

"Gun needs more pivot and arc. Then I could get off a shot. Fucking design flaw, if you ask me," Jordan added.

"We'll see about redesigning the vehicle once we get back home, okay?"

"Just get us straight, Captain."

Annie throttled the SRV up as fast as it would go and still stay on the twisting roadway, now close to a short, straight section.

But then another one-man vehicle appeared on the road in front of them. She jumped when Jordan fired forward and turned the speeder into a blazing, spinning ball of slag.

*Fucking Jordan—got eyes on the back of his head.*

She checked to onboard nav systems. The bad news: she was moving farther away from the portal. Once again, she wondered why the Builders—or whoever—had made such a complex system of interchanges and ramps. Part of a defense system for Hydra Salim? Or maybe it was simply a very busy hub at one time or another.

Annie glanced at the rearview display again just in time to see something that didn't make sense.

The speeder right there . . . behind them . . . still not firing, to the side, in the water . . . something huge and dark was moving fast along the road, tracking them like a predatory shadow.


In the gun turret, Jordan watched his pursuer intently, waiting for him to stop wobbling back and forth so he could actually hit it.

He could see a straight section ahead.

*C'mon*, Jordan thought. *Come to papa. Just need one clean shot.*

He jumped when a surge of sudden turbulence in the ocean off to his left hit the SRV.

His first thought was that a huge wave had heaved up and was about to break over them.

This one looked big enough to sweep the SRV and its pursuer into the ocean.

But that isn't what happened.

Instead, out of the churning gray water, a huge head—*bigger than the SRV itself*—broke the surface. It thrust up and out of the water, towering above them, balanced on a thick, elongated neck.

The underside of the animal was translucently pale, but everything happened so fast, Jordan could barely register it.

Then the thing *struck*.

Whipping its head around faster than should have been possible for something that size, it opened its mouth, exposing a red, gaping maw lined with huge, sharply honed teeth. With a quick, vicious snap of its body, the head darted forward like a striking cobra and snatched up the speeder.

And the speeder . . . simply . . . *vanished*.

Like it had never been there.

The water churned, throwing frothy whitecaps to the wind as the creature returned to the depths. A wave thick with red kelp sloshed over the road.

But that was the only sign that it had ever been there.

*That could have been us*, Jordan thought.


"What the hell just happened?" Annie was staring at the rearview screens.

One second, the pursuer was there.

The next . . . *gone*.

She tapped the screen to make sure it was still functional. The view of the road behind them was perfectly clear.

*So where's the speeder?*

"Jordan?" she said, more calmly than she felt. "What the hell just happened?"

Jordan's laughter came over the commlink, and then he said, "You—ahh, might want to take a higher road. Trust me on this."

"I'm getting a reading that there are more of the Runners up ahead. How you holding up?"

"Any ramp ahead and I'll be fine. Send as many as you want my way. Just because they're stupid enough not to shoot us down, doesn't mean I can't shoot *them*."

# 27

## SHOOTING GALLERY

Gotta give 'em credit. They're *tenacious bastards, whoever they are.*

Now Jordan was enjoying himself as he picked off their pursuers one after another.

*But why the hell aren't they shooting back? Even to cripple us, if they want to take the cargo or someone on board?*

He had no doubt they were Runners, and they were here to get their leader—Ivan—back alive.

"Look . . ."

He saw what lay ahead at the same instant Annie did.

They were moving in the direction of the portal now, the diversion down to the surface having worked . . . at least for the time being.

Jordan checked the nav systems and saw several routes to the Star Road entrance. He hoped Annie would take the quickest one and get them the hell out of here.

Once they were back on the Road, they should be safe, but could she shake these guys when they closed again? Could she evade them and could he shoot them all down before a well-placed shot crippled their vehicle?

The portal was close. But now, coming up on their rear . . .

The huge troop ship was moving up behind them.

Could Annie outrace it? Had to be too large to navigate the twists and turns of the road like SRV-66.

Smaller means faster . . . more agile.

But even as he watched, the troop ship opened, and more speeders dropped onto the road and started moving toward them.

*Small . . . agile.*

*Damn it!*

Eight . . . ten . . . fifteen and more were coming. More than he could count.

"All right, then . . ." he said as he squeezed the grips of the gun's controls, the palms of his hands dry.

This is what he lived for.

The speeders quickly closed the distance, but not all of them made it. Within the first thirty seconds, three were blasted out of existence, the wreckage falling to the ocean below.

But the road here was wide enough so they could zigzag back and forth, and Jordan couldn't predict all their moves.

And for most of them, their shields held.

He decided to hold fire. Wait to catch them on a turn, when their shields were exposed, and then: they started to shoot.

Streaks of white light shot from their forward cones, but these weren't kill shots, Jordan quickly realized.

*Going to wound us just enough.*

And as the speeders closed the gap between them, they stopped firing.

They weren't even going to risk going for the crippling shot . . . not if it meant disabling the SRV and having it lose control and drop off the ramp and into the sea.

*They may be crazy,* Jordan thought, *but they're certainly not stupid.*


Annie jumped with surprise when the commlink suddenly chirped.

Not Jordan's bandwidth.

She hit the button, and a face, blurred beyond recognition, popped up on her comm screen. She hit a button to run an ID scan but knew it wouldn't work. The scrambled signal would mix the data stream.

"Captain," the man said. His voice sounded unnervingly close in the confines of the cockpit. "Don't make this any harder on yourself than it has to be."

*Fuck you!* Annie thought, but instead said, "What do you mean by that?"

"Power down and pull over, or we'll burn you."

Annie stared at the face of the screen, knowing the commander could see her. She bit her lower lip as she slowly shook her head.

"Can I ask why you've opened fire on a civilian vehicle?" she said.

The commander of the troop ship leaned back and laughed.

"Isn't it obvious?"

"You're violating World Council law."

"We're a long way from the World Council, from Earth . . . Captain . . . Captain Scott, if I'm reading your transponder signal correctly."

A lengthening silence. And then: "We have nothing on board of interest," Annie said.

"How do you know what interests me?"

"We have a handful of passengers and a small amount of cargo. Medical supplies, mostly. Not worth the price you've already paid."

A laugh, this time deep and more sinister than humorous.

"How many men have you already lost?" Annie asked.

Thinking at the same time: *This has to be about Delgato.*

The commander laughed again and said, "I'll give your gunner credit. He's good. He should join us."

*Fat chance!*

With nothing more to say, Annie cut the communication and sped up, trying to put more distance between herself and the speeders. That lumbering tub of bolts would never catch her on its own, and hopefully Jordan could handle the speeders.

*Or I gotta outrun them.*

The SRV tore along the winding roads, but no matter what Annie did, she couldn't shake her pursuers. They popped up and swooped in, riding her . . . herding her . . .

Finally, frustrated, she flipped on the intercom and spoke to the passengers as calmly and carefully as she could.

"I need a volunteer. Anyone ever shoot a nose cannon?"

*Nahara or Rodriguez, maybe . . . Not the Chippie, and absolutely not the Seeker. Of course . . . there was one guy who could probably operate it, no problem. Delgato.*


Ruth froze when the captain's voice came over the speakers.

Like the other passengers, she'd been furiously knocked back and forth as the SRV sped over the winding roads. She was exhausted, like the rest of the passengers who hadn't slept in . . . how long?

And as shots flashed by the SRV, the heavy thump of the gun turret shook her bones.

*And now this? Asking for a volunteer?*

*Or what—we get captured . . . killed?*

She undid her safety straps and stood up. Clinging to the seatbacks, she made her way slowly to the front of the cabin.

"You. Nahara. How about you?" she asked, looking at the World Council exec.

He regarded her for a moment and then lowered his gaze as though ashamed.

"I-I'm just an executive."

He turned away.

"And you?"

She focused on the doctor—Rodriguez.

He shook his head even before she asked her question.

A sound off to her right drew her attention.

She looked at him—Ivan Delgato, the scourge of the Star Road, if she could believe the media.

His eyes were wide; his expression, pained.

Then, though she thought it impossible, he managed to say a single word.

"...I..."

That was all.

A sound like he was being strangled. Which he was. From what Ruth knew about neuro-collars, it was a miracle he could speak at all.

She held her breath and leaned closer.

"Don't strain yourself," she whispered.

But Ivan's face was infused with blood, veins bulging in his neck and forehead as he struggled to say more.

"...Take...this..."

A raw, ragged intake of breath.

"...off..."

Ruth looked around at the other passengers. Frantic.

*No help there.*

"Someone please. Help. This thing is strangling him!" she shouted to the others.

Then the exec, *Nahara*, shook his head again.

"None of my business," he finally said, softly. "And I'm not much of a fighter."

After a tense moment or two, Rodriguez stood up. Glaring at Nahara, he said, "Not much of a man, either. I'll do what I can."

With that, he walked up the few stairs to the cockpit door and rapped on it.

Within a second or two, the door opened, and he went inside.

• • •

Rodriguez's hands were sweating as he shut the cockpit door and stood there for a moment, staring in amazement at the complex array of navigation and communication screens, displays, and devices.

*Where to begin?*

"Okay, Doc, I doubt you've ever been inside a SRV cockpit or operated a pulse cannon before." Annie barely glanced up from her screens, her hands flying back and forth over the controls.

He shook his head.

"Have a seat. I'll talk you through it. When I have a—"

Without warning, she jerked the steering hard to the left, taking a narrower ramp.

"Sit down. Buckle up."

Rodriguez did as he was told and then watched, fighting back his fear as Annie steered the vehicle down a long, spiraling ramp. A feeling of vertigo swept through him. It looked like she was heading straight down toward the raging ocean.

*Is she trying to get us all killed?*

On one of the screens, Jordan—the gunner—was sitting in the aft turret, calmly swinging his cannon around and shooting. His face was expressionless.

The speeders chasing behind them were fast, and they easily dodged back and forth to avoid shots.

The shots that did hit exploded on the speeders' shields with bright flashes of orange plasma. Enough hits, and even the toughest shields would fail.

"The gun's control is there . . . on your left. Grip the handles, aim, and—*shit!*"

Another wrenching turn almost threw Rodriguez out of his seat.

"Aim and fire," Annie finished. "The trigger's the red button on the left handle. Above your thumb."

Without even thinking to take careful aim, Rodriguez pressed the trigger.

A streak of light shot from the forward cannon and hit the road about forty meters in front of them. Huge chunks of road compound exploded into dust.

An instant later, the SRV shuddered when it ran over the smoking crater his shot had made in the road.

"Easy there, cowboy," Annie said. "I said *aim* first."

Biting his lower lip, Rodriguez nodded.

Annie's expression was fixed, staring straight ahead as she piloted the twists and turns of the spiraling road. This particular loop led down and then straight up again. But here was their chance.

A last mad dash to the portal.

"Make sure you get someone in your sights before you pull the damn trigger."

*Technically, press, not pull,* Rodriguez thought, but he wasn't about to argue the point right now.

Rodriguez licked his lips and stared, amazed at the savage fury—and frightening beauty—of the ocean below them. Towering gray waves washed up and over the ramps and crashed in huge sprays against the pylons.

But this was no time to appreciate the view.

Up ahead, a one-man speeder suddenly appeared.

*Moving so fast.*

Rodriguez swung the gun up until the automatic targeting system blinked green. Then he fired . . .

And missed.

His shot went wide and tore through one of the pylon's support struts. Sparks exploded and flared as twisted hunks of molten metal and alloy exploded into the air. The gaping hole had to be at least four meters across.

"This thing's got punch."

The oncoming speeder was weaving from side to side, avoiding the fire and heading straight at them.

Rodriguez was sure they were going to collide head on.

But Annie darted onto another ramp, leaving that speeder behind until its pilot could turn around and get back into the chase.

"Take your time . . . this isn't rocket—or any other kind of science," Annie said in a quiet voice that almost made him believe he could do this. "It's just aim and shoot."

*Almost.*

Because then, his only thought was: *If it's left up to me, we're all dead meat.*


Jordan exhaled, frustrated.

The SRV zigged and zagged so much he still couldn't get off many clear shots, and the speeders were onto his tactics now and kept their noses darting left and right as much as possible.

*Steady there, Annie,* he thought. *Just for a bit.*

He couldn't see the troop ship through the turret, but his scanner indicated its approximate location.

What he saw made him smile.

"Annie, you've got him out of position," he said into the commlink.

"Say again?" Annie's voice crackled in his headset.

"We're between him and the portal. Check your readings. Jesus! Our shields aren't holding up."

"Not deionizing can't be helping," Annie said sharply.

*Had to be slowing the SRV down.*

"Can't do a damn thing about it now," Jordan replied.

A pause. Nothing. Then: "We're just going to have to make a run for it."

"That'd be my move."

On the scanner screen, Jordan watched as several dots moved in from three directions to cut them off, trying to drive them away from the portal.

He had no delusions about their odds.

Annie was a good pilot . . . a *great* pilot, but she couldn't do the impossible. These Runners were tenacious, dogged; they must *really* want whatever—*or whoever*—was onboard.

"Hey, Jordan. I'm gonna need you up front to clear the way if things get hot," Annie said over the commlink. "Going to have to forget the speeders. I think their captain knows what I'm gonna try."

"Be right there," Jordan said, already undoing his safety straps.

Within seconds, he was moving briskly up the aisle toward the cockpit. But at the front of the cabin, the Chippie grabbed at him.

"Want to chip up for me?" she asked, her eyes bright with excitement.

Jordan shrugged her hold off and raced to the cockpit door.


"Okay, Doc, head back and man the rear turret," Annie said to Rodriguez. "Works just like this one. Only bigger."

"And try not to shoot our own ass off," Jordan added.

"I can't do this anymore. I'm useless."

He looked like a lost child.

"Get your *ass* back there and do whatever you can! It doesn't have to be fancy. Just keep shooting to let them know we're not going down without a fight."

"We haven't already proven that?" Rodriguez said. When no one reacted, he left the cockpit.

As soon as Rodriguez was gone, the door slamming shut behind him, the atmosphere in the cockpit changed. Annie was focused on her piloting and the signals coming in on various displays and scanners.

"That asshole ain't worth spit," Jordan muttered.

Annie looked at the screens, moving from one to the other.

Dozens of speeders showed on her display, all angling toward them from several directions at once.

It looked like they'd easily intercept SRV-66 before Annie got anywhere near the portal.

"Okay, Jordan. It's showtime."

With the portal so close, they entered a gauntlet.

# 28

## ROAD TEST

*Rodriguez sat down in the* aft gun turret.

He grabbed the only thing that made sense to him—a headset—and snapped it on.

"You kidding me? What do I do back here? This is—"

"Rodriguez. *Quiet!*" Jordan said. "And listen up."

It felt as if the gunner was speaking right against his ear.

"Just grab the stick in front of you, right between your legs."

Rodriguez took the stick, and the twin barrels of the main gun and the turret started to move together.

"Whoa—I'm moving."

"No shit. You move in the same direction as the guns. Now, when you see something coming at you, just press the button to fire."

Rodriguez pressed the button. He blasted into a section of the ramp, and a smoldering crater appeared.

"At a target, Rodriguez. A *target.*"

He nodded, his heart beating fast in his throat, and said, "Got it. Yeah."

"Good."

And Jordan vanished from the screen.


"So close," Annie said. "But they're all over the place."

She looked at Jordan as his head swiveled from the cockpit window to the screens. Back and forth. Up and down. Calculating so much, so fast.

"Gotta wait. Let 'em get a bit closer."

Annie knew better than to question her gunner's tactics. She had the SRV running full out. Let him do his job.

But she'd have to ease up a bit before they hit the portal. No telling what the Road was like on the other side.

"Okay," Jordan said calmly, and then he started firing.

And Annie, even with her eyes locked on the ramp, adjusting her SRV as it rolled toward the portal, watched the nearest speeder burst into flames. Direct hit on its core.

Even better—the flaming metal mess careened into one of the other speeders and took it out.

"Nice one," she said.

Then more blasts. Some of the speeders swerved to avoid the SRV's shots.

But by getting close, they now had fewer options, fewer turns and ramps to take.

If one speeder dodged, the other had to sail on—exposed.

"Three down," Jordan said.

*And at least four . . . five more coming.*

And then some started hitting the SRV.

"Hitting us in the rear," Jordan said. Then: "Rodriguez . . . you have permission to fire . . . *amigo.*"

Jordan went back to picking off the speeders with only seconds left before SRV-66 entered—or tried to enter—the Star Road.

Rodriguez's frantic aiming had the gun turret swinging around wildly, his shots nowhere near hitting the two speeders racing after the SRV, firing away.

*Can't do this*, he thought. *Can't do this.*

He felt nauseous, and when he burped, a thick, sour taste filled his mouth.

*I'm a scientist . . . not some space warrior.*

*This is above my pay grade.*

He chuckled at that and, for a moment, stopped overthinking the shots. Now he moved, fired and—amazingly—a speeder burst into flames and crashed into the ramp, skidding and spinning around, sending up a shower of sparks.

"I *got* one!"

"So get more," Jordan said calmly.

The adrenaline—a new feeling for Rodriguez—raced through him now. He felt positively high.

Which is when he turned to target the other speeder and saw that—instead—the other speeder had *him* in its sights.

"No," Rodriguez said.

He pressed his button.

And the two opposing guns fired at the same time.

Rodriguez got off a shot; a hit but not fatal.

But the enemy speeder aimed dead-center on the turret and fired back.

The blast rocked the SRV, kicking it ahead, and the hit to the gun turret sent a shower of sparks raining down on Rodriguez. Hissing specks stung his exposed skin while the rocking SRV shook him back and forth like a rag doll.

His hands went up to cover his burning face.

Releasing the gun, he wiped away the painful glowing bits of metal and plastic from his hands and face.


Jordan tapped his screen.

"Rodriguez took a hit. We gotta get him out of there."

"No," Annie said quickly. "Stay at your post."

Jordan had cleared the last of the latest wave of speeders. But more were coming. Fast. The portal entry lay directly ahead, its churning rollers growing brilliant in the dim sunlight.

"You can't walk back there during a portal entry. Let's get through—then you can pull him out."

Jordan didn't argue.

She liked that about him.

He had his opinions, but he took an order as if he were still in the military.

"Here we go."

The screen showed the shimmering multicolored wringers of the portal while the cockpit window showed only a crazy jump into empty space.

"Now . . ." Annie said.

And the SRV left the near-space of Hydra Salim. After a stomach-churning moment of weightlessness, they were suddenly back on the Star Road.


The first thing Annie did was look at the screens, checking to see if they were being followed.

"I think . . . we did it."

"Okay, let me get Rodriguez out. Maybe one of the passengers can bandage him up."

"Right."

Jordan unsnapped his harness and left the cockpit.

And Annie thought, *Did we really just outrun them? Will that battle cruiser give up?*

Doubtful.

If it did, though, this was one hell of a lucky day.

She looked down to a screen showing the gun turret. Jordan was freeing Rodriguez from the debris covering the gun seat, hauling him out.

Not much blood.

That's good.

*Face is a mess though . . .*

Then she picked up movement on the aft screen.

And not just *movement.*

The Runner's battle crusier filled the screen.

*Too damn good to be true,* Annie thought.

Reality was now chewing on her ass.

And she sat there without a fore or an aft gunner.

What was the expression?

*A sitting duck.*

Even moving at hyper-speed, it was like she wasn't moving at all.


Jordan eased Rodriguez into an empty seat at the rear of the cabin.

"How bad am I hit?" He touched his face. "Am I bleeding?"

"Superficial wounds, Doc. You got singed. You'll be all right."

He gave the man, who was acting like he was breathing his last, a hearty pat on his shoulder.

"You done good, Doc. Taking out two speeders. Something to tell your grandchildren."

"If I ever have any—"

Then the intercom sounded.

"Jordan. We got company."

His smile faded.

"Can someone come back here and help Rodriguez? Tend to his wounds? First aid's right up here."

He tapped an unlocked overhead compartment.

Sinjira stood up, looking scared, but she moved toward Rodriguez.

"I will."

Surprised that the Chippie would offer, Jordan nodded and then ran back to the rear gun turret, fearing the worst.

Ruth looked at Ivan, slumped in his seat and rocking from side to side as the SRV constantly jigged left and right.

He could move his eyes.

And what she saw there—what she *thought* she saw there—made her reach out and place a hand gently on his wrist. She pressed her index and middle fingers down to feel his pulse. It was slow. Once every three or four seconds.

No matter what anyone else thought about him, this Ivan Delgato, she sensed nothing but honesty and goodness coming from him.

And she wouldn't be where she was, traveling across space to find answers about not just the Road, but about the universe if she hadn't learned to trust her feelings.

The vehicle rocked again. Hard.

Her hand tightened on his wrist.

His head immobile, his eyes strayed left, looking directly at her.

"Ivan," she whispered. "I'm sorry you—"

His lips opened.

Also in slow motion as if it was torturously difficult, fighting the control of the neuro-collar.

Open lips. A pause. Then: "I—"

A word. His eyes wide.

Then: "Can."

The next word took so much time, a tiny gust of air escaping through the narrow slit of his open mouth.

"Shoot . . ."

Ruth nodded and looked around.

"He's offering to help," she said.

*And we need all the help we can get.*

She nodded at Ivan and stood up and said, louder, "He's offering to help!"

"Damn, Jordan. Look at this . . ."

On the screen, the battle cruiser was behind them. And as they watched, a huge hatch opened up, and more speeders streamed out like angry hornets leaving a nest—two, four, six in formation at first, then dozens, splitting up, weaving . . . bobbing.

Jordan had been blasting at the cruiser itself to no effect, but now he had targets he could take out.

Which he did with typical efficiency.

But for each speeder he nailed, another pair flew out of the cruiser.

*Only a matter of time before they wear us down.*

But then there came a sound.

Unfamiliar.

A heavy clanking noise to the right . . . just behind the cockpit housing.

A whining noise, like—

*Drilling!*

She knew immediately what it was. A grappling hook of some kind. A drill, burrowing into the hull of the SRV's metal plating—plating that could handle meteors, even direct blasts from pulse cannons—but could, with the right drill bit, be penetrated.

If the drill didn't cause the whole ship to depressurize, any rupture would force the ship into self-protective compartment-by-compartment shutdown.

And the SRV would stop . . . dead.

*Prime eating for the Road Bugs.*

"For fuck's sake," she said.

"Annie?"

Jordan, so close to his gun's noisy blasts, might not have heard the drilling into the side of the hull.

"We've been grappled, Jordan."

"Thought so," he said. A pause. Then: "Only one thing to do."

"Yeah, only thing is . . . I've never done it."

"Seriously?"

"What can I say? I'm a cautious pilot."

They were both silent for a few seconds, the drilling growing louder, setting Annie's teeth on edge.

"No time like the present to learn a new trick," Jordan said.

Annie nodded. She grabbed the wheel tighter, checked her speed, and sucked in a breath.

# FOUR

# SECRETS AND LIES

# 29

BETRAYAL

*Annie let her breath out* slowly.

And then cut the wheel hard to port while hitting the retro-thrust.

The SRV did what any other vehicle on any other "road" would do.

It turned over, rolling as she increased her speed, gunning the engine, giving as much spin to the roll as she could.

Annie held on tight to the controls, and everyone inside SRV-66 turned ninety degrees, then completely upside down, and then: a grinding, crashing sound . . . the shriek of metal ripping apart.

The speeder that had attached itself to the SRV was crushed into the surface of the Road.

Not much left, not even for the Road Bugs.

The explosive multicolored sparks from the screaming metal flew forward, nearly blinding Annie as glowing pieces of the speeder sprayed like golden raindrops across the cockpit window.

The barrel roll continued even as the SRV dragged the remains of its attacker under it, pressing it harder against the Road.

More sparks, exploding in vibrant showers of light, and then the SRV righted itself.

Amid the crazed mayhem of the barrel roll, that annoying sound was gone.

Now came the tricky part . . .

Could Annie get the vehicle running straight again when it returned to a level position on the Road?

Theoretically, she knew how to do this. She had to go slowly, play with the controls to keep the SRV from flying off into what looked on either side like the absolute void of space.

Her pulse throbbed, the blood pounding in her skull.

But she held steady, turning slowly. *Don't overreact.* And the SRV came around level. She played the wheel to the right, then to the left. The SRV banged back and forth, trying to get some kind of traction on the Road.

And then, with a gentle thump, it settled down on the Road and was running straight.

It was quiet.

No drilling sound.

"Impressive," Jordan said.

A pause.

And she had to agree.

"Unbelievable."

"First time for everything."

On the screen, she could see that while Jordan was holding a number of speeders at bay, more were creeping up along both sides of the vehicle. The speeders were bristling with spiderlike arms—more drills.

*So that's how the Runners take down their prey.*

With less mass, the speeders moved faster than the SRV on the Road. They steadily closed the gap, and the helpless waiting game continued.

If one or more attached to her, could she pull off another barrel roll?

Unbelievable or not, she would have to try.

A light tap on her shoulder made her jump. Then a voice. And a single word.

"Captain?"


A quick look.

*Ruth Corso.*

"Back to your seat, Ms. Corso. We're still—"

"He spoke." Annie shook her head. Confused.

"Ivan . . . he spoke."

*With a neuro-collar on? Not possible.*

"He said, 'I can shoot.'"

Annie grit her teeth and nodded.

Thinking: *What he's really saying is "Set me free."*

*To help or . . . what?*

She looked at Jordan on the screen, overwhelmed by speeders slipping past him like a stream of running rats.

The shields all over the ship were decreasing, nearly drained.

*Ivan can shoot, but can I trust him?*

*He's the reason we're being attacked.*

She had to make a decision. Fast. And she was good at that.

She took a key from her side pocket.

"It releases the collar. He's going to be weak, sluggish at first, but tell him to get the hell up here, pronto!"

Gripping the key, Ruth returned to the one-time leader of the Runners, amazed to think he might be their only hope . . . or quite possibly their destruction.

Rodriguez winced and squinted into the mirror as he checked his wounds. The left side of his face was flecked with the electric burns that oozed blood and pus.

"Looks pretty bad to me."

Sinjira swatted the mirror away and leaned forward, smiling as she daubed antiseptic on his wounds.

"You'll live. I've seen worse, umm after a bad night in SoHo."

Rodriguez looked as though he didn't believe her.

She raised a hand to his face. Touched his cheek. Not a bad-looking guy. Though she liked more *man* in her men.

*Lots more.*

"Just flecks. Superficial stuff."

"And what was wrong with the SRV? What was with that turn?"

"Beats me, Doc. Just be glad we were both strapped in. Too bad I didn't get it on a chip, though. That *was* . . . unique."

"I like my stomach under my ribs, thank you," Rodriguez said.

Sinjira dabbed a few more spots with ointment that immediately stopped any oozing from the burns.

"And I think . . . I need a new chip."

She reached into her side pocket pouch to grab a chip because she was sure this show wasn't over yet . . . especially when Ruth Corso came down from the cockpit and unlocked Ivan Delgato from his neck collar.

"Really? You're freeing him?"

"Captain's orders."

The collar snapped free. Ruth helped Ivan stand up. He looked shaky, to say the least.

Ivan blinked, turned his neck left and right as if making sure it still worked. Then he raised his arms and stretched, but he looked as weak as a baby.

Sinjira heard Ruth say: "Captain wants you. Up front."

Ivan took a step forward and nearly collapsed into another seat. Then, stiffening his legs, he moved as fast as he could, weaving like a drunk as the SRV rocked left and right. He almost fell again as he started up the short flight of stairs.

Sinjira looked at Rodriguez

"Gotta say we are having ourselves quite the Road trip. . . ."


Annie glanced up as Ivan entered the cockpit.

"Against my better judgment, Delgato, I'm giving you the gunner's seat. Your head clear enough?"

Ivan nodded, but he was clearly pained. Disoriented.

"Start firing as soon as you can focus."

She tended to the controls but kept glancing back at him, not moving, just standing there.

"You hear what I said? Sit your ass down and start—"

Finally, he moved.

Reaching smoothly down to his right leg, he quickly produced a small handgun. It wasn't much bigger than a deck of cards.

"What the hell?"

Annie started to ease forward to un-holster her own sidearm.

Ivan shook his head. "I wouldn't if I were you. This is small, but it packs a good punch."

"Jordan will—"

"Will do what he has to. I know. But for now, open a secure link to the battle cruiser commander."

Annie didn't move. She listened to the quiet thumping in her ears.

"Did I forget to say *now*?"


Ivan kept the small gun pointed directly at the captain's head. Leaning forward, he removed her sidearm and tucked it into the waistband of his pants.

Finally, defeated, Annie heaved a sigh and then threw a switch. The ship's channel lit up the screen, and the speakers chirped.

"Battle cruiser Commander . . . this is Captain Scott of the SRV-66."

The screen at the top of the cockpit flickered to life, and the battle cruiser commander's holographic image appeared.

"I'll take it from here," Ivan said to Annie. And then: "Commander, this is Ivan Delgato. I've taken charge of this SRV."

On the projection, the commander's eyes widened. He looked confused. "Delgato? You don't look like—"

"A bit of reconstructive surgery, courtesy of the World Council."

The battle cruiser commander still didn't look convinced.

"I *am* Ivan Delgato . . . and I have this SRV and its captain under my control."

"How am I supposed to—?"

"Order your speeders to stand down. *Now!*" He glanced at Annie as he drew the word out. "Get them back into your bay. Tell me, is my brother aboard?"

The commander turned away, barked an order, then turned to face the screen.

"Kyros gave us orders to bring you to him. Alive if possible."

"Oh, I'm very much alive. What's the next way station off-ramp?"

"Bottes Six. Not far."

"Follow us there." To Annie: "Program for an unscheduled stop at Bottes Six." To the commander again: "You can take possession of this ship and its passengers and contents if you'd like."

"And what do you want us to do with them?"

Ivan leaned back and laughed, then glared at Annie to make sure he had her undivided attention. The gun barrel was mere inches from her forehead.

"With this vehicle? Its passengers and crew? Do whatever you want. Blow 'em all to hell for all I care. Makes no difference to me."

After a short pause: "Yes, sir. We're setting in a course to track you to Bottes Six."

"Good. We'll talk more once we're on the tarmac."

Then to Annie: "Cut the link."

Annie hit a switch.

"Now what?" she said, not a trace of nervousness in her voice.

*The woman's tough,* Ivan thought.

"You're actually going to hand us over to those killers?"

On the screen, Ivan saw Jordan watching as the speeders peeled away. Then he moved down to his screen that showed the cockpit and Annie.

But not the gun.

"Tell your gunner to come up here asap. And be careful. I'd hate to have to pull this trigger. At close range like this? It'd make quite a mess."

Annie took a quick breath. Leaning forward, she keyed the commlink.

"Jordan, get your ass up here now."


By the time the gunner entered the cockpit, Ivan had taken to the wall beside the hatch, so at first the gunner would only see his captain sitting in her command seat.

"What the hell happened? Where's Delgato?"

Jordan had his sidearm out as he entered.

*Good instincts*, Ivan thought

"Jordan," Ivan said quietly.

The gunner spun around, his gun aimed at Ivan . . . who kept a steady bead on Annie's head even as he looked at the gunner.

"Captain?"

Annie took a breath. "I think it's best if you stand down, Jordan."

The gunner didn't move. Didn't flinch.

"Jordan! I said . . . stand *down!*"

Finally, Jordan lowered his weapon.

"Good," Ivan said, reaching out and taking it from his hand. Jordan held his grip on it, not letting go for a tense second or two.

"Nice to see you both can be reasonable. Now take your seat while we get off the Road."

"Off the Road?"

"Bottes Six," Annie said quietly. "They want Ivan."

"And us?"

Annie lowered her eyes and said nothing.

"Okay, Captain Scott," Ivan said. "Get us to Bottes Six."

# 30

## THE TRUTH

### [PART TWO]

*Annie eased the power up* as the SRV hit the off-ramp.

Unlike the twisting maze of the station on Hydra Salim, this way station had a flat, straight plane converging on a small runway with a tiny control tower.

There was no sign of human activity anywhere. No one asked for their ID or was tracking their transponder or giving them landing instructions. Annie assumed that the Runners had already taken out whatever few poor bastards worked on this dismal outpost.

"They'll get you again," Annie said, pulling back and slowing down the SRV. "The World Council, I mean."

"We'll see about that," Ivan said dismissively.

"Screw the WC. I'll get you, you son of a bitch," Jordan said.

Ivan looked at him but said nothing.

He focused on the screens over their shoulders, his pulse gun aimed steadily at the back of Annie's head. Their landing on the tarmac was smooth and, on the rearview display, he saw the battle cruiser trailing behind them, lumbering like a behemoth on such a small ramp.

Annie brought the SRV to a gradual stop. Her grip on the controls tight, her knuckles white knobs.

"Okay," Ivan said. "Wait until the cruiser comes to a full stop. Then open the commlink."

Annie flipped some switches to start powering down the SRV.

And Ivan quickly shot out: "*No!* Leave her running."

"They'll notice if we don't power down."

"Maybe not. And you. Jordan." He had the gunner's full attention. "Don't get any last-ditch heroic ideas about shooting it out, 'kay?"

Jordan eyed him steadily, coldly sizing him up.

*For a coffin,* no doubt.

"All you'll accomplish is seeing your captain's brains decorating the controls. If I'm fast enough, yours as well."

"You're a son of a—"

Before he finished, the commlink chirped.

"Ivan Delgato, I'm bringing our cruiser alongside the SRV."

"In front, Commander. Move your ship directly in front of the SRV."

A pause.

*Confusion perhaps?*

"I'm your commanding officer," Ivan said sternly. "That's an order."

Then: "Yes, sir."


The cruiser slowly rolled past the SRV, towering over it and casting a thick wash of shadow across the tarmac as it passed before finally coming to a stop in front of them.

*Piece of cake for the forward gun,* Annie thought.

"You can—" the commander started to say.

"Commander." Ivan's voice was firm. In control. "Bring a squad out to take possession of this vehicle, its cargo, and its passengers."

"And do what?"

Annie shivered when she heard Ivan laugh.

"Like I said. Whatever the hell you want. But I can't stand here all day holding a gun to their heads. Get a move on."

"We're heading out even as we speak."

Then silence in the cockpit as they waited. Sweat ran down Annie's neck, and she was thinking: *Is there anything,* anything, *Jordan and I can do?*

She remembered all too well what had been done to all those people on the stations along the way. The death from the warrows. The devastation on Hydra Salim.

*No question what's going to happen to us.*

She thought: *A last-ditch hopeless effort may be the only card I have left to play.*

Jordan was thinking the same thing, she knew.

Annie tried to think through her limited possibilities.

They didn't have many . . . but the SRV's engines were still running.


Ivan watched as the battle cruiser's hatch opened, a giant clamshell, slowly sliding open, wide enough to drive the SRV into its massive cargo bay.

The cruiser's commander appeared first, walking . . . strutting, leading two rows of Runners—twenty soldiers in all, each one holding a pulse rifle at the ready.

*Good,* Ivan thought, *not too many.*

For a moment, he scanned their faces.

*Do I know any of them? Have I led any of these Runners?*

Before they turned into a paranoid homicidal organization that seemed intent on turning the Road into one endless, bloody battlefield.

But the faces were all young. Hard faces. Chiseled. Good material for the type of destruction best carried out by those who don't question orders.

Maybe Kyros had purged the ranks of any loyalists—Runners who would question this "war" against the World Council, his attempt to grab power and hold on to it with the threat of death.

"You bastard," Annie muttered as the line of Runners marched closer, their figures resolving from the heat haze.

Ivan noticed Jordan's hand drifting slowly toward the pulse cannon controls.

"I wouldn't do that."

Outside, the commander raised his right hand to the headset on his helmet.

"Prepare to be boarded."

His voice filled the cockpit.

Ivan could sense Annie and Jordan both tensing up, waiting for the order that would expose their ship—and her passengers—to whatever hell the Runner commander decided to inflict on them.

"Jordan," Ivan said, his voice mild—pleasant.

The gunner turned and glared at him.

Ivan handed his gun back over to him.

The gunner looked at his handgun, stunned—then at Ivan.

"You son of a bitch," he said as a slow smile crept across his face.

"There they are," Ivan said, his voice sounding hollow even to his own ears. He wondered again if he was betraying any men who had served him so loyally.

"Look at all those Runners . . ." After a brief, stunned silence, Ivan said, "Do what you do best."

Jordan snatched his gun and jammed it back into his holster while, in one fluid move, he turned back to the cockpit window.

And grabbed the controls for the forward gun.

And then, with blasts rocketing out of the SRV, the line of Runners—out in the open—was exposed.

The commander spun around and fell to the ground like a discarded toy. A line of dust kicked up where the pulse cannon ripped into the sand and asphalt a few meters in front of the line of men.

Jordan's blasts swept viciously back and forth across the line.

All of the men—*well-trained*, Ivan noticed—hit the tarmac, flattening themselves to make the smallest targets possible. Some ran left and right, dodging for cover.

It took only a few seconds. The air filled with dust.

Only the commander lay dead on the ground, red seeping from his head into the sand.

"If I were you, I'd go for their main guns," Ivan said. "Her shields are down with the loading bay door open."

Jordan didn't need the prompt.

He was already moving his sights up from the now-pinned boarding party to the four turret guns on the front and side of the cruiser.

No fire came from any of them . . . and by the time anyone could get to them and power up, each gun had been turned into a twisted, charred crater of glowing, smoking metal.

"Good eye," Ivan said, as if Jordan needed to be told. "But I noticed you didn't take out any men, except for the commander."

"Yeah. I won't kill anyone in cold blood no matter how much they might deserve it."

Ivan raised an eyebrow.

There was more to Jordan than he thought.

Then: "Okay, Captain . . . I'd say it's time you got us the hell out of here."

"Agreed."

Annie revved up the SRV's engine even as Jordan kept puckering the cruiser with blasts. He aimed at—and hit—the forward wheel carriage. The huge battle cruiser lurched heavily to one side, threatening to topple over like a wounded elephant. Support struts snapped like toothpicks.

Annie glanced at Ivan, not saying a word.

"You're a man of many surprises, Mr. Delgato," Jordan said.

Ivan looked at him and laughed but said nothing.

Annie turned the SRV around, no longer threatened now that the battle cruiser was crippled where it stood. And then the SRV pulled away from the burning wreckage, heading toward a ramp that led to the way station's nearby portal.

Jordan looked a tad frustrated, now that there wasn't anything left to shoot at. Maybe it had been too easy.

Ivan grabbed a rail to steady himself as the SRV lunged forward, engine whining.

"I still have to get those panels deionized," Annie said, frustration and worry in her voice.

Behind them, a thick column of black smoke billowed into the sky from the burning battle cruiser. Men were running around, their figures diminishing rapidly as Annie increased the SRV's speed.

"There," Sinjira said to Rodriguez. "You should be fine."

"What's the hell's going on?" he said. "We're leaving already?"

Sinjira slid into the seat across the aisle from the scientist and buckled in.

"Appears that way."

"What was all that shooting about? I thought we were being boarded, that the Runners had . . ."

Sinjira raised her eyebrows. "Go figure, Doc."

Then she turned to look at the cockpit door. Ivan hadn't returned to the passenger cabin yet.

*What's happening up there?* she wondered. *Is he helping the captain get away?*

If so . . . then the woman sitting up front, Ruth, the wide-eyed Seeker, had done something that saved all their lives.

*Might need to reevaluate her,* Sinjira thought, but for now, all she could think was how tired she was. She tried to settle into her seat as the G-forces increased.

*Reevaluate her, and Ivan, and Rodriguez, and—*

Another thought, this one unexpected . . .

*Maybe even myself.*

*Look at me playing a nurse. Caring for the wounded.*

*Will wonders ever cease?*

Apparently not on this trip.

Another, stronger wave of exhaustion washed over her. Maybe once they got back onto the Road, she and the rest of them could catch up on some much-needed sleep.

Maybe . . . but not likely.

"Hang on tight," Annie said to Ivan. "It isn't recommended that you enter a portal standing up."

Her eyes were fixed on the screens and the fluctuating readings, checking the readouts and displays to see if the battle had left the SRV with any fatal weaknesses. Ivan spoke, his voice low.

"Done it before. Builds character."

"Um . . . I bet."

"Hows the deionization?" Jordan asked.

"Fluctuating all over the board." Annie looked grim. "We'll be lucky if we don't burn her out on this next stretch."

And then they entered the spinning luminescent wringers. After a momentary feeling of disorientation as everything in the universe dilated, they were out of the portal and onto the Star Road again.

This section of the Star Road appeared to be endlessly straight, as though it might never curve one way or the other again.

*Good time for a nap, after everything we've been through.*

"Everything looking good?" Jordan asked. He stifled a yawn behind his hand and shook his head.

"Amazingly, yes. The deflectors still show too much heat buildup. But the core's within safety parameters. If we keep our speed down, we should be okay until we get to—"

She stopped.

Ivan had let go of the railing and come up behind her, looking at the screens over her shoulder.

"Do you mind?" she asked.

"It's just . . . I've never been in a SRV cockpit before," he said.

Annie shook her head, amused.

"Well, we should be okay until we get to Omega Nine. No more stops."

She glanced to Ivan.

"I guess we . . . *you* still want to go there, right? Even after what just happened?"

He nodded. "Now more than ever."

The Road was straight, no speeders, no battle cruiser, no Road Bugs. Jordan turned to Ivan.

"That was some trick you pulled back there. Had me a touch nervous for a while."

"It worked. That's what counts."

"True enough. But you could have gotten us all killed."

"I didn't, though, did I?"

A pause as everyone adjusted to the feel of the Road.

"I had to convince you if I was going to convince the commander."

"But they're after *you*," Annie said. "They were coming to free you. Isn't that what you want?"

She looked at Jordan. "I don't get it. Do you?"

Then back to Ivan. "So why don't you explain, nice and slow, so even Jordan will understand."

"Up yours," Jordan said.

Ivan grinned.

*He's enjoying this*, she thought. And she reminded herself that he had at one time been the leader of the Runners.

Nothing more than a pirate of the Road.

And yet . . .

*He just saved our lives—again.*

Her guess was he had his reasons, and they probably had nothing do with the lives of the people on the SRV. In the end, they were all probably expendable.

"Okay. Story time," Ivan said, rubbing his hands together. "This time, a true tale. And why we need to get to Omega Nine . . ."


Annie made sure the cockpit door was bolted. Until she knew Ivan's story, she didn't want anyone else hearing it.

*This trip's been crazy and bloody enough as it is.*

Annie nodded. Jordan sniffed and shook his head, eyes focused ahead on the Road.

"After my conviction—for treason—the head of covert operations for the World Council met with me and offered me a deal."

Annie was already skeptical.

"I could be released—I *would* be released—if I did something for the World Council."

Jordan shook his head. "So while everyone's thinking Ivan Delgato, the ruthless leader of the Runners, has been sent to an off-world penal colony, the council is cutting deals?"

"I might question the word 'ruthless.' Some people don't think the World Council has the right to control the Road. Even some council members. People want the Road open and free . . . to everyone who wants to take the risks."

"Yeah. I heard that speech before," Jordan said. "You can save it."

"What did they ask you to do?" Annie asked, still not convinced.

"Ever hear the expression: 'The enemy of my enemy is my friend?'"

Annie nodded.

"They let me go so I could cut a deal with my brother Kyros. Or stop him. He took over leadership of the Runners after I was captured. But as soon as he did, things started changing."

"No shit," Jordan said.

"The council saw that my capture didn't weaken the Runners. It only made them stronger. And now under Kyros, worse. What was that word you used, Jordan?"

"Ruthless?"

"Yeah. Ruthless. The Runners attacked mining operations, and they not only raided them for their ores and heavy metals. The death and destruction left behind were warnings. These weren't the Runners I used to lead."

"So you took the deal to get your freedom?" Annie said.

"Yes—and no. I didn't want to spend the rest of my days on some barren prison planet. But also"—he glanced at Jordan—"despite what you might think, this wasn't the organization I led. Something went wrong, and all because of my brother."

"A *lot* went wrong," Annie said. "You're responsible for the deaths of a lot of people."

"Not me. Kyros. I was in prison, awaiting trial for a long time. I had plenty of time to wonder about what had changed him. Changed the Runners. If that was my legacy, I needed to find out and—if possible—stop it."

"So the deal was, I would go to Omega Nine, talk peace with Kyros. Offer him and the Runners a pardon from the World Council. If he doesn't take it? I'm ready to do whatever I have to."

"You can't reason with an animal," Jordan said.

"He wasn't always like that," Ivan said, turning to him. "Something's changed."

"And we're going to Omega Nine for what could be"—Annie shook her head slowly—"a showdown?"

"I take it you don't like the idea of that?" Ivan said with a grin.

Annie didn't smile, thinking, *This isn't what I signed up for.*

But then . . . something was nagging at her. Something still didn't fit.

"Hang on," she said. "Your solo SRV breakdown, then the cruiser coming to get you . . . it doesn't add up."

Ivan nodded.

"Didn't for me, either. Not at first. But then, when I watched our gunner here blow that boarding party away, I finally got it."

"Go on," she said.

"I don't think you're going to like it. . . ."

# 31

## QUESTIONS

*Ivan looked at the shimmering* ribbon of Road un-spooling ahead.

So peaceful. So hypnotic. It was as if they were sailing a calm, flat sea, not racing halfway across the galaxy at seemingly impossible speeds.

"The plan was I would go to Kyros, unannounced, in the solo SRV."

"After changing your face?" Jordan asked.

"Just some quick minor stuff so if I had to stop, hopefully I wouldn't be recognized."

"Yeah, *hopefully*," Jordan said. "I had my suspicions right away."

"And your solo failed because . . . ?" Annie asked.

"That's where it gets interesting," Ivan said, frowning. "The vehicle had been thoroughly checked out. Vehicle cores don't just 'fail' like that. That's when I knew something else was going on."

He looked at them as they listened to the story.

It looked like they believed him.

*And that's good. I will definitely need their help before all of this is over.*

"Someone sabotaged my solo. I checked it out myself just before I left, and it was perfect. No way I would have missed that someone had tampered with it. But somehow . . . *someone* got to it before I left. They set me up to be Road kill."

"Why? If you had an agreement with the World Council?" Annie said.

"Yeah. The World Council wanted me to make peace with the Runners, with my brother . . . but someone who was privy to our deal *didn't* want that to happen. I figured it had to be someone deep inside the World Council."

"That's the only thing that seems to make sense," Annie said.

"If you hadn't come along when you did? The Road Bugs would've gotten me. End of story. Mission—failure."

"And your brother, he'd be able to go on doing what he's doing. Killing. Destroying—" Annie said.

"King of the Road. No one—not even the World Council—could stop him."

Jordan shook his head and said, "There's still one thing I don't get."

"Only one? Wish I could say the same," Ivan said.

"If your brother wants you dead, why didn't he wipe us out back there on Hydra Salim? Why not blow our SRV to smithereens and be done with it? Instead, he—"

"He—or at least the captain of the cruiser chasing us—wanted to get me alive. But if he thinks I'm a traitor to the Runners—or wanting to take charge again." He let the thought hang there for a few seconds.

Annie checked the controls. The SRV was rolling along just fine on autopilot now. She looked back at Ivan.

"Any theories?"

Another tight smile.

"A few."

Ivan was enjoying trying to figure it all out. He enjoyed trying to crack the mystery, looking at possibilities. Maybe that's why he loved leading the Runners. Sometimes he dealt with unknowns better than he did the known.

"Theory one: Kyros wants me alive because he wants to do something with me."

"Beyond killing you, you mean?"

"That'd be too easy," Ivan said.

"From what I've seen, not so easy," Jordan said quietly, almost to himself.

"Maybe he thinks he needs to kill me himself, some crazy idea he has to make sure everyone knows he's the true leader now. So maybe he was worried that something might happen along the way . . . that he'd miss his opportunity of bringing me to my knees in front of all the Runners."

"Interesting," Jordan said. "Makes me wonder why you—or we—would want to keep going to Omega Nine."

"I know. But here's theory number two."

He had their total attention now, but he could see that both of them were tired. Worn out. He wasn't feeling all that frosty, either.

"There's something on this ship that Kyros wants. Otherwise, he would have had it destroyed."

"Or someone," Jordan said.

Annie's eyes widened.

"Yeah. And whatever it is, he needs it more than he needs me dead."

"Makes sense," Jordan said. "What would it be?"

"Did either of you ever wonder how they knew I'd been picked up by your SRV?"

Absolute silence for a long time.

*Apparently not.*

"Far as I can tell, there's only one place . . . one time that any word of that could have leaked out."

Now Jordan nodded. "The Nakai Way Station."

"Uh-huh. When we were dealing with the warrows, someone got a message pod out. We know it wasn't either of you. And you know it wasn't me. With Sinjira and Ruth both waiting in the SRV, that leaves . . ."

Annie stood up, her face set, this theory not sitting well.

"Nahara or Rodriguez."

"Unless it was McGowan . . ."

Annie looked long and hard at Ivan.

"Whoever sent that pod has something your brother wants more than he wants you dead."

It took some time for that to sink in for all of them.

"So it would appear."

"And what could it be?"

Ivan shrugged. "Your guess is as good as mine. If you were Kyros, if *you* were leading the Runners, what would you want? And then who could give it to you?"

She turned to her gunner.

"Jordan, I'm going below with Ivan. You okay here?"

He nodded. "The Road's smooth up ahead for a few hours, anyway." Then . . . an uncharacteristic smile from the gunner. "I'm disappointed I'm going to miss the next scene, though."

Ivan reached out and gave the gunner a tap on his shoulder.

"Don't worry. You can watch it on the screen."

Then he turned and followed Annie down the steps to the passengers' cabin.


Annie took a breath before she opened the hatch.

"I hope you're right about this. Otherwise it's a serious violation of passengers' rights."

"Not to mention looking a touch paranoid," Ivan said. "Could be we have a mix of theory one and two here. Either way, we'll know soon enough."

She nodded. Braced herself.

As captain, what was about to happen next was all her responsibility.

She opened the cockpit door and walked down the steps. The cabin lights were dimmed in case anyone was trying to sleep. As if sleep was even possible. But it'd been a long trip so far, and they still had a ways to go.

Sinjira was sitting next to Rodriguez, both of them leaning back, their eyes closed.

Ruth, though, sat straight up, wide awake. She flashed Ivan a smile when he came down the steps behind Annie.

As he walked toward the seats, she undid her safety harness and stood up.

"You're okay? They"—she looked directly at Annie—"believed you."

"We're all on the same page, Ruth," he said. "And—"

When he looked at Ruth, Annie had a sudden thought.

*Is there something going on between these two?*

*The Runner leader and a Seeker . . . Pirate and mystic.*

There was a definite vibe.

*Stranger things have happened.*

"—if you hadn't trusted me," Ivan said, "released me when you did . . . *You're* the one who saved us. Not me."

Ruth Corso smiled and put a hand on Ivan's arm. The touch lingered.

"I can sense things about people . . . See them for who they really are," she said.

Annie stood there for a moment, the two of them seemingly oblivious to her presence.

And thinking, *Later. Right now, we have a traitor to smoke out.*

Ivan fired a quick glance at Annie. Back to Ruth. Smiling.

Annie nodded at Nahara, strapped into his seat. His eyes shut. His breathing shallow and steady.

*Asleep? Resting? Or faking it?*

Maybe this conversation between Ruth and Ivan was good. It made everything seem ordinary . . . routine.

No sense of urgency.

Annie felt Ivan's eyes on her as she walked to Nahara and leaned over him.

With a nod to Ruth, Ivan took a few steps so he was standing directly behind Annie.

"Mr. Nahara," Annie said, shaking his arm gently.

*Nothing.*

A bit louder.

"Mr. *Nahara?*"

His eyes slid open. Mere slits. But perfectly clear. She had the distinct impression he hadn't been sleeping at all.

*Closing his eyes . . . wishing this would all go away.*

No, he'd been feigning sleep.

*Because maybe if you have a secret—a secret that's against the law—maybe you'd find it awfully hard to sleep.*

"How are you feeling?"

"Feeling?"

He licked his lips. Sat up a bit in his seat.

"Your leg . . . those bites."

"Oh, my leg. Yeah. Right." He cleared his throat and sat up as best he could with the safety harness on.

"Not bad. Still some pain, but I can manage. I should be fine until we can get to a med center. Omega Nine, they have a full—"

Annie patted him on the shoulder and smiled, cutting him off.

"Glad to hear it. Oh. One more thing . . ."

Her hand now clamped his shoulder. Hard enough to make him wince. Ivan was hovering close behind her.

*Glad he's got my back,* she thought.

"We need to know who you sent that message pod to and what it contained."

Now Nahara's eyes widened, maybe taking in the fact that Ivan wasn't simply standing there listening—an innocent bystander.

He had a pulse pistol in his hand. Lowered. But at the ready.

"Message pod?"

Lulled by Nahara's apparent grogginess, Annie missed the next move as his right hand dropped down to his lap and undid his safety harness. The click of the latch sounded unusually loud.

Ivan shifted behind her, but Nahara moved remarkably fast, considering the pain he had to be feeling from his leg wounds.

In a flash, Nahara pulled a gun from a holster strapped to his right leg.

He sprang to his feet, grabbed Annie by the throat, and spun her around, so they were both facing Ivan.

The gun pressed into the back of Annie's head just above her right ear.

Ivan's voice was low and measured. "Mr. Nahara. We *know* it was you. And we also know why."

Nahara was silent, but his expression said: *Oh, do tell.*

"Put down the gun, and we'll talk."

Nahara snorted.

"You won't get much farther without your pilot."

"We have the copilot."

Annie looked calm, even with the gun pressing hard against her head.

"I know my brother," Ivan said.

"Your brother?" Nahara said, stunned.

Ivan nodded. He didn't want to have to act. Things could get messy with bystanders so close. "I know what Kyros wants and is capable of getting . . . especially from someone like you."


The gun metal felt hard against Annie's skull.

She knew, if Ivan went for a shot, a quick spasm in Nahara's hand could no doubt squeeze the trigger.

Her brains and fragments of her skull would decorate the wall.

*I'm getting a bit tired of having guns pointed at me*, she thought.

But Nahara's eyes, wild and wide, stayed on Ivan.

*Theory number two is looking pretty damned good about now*, Annie thought.

"I don't know anything about your brother or what he might want. I—"

If there was an opportune moment to make a move, Annie knew this was it.

She lurched forward—dropping her head—and swung her arm around where she knew the gun would be.

With a quick chopping motion, she brought her forearm up, sweeping Nahara's hand. Ivan stepped around Annie, knocking her aside as he closed his hand around Nahara's, putting his thumb between the trigger and the trigger guard.

"No shooting today, *compadre*," he said evenly.

With a quick twist of his wrist, like he was removing a bottle cap, he gave Nahara's hand a sharp turn. Something in Nahara's arm snapped, and the gun dropped free.

With a grunt, Annie saw Ivan push Nahara back into his seat.

The man let out a loud puff of air when he landed. He gripped his wrist, which had gone limp.

"You broke my damn wrist!"

"Be grateful that's all I broke."

Annie straightened up and brushed herself off. Composing herself.

"Collar him?" Ivan asked.

"No other choice," she said.

She walked over to the compartment by the cockpit entrance, opened it, and grabbed the neuro-collar.

When she returned, Ivan had his hand closed around Nahara's throat, pushing his head back against the headrest.

"Just restraining him until you get him collared," he said, even though he looked like he was ready to twist Nahara's head off his neck.

Nahara stared at him, bug-eyed.

His tongue hanging out of one side of his mouth like a thick, pink slug wedged between his teeth.

Annie wrapped the collar around Nahara's neck and snapped it tightly. Then she activated it. A green light came on, and Nahara sagged in his seat like a sack of potatoes, instantly immobilized.

"All righty, then," Ivan said, turning back to Nahara. "Let's see what you've got that my brother wants so badly." A glance back to Annie. "Am I violating any passenger's rights or anything?"

"Violate away," she said.

Ivan turned back to the immobilized man.

"I already have a pretty good idea what it is . . ."

And Annie stepped back as Ivan started patting down the Road Authority officer, rifling through his pockets and patting his body up one side and down the other, all the way to his shoes.

Ivan stopped.

And grinned.

"Bingo," he said softly.

# 32

## THE DATA CRYSTAL

*Annie watched Ivan rip open* the hidden pocket sewn into the left leg cuff of Nahara's pants.

A small, transparent cube dropped into the palm of his hand. Grinning broadly, he straightened up and then handed it to her.

"I'm guessing you don't have to worry about any lawsuit from him," he said, looking at Nahara. "What's the jail time for smuggling?"

"All depends on what's on that data crystal," she said, taking it from Ivan.

"Then let's go look."

Back in the cockpit, with Jordan watching and Ivan leaning against the door frame in the entryway, Annie held the data crystal up high, between her thumb and forefinger, and rotated it slowly.

It glistened like a wet diamond; but its surface was curiously cold and dry.

"I'm guessing this isn't just *any* data crystal. Can you—"

She kept staring at the smooth, clear crystal, studying it . . . watching the light play along its facets, fragmenting into shimmering rainbows that danced across the cockpit walls and ceiling.

"Take a look?" she said. "Sure—"

Leaning over the console, she slid the crystal into an empty port near the SRV's systems screen.

She passed a hand over the console, and the stream of information about the SRV's engine—the waves of energy coming off the Road, all the temperature and atmospheric readouts that monitored every inch of the ship—all vanished.

And in its place, the logo of the World Council appeared.

Another wave, and the logo vanished, replaced by a data dump that flashed by before she could make heads or tails of it.

"Whoa. Do you *know* what you just did?" Ivan asked.

Annie shook her head.

"Unless I'm wrong . . . I think you just accessed World Council proprietary code without a password."

"That's not possible," Annie said. She looked at Jordan.

"It is if you alter the crystal," Jordan said. "And for a World Council data crystal, that's a felony with a mandatory life sentence."

The data was still streaming by, incomprehensible numbers and figures.

But Annie made no attempt to stop it.

"Okay. What's it about?"

Before anyone even could hazard a guess, the data stream suddenly stopped, and the screen filled with the World Council logo and the words: "Star Road—O/S 3.5."

Annie's hand was trembling as she reached out and brushed aside the screen floating in front of her.

A flickering flash of light, and then something amazing happened.

The cockpit of the SRV-66 disappeared, and in its place a three-dimensional display veined with tiny white lines floated above the console and then spread out to engulf them. It shimmered and sparkled with an undulating white glow.

Some of the lines were straight. Others curved in wild parabolas that weaved in and out of each other. Some ended in large knots that pulsed in regularly-timed beats.

The lines were moving subtly, and along some of the strands, tiny white blinking dots were moving.

"What the hell *is* this?" Annie looked around in wonder. All of the lines eventually terminated at glowing orbs.

With a sweep of her hand, she brought a section of the map—if that's what it was—closer. And then, in an inspired moment, she leaned over the computer console and entered her SRV transponder security code.

Immediately, a faint beeping sound began, and a single red dot on the fringe of the ball of intertwining lines began to blink.

"Is that what I think it is?" Jordan asked.

"It's us," Ivan said, leaning closer. The shimmering lights played across his face and body.

Annie nodded. She had the beginning of an idea . . . of what this was.

Jordan craned his head back to see the display better. He reached up as if to grab the tangled strands that spiraled above their heads, but the projection filtered through his fingers like water.

"Then here . . . this is Omega Nine," Jordan said, indicating a tiny orange dot.

No one said or did anything for a full minute.

Until, finally, Annie realized what made this all so amazing.

What they all had to be realizing.

"It's the entire Star Road system," she said quietly, staring in awe at the amazing complex of interesting and diverging lines and dots. "At least it's all of the *known* parts. Some segments simply end, as if a chunk of the map was missing."

"And here, at Omega Nine. Look. It's on the extreme fringe of what we know . . . what's been mapped so far."

"Yeah, but there are a lot of spurs, loops, whole chunks of Road I've never seen or even heard of before." Annie locked eyes with Ivan. A thrill ran through her.

*Think of the possibilities.*

"There's a lot here that the World Council never told us about."

"You—and everyone else," Ivan said. "Only a fraction of the routes open to vehicles? Which is exactly why we want total freedom of the Star Road."

Annie couldn't stop looking at the vast web of silvery lines radiating outward in what she saw now was an elaborate fractal design.

*Fascinating and beautiful.*

"So this is the entire operating system?" Jordan asked.

Annie nodded. "A copy, at least. And Nahara was going to deliver it to your brother."

"Dangerous stuff. And notice that Earth is nowhere near the center."

"So who mapped all of this?" Annie asked.

"Whoever—or whatever—made the Roads," Ivan said.

"Why are you using the past tense?" Annie said. "You so sure that they're not still out there? Not still making Roads?"

"Maybe you should join up with our Seeker back there."

"Not my type," Annie said, letting her gaze linger for a moment longer than necessary on Ivan.

Ivan laughed, ever the cool Runner. But it was clear that when he looked around inside the map, he, too, had experienced a feeling of awe and wonder.

"Incredible to see the the full scope of it all." Annie's voice was hushed.

Another slight brush of her hand brought forth a silvery spray of light . . . a near-infinite tangle of intersecting lines. At the fringes, they ran off into dense blackness, where they ended as though abruptly cut off.

"God," Annie said, still awestruck. "Where do they all go?"

Ivan used a swipe of his hand to bring the map back to show a close-up of the segments that connected their route to Omega Nine.

"This is . . . almost scary," Annie said.

"And incredibly valuable," Ivan added. "Think of it. Whoever has this OS can keep track of everything . . . all the traffic on every branch of the Star Road." He took a deep breath. "In the wrong hands . . ."

The thought stuck in Annie's mind as she tried to grasp just how serious this matter was. Even knowing that the OS existed with all these "secret" Roads would be a felony.

"It's a blueprint of the Star Road system . . . all the known routes . . . the cutoffs . . . the short cuts."

Ivan glanced at Jordan and said, "You could organize quite an attack— even an invasion, given the men, time, and equipment." He took a breath. "Like I said, dangerous stuff."

Annie nodded. "And it looks to me like this isn't the whole enchilada."

"That's clear. A full map would be immense. Maybe incomprehensible."

"Infinite . . ." Annie said quietly.

As if the power and implications of what she was looking at finally became too much to take, Annie reached over to the console and—with a few pinches of her fingers—shrunk the holographic image down to a more manageable size. The mass of Star Roads was now a small, luminous ball.

Then she pushed it back onto the flat screen.

*Less unnerving that way.*

Another brush of her hand across the screen, and the ship's data systems popped back up.

She took a breath.

*Good to have that gone.*

Ivan reached forward to remove the crystal, but Annie's hand shot out and clasped his wrist. With her other hand, she quickly took the data crystal from its port.

"We have to get this back to the World Council immediately."

"Hang on. Think it through," Ivan said. "Where did they get this?

Where did the council, the Road Authority, get the technology to run this entire navigation system?"

"We . . . *they*, I guess, found a terminal on Pluto, and they explored it and . . . and they developed it," Annie said.

She winced, hearing how rote it all sounded, like something she memorized in pilot school.

Her voice betrayed her doubts.

"Sure," Ivan said. He looked at Jordan, who was carefully following this discussion.

"And so you never wondered about the astonishing quantum leap in technology? All of a sudden, in the span of—what? A bit more than fifty years? And all of a sudden we have new nav systems and communications that can cross impossible distances of space—message pods, and ships— that let us use the so-called 'Star Road'?"

Annie hesitated. Not knowing what to say. Like she was on the precipice of a terrible truth.

Ivan took a breath. Annie waited.

The Runner's words were compelling.

"Someone else—not human—made the Roads and developed the technology. We all realize that, but we've never met them. But here's a thought. . . . What if they purposely gave us the technology for *us* to find *them*?"

"You're sounding like the Seeker who wants to find the Builders," Jordan said, grinning.

But Annie noticed that Ivan wasn't smiling at the idea.

"Yeah, I do, except . . . I think that may not be such a good thing after all."


There was absolute quiet for a few moments.

"I'll hold on to this, if you don't mind," Annie said, looking directly at Ivan, challenging him to disagree.

"Still don't trust me, huh? After all we've been through." A wide smile.

*He expected I'd take it.*

And as for trust?

He'd been the leader of the Runners—an outlaw group, and yet he had shot at his own people, disabled their vehicle that was out to destroy or board them. He let Jordan kill their commander. And helped them escape.

But maybe, with this crystal . . . could Ivan still want to be the Runner leader again?

"This is clearly top-secret World Council and Road Authority property," Annie said. "Nahara downloaded and stole it from the Road Authority's computers"—she squared her shoulders—"but as the duly appointed official representative here—"

Ivan laughed out loud. "Go on. Say it, Cap'n. You don't *trust* me."

She slipped the crystal into her jacket pocket.

"Sorry."

"So why did Nahara steal it?" Jordan asked.

Annie looked at Ivan, guessing he already had a theory.

And she was right.

Ivan took a breath.

"That's easy. He stole it to deliver to the same person who sabotaged my solo and who just tried to capture me and bring me back alive to Omega Nine."

"Kyros," Jordan said.

"Uh-huh, and—"

A warning beep suddenly sounded. Annie turned back to the cockpit window.

"Got some tricky curves coming up." To Jordan: "Maybe we'd best—"

"Yeah . . . back to work."

A nod to Ivan. "And you'd best head back to the cabin. Might get bumpy."

"Sure, but one more thing."

She could see, even now, that the Road had begun to rise up and fall, and the SRV was suddenly in need of some real piloting.

"What?" she asked over her shoulder, focusing on the Road ahead now.

"Kyros wants that crystal. We're going to Omega Nine. My guess is he's still there, and he'll do anything to get it."

"He's done quite a bit already," Jordan said, a sharp snap in his voice.

"We have our destination. We have our cargo for the settlement. Rodriguez needs to get there for whatever reason the council sent him."

"I hear you."

Annie nodded. "Right. So we're not turning around. As long as that's clear."

"I wouldn't have it any other way." Ivan started to leave but then stopped. "Just remember, you better be ready. Now you have some idea what my brother's capable of, but trust me—that's only a fraction."

Jordan sniffed.

"I already wish we had never found that crystal," Annie said.

Then, all was quiet.

And with the Road suddenly gone from an endless flat ribbon to something filled with twists and bumps, navigating unknown and unseen distortions of space and time, Ivan left the cockpit.

And Annie told herself: *Whatever's waiting for us on Omega Nine, we'll find out soon enough.*

"Just have to get us there in one piece," she whispered.

"You say something?" Jordan didn't look away from his screens.

Annie shook her head and held the wheel tightly as the Road became even more ragged.

"Nope."

# 33

## OMEGA NINE

*Time to sleep.*

Annie hadn't had even a nap in almost forty-eight hours.

*Forty-eight hours? Feels more like a week.*

"You got the stick?" she asked Jordan as she pulled the lever to lower her seat back. The footrest kicked up, and she was prone. The foam-filled cushion adjusted to her weight and position, surrounding her in comfort.

Jordan grunted, then said, "Yeah. Took a som-tab a couple of hours ago. I'm good."

"You sure?"

"I said I'm good."

Annie rolled her head up and down but still felt too wired to fall asleep quickly. Maybe a som-tab was the answer.

A lot to think about—transporting a thief with World Council materials, harboring and even abetting a supposedly convicted felon.

And a load of materials and passengers that she needed to deliver safely to their destination.

"Do you think the passengers are—"

"They're fine. Everyone's fine. Now get some rest. I got this."

Annie grunted and nestled her head into the seatback.

It did feel good to rest . . . to let her mind and body go.

And soon enough, she was in a deep asleep, so deep, she didn't even dream.

• • •

Sinjira—about to sleep—knew she would dream.

Chip enough, and dreams became a constant, merging with reality.

After helping Rodriguez—who didn't seem like such a bad guy, after all—she settled down to sleep.

The tension of the Road trip so far had weighed on her.

It was one thing to put on a front and live the life of an adrenaline-crazed Chippie, providing "experiences" for other people.

But now, out here, on the far edges of the Road, where shit got real very fast?

She closed her eyes and concentrated on her breathing . . . slow . . . steady . . . in . . . out . . .

She drifted in a warm, comfortable place. The white noise of the SRV lulled her deeper . . . deeper . . . until—

A face suddenly loomed up in front of her.

*"McGowan!"*

The image of the dead man's face resolved more clearly, and she saw not flesh and blood, but gears and flywheels and blinking lights, all merging to form the man's features.

*Not the real man!*

She sat up suddenly, a ragged intake of breath. The dream image vanishing.

Momentarily disoriented, she didn't know where she was. The light in the passengers' cabin had been dimmed, and everyone—everyone, that is, except that Seeker—was sound asleep.

Even her outcry hadn't awakened them.

"You all right?" the Seeker asked.

*It won't hurt you to be nice to her. She's just showing concern.*

Sinjira licked her lips, feeling their dry texture.

"Yeah," she said, her voice a froglike croak. "Just a . . ."

"Bad dream?"

The image of McGowan's face lingered in her memory, filling her with a feeling of dread.

It was all but impossible to describe, but she had the feeling it hadn't been a dream.

No. It had been a vision . . . or something.

Somehow she had experienced a kind of connection with the man she knew, for a fact, was dead.

"We all have ghosts inside us," Ruth said.

Sinjira nodded.

*A ghost. A phantom.*

*Or . . . something else?*

*A warning?*

One thing for sure, though—she wasn't going to get to sleep now.

So she popped a stim-cap.


The view out in front of SRV-66 suddenly changed.

The shimmering, rotating lights of the portal appeared in the distance. Jordan, starting to feel the strain of sleep deprivation himself, nudged Annie's shoulder.

"Hey. Captain. Time to wake up."

He watched Annie's eyes open, crusty with sleep and cloudy.

She could have used more sleep. But running the Road, you got used to grabbing a few winks when you could.

She looked confused for a moment. Then—in a flash—she was awake.

"How long was I out?"

"Few hours."

"Everything okay?"

"Couldn't be better."

He reached down and made slight adjustments in preparation for the jump through the portal.

"Passengers quiet?"

"Not a peep."

He nodded at the display showing the immobilized Nahara. His eyes were closed, but Jordan doubted he was asleep.

"But we're coming up on Omega Nine."

"Okay," Annie said, a chill hitting her gut. Then: "I'll take over from here."

Jordan nodded. The captain was back in charge.

Annie pressed a button on the side of her chair, and with a faint hum, the back and footrest retracted, shifting her to a sitting position.

Jordan, like Annie, wanted to drop their passengers and supplies, deal with Nahara as quickly as possible, and get the hell back on the Road to home.

*Maybe getting too old for this, wanting to get back to Earth.*

*Maybe this Road trip was just a bit too much fun.*

A fleeting thought. He knew well enough that he'd never settle down.

Maybe he was feeling low because—after the mad race out of Hydra Salim—now there wasn't *enough* going on.

Annie took over the controls, and he settled back in his chair.

"You strapped in?" Annie asked.

Jordan nodded, then watched as Annie flipped the button for the intercom.

"Attention passengers. We're approaching our final destination, Omega Nine. Please make sure your harnesses are secure. We'll be landing soon."

She keyed off the intercom.

Then Jordan saw something on the security screen.

A face had appeared at the cockpit door.

Ivan.

Eyebrows raised—a silent question—Jordan glanced at Annie and pointed at the screen.

"Let him in. Let's hear what he has to say."


"You like getting banged around on takeoffs and landings?" Annie asked, looking at him. "You heard my announcement. Take your—"

"I'm fine where I am," Ivan replied.

Up ahead, the spinning light of the approaching portal grew closer, filling the screens. Jordan ran through automatic readouts.

Annie stayed focused on piloting her SRV, adjusting speed and vector to make as smooth a landing as possible.

There was a moment where everything felt like it was shrinking... contracting into an infinitely small point, and then—like *that*—they were through the portal and on the runway.

A glance at Ivan, who was tightening his grip to keep from swaying around too much.

The sudden glare of sunlight stung Annie's eyes, making them water; but through the blur, she could make out the terminal building in the distance.

Beyond the terminal, a ring of jagged mountains rose up into the sky like a ring of rotten teeth. The sky was clear and had a greenish tinge like algae in a pond.

"Long runway," Annie said.

"Planet this far out of system... got plenty of room to stretch out," Ivan said.

Annie leaned forward and flipped the switch on the commlink, but as she cleared her throat, preparing to speak, Ivan stopped her.

A gentle touch on the back of her hand.

She looked up at him. He bit his lower lip and shook his head.

"I wouldn't just yet, until we see what's what . . . that way."

He pointed, and Annie steered the SRV up the runaway toward the far end of the terminal.

Its engines roared in the sudden stillness. Brakes squealing . . . wheels thundering on the tarmac, kicking up a plume of dust that rose into the oddly green-tinted sky.

Now Ivan leaned closer to the control, his fingers poised over the nav system.

Before he touched the screen, though, he looked Annie straight in the eyes. Close.

"May I?" he asked.

She nodded slowly.

*Trust.*

At least for now.


Ivan's fingers slid back and forth as he entered a code.

Annie was watching his every move. Did she trust him or not? He could feel her apprehension. He also noticed that Jordan's right hand never strayed far from his sidearm.

"Go to these coordinates," Ivan said, his voice light, not betraying that he'd read her concern.

Annie gave him another, longer look.

Then she nodded and hit ENTER. Making minor adjustments, she had to use both hands to steer the vehicle as it left the smooth ramp and headed out across the wide, rock-strewn plain.

Ivan had been here before—too many times.

This desolate rock.

He wondered how it would all end, but satisfied himself that the answer wouldn't be long in coming.


Ruth wondered what Ivan was doing up in the cockpit.

*Do they have him under arrest again? Collared? And they don't want me to know?*

*Or has he done something horrible to the pilot and gunner?*

"Why aren't we heading to the terminal?" she asked.

Nahara couldn't respond. It looked like it took immense effort simply for him to shift his eyes.

Rodriguez was busy going through his attaché case, as if taking inventory.

And Sinjira—Sinjira was sitting, her eyes glued to the portal, no doubt recording everything she could.

Ruth swayed in her seat as SRV-66 bumped across the rocky terrain, dodging the larger boulders. She saw things, scurrying into hiding. Off in the distance, she could barely make out the winding blue ribbon of a river.

Behind the terminal, she noticed a few buildings—the beginning of a settlement.

*But why are we moving* away *from it?*

Craning her head forward, she tried to see where they were heading, but the angle was bad, and the curvature of the window's Plexi distorted her view.

"Does anyone know where we're going?"

"The captain better," Sinjira said with a lilting laugh.

Ruth didn't like the nervous edge in her own voice, but there it was.

*And no one saying anything else.*

Something had happened—was happening—and they weren't going to get off at their regularly scheduled stop.

Ruth would have undone her safety belt and gone up to the cockpit, knocked on the cabin door, and asked what was happening. But the SRV kept bouncing jerkily over the extremely rough terrain, weaving and swaying from side to side.

And all the while, her tension was mounting because she couldn't stop thinking that, however bad things had been, they were going to get even worse.


Ivan stared straight ahead at the forward view.

"Damn," he muttered.

Jordan stayed silent. Aware, alert. Ivan had come to expect that.

"What is it?" Annie asked.

"This place . . . I know it. Not exactly like coming home, but"—he struggled to put into words what he was feeling—"as close as I ever got with the Runners. But now I don't belong here anymore."

They kept rumbling across the rough terrain, the terminal and surrounding settlement having vanished in the shimmering green heat haze behind them.

The road—a barely discernible rocky track—wound its way up into the mountains, taking sharp switchbacks that Annie had trouble negotiating.

"Narrow pass ahead," Ivan said. "Keeps it limited to smaller vessels."

"All right. Any chance you can tell us where we're going?"

Ivan smiled. He was almost tempted to bring her up to speed. But—

*Always good to keep an edge.*

"You know," Jordan said, his voice flat, "all this dust won't help our de-ionization units."

"We're almost there."

"What about the atmospherics?" Annie asked.

"As close to Earth normal as you could ask for," Jordan said. "Interesting, though. Oxygen's a little high." He looked out the side portal. "Might help with our breathing this high up, but you may feel a bit giddy at first."

"Giddy . . ." Annie said.

Ivan nodded and added, "Yeah. Gravity's a bit above Earth norm, too, so you might feel a bit heavy."

Jordan—without looking away from his scanners—said, "I exercise on Grav 1.5."

*Figures,* Ivan thought.

As they got closer, anxiety steadily built up inside him.

*Steady,* he thought.

Whatever lay ahead, whatever unknowns, filled him with emotions he hadn't experienced in . . . , he didn't want to think about how long.

All he knew was, he was a much different man from the one who had been captured and thrown into prison.

They entered a narrow defile when Ivan signaled Annie to cut the engines and run on electric backup.

"Nice and quiet," he said.

Annie nodded, saying nothing.

Her anticipation had to be building up, too.

But not Jordan.

Like a stone, staring straight ahead as the road unspooled before them.

Then Annie asked: "You think anyone will notice the funnel of dust we're kicking up behind us?"

Ivan glanced at the rearview.

*Shit.*

He grimaced and shook his head.

"So much for the element of surprise," he said.

"So Kyros knows we're coming . . . probably already knows we're here," Jordan said.

"That is if your brother's even on this planet."

Annie shot Ivan a quick, questioning look that clearly communicated exactly how much she wasn't liking this so far.

"We'll find out one way or another soon enough. Our—the Runners'— camp is just around the cliff up ahead."

The control board sounded an alarm and started flashing a reading that their destination lay half a kilometer away.

"Okay. Let's take this nice and easy, now," Ivan said. His hand dropped to the pulse pistol on his hip.

Realizing he was hovering over the controls like he was the instructor, and Annie the student, Ivan straightened up and stared at the view ahead.

All so familiar, painfully so because of all the hopes and dreams they'd fought for.

But now—returning like this—it all looked so small.

And now, knowing how large the Star Road system truly was made his and the Runners' hopes and dreams seem pathetic . . . ridiculous.

They rounded the bend, and there it was up ahead, the Runners' base camp.

"That's it?" Jordan said. A smile twitched one side of his mouth. "Not what I expected."

A few buildings with a dirt street running down the middle.

Only one thing was at all impressive: On the far side of the makeshift "town" was row upon row of vehicles—speeders, Road ships, cargo ships, a decommissioned battle cruiser, and other personal and crewed vessels.

*Yes. The Runners were here.*

*And Kyros, too.*

And yet—like every station they'd stopped at so far this trip—the place looked deserted.

"No welcome committee, hmm?" Jordan asked.

"My guess is they're watching us."

Ivan started to reach forward. Then stopped himself. He looked at Annie, his hand poised above the commlink.

"May I?"

Annie shrugged. "It's your party."

Ivan picked up the headset, but Annie stopped him before he put it on.

"Keep it on speaker so Jordan and I can hear."

Ivan caught the nod of approval Jordan gave her.

"Sure," he said.

He flicked the switch. A green light came on, and he leaned close to the microphone.

"Kyros. You there?"

*Nothing.*

"Kyros! I know you're listening."

He made a few adjustments. Looked at Annie.

"We're broadcasting full spectrum," she said "If he's out there, he can—"

A sudden wash of loud static filled the cockpit, but then nothing.

"Do you read me, Kyros. This is—"

"I know . . . who this is." The voice was low, almost sleepy-sounding—instantly recognizable.

Ivan locked eyes with Annie and nodded. Then he cleared his throat. "Brother. We have to talk."

# FIVE

OMEGA NINE

# 34

## AN INVITATION

*"Can we get a visual?"* Annie whispered, leaning close.

Ivan shrugged, knowing that Kyros could hear her as well.

"Who's your company?"

The voice, no more than a growl. Like he was drugged.

"No one you'd know," Ivan replied. "For now, it's just you and me."

Kyros laughed. More of a cough.

A faint click came over the speaker, and then a low hum filled the cockpit. Within seconds, a clear hologram of Kyros drifted in front of them.

He looked about the same as he had two years ago. A bit heavier, maybe. His hair longer. Unkempt.

The way he sat? Confident. Like a king. An all-powerful ruler.

Leaning back with both hands clasped on the arms of his chair.

And the chair. Strange. Not designed for a human. Someone or something much larger, taller.

*An alien design?*

Within the arc of the hologram, Ivan could also see that Kyros sat at a semicircular console. But like the chair, totally unknown and unfamiliar.

*What the hell is it?*

"Did you go *soft* in prison, brother? Get stupid? Lose your edge?"

Ivan caught a strange reverberation—a quaver—in his brother's voice.

*Is that from the transmission equipment or is it the room he's in?*

"What do you mean?" Ivan asked. His muscles tensed. He didn't like what he was seeing—the odd arrogance of his brother, the strange chair, whatever the machine was he sat beside.

"There's nothing left to talk about."

"What happened here? At the camp? Where are my men?"

"*Your* men?" Kyros let out a sharp burst of laughter. "Brother, you *betrayed* your men. You double-crossed us all."

Ivan shook his head.

"I did no—"

"You sold us out to the World Council."

*Well, that game's over. Time to put all the cards on the table.*

And as he stared at the lifelike holo, he realized that something else had changed about Kyros. Something internal, not visible.

And in his gut, Ivan knew his brother was *much* more dangerous.

*No point in pretending.*

"You're right. I made a deal." It took considerable effort to keep his voice neutral. "Not just for my life, but for *all* of our lives."

Kyros's laughter rose even louder, the sound swelling.

*Insane.*

His face turned bright red.

"You don't fucking get it, do you, brother?"

"Get what?"

"That you no longer command the Runners. I do."

"Hang on. Listen. We've been granted a pardon—total amnesty. All of us. We're free to go anywh—"

"Anywhere except wherever the hell we want to go on the Star Road."

Kyros's face was livid now.

"All along—as soon as you got yourself captured, I suspected you'd do this." Kyros trembled, staring straight into the camera lens. "That's why we had to set a few examples along the way to prove that the Runners weren't broken."

Kyros's tongue snaked out of his mouth.

"That we aren't *all* gutless traitors."

"The pack of warrows in the way station?" Ivan said. "Looked pretty gutless to me."

"They did the job we wanted done." Kyros took a deep breath. Shifted in the massive seat.

"And you—I don't need your *approval*, brother. In fact, there's only one thing I need that you have."

Kyros gripped both chair arms tightly as he glared into the camera.

*Has he really gone insane?* Ivan wondered.

"And what would that be?"

"Send me Nahara within two hours, or you and everyone on board that bucket of bolts will be incinerated."

"No," Ivan said sharply. "First, we talk. You and me. Face-to-face. *Then* you can have Nahara."

"You don't have any cards to play here!"

"I have Nahara."

Kyros, wide-eyed with rage, veins throbbing in his neck, pounded his console. Then he leaned back in his chair and rubbed his cheeks with the flats of his hands. When he gazed up at the ceiling, the view of the hologram made it look as if his eyes had rolled back in his head, exposing nothing but the whites.

*Madness.*

Finally: "All right then, brother. We'll talk." A hollow laugh. "Maybe you can convince me to accept this *amnesty* of yours."

*As if I can't tell he wants to kill me the instant he sees me,* Ivan thought.

"Where are you?"

Ivan still couldn't make out his brother's surroundings. He shifted back and forth while gazing at the hologram, but the image held tight on Kyros.

His brother smiled.

"See that cave opening due west of the settlement?" A pause. "Let me send you coordinates."

He turned around and tapped something on a keypad out of sight.

Ivan glanced at Annie, who checked the readings and then pointed toward the range of mountains off to the port side.

"Got it," she whispered.

Ivan felt a nudge on his shoulder and, turning, saw Jordan pointing to another screen, scanning the rocky slope that towered into the green-tinged sky.

After a few sweeps, the movement stopped.

He saw something—a dark, gaping opening.

"You're in the old mine? I checked that out a long time ago."

"You didn't check carefully enough," Kyros said. "That's your problem. You quit too easily, Ivan." A beat. "Wait and see."

And there was that loud, braying laugh again.

"So what are you waiting for? Come on up and visit me. Alone!"

"You know better than that," Ivan replied.

"You want to bring your friends along? Fine. Dangerous cave, though. You never know what might happen."

With that, Kyros leaned forward, his arm moved, and then the hologram dissolved in a static-filled hiss.

"Well," Ivan said, straightening up. "That's my brother."

Neither Annie nor Jordan said anything.

Then he added: "What say we go find the bastard."

# 35

## EXPEDITION

*Jordan knelt down on one* knee, his face close to Nahara's. The man's breath, like sour vinegar, was warm on his cheek.

"You nice and comfy there, you worthless piece of shit?"

He grabbed Nahara's right arm and raised it until it was level with his shoulders. Then he let it drop. It sounded like a dead fish hitting the floor when it slapped down on his lap.

Jordan would have paid money to haul off and punch the guy—repeatedly—until his face looked like strawberry marmalade.

Someone came up behind him and tapped him lightly on the shoulder. Jordan sprang to his feet and turned.

Annie frowned at him as she leaned away.

"You're above taunting a prisoner," she said.

Jordan grinned. "Just making sure he's secure, Captain." He looked back at Nahara. "And I'm not keen on leaving him here like this."

"You got a better idea? Looks like the collar's working."

"Kill him? Say he was trying to escape."

Annie shook her head. "Like I said. You're better than that. Come on. We're ready for the EVA."

Jordan looked at her. Then back at Nahara.

"In a minute," he said.

After she was gone, Jordan went to the supply compartment and took out a length of nylon rope. He quickly bound Nahara's hands and feet to the seat supports.

Once that was done, he straightened up and said, "Stay nice and snug until I get back. Okay?"

And then—for good measure—he punched Nahara once in the face.

Hard enough to make something in his face or neck crack.

"Grab as much of that filament line as you can find," Ivan said. "And full spectrum goggles if you have them. Gonna be dark."

"Lemme check," Annie said, and she hurried out of the storage and back to the passengers' cabin.

"That was McGowan's," Sinjira said, indicating the loops of filament line Ivan had picked up.

"He'd probably be glad to see it put to good use."

He—along with Annie, Jordan, Ruth, Rodriguez, and Sinjira—were scrambling around the SRV's cargo hold, suiting up and equipping themselves for the hike up to, *and into*, the cave where his brother was waiting.

Waiting . . . for what? To trap them and kill them?

*So it's down to this . . . brother against brother.*

And then: *What's he got waiting for us up there?*

"We're going to have to be on our toes," he said. "We have no idea how many Runners are up there or how hard they'll fight for my brother. If I can talk to them . . . convince them that—"

"They can talk to *this*," Jordan said, slapping the butt of his pulse rifle as he entered the cargo area. He had double holsters strapped to his waist, each slinging a meg-10 pulse pistol with extra chargers.

*Imposing.*

*Got any flash grenades . . . maybe a nuke to go with that?* Ivan thought but didn't say.

No use antagonizing the man he was going to count on most. He already seemed on edge about something.

"I'm sure you'll get your chance," Ivan said calmly.

Then he turned to Annie. "What other equipment do we have?"

"What do we need?"

Ivan made a quick inventory of what they had so far: lights, helmets, goggles, filament line and collapsed grappling hooks, flashlights, dehydrated food packs, canteens of water, and guns . . . plenty of guns and chargers for everyone, except Ruth and Sinjira. Both of them refused to be armed.

*Probably safer that way.*

*Good to know one's limits.*

"We can take on an army," Annie said, but Ivan wasn't reassured.

He couldn't get rid of the nagging feeling that they'd forgotten *some-thing* . . . something vital.

He also wished he had been able to convince Ruth to stay behind with the SRV and keep watch on Nahara.

"You'll be safer," he had said more than once. "Lock the hatch until we get back. No one will bother you.'"

But she had refused . . . insisted.

Jordan, too, appeared to be rattled that she was coming along. Ivan wondered—again—what there might be between them . . . and if it was over.

As for Sinjira, he could understand why she'd want to tag along. She'd be recording her ass off. There were few—if any—chips available of first-hand explorations on distant planets. Add the chance for a firefight, and it could be a classic chip.

And Rodriguez?

Come along or stay behind—either way, he'd be more hindrance than help.

Jordan, Annie. He could trust them with his life. He had already.

"I'm still not sure why we're doing this," Annie said as she returned to the cargo hold. She tightened a belt of pulse chargers around her waist.

"We have—" She looked around, making sure no one else could hear them. Then she leaned closer and whispered, "We have the data crystal your brother wants. I don't see why we don't wait him out. Make *him* come to *us.*"

Ivan shook his head.

"Hell," Annie said, "we could start back to Earth today. Right now. Give the data crystal to the World Council. Deliver Nahara to them. Explain what happened. They'd get a couple of troop ships out here *pronto.* Enough to bring the whole damned mountain down on his head."

She took a breath.

"We don't have to do this."

"And if Kyros leaves? What if he plans more attacks on other stations . . . or an ambush for us? Can we even get away if we want to?"

Another shake of his head.

"I doubt it," Ivan said.

Annie hesitated. Then: "I *certainly* don't like the idea of civilians coming along. This isn't some damn picnic."

"But they're not your responsibility anymore. They're not on your ship, so you can't tell them what or what not to do. Better that they're with us than alone."

Distracted for a moment, Ivan shifted his gaze over to Sinjira, struck for a moment by just how beautiful she looked as she raised her arms above her head and stretched her shoulders back to heft a backpack with Rodriguez's help.

She caught Ivan looking at her and shot him a wide smile.

"And Rodriguez," Annie was saying. "At least he's on official business. But we've seen how totally useless he is in a pinch."

Ivan grinned at that. Then he double-checked his weapons belt and adjusted his backpack.

He smiled at Annie and said, "Come on. It's time to meet my brother."

Rodriguez started having second—and third and fourth—thoughts as they trudged in single file up the winding mountain trail.

The wind blew dust into his face. It stuck to his arms and clothes with a slick, oily feel. The green sky was filled with towering yellow clouds that, for all he knew, meant a storm might be coming.

*Let's get into that fucking cave and get this over with.*

Delgato was leading them . . . of course.

Even on the steep trail, Ivan walked with a swagger that Rodriguez found irritating.

*He's a criminal!*

No matter—he was about to learn the truth behind the cover story of a plague on Omega Nine.

The problem was, without getting his final briefing pod when they were on Hydra Salim, he—like the rest of them—had no idea what they were walking into.

And for all he knew, it would be a lot worse than any plague.

He noticed how close Ruth stayed to Ivan.

Following Ruth was the Chippie, who remained blessedly silent, for the most part, as she looked around, recording everything she saw, heard, smelled, and felt.

The SRV captain—Annie—was next, and behind Rodriguez, Jordan brought up the rear.

Whenever Rodriguez glanced over his shoulder at the gunner, he saw the man carrying his pulse rifle at the ready, swinging it from side to side as he scanned the area.

*Wary . . . like a hunting warrow . . .*

*And what the hell am I doing here?*

Without final orders, his first priority would have been to get back to the way station. If the message system was intact, he should send a message back to the World Council and get them to clarify his orders.

*I'm out here because it's clear now what killed everyone on Omega Nine.*

*Kyros and the Runners.*

He kept thinking this as he trudged along, placing one foot in front of the other with mind-numbing monotony.

More than three Earth hours of hiking passed under the blazing hot sun.

The clouds had long since blown away, and the emerald sky was clear.

Ivan looked up at the larger of the twin pock-faced moons hovering low on the horizon. A thin, ivory sickle. He took a breath, but the air was hot and dry, burning the insides of his nose.

He kept checking to see how Ruth was holding up, surprised by her stamina.

*More guts than I'd expected.*

The extra gravity was weighing them down, and he could see how exhausted she was.

But she never complained or even asked to stop for a rest.

Not until the others did.

The cave mouth, nearly halfway up the mountain—their destination— came in and out of view as they moved.

Years ago, when the Runners first established a base here, Ivan had come up with an exploratory party, but they hadn't found much of interest.

Just a large limestone cave that some indigenous life form used as a den.

*But then we didn't go very deep. . . . We didn't go all the way in.*

*And Kyros found something.*

Finally, exhausted, they arrived at the ledge outside the cave just as the sun began slipping below the distant horizon. The sky was a deeper green now.

Ivan was surprised to see evidence of activity up here.

Debris . . . piles of dirt and huge chunks of castaway stone were piled outside the entrance.

"Good place for an ambush," Jordan said, the last to join the group.

Ivan shook his head.

"He wants us . . . me, anyway, alive. Knowing my brother, I'd say he's not likely to go for a direct assault."

"Why's that?" Annie asked.

Like Jordan, she never stopped looking around, as though she expected an attack at any moment.

"For one, we have what he wants. You have it, right, Annie?"

She nodded and patted a pants pocket.

Ivan thought to ask her if he could see it. Just to make sure.

*Trust.*

But he wouldn't put it past her to bring a fake.

Maybe that's what he would have done.

"And two. He knows he has us on his terms."

Jordan took a breath, clearly not happy with that. The gunner looked like he was about to say something, but instead he simply looked at Ivan, then away.

Ivan made a show of checking his weapon and then addressed the group.

"We ready?"

"For what?" Rodriguez said, his voice shaking, his eyes darting back and forth.

*Guy's close to losing it, and we're not even in the cave yet.*

"Okay," Ivan said, letting out the breath he hadn't realized he'd been holding. "Let's go see what my brother's been up to."

# 36

## TRIP WIRE

*This sucks! Nahara kept thinking.*

He'd seen enough people in neuro-collars before, but he'd never experienced it.

The worst part was that his mind remained perfectly lucid. He could hear and see and smell *everything*, but his sense of touch was gone.

He knew—rationally—that he was sitting in an SRV seat, but he had no sensation of his weight on the seat . . . or the seat pressing against him.

When the gunner had punched him—*sucker punched*—his head had rocked back, but there hadn't been the slightest flicker of pain.

Spots of blood drying to a dark brick red splattered his shirtsleeve.

It took immense effort simply to move his eyes, and the inability to blink made them sting. He measured the impossibly slow passage of time by the progress of the sun and shadow that moved so damned slowly across the cabin wall and floor.

He had no idea how long he'd been here.

There hadn't been a "night," but then again, he had no idea what this planet's rotational rate was. A "day" could last hours or weeks beyond the standard twenty-four.

All the while, his anger—at Jordan and Annie, and at Kyros for luring him into this, and the others, the ones in the World Council who had arranged this transfer of data—grew stronger.

But no blame for himself.

He had a chance to make a fortune. To escape his life, his family, the work for the authority, so dull and boring.

*He could escape.*

He lost himself in such thoughts . . .

But then at some point in the meaningless, timelessness of his situation, he saw something.

At first, he didn't believe it.

He was convinced a shadow had passed across the sun or that his vision was going after being strained for so long.

But a timeless moment later, he knew what he was seeing was real.

A shadow was cast across the floor at his feet, and up onto the wall. It was elongated but clearly the head and shoulders of a person.

And then—bracing himself for whatever was about to happen—the SRV hatch door was forced open.

He had company.

"You sure you don't want to sit this one out, Doc?" Sinjira asked as she turned to face Rodriguez.

He regarded her with a look she had seen all too often in her dealings with people—especially men, but more than her fair share of women, too.

"Are you kidding? Stay here by myself?"

She adjusted the chip in the node on her head and checked the levels on her handheld.

"This is going to be KC."

"KC?"

"Killer content . . ."

"Everyone ready?"

Ivan's voice, sharp and sudden, echoed in the cave opening.

Sinjira turned to face him.

*The cave entrance ahead.*

Rodriguez took a step back and, waving his hand loosely, indicated that she should go in front of him.

*Polite . . . or a coward who wants to be at the back of the line in case shit gets real?*

It didn't matter because Sinjira was feeling just the opposite.

She wanted to be as close to the action as possible.

"I'm all set, boss. Cannot wait."

Ivan nodded, turned, and then led them into the cave.

● ● ●

Ivan saw the body first.

Huge . . . probably four meters tall, stretched out to its full height.

The good news: it was dead.

The bad news: he had no idea what species it was . . . had never seen anything like it before in all his travels.

He stopped short, so abruptly that Ruth bumped into him.

If the creature had been alive, the impact would have knocked his aim off.

*I'll have to mention that to her . . . watch out for my gun.*

Ruth let out a surprised gasp as Ivan played his flashlight beam across the dead alien.

It was hideous. The closest thing Ivan could compare it to was an iguana . . . a four-meter-long iguana with desiccated openings covering its body.

Evidently, it had been dead for some time. Its punctured, scaly skin was rotting and peeling away.

*Apparently not tasty to scavengers*, Ivan thought.

The belly of the creature had also split open, exposing a waxy, red honeycombed internal structure, looking more like shiny stone than flesh. The visible organs all black with rot . . . and then Ivan saw that those organs were dotted with thumb-sized white "worms."

Waxy tubes the size of small snakes.

"What is it?" Ruth asked. She sounded so scared, even with it dead.

"Not sure," he replied. "Nasty, hmm?"

Ruth moved closer, bending at the waist to inspect it.

"Uh, it looks dead, but still I wouldn't get *too* close."

Her eyes looked at the seething mass of white worms, consuming what was left of the rotting flesh.

Annie stayed back, gun lowered at the thing as if expecting the worms to jump up at her.

Ivan saw her swing her flashlight beam around, pistol aimed, taking it all in.

"What the hell is this place?" she asked.

"Years ago, we camped up here . . . when we first arrived," Ivan said.

"The Runners?"

Ivan nodded.

"Looks like there's been some excavating going on since then."

Ivan nodded again as he directed his flashlight beam toward the back of the cave, the light swallowed by the darkness.

The cave floor up ahead was littered with numerous motionless forms.

"We . . . the Runners used Omega Nine as a base for a while . . . until the miners showed up."

"What happened then?" Ruth asked.

Ivan shrugged.

"Nothing for a while. We left them alone. They left us alone."

"So what's in here?" Annie asked. She took a few tentative steps forward, her flashlight beam playing across the assortment of corpses. Dozens of different alien species in various stages of decay.

"Beats the hell out of me. It wasn't like this by the time I went to prison." A breath. The air . . . even *that* smelled different here. "And Kyros didn't bother to send me any updates."

Keeping a safe distance, Ivan led the party around the first corpse. But there were more ahead.

Plenty more.

Five of the corpses looked like fish with thick, heavily muscled legs and short arms.

*Don't see that every day!* Ivan thought.

Several others were more vaguely humanoid—a few as tall as five meters; others, short, dwarfish.

Some wore clothes of different material and styles. An assortment of equipment—some familiar, but not all—lay scattered across the dirt floor. The stench of rot was thick.

"You know what it looks like?" Jordan said from the rear of the group.

"What?"

"Like all these creatures were coming in, going deeper into the cave when someone—"

"Or some*thing*," Ivan said.

"Yeah, or something stopped them dead in their tracks."

"Like us."

Ivan nodded at that.

*What killed them?*

He looked at the corpses for indications of how they had died but saw no obvious wounds. Of course, with the decomposition, it was impossible to tell.

"Is that a light up ahead?" Ruth asked, drawing everyone's attention away from the alien corpses.

Ivan switched off his flashlight and peered ahead.

Sure enough a faint iridescent red glow filled the back of the cavern, washing the stone walls like paint.

"Miners' lights?" Ivan said.

"You think miners came in here and and did this?" Ruth asked.

Ivan shook his head. "Not likely. Maybe Kyros and the boys killed the miners, took their lights."

"The boys?" Jordan sniffed and spat onto the cave floor. *"Runners,* you mean."

Ivan nodded and then continued moving forward; the others followed, their pace slow now.

And, after a few twists and turns in the passage, they entered a wide area where both of the walls, hacked out of the stone, were lined with strips of cold, fluorescent mine-shaft lights.

"Someone's been busy," Ivan said.

No one laughed.

He turned to Ruth and said, "Okay. Things might get interesting. So don't follow so closely. You might mess up my aim if I have to shoot fast."

Ruth nodded her understanding.

"See those? I recognize a few of these species," Rodriguez said. "From pictures, anyway. Certainly not native to Omega Nine."

Ivan took a shallow breath, trying not to inhale the smell too deeply.

They moved slowly, all of them tensed and waiting for . . .

*What?* Ivan wondered.

*For whatever had killed these creatures . . . or for these aliens to attack and . . . kill us?*

The air in the cave turned cool, but a trickle of sweat ran down his neck.

"Hold on. Something up ahead," he said when he noticed the lights were getting brighter as if reflected by—mirrors.

Ivan was the first to round the corner, the others following close behind.

Before them was a large, round stone chamber, a massive room more than twenty meters wide.

And sure enough, the walls were covered by a variety of mirrors of varying sizes, placed at various angles. The effect was that of an old-fashioned fun house on a huge scale.

Reflections doubled and redoubled, receding to infinity and creating a weird dizzying effect, but behind—or inside—the mirrors, the view was still dark.

The effect was confusing, disorienting.

Behind the criss-cross of lights, Ivan thought he caught a hint of motion in the darkness. It was reflected, so he wasn't sure exactly where it was, but there was someone . . .

*His brother? One of the Runners?*

He raised and fired his pulse pistol.

The blast of energy shot out, punching one mirror, shattering it and leaving a large spiderweb pattern. But the flare of the blast reflected off the mirrors and ricocheted with a sizzle back and forth and all around the chamber.

Before the zigzagging light faded, it sliced the air inches from Jordan's head.

The gunner dropped to the cave floor and rolled to one side to avoid it. As he got up onto his knees, he glanced back at Ivan.

"Let's not do that again unless we have to," Jordan said quietly.

"Agreed."

Annie came up close to the two of them. "What the hell is this place?"

"Something to stop us, give us something to think about?" Ivan said.

Ruth, Sinjira, and Rodriguez were all hanging back.

"Let's take this nice and slow."

Ivan started leading them into the room again.

And as he did, the infinite reflections shifted in all directions, creating a dizzying optical illusion.

Dozens, maybe hundreds of their reflections moved across the mirrors' surfaces.

"Did anyone else see something . . . in the shadows?" Ivan asked.

*Had it been an illusion? More fun in this hall of mirrors?*

"See what?" Annie said, looking from reflection to reflection, poised, ready for an attack. The darkness in the background of the mirrors created depth to the reflections.

"I thought I saw . . . *dunno* . . . someone, maybe."

His voice drifted off as he moved forward, hanging close to the wall, gun ready. He waved the others to follow, but they were hanging back. Cautious.

Then: "Ivan . . ." Ruth's voice rose sharply. "On your leg. Your left leg."

Ivan looked down and saw the tiny spot of a red laser beam moving slowly up his leg toward his crotch. It crossed his hip and then centered on his chest.

He turned quickly to one side an instant before a bolt of blue light flashed through the air.

It hit the mirror behind him and reflected in an intersecting pattern of light that instantly filled the room with dozens—hundreds—of deadly blue beams.

The air was filled with the stinging smell of ozone.

Wherever the blue beam hit the cave floor, it kicked up an explosive line of rocks and dust.

Ruth and everyone else froze where they stood.

Ivan raised his rifle slowly and looked around.

Not moving. Breathing hard . . . thinking.

"Nobody move." His voice was not as steady as he would have liked. Everyone—even Jordan—had stopped in their tracks.

"What the hell?" Annie asked.

"The thing's motion activated," Ivan said.

He narrowed his eyes and scanned the surfaces of the mirrors, trying to see not the reflections, but the darkness behind them . . . and the figure, reflected dozens of times, that he knew was lurking somewhere behind one of the mirrors.

"See? There," he called out, pointing to his left.

The shadowy figure moved, but as soon as Ivan focused on it, it appeared in several other mirrors, moving around the room in various directions.

*Had to be Kyros, crazed, toying with them. Hiding behind the mirrors.*

*But which one?*

"I don't like this," Jordan said.

"Did anyone see where that figure came from?" Ivan shouted.

"From the left, I thought," Annie said.

"N-no." Rodriguez rubbed his upper lip. "I'm pretty sure it came from in front of us."

"I was sure it came from the right," Sinjira said.

"All right! All right!" Ivan said. He stared at the chip in the side of Sinjira's head. Blinking. Recording.

*Maybe record us all dying for someone else to find . . . if they can.*

"Ivan, we can't just stay here doing nothing," Jordan said.

Ivan nodded.

They *had* to do something.

Moving slowly, he knelt down until he could touch the floor. Scooping up a handful of dirt, he straightened up and then, with a swift motion, he threw the dirt into the air and ducked to one side.

The bolt of blue light shot out again, and the blast reflected off the multiple mirrors in a crazy web pattern.

One bolt grazed Annie, tearing through her shirtsleeve and the strap of her backpack.

She let out a yelp of pain but didn't react—didn't move.

From his crouch, Ivan saw something amazing.

It was drifting in the dust, for only a moment, suspended in the room, a matrix of thin, intersecting red laser beams filling the room with a dense web.

"Okay," Ivan said. "I got it."

"Right," Jordan said. "If we break a beam, the lasers shoots."

Annie was looking frustrated.

The dust slowly settled, and the red laser beams gradually disappeared. Ivan—standing there motionless—wondered how the hell they could make it through this trap without someone tripping the bolts again.

They'd been lucky so far. The one reflected shot had caused only a minor wound to Annie.

They might not be so lucky a third time.

"You notice something?" Jordan said from the back of the line. His reflection was multiplied in the fun house mirrors—like everyone else's.

"What's that?" Ivan asked.

"Up there." He pointed. "Look at that mirror array. It's all coming from up there."

Ivan leaned forward, straining to see the dark vault overhead.

"The motion detector? Looks like it's shielded pretty good," he said. He glanced at Sinjira and said, "You getting all this, Chippie?"

"Every second," she said with a totally neutral voice.

*She's like Jordan. Ice water in her veins when she's doing what she likes best.*

Ivan realized that the motion detector had to be shielded from every corner of the room so it wouldn't get blasted. There was a narrow opening directly beneath it.

*Must use a prism there to scatter the light and mirrors amplify the blasts.*

Ivan slowly raised his arm, aiming his pistol at the ceiling, hoping he didn't break one of the now-invisible laser beams as he moved. Taking careful aim, dead center, he squeezed the trigger.

The gun hissed, and the pulse hit something.

But not the aiming or the firing mechanisms above them.

A bright beam of light and a dense puff of smoke spilled down.

"Hold on. Stop!" Jordan said.

Moving as slowly as Ivan had, Jordan took off his backpack and unzipped a side pouch. He reached inside and took out a small, metal tube. An emergency flare.

"Packed for every occasion, huh?" Ivan said with a chuckle. He already realized what Jordan was planning to do.

"Always," Jordan said without emotion.

Ivan watched as Jordan twisted the small metal cover.

A brief scratching sound, and then the flare started spewing out bright red light and a dense billow of white smoke.

Kneeling down, Jordan rolled the burning flare into the center of the room. Everyone waited and watched, fascinated, as the smoke expanded to fill the room. It stung their eyes, but the straight red lines of laser lights—the trip wires—became clearly visible.

"Everyone okay?" Ivan called out. "All right then."

*How long will our luck hold up?*

"Don't break any of the beams," Jordan said. "You should be okay."

He pointed up, indicating the apex of the chamber. The web of red laser lines all emanated from it.

*Easier said than done.*

"Everyone," Jordan said, "stay where you are."

Before anyone—even Ivan—could react, Jordan darted forward. He ran in a low crouch, nimbly dodging and jumping over the red beams until he was about three meters from the exact center of the room.

There, the web of laser light became too dense for anyone to avoid.

But he didn't stop moving.

He dropped down to the floor and then rolled once . . . twice . . . three times, until he was on his back, directly under the apex.

He raised his pistol and shot.

Once.

A loud crackling sound filled the room, as if someone had dropped a container of glasses. A bolt of blue light shot straight down at him, searing the floor inches from his head, but he moved fast enough to avoid it.

But even as the dust was settling, Jordan flipped over onto his stomach and jackknifed to his feet.

Ivan was grinning at him.

"Impressive."

The red laser beams and their numerous reflections—not to mention the pulses of deadly light—had vanished in an instant.

Jordan was panting.

Drops of sweat carved streaks in the dirt on his face as he walked back to them.

He and Ivan locked eyes for a moment. Then: "You spend your downtime practicing those moves?" Ivan said.

Jordan smiled and said, "I didn't want you to get all the glory."

Ivan laughed and slapped him on the back.

"Great work, Jordan. Really. Took balls."

Jordan didn't even nod. Then he said: "Lead on."

Ivan turned, ready to take them as far into this alien cave as they would have to go.

# 37

## NOISE

"*Got a question for you,*" Annie said as she and Ivan walked side by side down the wide cave passageway. The air was dusty and dry. Ruth walked on his other side, brushing up against him every now and then . . . accidentally or on purpose, he wasn't sure.

"What's that?" Ivan said.

"So you didn't know about any of *this*?"

"The lasers and mirrors?"

Annie nodded.

"Never got this far in. The cave mouth was blocked up." He took a breath. "All new to me."

"What is it, then?" Ruth said. "Who do you think made it—that mirror room and those lasers?"

Annie watched Ivan turn to Ruth, then back to her.

"Good question," Annie said.

Like Ivan, she had her gun at the ready and kept looking around. Their voices echoed oddly in the tunnel.

"Not the miners. Not the Runners. No way they made this. Way too sophisticated, even for Kyros," Ivan said.

"And there may be more," Annie said.

"Bound to be," Ivan said.

The passageway narrowed and widened and then narrowed again until they entered another wide room.

"No mirrors here, at least," Ivan said.

He held up his hand to get everyone to halt.

He had a *feeling.*

Something . . . was ahead.


"This is weirding me out," Sinjira said, unable to mask her anxiety.

She had been recording all along, and she knew she had some killer content. But now something wasn't right.

"That . . ."

She pointed to one side, and everyone looked at a far corner of the room. The light was weaker there, but she could make out a splotch on the ragged rock wall about ten meters to their left.

Darker than the stone, and not moving.

*Not anymore, anyway.*

The others followed a few paces behind her as she entered the darkened area and approached whatever it was.

Everyone except Jordan.

"We got no time for this. We have to keep going," he said.

Sinjira noticed how *different* his voice sounded in the cavern. Not muffled, really, and it didn't echo. But it sounded altered.

Dead.

Stopping less than a meter from the thing on the wall, Sinjira fixed it in the beam of her flashlight. Cocking her head from side to side, she looked at it . . . studied it . . . but, most important, listened . . . and recorded.

*Something definitely isn't right here.*

The others, milling around behind her, shuffled their feet impatiently, getting frustrated at the delay.

Try as she might, she couldn't figure out what it was.

"Sinjira. We don't really have time for any sightseeing," Jordan called out.

But she didn't move. She wanted to—she *had* to—figure out what was going on here.

"This . . . I think it's alive," she finally said. "At least it used to be."

It wasn't any kind of creature, though, no cave bat or other life form that nested in the recesses of the cave.

But she was positive it had once been alive.

And there were more.

"God," she whispered as she shifted her light beam into the deeper recesses and saw more splotches. Ten . . . twenty . . . easily more than thirty. And all of them irregular, some crusted with dried blood of various hues.

"What the hell—" Ivan said, moving behind her.

Now that she looked around, Sinjira saw evidence everywhere of *something* that had died and was now part of the wall.

"Okay. Let's have a look," Rodriguez said, coming up next to her. He took a small instrument from the breast pocket of his jacket and held it up to the splotch.

Lights flashed and the tiny machine made a faint clicking sound. Then there was a short beep.

Rodriguez looked at the instrument, then at Sinjira.

"Hang on," he said. "This is similar to protoplasm but it's not human or any other known species tissue. It's not a living organism."

"Maybe just a piece of it?" Sinjira said as she directed her flashlight beam upward at the ceiling as if expecting to see some hideous nightmare creature lurking up there . . . preparing to pounce.

Without warning, the lens of her flashlight shattered. The light flared and then went out. Shards of broken glass made faint tinkling sounds as they fell to the floor at her feet.

"What just happened?" Ivan asked, but Sinjira could only shake her head, confused.

"Can you hear that?" she asked.

The sound was faint at first, a high-frequency whistling that grew steadily louder when she listened carefully.

She looked around at the blank stares of the people around her. They didn't understand. They didn't hear. Her voice was halting as she spoke.

"Look! My chip is picking up some kind of noise."

"What do you mean, noise?" Ivan looked around. "I don't hear a—"

As if in answer, the lens of his flashlight suddenly exploded and went out, too, in a shower of glass.

The corner of the cavern was darker now with two less lights. Sinjira's feeling of uneasiness was quickly shifting into genuine fear.

*What the hell is going on here?*

She jumped and let out a piercing squeal when Rodriguez's flashlight lens exploded.

And then Ruth's . . . and finally Jordan's.

Sinjira felt panicked as she tried to understand whatever this was that her chip was picking up, and that could shatter their flashlights.

"Wait a second," Ivan said. "I think I can—"

He cupped his hands to his ears and turned his head back and forth as though trying to locate the origin of whatever the sound was.

"You hear it, too?" Sinjira asked.

Ivan waited, then nodded slowly.

"I think so. Just barely . . ."

"I don't hear anything," Rodriguez said. "You're probably just . . ."

His voice trailed off, and he scrunched up his face as he, too, listened.

Sinjira kept wheeling her head left and right, trying to pinpoint the source of the sound.

Right now it seemed to surround her.

Rising higher.

Turning even more shrill.

She licked her lips, aware of the dry, crusty texture. When she wiped the flat of her hand across her face, she felt something sticky.

She let out a faint groan when she saw the streak of blood on her palm.

*No!*

The sound was inside her head now. If it didn't stop soon, it would drive her crazy.

"We have to . . . get out of here!" she shouted, surprised by the strength of her voice. "There's some kind of—"

"The sound's painful," Ivan said, shaking his head as if he had water in his ears. "Anyone else hear it?"

Sinjira watched as each of them looked hurt . . . crippled by the noise.

Suddenly, Ruth doubled over and grabbed her head with both hands. Blood was streaming from both of her nostrils. It glistened darkly in the dim light.

Sinjira looked down at her chip. Still recording, but the levels were all wrong.

"This is going off the scale, way past any UHF. The noise isn't even close to normal frequencies."

First Ruth, then Rodriguez fell to their knees, clutching their heads. Ivan came up to Ruth, covering his ears.

"It's a trap," he said. "The sound . . ."

*Like the mirrors with light, only now it was sound.*

"We have to get away from it," Ruth said. Blood ran freely from her nose to the edge of her chin.

By now, everyone was blocking their ears with their hands, but Sinjira could feel the sound still swelling, building up pressure inside her brain.

Covering their ears would do nothing.

This sound could penetrate their skulls.

She looked at the trickle of blood leaking between Jordan's fingers as he covered his ears.

Ivan walked over and yanked Ruth and Rodriguez to their feet. He started dragging them away, back to the main room, forcing them to run.

Sinjira, with Jordan following, ran after them.

Their footsteps made harsh, hissing sounds in the dust as they ran, sprinting as fast as they could to put as much distance as possible between them and the origin of that high-frequency sound.

*How far will we have to get away from it before it won't affect us?*

Ivan ran as fast as he could, dragging Ruth and Rodriguez. Like them, he was nearly immobilized by the sound but kept pushing.

Behind them was Annie, Sinjira, and—finally—Jordan, perhaps bleeding the most, his ears shiny with red blood.

"Ingenious," Rodriguez said, gasping.

"What's that?" Ivan said, still pulling him along.

"A hypersonic defense system," Rodriguez went on. "If we had stayed there much longer, the sound—basically inaudible, like an old-fashioned dog whistle—would have ruptured our blood vessels, maybe even cracked our skulls, made our heads explode."

"Like what was on the wall," Sinjira said.

"Yeah. Fucking brilliant," Annie said, panting as she ran, her fists clenched and pumping like pistons.

"Can you still read it on your chip?" Ivan asked Sinjira.

She nodded and said, "It's fainter . . . but still there."

Ivan thought: *What if there was another trap up ahead?*

It could be that the UHF noise hadn't been designed to kill . . . only to annoy them and make them run faster, herding them like animals, straight into another trap.

*Gotta watch it . . . be ready.*

He was still holding Ruth's hand, even though they had passed the danger.

As they ran along, he was surprised how good this felt.

*Her hand in mine.*

As they navigated the twists and turns of the cavern, he checked on Jordan and Annie, his backup.

Both appeared to have recovered, a little anyway, although Jordan's neck was streaked with blood.

*Have to be ready for whatever's ahead.*

Then . . . he tensed when, up ahead, he saw that the cavern looked like it had come to an end.

*A dead end . . . or worse?*

He slowed his pace, and Ruth, breathing heavily behind him, slowed down as well. Even when they stopped, Ivan noticed how neither of them let go of the other's hand.

The cavern narrowed down, and there was a wall of blackness ahead.

"Hold up!" he shouted, and now—finally—he reluctantly let go of Ruth's hand.

Sinjira and the rest of them came to a halt.

"What is it?" Annie asked.

"Dead end. Maybe," Ivan said.

Up ahead, he saw a dark entryway, blocked by three huge stones, stacked one on top of the other . . . like stairs.

At the top, a platform.

Ivan approached the opening, staring into the darkness beyond. Jordan came up beside him and lit a flare.

"Looks like it drops off on the other side," Ivan said. "I wish we still had a flashlight that worked."

Ivan climbed the three large stone steps to the top of the platform. Once he was at the top, he looked down.

And saw nothing but darkness.

"Shit."

"What is it?" Jordan asked, striding up the stairs behind him. They both peered down into what might as well have been a bottomless pit.

"Too dark even for the goggles."

"Totally black."

"Got another flare?" Ivan asked.

Without a word, Jordan slung his backpack off and opened the top flap.

"Only a few left," the gunner said.

As Jordan took out a flare, Ivan asked, "How many?"

"Seven . . . counting this one."

Ivan nodded, thinking.

Jordan took out three flares and handed them to Ivan.

"Share and share alike."

"Thanks," Ivan said as he slipped them into his backpack and zipped it shut.

He watched as Jordan struck the second flare and held it above his head. The sputtering red glow filled the cavern as sparks spilled to the floor and a thick billow of smoke rose to the dark reaches of the cave ceiling. How far up it went was anyone's guess.

The sudden brightness momentarily blinded Ivan, but when he looked down, he could see . . .

"I'll be a son of a bitch," he said as he and Jordan stared down at the long flight of stone steps spiraling down into the depths below.

Ivan looked back at the others and called out. "There's a stairway. We have to go down."

*Is that all this is?* he wondered.

He took the first step down, placing his foot solidly on the wide stone.

And in an instant, it disappeared . . . like a light winking off.

Thrown off balance, Ivan lurched forward and began to fall.

# 38

## THE STEPS

*As Ivan's momentum carried him* forward, Ruth let out a piercing scream and Jordan dove forward. He missed Ivan's arm, but his fingers snagged his jacket collar.

It wasn't much . . .

But it was enough.

Ivan twisted around to face Jordan. His arms shot up and out as his hands and forearms slapped the top edge of the cave floor. Grit from the cave floor rained down into his face.

For a few seconds—seconds that seemed like minutes—he dangled with his legs kicking freely in empty space.

He grunted, looking up at Jordan and Ruth and the others.

"Uh . . . a little help here'd be nice?" he said, his breath puffing hard with the effort of hanging on.

Jordan held the flare high so Annie and Rodriguez could see what they were doing as they knelt down on either side of Ivan and got a good grip on him. Hands wedged under his armpits, they lifted him up, dragging him slowly until his knees scraped against the cave floor.

"Thanks," he said, panting from the effort as he straightened up and brushed himself off.

He noticed the blood still leaking from Ruth's ear and reached out to touch her on the shoulder.

"You all right?" he asked.

A quick nod. Ivan turned to face the others.

"Okay. Want my guess about what's going on here?"

For a moment, they stood there quiet. Stumped. Then: "It's another part of the defense system."

"Defense system?" Annie echoed, moving close.

"I mean, this is all a deadly game for someone."

"Your brother, you mean," Jordan said.

"No doubt he's enjoying it. But I don't think he had anything to do with making any of this. It's too ingenious. And my guess—probably alien."

Ivan looked around.

"Kyros must have found this place and now he's using it against us. And whoever made these traps was sure as hell protecting something pretty damn important."

"And each part of it," Annie said, "is luring us deeper in—"

"If it doesn't kill us first," Jordan said.

"Yeah," Ivan said. "Designed to kill any interlopers. Like us. That is, unless we can figure out the traps."

"So it's like a test?" Ruth said quietly.

The flare sputtering in Jordan's hand tossed red sparks onto the dirt floor.

"Pass the tests, and it drives us deeper and deeper into the cave," Ivan said. "And I suspect whatever's down here that's valuable my brother has already found."

He looked at Annie. She'd been unshakeable as far as he had seen so far. Now? Her face was set, grim.

*Stay with me*, he thought.

"W-we should stop then," Rodriguez said. "I am *not* going to be herded like an animal to the slaughter. I say we go back."

Ivan turned on him, hoping to make it perfectly clear.

*There is no going back. No turning around.*

"I say we get out of here while we can," Rodriguez continued. "We can find some other way to deal with your brother if he's even down here."

Ivan tensed, resisting the temptation to punch him.

"Oh, he's down here all right," he said.

*Will the doc get the hint to shut the fuck up before he freaks everyone out?*

"You think you get to call the shots, Doc?" Ivan kept his voice low, commanding. And Rodriguez took a quick step back. His expression froze as he looked around searching for support from someone . . . anyone.

"What?" he said. "You all want to die down here?" He pointed at the stairway. "If we had panicked and been running away from that UHF, not being careful, not looking where we were going, we would all have gone off the edge when we reached these steps."

"Are you about done?" Ivan said, taking a step closer.

"Easy there, Ivan," Jordan said.

"That room back there." Rodriguez's face flushed. "That stuff that was stuck on the walls? You know what it was, right?"

Before anyone could answer, he finished it for them.

"It's whatever was left of whoever came down here. That high sonic frequency shattered their skulls. And it would have done the same to us if we hadn't run."

"No one's dead," Ivan said.

He looked around, taking the temperature of the group.

"Not yet!"

"It's talk like that that'll get us killed. Fear, Doctor. Trust me. Fear kills."

And Rodriguez definitely looked afraid when Ivan stepped closer.

Rodriguez looked at Annie, as if expecting her to back him up, protect him.

"I say we put it to a vote," he said.

Before he could finish, Ivan backhanded him across the mouth, a hard, loud smack that drew blood.

"Leave if you want, Doc," Ivan said softly, evenly. "But I say we're safer if we stick together."

Wiping blood away with the back of his hand, Rodriguez looked at Annie.

"And you're going to just stand there and let him treat one of your passengers like this?"

Annie glanced at Ivan. Then shook her head.

"You're not my responsibility anymore, so"—a shrug—"I'm fine with letting Ivan *and* Jordan take command."

Ivan cocked an eyebrow at her.

*Jordan, too? When did I say anything about Jordan being in charge?* he wanted to ask but didn't.

"Okay," Ivan said. "It's decided, then. We have to calm the fuck down and figure this out."

In the sputtering red light of the flare, he looked down the long flight of stairs. They took a long, sweeping curve around to the right and disappeared down into darkness.

Who knew how far down they went . . . or if they were even really there?

*Are all of the steps an illusion or just some of them?*

Ivan dropped onto his hands and knees and waved his hand in the empty space where the step had been. He leaned out, feeling around the edges.

"This step's definitely not there." He leaned out even farther, looking left and right, but it was impossible to see into the deep shadows. "There's no indication it was some kind of projection, so my guess is, the step was real—just not supported."

"We never heard it hit the floor down below," Ruth said.

Ivan nodded. "True. But we were so surprised, we weren't really listening for it, either."

He leaned as far forward as he could go and slapped the second step in front of him.

His hand hit hard stone. This one was solid.

"Okay," he said, easing back onto the platform.

"It won't be if it drops away as soon as you stand on it," Ruth said, sounding worried.

Ivan sat back on his heels and ran his fingers through his hair.

"I'm thinking the first step was a holographic projection. Never really there. No one would create a trap where a real stone would fall and have to be reset every time someone tripped it."

"Maybe," Jordan said, "but how do we know which steps are real . . . or if any of them will support us?"

Ivan stared down the long, winding stairway, thinking.

"That flare about done?" he asked Jordan.

He held out his hand.

Jordan studied the flare for a moment and then gave it to him.

Ivan gripped it loosely, feeling the heat of the burning metal tube. Then he leaned over the gap and gently tossed it onto the second step.

It hit the wide stone block with a loud, metallic ringing sound.

The stone step didn't disappear. Then the flare rolled and dropped onto the next level.

Same thing.

The stair remained where it was.

The fourth step didn't fall or disappear, either.

But when the flare rolled onto the fifth step, that one winked out of existence with a faint electronic hum.

And the flare dropped, spinning end over end until it disappeared into the dark abyss.

"Long way down," Jordan said once the light was gone.

Ivan nodded. "Hate to fall."

He took a breath. "Okay, then" he said. "The first step and the fifth step weren't real. If this is some kind of puzzle, it'd be too easy for every other step to be the fake one, right? So"—he shook his head—"the only way to find out is to go down them . . . step by step."

"You're out of your mind," Rodriguez said. He was daubing at his split lip, licking the blood off his fingertips. "You'll get us all killed."

Ivan stood up and brushed his hands on his jacket.

"You know, Doc, I was kinda thinking of asking *you* to lead the way."

Rodriguez backed away.

Ivan smiled and, turning to the others, said, "So who has the fiber cable?"

Jordan stepped forward, unzipped his backpack, and took out a length of thickly coiled cable.

Ivan held the man's gaze as they each held the cable tightly.

"You want to play hero?" Ivan asked.

Jordan smiled and let go of the cable.

"All right, then. We loop this around ourselves and start down one at a time, single file, giving plenty of slack. I'll take the lead."

While he was talking, he unspooled the end of the fiber cable and, with Ruth's help, tied it around his chest, keeping the loop snug under his armpits.

"You don't have to do this, you know," she whispered, her voice soft, her breath warm against the side of his face. "Maybe Rodriguez is right. Maybe we should all go back."

Ivan took a breath.

A thought.

Obvious. So clear.

*She cares for me. And maybe I care for her.*

There it was. But he had sensed all along that there was also something going on between her and Jordan.

Should he back off?

Finally, while playing out the fiber from the coil, he called out, "All right. Who's next?"

Before anyone could speak, Ruth said, "Me."

She took the fiber line and tied it securely around her chest the way Ivan had.

Ivan checked to make sure it was secure. Then he played out more fiber, so Annie and then Sinjira could tie it around themselves.

When it was Rodriguez's turn, he took a step back and held up his hands.

"No fucking *way* I'm doing that."

Jordan glanced at Ivan, who nodded. Then Jordan raised his pistol and pointed it at him.

"You have a simple choice to make here, Doc."

Rodriguez's face was pale even in the glow of another flare.

Ivan thought the doctor was going to stand his ground and not tie on, but finally, he took the fiber and looped it twice around his chest. Jordan checked it, giving it an extra hard tug.

"If one of us goes, we all go, huh?"

"One for all, and all for one," Ivan said with a smile.

Lastly, Jordan tied on, making sure there was plenty of slack between him and Rodriguez.

When they were done, they were each spaced a couple of meters apart.

Ivan went down the line, checking everybody. Satisfied, he sucked in a quick breath and jumped over the first gap to land on the second step.

The solid one.

It held.

"All right," he said, only slightly relieved. "Let's see how many steps there are to this hell."

*These idiots are all gonna fall and drag me down with them.*

Rodriguez trembled as he climbed up the three stone stairs and prepared to step over the gap and onto the second—and first solid—step.

He made sure to keep plenty of slack between him and Sinjira in front and Jordan behind.

If someone fell, he wanted as much time as possible to drop to the ground and find something—*anything*—to hold on so he wouldn't be dragged down into the abyss.

"H-how do we know any of these steps are safe?" he called out, his voice echoing weirdly in the wide stairway.

He could still taste the blood in his mouth and spat.

Up ahead, Ivan carried a flare, holding it high.

Behind him, another flare—carried by Jordan—sputtered as it spewed smoke. The red glow from both flares was as thick as paint, casting wavering double shadows across the rough-cut stone walls and descending steps.

"How many flares do you have left?" he wondered.

No answer.

"If we run out before we reach bottom, what then?"

Jordan said, "Relax, Doc. We're still alive so far, *ain't* we?"

Rodriguez inhaled the dry cavern air and adjusted the rope around his chest.

Then he took his first step down.

Four people in front of him. They stretched out in a long line, carefully making their way down. Up ahead, Ivan paused and checked each step before putting his full weight on it.

*It pays to be paranoid*, he thought but didn't say.

Some steps disappeared with a crackling hiss while others remained solid.

*So far. What if they, too, gave out once they were all on them?*

They inched along, taking their time, until both Jordan's and Ivan's flares eventually burned out.

Before his was entirely gone, Jordan tossed it over the edge. Rodriguez looked back and watched it disappear, sucked down until it disappeared into the darkness below.

And then gone.

When Jordan lit another one, Rodriguez was momentarily blinded by the sudden burst of light in the darkness. Blinking his eyes, he turned away.

That's when he saw on the wall—

*Symbols.*

"Hang on," he shouted, loud enough for everyone to draw to a stop. The line went slack.

"What now?" Jordan asked.

"Look here. On the wall."

Rodriguez scanned the cave wall. The symbols were carved into the rock wall about six meters above each step.

They were difficult to see with the light flickering.

"This could be important," he said.

The numbers or letters or whatever had obviously been carved into the rock on purpose. Old, like ancient petroglyphs, worn by erosion.

But that was strange, too. There was no "weather" down here to cause erosion—unless this stairway had been filled with floodwater in the past.

A long time ago. Long after these symbols had been carved.

He wondered who had been down here first, exploring this cave, making those marks.

And how long ago?

*But what are these symbols for? What do they indicate?*

They couldn't be random. There had to be a reason, and as Rodriguez studied them, he noticed that certain ones repeated farther down.

*Letters? Numbers?*

"There's a pattern here," he whispered, as much to himself as to the others.

With the flare sputtering in his hand, Jordan moved down to the step next to him.

"We don't have all day here, Doc," he said.

"I know, I know." Rodriguez gave him a quick nod, irritated that he had broken his concentration. "Just give me a few seconds. There's definitely something here . . . something . . ."

His voice trailed off as he stared at the carving while rubbing the sharp edge of his jaw.

"These flares won't last forever," Ivan called up from below.

"Just wait a minute!" Rodriguez shouted back, surprised that his fear had been replaced now with a determination to understand.

He guessed he might even seem deranged as he looked back and forth, up and down the stairs, all the while counting on his fingers and muttering to himself until—finally—he snapped his fingers.

"Got it," he said. "I understand!"

"Understand what?" Jordan said, but Rodriguez looked at Sinjira, staring at the symbols, recording everything. He turned to her.

"Put this one in a special file, sweetheart," he said, leaning close and mugging for her. "Label it 'genius at work.'"

She looked at him, one eyebrow raised.

"Can we get moving?" Ivan hollered.

"Faster than ever now," Rodriguez shouted back.

He was feeling so confident—or maybe suicidal—he loosened the rope around his chest, wiggled out of the loop, and started striding down the stairs, stepping over the gaps while counting out loud as he went.

When he was standing on the step beside Ivan, the ex-runner grabbed him by the collar, yanking him off balance.

"Are you out of your mind? Are you trying to get us all killed?"

"Simple mathematics," Rodriguez replied, letting his smile widen.

"Explain," Annie said.

"Three steps up to the platform," he said. "Then a stairway leading down. Look back and count the steps that have disappeared so far. Anyone see a pattern?"

Ivan glared at him for a moment, then looked up the steps, counting the black gaps where stones had disappeared.

"None."

Ivan appeared to be in no mood for fooling around, but Rodriguez laughed in his face.

"One . . . four . . . one . . . nine . . . two . . . six . . . and five. Ring a bell? Anyone?" He looked up the stairs at the others, waiting.

Ivan shook his head as though he thought the man had lost his mind.

"So the next steps that will disappear as we go down will be three . . . five . . . eight . . . nine . . . seven . . . nine . . . et cetera."

"How do you know this?" Ruth asked.

"What do you mean, et cetera?" Ivan clenched his fist. "We don't have the time for games."

Annie said, "Yeah, Doc. I gotta admit you lost me here."

As if to prove Ivan's point, the flare Rodriguez held sputtered, the light gradually fading.

Before he dropped it over the edge, he fished another one from his backpack and lit it.

"It's *pi*," Rodriguez said. "The digits of *pi*. You know? The ratio between the circumference of a circle and its diameter?"

Ivan shook his head and said, "I gotta admit, I wasn't much of a math student."

"What a surprise." He laughed out loud. "You see, you divide the—"

"No. No . . . don't explain," Ivan said irritably. "If you can get us down these stairs any quicker, please, be my guest."

"Follow me then."

Rodriguez started down the stairs, moving fast and counting numbers out loud as he went.

"Four . . . six . . . two . . . six . . . four . . ."

"The guy's a damned nutcase," Ivan said, but he focused on Rodriguez as he made his way down the spiral stairway.

Then he and Ruth and the others followed along.

"Aren't you glad you didn't let him go back?" Ruth asked.

Ivan said, "I still may have to push him over the edge . . . if I can catch up with him."

Rodriguez's voice echoed from below, receding with the distance.

"Three . . . three . . . eight . . . two . . . seven . . . nine . . ."

*Mad. Crazy.*

*But correct.*

"Hey! Hold up! Not so fast," Ivan shouted.

When he looked at Ruth in the glow of the flare, he tried not to think how beautiful she looked.

*Focus.*

"Five . . . zero . . . two . . . eight . . . eight . . . four . . ."

"How long does this number—this *pi*—go on?"

"That's the thing of it," Ruth said. "Scientists using computers have carried out the division to millions of decimals, but it never ends. Apparently, it goes on forever."

*Forever.*

Ivan spat into one of the gaps as he stepped over it.

"Let's just hope this stairway doesn't."

# 39

## THE VINES ABOVE

*Ivan stopped.*

Suddenly, light—a rich blue glow—appeared up ahead and they weren't simply inside a chamber.

Quite clearly, they were deep inside this cavern, inside this mountain on Omega Nine where *someone* had left a series of connected chambers carved out of the stone. All tests.

And now, here, before them, was a mammoth corridor that looked more like the entrance to a magical city hidden deep inside the mountain.

Jordan came up from the rear and stopped beside Ivan.

"What do you think—another trap, another game?"

Ivan bit his lower lip and shook his head.

He looked back at the others. Annie's eyes were locked on the two of them. The others were looking around at the smooth curved walls that swelled and ballooned, growing larger as far as eyes could see.

"No. I think . . ."

Ivan looked around at the reverse funnel shape of this grand hallway.

". . . it's the entrance to . . . I'm not sure." He looked at Jordan and grinned. "I'm surprised not to see a sign saying, 'Abandon all hope.'"

Jordan shifted from one foot to the other. "What's that?"

"A poet, a long time ago, said that was the sign over the entrance to hell. 'Abandon all hope ye who enter herein.'"

"Nope. Never heard of it," Jordan said.

*Not surprising*, Ivan thought.

"Look. We passed the tests. We got through the traps, and we're in."

"In . . . where?" Ruth asked.

Ivan turned around and looked at her.

"Maybe something made by the Builders."

Ruth's eyes went wide.

"And now," Ivan said, "now that we made it inside this . . . I don't know . . . this building or chamber . . . or fortress . . . whatever . . . we can go on. Maybe no more traps."

Annie gave the slightest of nods.

*Hopefully,* Ivan thought.

But his hope quickly faded when he remembered that his brother was down here somewhere hiding, waiting. The traps up above were supposed to have killed them, and no doubt there would be more traps . . . and worse.

Ivan turned to Jordan, about to say, *Stay sharp. Eyes open.*

But that would be redundant.

He started moving forward, and now that circumstances appeared to be different—perhaps—the gunner walked by his side while the rest of them came up behind them.


Annie looked around at the passengers of the SRV, all following the two men in the front with their guns ready.

They were all here. Why?

Because they had no other option other than staying back with a crazed Nahara and waiting to see what happened? And the Star Road wasn't for people who sat around and waited for things to happen.

Annie wondered if any of them were having second thoughts.

She knew she sure as hell was. Give her the open Road, and her at the helm. *That's* what she wanted.

But she kept pace with the others, gun ready, as Sinjira and Ruth walked on either side of her now, having more in common—their fear—than their differences.

She kept glancing at Rodriguez behind her. He looked wide-eyed, but she guessed that, as a scientist, this all amazed him as much as it scared him.

Nobody spoke.

As the chamber opened even wider, the blue glow intensified, washing their faces. The light emanating from some mysterious power source, maybe the same source that had been used—how many eons ago?—to carve this massive entranceway out of stone.

No sound. No talking.

Until one of them—Sinjira, of course—heard the *humming.*


Sinjira moved up close to Ivan and Jordan, and touched them both on their elbows.

"You hear that?"

They stopped, and turned to her.

"Hear what?" Jordan said.

"Listen," she said.

Thinking: *Was she that much more sensitive than the others that she could hear, see, and feel things that just went right past them?*

"A hum. Very faint."

Ivan nodded.

"Another sonic trap?" he asked.

Sinjira shrugged and said, "Could be."

She wasn't sure he actually heard it or had simply grown to trust her instincts, her senses.

"Okay. Let's stay frosty. Until we can hear what you're hearing, okay?"

Sinjira nodded to Ivan.

But she didn't resume her position back with the others, thinking: *Let's stay close to the firepower.*

They moved even more cautiously, the party in slow motion.


"I hear it now," Ivan said.

The hum, not quite clear. Not irritating. Certainly not debilitating like the sonic attack they had suffered. Almost soothing.

A gentle, breezelike sound.

"Um . . . me, too," Jordan added.

Annie, a meter or so behind them, said, "Yup. Me, too. Any ideas what it is?"

That question, as they kept moving, resolved itself.

Ivan looked up to the smooth expanse of the now giant, sweeping arc of the ceiling of this entryway.

Vines hanging down.

Not exactly vines.

Hard to tell what they were in the blue light, these dark blue-green tendrils hanging from the ceiling of various lengths. They glowed with an eerie iridescence and vibrated constantly as if fitful breezes were blowing through the chamber.

But—of course—there was no breeze. Not this far down.

The vines shook ever so slightly, each acting independently. And as they shook, they created a gentle humming sound.

"What are they?" Annie said.

"They're absolutely beautiful," Sinjira said from behind Ivan, no doubt recording it all.

*Beautiful. Yes, but what are they . . . What do they do?*

He kept walking since the vines seemed to pose no imminent danger.

Other than swaying and vibrating, the vines didn't seem to react to their presence as they moved closer and then passed under them.

The faint hum remained gentle, soothing. The subtle, waving motion continued . . . but didn't increase.

"Guess they're okay" Jordan said.

Ivan wasn't so sure.

Ivan raised his hand, silently ordering everyone to halt. Then he pointed to the floor ahead.

Even though they were still far away from what littered the ground, he could tell what the indeterminate jumble actually was.

*When you've seen battles, when you've seen bodies piled high, you know.*

"What is it?" Jordan asked. His rifle was raised, sweeping the area.

Annie came up to his side. "What's wrong?"

Ivan gestured to the shapes that covered it as far as he could see in this weirdly lit chamber.

At some point, the mammoth entranceway curved to the right.

But in front of them . . .

*Bodies. Hundreds . . . thousands of bones.*

He had nothing to say . . . not without a closer look first.

He turned to Jordan.

"This is not looking good."

A nod from Jordan and he moved forward. Annie quickly moved forward, too.

They didn't have to tell the others to hang back, as obedient as school kids, the silent command to stay put easily enforced by the shapes of bodies ahead, dark shapes silhouetted against the blue light.

Ivan, Jordan, and Annie walked together, each instinctively moving their rifles to a ready position, sweeping from side to side, covering all possible approaches.

Until they reached the first of the bodies.

There were two figures. Humanoid, but clearly not human. Even in death, they were locked in a death battle, hands—or claws—wrapped around each other. One on a throat; the other with a clawlike hand meshed tightly against the other's face.

Their battle, frozen in time.

Such scenes were replicated everywhere they looked. More corpses locked in a wild melee . . . a fight to the finish. Some of the corpses looked as though they had exploded by massive gun or energy blasts. Others were desiccated masses with exposed brittle bones, their innards long ago rotting in the dry air, turning to dust.

Annie was the first to speak:

"What . . . the *hell* happened here?"

Ivan shook his head.

"A lot of different types. Aliens. Different species," he said. "It's like they . . . like they all came here from various planets to fight and they all died."

A chill ran up Ivan's back. The implications were staggering.

He had seen death and destruction. But this completely chilled him.

He looked up at the cavern ceiling. The vines were still vibrating harmlessly. The slight quivers still seeming somehow benevolent . . . welcoming.

But could the strange vines have anything to do with it?

A battle scene—but not really.

More like scores of scenes from many different battles, a jumbled war as untold alien creatures fought to the death.

Ivan looked ahead, beyond the vast field of dead, to something he had been too preoccupied to notice before.

The expansive walls of the side of the chamber were no longer widening.

And he saw something on those walls.

Without waiting for the others, Ivan started walking through the field of death.

SIX

THE MACHINE AWAKES

# 40

INSIDE

*Ivan moved forward, picking his* way carefully around the twisted figures lying on the ground as best he could; but there was no escaping the occasional step on a loose bit of bone or a fossilized twist of skin.

The crunch of his steps echoed hollowly in the chamber.

Jordan followed close behind.

"You see it, too, don't you?" Ivan asked.

"Uh-huh."

As they both moved forward for a better look.

"What the hell *is* this, Delgato? Best guess?"

Ivan shrugged.

The smooth walls of the cave entranceway gradually faded from rock to . . . what? Support struts and panels and various odds and ends of what looked like metal grew out of the wall until the insides of the cave looked more like a massive machine.

Huge polyhedral shapes filled the walls, all different sizes and colors. Some connected, others standing alone; some had toothlike protrusions as if they functioned like gears while others had sides as smooth as glass.

They were of varying sizes, but all were huge

As the others joined them, everyone were perfectly quiet . . . awestruck.

And that, Ivan guessed, was a good thing.

"I was hoping you had an idea, Jordan." He turned to Rodriguez. "You ever see anything like this, Doc?"

Rodriguez shook his head, his eyes wide with wonder . . . and curiosity.

Ivan looked back at the gunner, then the rest of their crew.

"I'd say we're inside some kind of machine."

"One that no longer works?" Annie offered.

"At least it isn't working right now."

Ivan looked to the right where a trio of hexagons, glowing blue like the walls they protruded from, were locked together, engaged and ready to start turning.

"Someone throws a switch somewhere," he said, "and they'll move, and . . ."

A shudder ran though him when he suddenly pictured his brother's hand on that switch.

"Yeah," Jordan said. "And do what?"

Annie kept looking around.

Sinjira muttering, "Wow," as she recorded everything. "Place is getting freakier by the minute."

"Getting?" Ivan answered.

"What about your brother?" Jordan said.

Ivan felt better, knowing he wasn't the only one thinking of Kyros.

"This is another trap. Gotta be," Ruth said, her voice high. "We nearly got killed trying to get down here, and then—"

"He surprises us with whatever the hell this is," Ivan finished for her.

Annie turned around, looking back at the vast expanse littered with so many dead bodies.

"Maybe we'll join *them*," she said.

Jordan shook his head. "And maybe not, but"—he turned to Ivan—"I say we get out of here *pronto*."

Ivan shook his head.

"You think if Kyros set up all these bodies, he'd simply let us walk out?"

He fished his commlink from his pocket and pressed the CALL button.

"Kyros? You in here? You hear me, brother?"

Nothing.

Not even static.

Sinjira, Rodriguez, and Ruth huddled close, their eyes wide as they waited and—like Ivan—wondered from which direction the surprise would ultimately come.

Ivan smiled reassuringly at Ruth, trying to chase some of the fear from her eyes.

Again, into the commlink: "Kyros?"

Still nothing.

Annie started: "Maybe he's not—"

Before she could finish her sentence, the speaker in Ivan's hand came to life. The voice was as clear as if Kyros was standing next to them.

"I'm right here, brother. Just a little bit farther, and we'll be reunited."

Ivan hit the MUTE on the device.

"Do we trust him?" he asked.

"He's your brother," Jordan said.

"Not much fucking choice here . . ."

He restored the link: "Show yourself, Kyros. I have what you want. The data crystal."

Kyros's laugh filled the room, sounding as if it wasn't coming only from the commlink.

Ivan had the brief impression that the vibrating vines overhead were transmitting, amplifying his laugh.

Looking from face to face, bathed in the weird blue light, Ivan and the others waited to hear what was so damned funny.


"You actually think I need *you* to bring me the crystal? I could have gotten Nahara and that crystal whenever I wanted."

"He sounds sick," Annie said quietly. "Deranged."

But not quietly enough for Kyros not to hear and respond.

"Sick, Captain Scott? *Really?* Why not come up here and see for yourself?"

Then the commlink went dead.

But the laughter still filled the serpentine chamber, gradually receding.

Because now the laughter wasn't coming over the commlink.

Now, the voice was coming from somewhere ahead of them.

"It's you, Ivan. *You* who I want to see, brother." He said the last word with such disdain, such venom, that it made Ivan's skin crawl, and his hands squeezed his rifle.

He turned to the others.

"Maybe you all better stay here, and I'll go ahead—"

"No chance," Annie said at the same time Jordan said, "You forget our deal?"

Ivan looked at them, not sure he remembered any "deal."

"No hero cards." Jordan looked at the other three passengers. "And no way we're leaving them behind."

"All for one?" Ivan said.

"And one for all," Jordan responded.

"And I thought you said you didn't read."

But any amusement was quickly cut off when Kyros's voice reverberated through the cavern with metal walls.

"I'm *waiting*, brother. You are *so* close."

Ivan nodded, accepting the inevitable.

He accepted that he didn't have any more cards to play. All he had was the trust in Jordan and Annie, and the solid weight of the pulse rifle in his hands.

Then he cupped his hands to his mouth and shouted as loud as he could, "Kyros, I'm coming!"

Silence . . . except for the vines, which were still humming.

A steady chorus in the quiet chamber.

Stating the obvious, Jordan said: "Guns ready?"

And Ivan led them forward, around the wide curve of the entrance and farther into what he now thought of as "the machine."


The long, winding corridor, like an umbilical cord, opened up into an enormous arena-sized room.

Even more astounding than the size of the open space was the huge object—if, indeed, it was a single object—that it housed.

It consisted of towering stacks of the mammoth polyhedral blocks stacked side by side and atop one another. Many had sharp edges and spiky projections that resembled blue ice spears darting out in a dozen different directions.

Above it all, bizarre, intricate clockwork machinery was turning . . . thousands of Mobius strip–like shapes turning and twisting. The walls all around were arrayed with blinking and flashing lights, and moving machinery that made low, arrhythmic sounds that shook the walls and air.

"This is—" Ivan started to say, but Ruth cut him off.

"The Builders . . ." Her voice was hushed with awe, and Ivan looked at the expression of awe and reverence on her face . . . the glow in her eyes.

"I'll tell you this," Ivan said as he started moving along. "My brother isn't any Builder."

As they moved cautiously out into the wide expanse of the arena, Ivan looked up at one wall and saw an opening. And inside that gap—a stone chair, more like a throne that all but engulfed the person sprawled on it.

And behind that person, a confusing and elaborate display of machinery, and in front, a control panel floated, suspended in the air.

The man in the chair—even at this distance—easy to recognize.

*Kyros.*

With a wave, Kyros moved the control panel aside, and standing up, began to clap his hands in a slow, steady cadence that was more mocking than laudatory.

"Well done, my brother. We'll *done.*"

Ivan said nothing as he stared at his brother, but he did notice that Jordan moved a short distance to one side. *Trying to flank him. Good . . .*

"I was surprised you survived all of the little safeguards."

Ivan stopped walking, thinking his brother looked *too* relaxed.

No tension. No alarm. Not even a weapon in hand.

Ivan wasn't fooled and didn't have to remind himself of the death and destruction Kyros had unleashed on the Road stations.

*He's insane*, Ivan thought. *Don't ever forget that.*

Then, moving forward, Kyros held out his hand. "I'll relieve you of that crystal now."

"I thought you wanted *me?*"

Even at this distance, Ivan detected a tight smile.

"Oh, I *have* you. Some of our people, the old-time Runners, are still loyal to you. But when they see you, they'll think that you betrayed them"—his voice rose—"when they *understand* that you are a goddamn traitor to the cause. They will see . . ."

Kyros's body appeared to be suddenly much larger, inflating like a balloon.

"That you *betrayed* the Runners. You betrayed our cause—the cause so many of us gave our lives for, they will *know*, and they will *demand* that you pay for what you've done!"

Kyros appeared to hover like a phantom above the stone floor.

Jordan kept moving off to one side.

"Steady," Ivan whispered.

Kyros clenched his fist and pointed it directly at Ivan, but his voice became quiet . . . steady . . . even sounding reasonable.

"Give me the crystal, Ivan, and I'll let them all live."

"How can I trust you?"

"You'll have to take my word for it."

"Doesn't sound like a bargain I'm willing to make." Ivan's grip tightened on his pulse rifle, but he sensed—no, he *knew*—Kyros had to have some kind of defensive shielding.

He was brave enough in battle, but he wouldn't risk such a confrontation . . . not without protection.

"I *will* have the crystal." The high note of insanity was back. "One way or another."

Ivan inched forward, a few steps closer.

Kyros didn't react.

Ivan sensed Jordan moving farther to the right. Not wanting to betray him, Ivan didn't glance at the gunner. He knew he could trust him to size up the situation and do what he had to do.

Then more movement. Annie. Shifting to the left.

The others—Ruth, Sinjira, and Rodriguez—remained perfectly still. This was their battle, too, but what could they do, unarmed?

Then Sinjira started moving away, slowly . . . distancing herself from the other two.

Kyros glared at them, his smile broad and toadlike.

When he moved, though, he didn't bring up a weapon.

Instead, his hand brushed something on the hovering control panel. Ribbons of arcing blue light glowed above the machine.

"Why do you want the crystal?" Ivan said.

"Why?" Kyros laughed to himself.

His hand now pointing straight up. The writing blue energy, looking incredibly like shimmering water, surrounded his hand like a glove. The energy rose toward the ceiling, snapping, twisting.

A sizzling hiss filled the area.

"Because of *this*, Ivan! *This* is what you and I and all of us have always dreamed of."

Ivan looked up and said as casually as he could, "And what would that be?"

Truth was, he was both amazed and confused by the weird energy that Kyros seemed—somehow—to control.

*Or did it control him?*

But as the blue plasma continued to rise, Ivan—never taking his eyes off his brother—got a first wave of understanding.

*Intuition.*

The amazing truth of what Kyros was pointing at . . .

He held his breath as Kyros laughed softly and then spoke.

# 41

## THE ENDLESS ROAD

*"You have no idea what* I'm capable of," Kyros said.

Ivan looked up at him.

Overhead, more of those subtly waving vines.

Humming louder now, and gradually lengthening as Kyros stood beneath them. Was he also getting larger? Or was it an illusion?

He stared at his brother.

"What *is* this place, Kyros?"

Ivan was aware that Annie and Jordan had each moved even farther to the right and left.

Had Kyros noticed as well?

So far, Kyros appeared to be unaware anyone was moving.

Even when Ivan started walking up the wide, stone steps toward him. Gun in hand.

His brother took another step away from the chair and the floating console and came down a step toward him.

He nodded to the dazzling array above them.

"The *Road*, Ivan. This entire thing. Right there. It's what we always—"

He moved even closer to Ivan.

"It's what we always *dreamed* of, brother. What we *fought* and died for! The open Road. And we have it now We have a map they left behind."

"A map?"

"Here. Floating above us."

Ivan shook his head and heard someone—Sinjira, he thought—gasp.

His brother had lost his mind. Drunk with power.

What would the Runners become, with that map, with the entire universe at their control, under the leadership of Kyros?

For a moment, though, Ivan had to agree. *Yes. This* is *what we always wanted.*

The open Road.

Freedom to go anywhere in the universe.

Escaping the crushing control of the World Council. Opportunity for everyone to succeed—or fail—using their own initiative.

But Ivan had rejected that.

He had accepted the World Council's offer.

And for him, his word—to Runners, to friends, to strangers, and even to the plutocrats on the World Council—was as solid as the ground he stood on.

"They offered amnesty, Kyros," he said. "We can stop the violence. We can stop running. We can bring them peace, and we can stop being chased and hunted."

Kyros stopped moving forward. Energy streamed around him like a gigantic cloak.

"Just as I thought," he said. "A traitor and a coward! That's why I had you come here, so the Runners could see what you have become!"

Kyros swiveled his head, looking left and right, and saw—or finally acknowledged—Annie and Jordan's flanking maneuver. He smiled, unworried.

Then he glared at the passengers standing behind Ivan, at Sinjira, slowly edging closer to the console, the Road map display, floating above it like an amorphous jelly.

"These people with you . . . They're proof you work for the World Council." His eyes flashed as he regarded Ivan. "You're a traitor. And you more than anyone else know what we do with traitors!"

*He's insane*, Ivan thought.

Whatever humanity Kyros might have had was gone. Something had happened. Something right here, in this place, with this machine.

But the window for doing something about it had long since closed, Ivan realized.

Kyros clearly had no interest in any amnesty or anyone's survival but his own.

"I'll take the data crystal now," Kyros said.

*Of course.*

The alien device that allowed new, undiscovered sections of the Star

Road to be accessed and traveled—a map of new Star Roads—would be useless without the full Star Road operating system.

Many, probably most people on Earth, if they thought about it, believed that the Road Authority had already discovered the full extent of the Star Road system.

The Seekers, like Ruth, were an embarrassment to sane society, asking their deep questions and looking for the original Star Road Builders.

This crystal, with its alien control system, proved otherwise.

To Kyros, it would bring immense, even dangerous power. The World Council would be weakened if not utterly destroyed.

And in its place?

Ivan knew he couldn't let that happen.

He glanced at Jordan, hoping the gunner knew what he was thinking.

He had to hope that Jordan was ready to move.

In a split second.

Kyros raised his hands above his head, and everything changed.


The gentle humming of the vines shifted to a higher pitch, like vibrating crystal, and then turned into screeching, mewling sounds as if suddenly awakened.

And while Ivan watched—helplessly—a single vine shot down, elongating, and, before he could react, wrapped around Ruth Corso's throat and yanked up.

She had to stand on the tips of her toes and even then was barely able to keep the strangling pressure of the vine from hanging her.

She opened her mouth, her eyes bugging out, as she tried to speak.

She could breathe, but only coughlike gasps emerged from her mouth.

"Let her go, Kyros!"

"I will—for the data crystal," he said.

Ivan looked at Ruth, then the others.

"And drop the gun, brother."

Ivan hesitated and then, slowly, placed it on the ground before him.

"That's better. Now . . ."

Sinjira stood below the floating console, looking all around it, down to the machine.

Close to Kyros. But he seemed to register that she was no threat.

Ivan wanted to tell her to get back, but he knew there was no telling her what to do.

"Let her go, Kyros, and I'll—"

Kyros shook his head. "Do we have to make this so unpleasant?" He smiled. "Give me the data crystal now, and I'll let her go. What is she to you, Ivan?" He laughed. "I thought you never had time for *friends*."

"Fuck you—"

"Ivan!" Annie shouted from his left. "Don't trust him. He'll—"

Ivan shot her a look that silenced her.

He was hoping she, like Jordan, could tell what he was thinking, what he was planning.

*Hang in there with me, Annie. Let's play this out so no one gets hurt.*

Ragged gulps were coming from Ruth as the vine pulled tighter, lifting her off her feet. She grabbed the vine, trying to pull it away and ease the pressure.

"She won't last long," Kyros said. "These nodules are lined on the inside with an array of needle-sharp spikes. Any second now, they're going to pierce her throat and head." He paused and then added, "It won't be pretty."

Another choking sound from Ruth.

A long pause, and then—finally—Ivan said, "All right. You win."

"I always do, brother."

Ivan started boldly up the steps, moving closer to Kyros. At the same time, he dug into his pocket, reaching for the data crystal Annie had given him.

He pulled it out slowly, making sure Kyros didn't think he might have a weapon, other than his pulse rifle on the ground behind him.

"Here it is." He held his hand out. "Now let her go."

Reaching down to his side, Kyros pulled out a gun and waved it back and forth, sweeping from Annie on one side to Jordan on the other.

"All of you. Drop your weapons," Kyros said, still waving the pistol from side to side as if drunk.

*I'm missing something here*, Ivan thought.

Kyros reached out and grabbed not the data crystal, but Ivan. He snagged his jacket and yanked him close, placing the barrel of his own gun against the side of Ivan's head.

With his other hand, he reached down to Ivan's hand holding the crystal.

A whisper into Ivan's ear.

The moment primal.

"Brother. You are such a disappointment."

Kyros yanked away the data crystal.

The barrel pressed against Ivan's temple so hard it hurt. Spikes of light and pain flashed behind his eyes.

"Let her go now, Kyros. I expect you to keep your word."

*Runners kept their word.*

Ivan had to hope *that* truth still held.

With the cold metal at his temple, he turned his head enough to see the vine slither off and away from Ruth.

She dropped to her knees, gasping and gagging. Pink-tinged spittle ran from her mouth to the stone floor.

Rodriguez, who until now had been frozen, a stone statue near the entrance to this giant arena, came quickly over to Ruth to help her.

Ivan rolled his eyes to one side, looking at Jordan.

His gun was now tilted at a 45-degree angle.

Their eyes locked.

Ivan thought: *I've grown to trust that guy, and they owe me their lives.*

*And now Jordan has a chance to prove himself.*

Kyros extended his arm and held the crystal out, admiring it, letting its facets catch and reflect the blue light.

Dragging Ivan with him, he moved back to the floating console and reached out toward a circular metal plate.

As soon as the crystal came into contact, the machine started scanning it. The Star Road map above began to twist, turn . . . reacting to the new data.

The massive polyhedral shapes that surrounded them on the walls began to vibrate and move.

*It's now or never,* Ivan thought.

He threw his weight to the right. The gun barrel slipped away from his head. He knew Kyros would move fast. He might be insane, but he also was as well-trained as Ivan.

But now was his best—and only—chance.

He clenched his fist tight and he swung with every ounce of strength he had.

The instant the blow connected, Ivan knew something was wrong.

It wasn't like punching air, but there was so little resistance that Ivan's body swung around . . . more than he had expected. The roundhouse kick he had intended to follow up with turned into a lurching step to regain his balance. The momentum almost brought him down.

And before he could react, a thunderous concussion slammed into the side of his head like a clap of thunder.

Ivan rocked back on his heels as a spray of white lights shot across his vision. Through his pain and confusion, a deep, crazed laugh filled the sudden vacuum.

"Nice try, brother," Kyros said. "I'm happy to see that you haven't gone totally soft."

Ivan's ears were ringing. As he twisted around and reached for his brother's throat, it felt as if he was fighting with an illusion, a hallucination.

The dark form in front of him swelled and roiled like a rapidly descending storm cloud.

*Another hit like that, and I'm done,* Ivan thought as he shook his head, struggling to clear it.

*No doubt about it.*

*One shot left . . .*

No panic . . . just a cold, hard assessment of where he was and what was happening.

But in a flash, he saw another opening.

Whether on purpose or by mistake, Kyros had dropped his left shoulder, lowering his guard.

And Ivan struck hard, his clenched right fist striking fast, catching Kyros on the edge of the jaw.

Although it wasn't much—it didn't feel like punching a person—it had an effect.

A stunned look of surprise crossed Kyros's face, and he staggered back. And fell.

Now reflexes took over, and Ivan lowered his head and slammed his shoulder into his brother's chest. They went down together.

*Like brothers should,* Ivan thought.

And Ivan hoped that—just like when they were kids—he could always beat his brother in a fistfight.

Grunting like an animal, he piled his weight onto Kyros to bring him down. But even as he did, he knew something was wrong.

There was no *substance* beneath him.

Straddling his brother's chest, Ivan cocked his fist back for another punch to Kyros's face, but he hesitated when he saw his brother looking up at him.

The weird smile on his face—placid, unconcerned—was unnerving . . . like this was all a game.

"You can't beat me, Ivan," he said. "It's not like when we were children."

*Can he read my mind?* Ivan thought.

Ivan brought his fist down hard, but before it connected, something shifted beneath him.

And then—somehow—Kyros was . . . *gone.*

Ivan couldn't check his punch, and his fist skinned against the hard, bare rock floor of the chamber.

He cried out with pain even as he raised his head and saw Kyros looming over him. A commanding smile was still plastered on Kyros's face as he raised his pistol and calmly aimed it at Ivan.

"It's all over," he said. His eyes seemed to glow with hatred. "You lost, brother."

Ivan got onto his hands and knees, shook his head as he began to stand up, but then, from far off—faintly—he heard someone.

*Is that Jordan?*

"Stay down!"

*He must have a shot,* was Ivan's one, clear thought as he dropped to the floor.

And Jordan took it.

He fired.

Once.

The blast caught Kyros on the shoulder, spinning him around. The gun fell from his hand. He staggered backward, slamming against the floating console.

"Sinjira!" Annie screamed.

The girl was apparently oblivious to what was happening around her. She was standing so close to the floating console . . . to Kyros.

Jordan fired again, although Ivan didn't think it was necessary.

The first shot had been perfect. It should have blown a hole in Kyros's chest.

Instead—

*Nothing.*

Kyros appeared slightly stunned but perfectly unharmed. No gaping wound.

As he got to his feet, Ivan wondered if Kyros was even there at all.

*This has gotta be an illusion . . . a holographic projection.*

But then Kyros spoke as Ivan backed up and scooped his own gun off the floor. Ivan knew holograms couldn't grab people and hold them.

"The tendrils," Kyros said. "The traps, the Star Road above—that's not all this machine can do. Not by a long shot."

Kyros spread his arms out wide, a crazed Christ-like gesture, as if he was embracing—or blessing—everything this place was.

Annie and Jordan moved closer to Ivan, standing with him, shoulder to shoulder now.

They all fired—

To no effect.

Sinjira started backing away, staggering. An expression of fear or pure terror and amazement on her face.

But she didn't move fast enough, and they all got to see exactly what this machine could do.

# 42

## NO ESCAPE

*The giant polyhedral cogs on* the walls began to turn one way, then the other, as if unlocking a combination to the inner workings of the machine.

The noise was deafening.

Annie turned to Ivan, shouting, "We have to get the *hell* out of here! Now!"

Ivan looked at Sinjira backing away but moving too slowly, back from the machine she had been looking at with such intensity.

And Kyros stood there, a man who should have been blown to pieces, unharmed, his eyes closed, his arms still outstretched.

While from the back of the machine, a filmy cloud arose and swirled around the machine, dancing, circling, engulfing Kyros.

Ivan—totally confused by what he saw happening to his brother.

Dark spots appeared on his flesh as the machine-made cloud twisted and writhed around him.

The small dots crawled and spread all over his body, some vanishing under the skin like fading tattoos while others emerged on his face, neck, and arms . . . popping up from the skin in rising bumps and ridges.

Only one image came to mind . . . one slim point of reference.

*Road Bugs.*

The way *they* moved, the machine-meets-organism way the Road Bugs scurried, but here they were moving over a human body instead of a machinery-littered section of the Star Road.

Sinjira finally snapped to and started running now, but she was knocked down by the rapidly expanding outer edge of the cyclonic cloud.

Knocked down, but crawling, she then scrambled back to her feet.

"Ivan," Annie said. The urgency in her voice was chilling.

Jordan quiet . . . looking . . . taking it all in.

But then Jordan went over to Sinjira, coming close to the cloud himself. He reached out, grabbing the Chippie's hand, and she staggered forward as if she had been suddenly propelled by the front end of a fast-moving truck.

"Now!" Jordan shouted.

Rodriguez was already running out, away from this madhouse with Ruth, supporting her as she still gasped to catch her breath.

Ivan started backing away as Jordan and Sinjira came up next to him. He aimed his pulse rifle.

Directly at his brother's head.

And then he started firing, at Kyros, at the cloud, blast after ineffective blast.

A head shot—amazingly—seemed to turn his brother's face into an ashen stump, but only for an instant.

In seconds, his face reappeared, smiling insanely.

With each shot, a hole would appear for a moment in the swirling cloud. Then swarms of the tiny black dots gushed out of it, and the holes would vanish.

As the shimmering storm cloud swirled even more wildly around Kyros, his face twisting, reacting to the shots for a moment, and then—as if waking from a dream—his body, maybe not his body anymore, effortlessly repaired itself.

With Annie in the lead and the others running away as fast as they could, Ivan kept firing his useless blasts, and then his brother's eyes locked on him.

This creature before him—who Ivan knew was no longer his brother—started walking slowly toward them.

The black storm cloud swirled around him, growing larger and wilder with each step.

He had said: "That's not all this machine can do," Ivan remembered.

Ivan ran, his arms pumping hard. His single, clear thought was that they'd be lucky to escape alive.


Ivan joined Jordan and Sinjira. She was hurt, but he couldn't see where. Maybe contact with that energy cloud had done something to her nervous system.

No matter what, she was seriously slowing them down.

They stopped, and lowered Sinjira to the ground as gently as they could.

"What's wrong?" Ivan said.

Jordan held her hand. Squeezed it.

But when Sinjira turned, her eyes were narrowed, like those of a little girl who'd gotten hurt playing in the park.

She looked sad . . . frightened . . . desperate.

She held out her other arm, and Ivan saw flecks of shimmering light that looked like minute flakes of metal covering her forearm.

And they were spreading . . .

*Like a frost, an icy morning leaving a crystalline sheen on a window, the first signs of a brutal winter to come.*

Ivan looked from her eyes to Jordan and to the arm again.

The growth—whatever it was—was slowly spreading.

"Jordan," Ivan said.

Both of them saw the obvious.

Jordan pulled out his handgun as this insane moment played out and, with his other hand, gave Sinjira's untainted hand a tight squeeze.

He leaned forward to her and whispered something to her tenderly. Jordan, the man who said little or nothing and never betrayed emotion.

Sinjira heard and nodded, biting her lower lip to keep from crying out.

"Is the pain bad?" Jordan asked softly.

She grimaced and nodded. Her eyes were as filmed as the cloud created by the machine.

Then Jordan positioned the handgun close to the infected arm, above the elbow where the skin was untouched so far.

And he pulled the trigger.

The shiny, silvery flakes swarming over Sinjira's lower arm blew away. Blood sprayed out of the wound.

Ivan quickly pulled off his jacket.

Jordan had dropped his gun.

Together they each took an end of the jacket and wrapped it tightly around the bloody stump.

Rodriguez had stopped running, Ruth was leaning against him, gasping.

Sinjira screamed, her feet kicking wildly.

Then Rodriguez said, in a cold, clinical voice, "These look like nanotrites. But if they are, they're way beyond anything we've developed."

"You've seen these?"

"Not exactly. They appear to be more alive than mere machine, but—"

Ivan looked at him blankly.

The scientist shaking, his face bathed in sweat as whatever he was saying faded away, the possible scientific explanation incomprehensible to Ivan.

*Sounds more like magic than science,* he thought, *but at a certain level, how can anyone tell them apart?*

He helped Jordan pull the makeshift tourniquet tighter.

Then Jordan scooped Sinjira up in his arms, settled her, and was ready to move.

As they started walking, Rodriguez was still near-babbling.

"Like nano-machines, those things on her. But I have no idea what that thing surrounding your brother was. It's like nothing, nothing I've ever—"

Rodriguez looked at Ruth, clearly approaching full hysteria.

"Okay, Doc. Let's just calm down and get the hell out of here. All right? We'll talk later."

With a quick nod, Rodriguez stopped jabbering.

Ivan led the way, getting them to move as fast as they could, now reaching the place where the legion of dead bodies were sprawled on the floor. The cave exit was still a long way off.

Then he heard a voice, bellowing from behind them, echoing and amplified in the vast reaches of the cavern.

Kyros.

"There's no escape, Ivan!"

*Why not?* Ivan wondered.

They could work their way through the traps, now that they knew how they worked, so why *couldn't* they get away from Kyros, who didn't even appear to be hurrying to catch up with them?

*Why such confidence? It was as if he knew a secret . . . had another surprise in store for them.*

Then Ivan heard a sound.

The vines above them were stirring.

The low, throbbing hum quickly blended into a high-pitched buzz. The gentle swaying of the vines quickly changed into the wild lashing of loose lines . . . like an old-time sailing ship's rigging, whipping around in a storm.

They reached down . . . down to the vast field littered with the dead bodies locked in their eternal struggle.

Or so one would have thought.

Ivan looked up ahead, then back the way they had come, and then ahead again.

The way out was still so far away.

*"No escape . . ."*

And then, to his horror, Ivan saw what Kyros meant.

# 43

## THEY RISE

*Ivan's first thought was that* the vines lashing overhead were about to reach down and attack them, wrap around them, and kill them.

But that wasn't it at all.

As the vines swayed and snapped back and forth, they shot down spiky protrusions on long threads that emerged from inside the stalks.

But instead of attacking them, the thorns broke loose and showered down onto the field of corpses on this silent alien battleground.

They rained down onto the species, known and unrecognizable.

Ivan and his crew were moving as fast as they could, but Sinjira kept slowing Jordan down as they dodged through the spiky thorns that continued to fall down onto the corpses.

And as the thorns fell, they erupted like thousands of metallic larval sacs bursting open while a dark ooze spilled out, filling the room with a nauseating smell.

The ooze looked like the same miniscule black nano-machines that had swept over and around Kyros.

Within seconds, they covered the alien bodies, seeping into the desiccated, fossilized skin and rotting innards, painting the exposed organs and bones.

And then the bodies began to move, stirring, at first like dry leaves being swept up by a powerful wind.

"Come on! Keep moving!" Ivan said, but he realized his voice had been too low; the horror of what he was seeing so immense.

So now he shouted, his yell filling the cavern.

"Keep! Moving!"

But what could they do with Jordan, Sinjira, even Ruth stumbling and falling as they ran?

Annie turned and looked back at them as she ran, seeing the same horror show unfolding in the cavern.

The bodies were no longer dry leaves vibrating in an icy autumn wind . . .

Now, they were *rising*, pulling up a knee here, raising an arm or a head there . . . even, *Christ*, when half the skull was missing or had a massive hole in it from whatever had destroyed the once-living brain.

These dead beings were moving—unnaturally alive—whether by science or magic, it didn't matter.

A dozen or more staggered to their feet as more and more spiky thorns fell all around, each hit causing another body to be quickly covered by the blackish "nano-trites" that animated them.

At the far end of the cavern, Ivan saw his brother, still surrounded by the luminescent cloud.

He strode toward them with a slow, steady pace, following in the wake of this unnatural army. He was heading straight toward Ivan, relentlessly.

*Kyros more alien, more machine now than human.*

And he was the master, the controller of all of this.

Looking ahead, he saw Jordan stop and put Sinjira down for a moment.

Without missing a beat, Jordan slung his gun over his shoulder so he could still hold it and shoot when he had to.

Once again, he picked up Sinjira, scooping her up and carrying her like a baby as he tried to pick up his pace to elude this undead army.

By now, scores if not hundreds of them were rising up, but Ivan wasn't about to stand there and count them.

Whatever their conflicts with one another had been before, they were gone now . . . vanished as they moved toward Ivan, Annie, Jordan, Rodriguez, and Ruth.

Ruth walked beside Jordan, holding Sinjira's dangling hand.

Ivan thought: *As slow as they move now . . . once we hit the traps, they'll catch us.*

He came up beside Jordan, now also flanked by Annie.

And for a few stomach-turning seconds, amid the rising of corpses, no one said anything.

•   •   •

"Run," Ivan finally said, his voice hard with command. "As best you can!"

And then he turned and started firing, spraying massive pulse blasts at this army of the alien undead.

Some shots blew off what remained of heads and other body parts. Some shots seared into their chests and abdomens and blasted off arms and leg.

It made no difference.

They simply continued moving forward, crawling and writhing on the ground, making better progress than they did walking upright.

If a body was split in two, both halves continued their grim movement forward.

"I hate to say it, but it looks fucking hopeless," Ivan said.

Which is when Sinjira opened her pain-glazed eyes. Mere slits. Hazy, as if she had been sleeping or was drugged.

She raised her gaze to a dark corner of the cavern—a narrow opening that led off to one side, seemingly back into the mountain itself.

"That way," she said, her voice no more than a croak.

Jordan, struggling to carry her, ignored what she said.

But Ivan heard the urgency in her voice and said, "What do you mean?"

He looked at Ruth, who was also following the conversation. They were approaching the bottom of the mathematical steps, which they could navigate, now knowing the secret, assuming the pattern hadn't changed.

But they were moving so slowly, the undead army would be all over them, tearing at them before they were halfway up.

And would they infect them with the same nano-machines, turning them into . . . who knew what?

*Maybe,* Ivan thought, *that's when we turn against each other like they did, in a mad and ultimately futile struggle to survive. Even death wouldn't be a release.*

"Trust me," Sinjira said. "They're already . . . inside me. I *know.* Go *that* way."

Jordan was simply soldiering on, carrying Sinjira and intent on only one thing—getting out of this cave.

Ivan tapped him on the shoulder.

"Jordan."

Ruth was still looking at him, fear written all over her face, but also something else . . . Determination.

Then louder: "Jordan. *Stop!* She said—"

Sinjira could barely raise her head.

"I can *feel* another way out. A hidden passage. Over there."

Another slight nod.

"Our only chance, gunner," Ivan said.

Jordan was clearly torn. For him, forward was the only option. Always. Not back, and certainly not *deeper* into the darkness.

"I—"

Sinjira was barely able to speak.

"I can *feel* it."

Then a nod, as the gunner turned.

Annie looked to Rodriguez, who had run ahead, toward the stairs, no doubt thinking if he was out front, he'd be safe.

Maybe he'd be the only *one* they *wouldn't* get.

"Rodriguez, no. This way!" Ivan shouted, but Rodriguez froze.

The army of undead was only meters away.

Their animated body parts and old bones made a clunky carousel of sound, and the stench in the air was nauseating.

Rodriguez didn't move.

*His choice*, Ivan thought.

But then, finally Rodriguez took a step back toward them.

Jordan was already clambering up to the side toward the dark opening Sinjira had indicated.

Except as Ivan followed, with Annie a few paces behind, he had to wonder at her words. *"They're already inside me."*

*The nano-machines?*

Could they also lead her in the wrong direction?

Could what they were about to do actually seal their fate by luring them into a dead end where there was only one way this battle could end?

*We're about to find out*, Ivan thought, resigned.

Jordan and Sinjira disappeared into the narrow opening.

Ivan looked at Ruth, Annie, and Rodriguez.

His expression said it all: *It's anybody's guess.*

And they followed them into the darkness.

# 44

## A HUMAN SACRIFICE

*Ivan looked back at the* others following him into the tunnel, scrambling in the dark. The way ahead sloped steeply upward, the path littered with massive boulders with sharp jagged edges. Only weak flecks of the blue light here.

Just enough light so they could see the handholds . . . and where to step.

*This could be a way out,* he thought, *but it feels like a trap.*

Jordan, laboring with Sinjira in his arms, still turned and tried to get off a few blasts, but her dead weight was having an impact on him. Wearing him down.

And the way everyone clustered together as they moved as fast as they could through the tunnel made getting clear shots at the advancing horde almost impossible.

They needed time to regroup.

Ivan could see only one thing to do as the army of undead followed them.

"Jordan—"

The gunner looked at him.

"Give me two grenades."

Jordan smiled thinly.

"Hero time?"

Ivan said the next words as if it was so clear, so obvious.

"If we don't stop them here, we're all dead."

Jordan let Sinjira slip down to the ground. She looked totally exhausted, her face marked with the intense pain.

"My grenades," Jordan said, "my job."

"We don't have time to discuss this."

Annie joined them but remained silent, other than breathing hard, letting the two of them argue over who was about to die.

Then a small voice from the ground spoke.

"Jordan . . ."

Stopping them cold.

Sinjira held up the stump of her arm.

Even in the dim light, they all could see the shiny flakes of the nanomachines spreading past the tourniquet and up to her shoulder.


No one said a word.

The next voice was hers.

"Doc," she said. "Hit me with a stim."

Rodriguez fumbled in his backpack, but Jordan got between them.

"There's no way in hell you're going to—"

"Hit me . . . with . . . a *god . . . damn . . . stim!*"

By this time, Rodriguez had fished a small packet from his backpack.

He looked from Annie to Ivan to Jordan and then to Sinjira. Her face was set in a rictus of pain.

"Do it!" she said between clenched teeth.

Ivan watched Rodriguez rip the package open and take out a needle.

Annie looked down the slope and said, "They're almost here. We have to—"

Staring at Rodriguez, Ivan nodded, and Jordan, seething with fury, stepped aside.

Rodriguez leaned down and prepared to inject Sinjira in her good arm, but with a heavy effort, she shook her head and then tilted it to one side, exposing her neck.

A bulging vein caught the scant light.

"Here," she said. "It'll hit quicker."

A moment's hesitation.

"Just fucking *do* it!"

Then Rodriguez touched the vein with the tip of the needle. As everyone watched, the auto-plunger shot the stimulant into her bloodstream.

All the while, Jordan was shaking his head.

His eyes glazed.

Just then, the first of the shambling army of zombies turned the corner and witnessed a scene that would have appeared—if they had any thoughts at all—to be the group of humans waiting to die.

Ivan watched Annie move closer to the undead, mowing down the first row, sending their revived body parts flying.

Thankfully at this range and when totally shattered by the pulse blasts those body parts stopped moving.

*Maybe they have to be close to those vines*, he thought.

A faint trace of hope as he turned to Sinjira who—amazingly—was standing up.

She looked at Ivan and Jordan, then at her arm and the discoloration creeping up past her shoulder now.

"Give me the grenades," she said to Jordan.

He shook his head.

"Hell no. You'll die."

Ivan had figured out something that must not have dawned on Jordan yet.

Sinjira knew it was already too late.

She pulled the chip from the node in her head, the stim giving her the strength to stand, to move.

To Ivan: "Take this. I got it all."

Annie, down below, shouted, "There's more coming!"

"*All* of it?" Ivan said, astounded. Did she mean—?

Sinjira struggled to talk. She probably had only seconds left of coherent conversation, but it was clear what she was thinking.

"When it was floating overhead," she said. "I recorded the Star Road Map. It's all there."

She pressed the chip into Ivan's hand, his fingers touching hers in the exchange. They were ice-cold.

To Jordan, she said, "I'm already dead. The ultimate trip, they say, right? That's why they save it for last."

"You don't have to do this," Jordan said, his voice cracking. "We can get you to the medical facility—"

"*Stop* it. You're only making this harder for me." She swayed on her feet, struggling to stand. "Let me stop them. Let me give you a chance."

And Ivan saw in Jordan's eyes that he—Jordan—finally accepted her logic.

Annie's pulse blasts were deafening in the narrow tunnel.

Jordan handed the two grenades to Sinjira.

She smiled and then, leaning forward, kissed him on the mouth.

"Y'know . . . we could have made some interesting chips together."

The she turned to Ivan and said, "Now get everyone the hell out of here. Just follow this tunnel. Trust me. It'll get you out of here."

Ivan nodded.

He yelled down to Annie, who was kneeling and ready for the next wave of undead to charge them.

*"Annie!"*

As Annie scrambled back, Sinjira, looking unsteady on her feet, started walking down to meet the army streaming toward them. Kyros, hanging in the back, was shouting commands, urging them on.

Ivan started up the incline as fast as he could go. Jordan, unencumbered by Sinjira, was guarding the rear, making sure Annie made it up the slope.

Annie was a short distance behind him. Jordan waved her to hurry, shouting, "Go! Get the hell out of here!"

Ruth helped Rodriguez keep up with the retreat.

The Seeker showing that she had a level of strength maybe she didn't even realize until now.

More twists and turns, more climbing, making their way as fast as they could through the narrow tunnel until up ahead, Ivan saw a faint trace of light—daylight. It *had* to be an opening.

*Nearly there . . . Hope.*

And then—as if to remind everyone of the price they were paying—an orange flash lit up the tunnel behind them, followed by the concussive blast of a thermite grenade.

*Sinjira*, Jordan thought, genuinely pained by the thought of her sacrifice.

They kept running, the ground leveling out now . . . the opening . . . the cave mouth of the hidden entrance.

But Ivan tensed and looked back the way they had come, waiting to see and hear the second blast.

And then it came—flashing and roaring—too close.

Rocks and dirt fell from the ceiling, and a wave of searing heat rolled over them, charring their eyes and lungs.

For an instant, the explosive cloud filled the cave, obliterating the walls and the entrance.

Ivan was sure that the second blast was going to bring the entire mountain down on them.

They all ran as a deep-throated rumble of shifting stone and earth filled the cave.

As the smoke cleared, Ivan saw only a few more meters ahead the odd glow of the sun beaming down on the mountain's side.

All of them were coughing, their ears ringing. They waved away the swirling dust as best they could and staggered out into the open as a dense cloud of dust belched from inside the mountain.

Jordan—the last to leave.

He held his pulse rifle at the ready, but there was no need. The ceiling of the cave had come down, sealing off Kyros and his undead army, at least for now.

Ivan stood and watched with the others as Jordan finally turned and walked away.

Ivan waited, looking at Jordan, not wanting to break the silence.

Finally: "That was a brave thing she did."

"She saved our lives," Ruth said.

Jordan looked around at all of them, his mouth a thin line on his dirt-smeared face.

"That's the thing about people," Jordan finally said. "You just never know."

Then Ivan, with Jordan at his side, went back to the cave mouth to make sure it was sealed.

"Nothing's getting through that," Ivan said.

Jordan was silent as he studied the wall of rock.

"She brought the whole damn thing down."

"On all of them, even my brother."

Jordan kept staring at the opening and then added, "And that fucking machine, whatever the hell it was."

The gunner turned and walked away, and when he came abreast of him, Ivan said, "You think so? You think it's all sealed?"

"No way to know for sure."

*Maybe it was over.*

*But being absolutely sure?*

*Not possible.*

Ivan shrugged.

And he saw Jordan glance at Ruth, his face lined with worry.

*So what is it between the two of them?*

Then Jordan walked over to Ruth. He put his hand on her shoulder. She patted it.

*Yeah,* Ivan thought. *It makes total sense that they know each other . . . that they had a relationship that still might not be over.*

And then one last thought: *We're all done here.*

He turned and walked away.


The cave had let them out to a spot high above what had once been a miners' camp.

Ivan looked down the forested slope at the now-empty camp, then back at the cave opening.

He tried to ignore Ruth as she walked away from Jordan and approached him.

"Think there might still be some explosives down there?" he asked Annie, who was walking a few paces behind him.

"If not," she said, "I'm sure Jordan wouldn't mind a little target practice if we bring the SRV around this side of the mountain."

Jordan stopped beside them and also looked down at the camp.

"Miners. Tunnels. Gotta be explosives, right?"

"One would guess," Ivan said as he started down a narrow, winding path to the camp while he shouted back to Annie.

"Lead the others back to the SRV. Jordan and I can handle this."

They got to the camp and looked around. One rickety shed contained several crates of explosives, all powerful timed devices.

Jordan opened a crate.

"How many?"

Ivan stared at the neat line of explosives.

"I think one box should do it."

Ivan grabbed one end of a box, and Jordan the other.

It took some effort to go back up the steep incline, but they finally arrived at the cave opening.

Chalky dust still swirled in the air like a smoke haze.

"Explosives aren't exactly my area of expertise," Ivan said.

"Me, either. But I'm guessing we can't go wrong filling the mouth of the cave with them, right?"

"As long as we give ourselves enough time to get away."

They set the box down on the ledge outside the cave mouth.

Ivan took a few of the explosive devices, studied them for a few seconds, and then walked as far as he could into the cave opening.

Sinjira's sacrifice may have stopped the undead army, but this would be an added guarantee.

Now, with Jordan on one side, and him on the other, they lined the mouth of the cave with a dozen explosives.

"Set 'em for ten minutes?" Jordan asked.

"Your guess is as good as mine," Ivan said.

*Should be enough time.*

He entered the time on the digital display of each explosive. Then hit the ignition button.

Ivan looked at Jordan, who had finished arming his set of explosives at the same time he had.

He remembered when he and Kyros were little kids, messing around with firecrackers on the Fourth of July, exploding neighbors' garbage cans and mailboxes.

*A world away.*

They nodded to each other and then turned and started running down the mountain trail, heading as fast as they could away from the cave.

As he ran, Ivan wondered if—even now—they would make it past the miners' camp and back to the SRV.

By the time the ground leveled out and the trail was wider and more clearly defined, they broke into a desperate run.

Ivan laughed as he ran, and even Jordan appeared to be enjoying himself.

In the distance, they could see the SRV parked in the glaring light of the sun.

And then the ground began to shake, throwing Ivan and Jordan off balance. They both fell, sprawling in the brush that lined the trail. And the mountain towering above them trembled and then roared as the explosives went off in a rapid series.

They might not be at a safe distance yet, but both of them stayed where they were on the ground and watched the display.

The mountain erupted in a fiery display that sent a roiling cloud of dust and huge slabs of rock into the air and then tumbling down the mountainside. A few began a crazy slide to the ground below, plowing into the trees, leveling them along with the deserted miners' camp.

*Was the passageway sealed now?*

*Were all the horrors and mysteries inside locked away forever?*

No way to know.

*We just have to hope,* Ivan thought.

With the SRV in sight, he and Jordan got up, brushed themselves off, and started down the trail, both of them the silent . . . both of them knowing this still wasn't over.

# 45

## NAHARA

*Ivan entered the cabin of* the SRV to see everyone else seated, looking exhausted and tense.

Jordan entered behind him and stopped in the doorway, leaning an arm on the frame and panting with exhaustion.

At the rear of the vehicle, Nahara was holding a gun, which was aimed directly at Annie's head.

Jordan looked up, saw what was happening, and started to move. Raised his rifle.

"Easy there, gunner," Nahara said. "I wouldn't want to hurt anyone because you go and do something stupid."

"Looks like you already have," Jordan said as he lowered his rifle.

"Good. Now just . . . put your weapons on the floor. Your pistols, too, Delgato."

Ivan gently laid his rifle down, the stock positioned so he could grab it easily if he got the chance.

Did Nahara know that he had a handgun stuck under his belt at the back?

"How did you—?"

"Get free of the neuro-collar? Turns out one of your Runner friends came by to check things out. Figured that any friend of Kyros was a friend of his."

Ivan noticed that Nahara was still wearing the leg shackles.

•   •   •

When they were steps away from the SRV, Ivan thought, *There are things we have to deal with.*

*The Runners were no doubt waiting to see what their leader would command them to do now.*

When that was done, Ivan could be free, especially now that he was sure there was most definitely something between Ruth and Jordan.

And the right thing for him to do was to walk away.

He was good at that.

*Being alone. The way things should be.*

*And free. What would he do with all that freedom?*

For now he didn't have a clue.

"Didn't have the key for these, though." Nahara's stare was icy. "I assume one of you does? My guess would be our captain."

Ivan shrugged.

"So whoever has the key, come over here and undo the shackles. Oh, and the data crystal, too."

Ivan shook his head. Annie and the others all had their eyes on him. They looked scared, but Ivan was sure Jordan would back his play . . . whatever it was.

"You really have it in you to kill innocent people?"

*"Now!"* Nahara shouted, his voice more of a bark. "Someone give me the damn *key*!"

Ivan started to dig in his right pocket, pretending to fetch it.

"Nice and slow," Nahara said. "No tricks. No surprises. There's no telling what a mistaken move might trigger."

"Right," Ivan said. "Got it. Nice and slow . . ."

A quick glance at Jordan.

Both of them probably thinking the same thing.

*What was the way out of this?*

What would Nahara do once he learned what had happened to Kyros?

Slowly, Ivan slipped his hand in and pulled out the key to the ankle chains.

"Good. Now, walk up here and hand it to me nice and gentle."

Ivan took a quick breath. If there was going to be an opportunity, it would be coming soon.

But first—

"You can give it up, Nahara," Ivan said. "Kyros is dead . . . buried under that mountain. Your deal, whatever it was, is off."

"Oh? I should give up?" A laugh, low and hollow. "And what do I look forward to? A life on a prison planet? Some dismal dark rock?" He shook his head. "No, I don't think so."

"You could beg for clemency."

"I don't beg!"

Ivan kept moving forward slowly while engaging Nahara.

"Do you really think I'd get it? Stealing the Star Road OS?" Nahara shook his head. "I'm not stupid."

*But you are distracted,* Ivan thought.

Time to turn up the agitation a notch.

Ivan stopped, paces away.

"The data crystal. That's gone, too," he said. "It's buried up there along with my brother."

Nahara's face went pale, his eyes narrowing. Ivan knew that chip would have been his bargaining chip, something he could have used anywhere in the universe.

Now—without it—what did he have?

"You're lying."

Ivan shook his head and held his hands up like he was surrendering.

"I wish I was," he said. He glanced at the others. "Ask anyone. It's gone. Like it never existed."

Nahara's eyes darted wildly from side to side.

A rat trying to chew a new escape hole.

A way out.

Ivan gave the key a little toss in the air and caught it in the palm of his hand.

"So, you can have this for all the good it'll do."

But instead of handing the key to Nahara, he threw it to him. Instinctively Nahara's free hand flew out to catch it, and—

Jordan moved.

Ivan leaped forward to tackle Nahara, but the man stepped back, catching onto the game, stumbling backward.

Then, seeing Jordan reaching for his rifle, Nahara fired.

Jordan tried to dodge to the side, but the blast caught him in the shoulder, sending him spinning around to drop on the floor.

Ivan moved fast, digging around his back and pulling out his handgun as Nahara moved to aim his own pistol at him.

A race to see whose barrel would be on target first.

But Ivan moved smoothly, and his handgun came up while Nahara was still trying to get a shot off.

"Should have taken the deal," Ivan said as he fired.

The shot hit Nahara in the throat, throwing his head back in a shower of blood and shattered bone. His eyes went wide, as if surprised as they bulged out of his head.

Nahara never got his second shot off.

Eyes still wide, he looked up at Ivan, leaning over him, and tried to say something. But nothing would come out of his ruined throat.

His plans for incredible wealth and unimagined freedom ended in a widening pool of his own blood.

As if preserving the solemnity of the moment, no one moved or said a word for several seconds.

Then, the first sound.

Ruth sobbing.

Annie calling Jordan's name, hurrying to tend to his wound.

Rodriguez glued to his seat as Ivan got up and turned around.

It felt like it was over.

Whatever this journey had been about, it had—finally—come to an end. There was just one more loose end to tie up—the Runners.

He stared blankly at Ruth, sobbing, tears streaming down her face as she leaned over Jordan.

*She may be out of my life,* Ivan thought bitterly, *but one more thing—perhaps the most important of all—is still ahead.*

# 46

## DEPARTURES

"*Is this what you want?*" Ivan shouted.

He stood on a wooden platform and stared out at the several dozens of faces that looked up to him.

Torchlights flickered, casting a rich orange glow across the crowd of Runners.

"You want to be branded murderers, hunted like animals?"

"We already are!" someone shouted, and a roar swept the crowd.

Still, Ivan couldn't get the real temperature of the gathering—his last as leader of the Runners, no matter what.

"Yes. But all we ever wanted was freedom of the Road. Now, we have it for the taking."

"They made us outlaws!"

The voice—the same one—rose up from the crowd in the brief silence. Ivan looked around, trying to see who dared interrupt him.

*Is he trying to stir the mob to violence?*

The voice had been familiar, but Ivan couldn't place it. Finally, the crowd parted, and a single figure, dark in silhouette, stepped forward.

Edgar Cullen.

*An old crewmate, with the Runners from the beginning.*

*As much as as leader,* Ivan thought, *as I am.*

"Cullen," Ivan said. A trusty warrior, too. They had fought together since the founding of the Runners, often side by side.

Cullen was afraid of nothing.

"Ivan, what makes you think you can trust them? The World Council?"

He spat onto the ground.

*At least he didn't spit at me,* Ivan thought.

"They gave their word."

"You trust that?" Cullen shouted.

"And you have *my* word. Full amnesty for everyone who turns themselves in. You keep your road vehicles. You keep your weapons. The hunt ends."

Another, louder murmur spread through the crowd; but all eyes were on Ivan and Edgar Cullen.

*Delicate,* Ivan thought. *Could go either way.*

In the time he'd been in jail, Ivan could see the effects his brother's rule had had on the Runners. Such high levels of hostility . . . and maybe a sense of persecution and frustration that could only lead to more senseless violence.

*Got to tamp it down now, now or never,* Ivan told himself.

"You know me, Cullen. We fought side by side for years, and more than once I saved your ass, and you saved mine."

"True," Cullen said, nodding his approval. "That was then, before you became a prisoner. Before you worked for the World Council."

A roar of laughter from the crowd.

"I won't deny it."

"It's nothing but a World Council trick," someone suddenly yelled.

"They'll want our ships, our guns!" someone else shouted.

Another voice: "We can't trust you!"

Ivan watched as Cullen moved closer, standing close to the foot of the platform. He might not be a natural-born leader, but he had strength and charisma . . . and influence.

If he could persuade Cullen, Ivan knew he had a chance to sway the rest of them.

"Listen to me. I have it in writing from the Director of the World Council himself. I met with him!"

"Prove it!"

"Show us the paper!"

"To hell with the World Council!"

*I'm losing them,* Ivan thought, and he looked down at Cullen, who seemed determined to hold back and let the other Runners have their say.

"I can't—I *won't* tell all of you what to do." Ivan had to shout to be heard above the noisy crowd. "But your freedom—freedom on the Road—is here for the taking."

He shook his head. His words seemed useless in the face of the mob mentality here.

*Useless*, he thought.

He started to leave the stage, prepared to be harangued, insulted . . . even attacked.

And then a voice boomed out as loud as a cannon.

"Hold on! We're not done."

*Ahah. The moment of truth.*

"Yes we are," Ivan said, facing Cullen for a long, tense moment. "At least I am."

Cullen's face was grim, expressionless as he gripped the edge of the stage and vaulted up onto it.

Placing his massive hand on Ivan's shoulder, he stopped him in his tracks. Ivan turned, ready to face this man who might be the new leader of the Runners.

Cullen just looked, nodding, a savage glint in his eyes as he held Ivan still.

Ivan had his gun at his side. Jordan and the others were out there watching. They could shoot it out, but what purpose would that serve?

*Except I'll go down firing!*

Ivan looked from Cullen to the crowd of Runners.

The old warrior stared at Ivan for a long moment, and then a faint smile twitched at the corners of his mouth.

He cleared his throat, turned, and faced the crowd.

"Many of us have known Ivan for a lot of years," he said. "Some of you new recruits only know him by reputation. But I've fought and run with him across half the universe."

He paused.

Not a sound came from the crowd.

And then: "Ivan's always been a good leader—a man of his word."

A pause, a deep breath by this bear of a man. "I trust him. Let's make peace now while we still have our hides. I say we accept this amnesty!"

Stunned, Ivan looked at Cullen as his grin widened, exposing a row of brownish, irregular teeth that still somehow caught the flickering torchlight.

Silence.

And then, slowly, like a swell moving through a sea, the first cheers, then more until the wild cheers exploded from the crowd, and a name bellowed out and became a chant.

*"Ivan! Ivan! Ivan!"*

●  ●  ●

Dawn came fast to Omega Nine.

SRV-66 gleamed in the strange green glow of the rising sun as Ivan, freshly washed and wearing clean clothes for the first time in many days, emerged from one of the Runners' cabins.

He noted activity around the SRV, and walked over to see what was going on.

Annie stood up on one of the cowlings, furiously scrubbing the deionized filters clean.

"Leaving soon, huh?" Ivan said, squinting and looking up at her. She was a dark silhouette against the green sky.

Annie wiped her hair from her forehead with the back of her hand and said, "That's the plan. So are you, I hear."

"Who'd you hear that from?"

Annie smiled but said nothing. Ivan guessed maybe a Runner or two had booked passage with her, back to Earth.

They were free now. Free to live, to roam the Road—or to return to Earth.

"How's Jordan doing? Any better?"

Annie put down her scrubber and looked down at him.

"The wound doesn't look infected. Rodriguez says he'll be fine. Just out of commission for a while. You can imagine how he's taking that."

Ivan laughed. "Yes, I can."

"Ruth's been tending him for the past twenty-four hours."

*Ruth.*

Annie's words stung, but she didn't show any sign that she knew Ivan had grown to care.

And Ivan wasn't going to say anything now. He wouldn't let it show.

As if on cue, the SRV hatch opened, and Jordan appeared in the doorway, leaning on Ruth, who smiled faintly as she looked at Ivan.

Her arm was wrapped tightly around Jordan's waist.

"Speak of the devil," Ivan said. "How you doing there, gunner?"

He addressed Jordan, but he couldn't stop staring at Ruth. She looked translucent in the green glow of the planet's early-morning sunlight.

Radiant and beautiful.

*Funny how things creep up on you.*

*And then you're just a bit too late.*

They started down the ramp, side by side. Rodriguez hovered in the doorway.

"So," Ivan said, still not looking away from Ruth.

How could he?

She looked amazing.

"So?" Jordan said. "What are your plans now?"

Ivan nodded back at the Runners' camp.

"After we get organized here and send message pods back to the World Council accepting their offer, I think I'll see what's out there." He looked up. "It's a big universe."

Jordan asked a question that Ivan kept thinking about: "And what if Kyros is still alive?"

*Kyros. Buried alive.*

*But buried with those things inside him.*

*Is he really dead . . . or is he trapped under that mountain, sealed away like an insane Egyptian pharaoh?*

Ivan said, "I'll worry about that when—*if*—he shows up." He gestured toward the mountain. "He's got a lot of rock to claw through."

"And a lot of technology we don't understand at his disposal," Jordan said.

"If he's alive."

"Big if."

Ruth took a few steps forward but then stopped. As much as it pained him to do so, Ivan had to say something to her.

"And how about you, Ruth? Have you had enough *seeking* for the time being?"

She started to say something but then stopped. He could clearly see something warring inside her.

*What is it?*

*Does she still want to find the Builders after all she's been through?*

"I was thinking"—her voice faded, but then she braced her shoulders and continued—"hoping I could go with you."

Ivan froze.

*What?*

Had he heard correctly? And he was all set to head out solo.

On his own.

Like always.

"What do you mean?" he asked, surprised that he didn't stammer.

Ruth turned and nodded at Jordan, who was holding on to the ramp railing for support.

"Now that I know my brother's going to be all right, I thought maybe

I . . . that you and I could—" She shrugged, but a single word echoed in Ivan's head.

*Brother?*

Ivan thought: *I must be so dense.*

Her voice faded away, and she ended with another shrug before saying, "That is, if you want me with you."

Even then, Ivan knew that it would take him a long time . . . maybe the rest of his life . . . to try to describe what her simple words meant to him at that moment.

*Been alone for a long time.*

*Now—imagine not being alone.*

He tried not to let his confusion show.

"Your brother? Jordan is your *brother?*"

Ruth bit down on her lower lip and nodded.

"Yeah. We've been distant. Same family, but so different."

"A gunner. And a Seeker. Different isn't quite the word."

"Right. But after all this I'm glad I got to see and know who he really is."

"You, too," Jordan said, managing a smile.

With that, Ruth strode down the ramp and came to a stop in front of Ivan, facing him.

She watched, amazed, as he raised his arms and took hold of both of her shoulders, now staring right into those blue-green eyes.

*A man could get used to them*, he thought.

Jordan interrupted. "Don't you think you'd better send out a message pod to Mom and Dad first?"

Ruth turned to her brother. "You're going back to Earth with Annie. You can tell them yourself."

Then she turned to Ivan again and said, "Well . . . do you want me to come along?"

"What? Yeah. Of course I do."


"So—" Ruth said later that day after she'd packed, and they all said their farewells.

She settled into the seat of the small SRV Ivan had commandeered from the Runners and pulled the safety harness taut.

"Where are we off to first?"

Ivan smiled as he reached into his pocket and produced a small chip.

"Wait a second. Is that a chip?"

Ivan nodded.

"You don't mean—"

Ivan's smile widened.

"Sinjira's," he said. "A copy."

"From the cave? When Kyros displayed the Star Road map?"

Ivan nodded.

"She recorded the whole thing."

"And now . . . now you have it all."

"As much as there was on the chip. A lot of Road to explore. Who knows what's out there?"

"But, won't you need—"

"The Road Operating System? Got that, too."

"Wait a second. You mean you have Nahara's data crystal? I thought it was illegal to . . ."

"It is," Ivan said. He was now smiling so hard it hurt as he shook his head. "It's a World Council felony. But I *did* manage to make a copy of it."

"You are . . . something else."

"And now I—*we*—have a whole new map of Star Roads no one, no one human, anyway, has ever traveled."

She stared at him like she still wasn't sure about him.

"I figure," he said, "if you're gonna be an outlaw, you might as well really *be* an outlaw."

"So you're not fully reformed," Ruth said.

But then she broke into a smile . . . and then she laughed.

"I can't believe it. I'm running away with an outlaw!"

"What good is a Star Road map if you're not going to use it, right?"

And by the expression on her face, he knew that Ruth was obviously just beginning to realize the possibilities, the infinite possibilities that lay out there ahead of them.

Soon, Omega Nine would be a distant memory.

And Ivan—for one—couldn't wait to see what happened next.

The portals ahead, the strange worlds, the civilizations—living and dead.

Who knew what lay ahead?

There was only one way to find out.

He took Ruth's hand.

It was time to leave.

Time to get back on the Star Road . . . where the unknown was waiting for them.

# AFTERWORD

Normally, I imagine that an afterword to a novel written by two authors would also be written by the same two people. But that won't be the case here.

I first met Rick Hautala about twenty-five years ago when he called to say that he had read my second novel, really enjoyed it, and would be sending a blurb to my editor, Ginjer Buchanan at Berkley. We talked for a long time, the conversation flowing, the friendship—even by phone—suddenly "there."

Thus began the decades of calls and conversations we've had, often daily, about life, about writing, about the things we loved, about our struggles, and, amid all that somewhat serious stuff, about things that made us both laugh.

Sometimes we met, such as at the NEcon convention in Rhode Island, mecca for many horror writers, or when Rick would bring his then-young family to visit my wife, Ann, and me in Katonah, New York. Or when we had a big "writer's picnic" on my deck and Rick would be there, smile on his face, happy with a cold beer and a cigar.

Once he came to New York so we could visit some of our mutual editors, and taking the boy from Maine into the wilds of New York City was something to see. I might as well have taken him to Jurassic Park. The city wasn't for him.

We had never worked together. Until, almost improbably—considering its convoluted history—*Star Road* happened, and we contracted to write a

SF epic for our editor, Brendan Deneen of Thomas Dunne Books. Old-school space opera, the type we grew up on, the type we had loved. And we set out not just writing it together; we had fun together, dodging space monsters and staging massive gun battles on the outer, unknown reaches of the amazing Star Road.

As you may guess, Rick is gone. Too early. Too soon. A shocking reminder that something can go wrong with your heart, and suddenly . . . the laughs, the talks, the smiles, the beers all vanish. I'll never be the same, pretty sure about that. The phone ringing just doesn't feel the same.

But we have *Star Road*. Right here, in your hands. When two friends decided to head out to space together, and yes, with just the right amount of time to finish the trip . . . they got there together.

—Matthew Costello